T0119614

Swedish Folktales and Legends

Swedish Folktales and Legends

Translated and Edited by

Lone Thygesen Blecher and George Blecher

MINNESOTA

University of Minnesota Press

Minneapolis

Copyright 1993 by G & L Blecher Inc.

Published by arrangement with Pantheon Books, a division of Random House, Inc.

First University of Minnesota Press edition, 2004

Book design by M. Kirsten Bearse

Every effort has been made to obtain permission to reprint previously published material in this book. If any proper acknowledgment has not been made, we encourage copyright holders to notify us.

All rights reserved. No part of this publication may be reproduced, stored in a retrieval system, or transmitted, in any form or by any means, electronic, mechanical, photocopying, recording, or otherwise, without the prior written permission of the publisher.

Published by the University of Minnesota Press
111 Third Avenue South, Suite 290
Minneapolis, MN 55401-2520
http//www.upress.umn.edu

Library of Congress Cataloging-in-Publication Data

Swedish folktales and legends / translated and edited by Lone Thygesen Blecher and George Blecher.— 1st University of Minnesota Press ed.
    p.   cm.
Includes bibliographical references.
ISBN 0-8166-4575-2 (pb : alk. paper)
    1. Tales—Sweden.   2. Legends—Sweden.   I. Blecher, Lone Thygesen.   II. Blecher, George.
    GR225.S87 2004
    398.2'09485—dc22

                                      2004013008

Printed in the United States of America on acid-free paper

The University of Minnesota is an equal-opportunity educator and employer.

27 26 25 24 23 22 21   10 9 8 7 6 5 4

Dedicated to our children,
Lilly-Marie and Haldan

Contents

Acknowledgments   *xiii*
Introduction   *xv*

Animal Tales   *1*

Small Birds Can Kill Too!   *3*
The Rooster Wins the Race   *3*
The Fox, the Bear, and the Honeycomb   *4*
How the Bear Got His Stubby Tail   *5*
The Fox and the Rowanberries   *7*
"They're Sour," Said the Fox   *8*
The Fox and the Crane Invite Each Other to Dinner   *8*
Why the Hare Has a Cleft Lip   *9*
If It Were Summer . . .   *9*
The Wolf and the Fox   *10*
The Wolf Who Wanted to Become Stronger   *10*
The Billy Goat and the Wolf   *11*
Hold the Wolf by the Tail   *12*

Trolls, Giants, Ghosts, and Other Beings   *13*

To Squeeze Water from a Stone   *15*
The Girl Who Wouldn't Spin   *17*
The Boy Who Worked for the Giant   *19*
Little Hans   *25*
Onen in the Mountain   *30*
The Gullible Troll   *34*
The Clever Boy   *35*
The *Bäckahäst* (legend)   *36*
The *Skogsrå* at Lapptjärns Mountain (legend)   *39*
To Catch Smoke (legend)   *40*
The Tale of the Troll Woman (legend)   *42*
The Tale of Speke (legend)   *43*
The Gypsy Girl and Her Dead Fiancé (legend)   *43*

Hobergsgubben (legend)   *46*
The Trolls and the Bear (legend)   *47*
The Giant's Toy (legend)   *49*

True Dummies and Clever Folk   *53*

The Tale of the Crooked Creature   *55*
Wise Klara   *56*
The Stupid Boy Who Didn't Know About Women   *59*
Counting the Stars in Heaven   *60*
Fools   *61*
The Princess of Catburg   *62*
Pretend to Eat, Pretend to Work   *66*
Lazy Masse   *67*
Big Tomma and Heikin Pieti   *70*
For Long Springday   *73*
The Students and the Eclipse of the Moon   *74*
The Numbskull Who Thought He Married a Man   *75*
Tälje Fools   *76*
The Thief's Three Masterpieces   *80*
The Girl and the Calf's Eyes (legend)   *88*
The King, the Headsman, and the Twelve Robbers
    (legend)   *89*
Twelve Men in the Forest (legend)   *92*
The Wise Daughter (legend)   *93*
Bellman Stories (legend)   *93*

How to Win the Princess   *97*

Twigmouthius, Cowbellowantus, Perchnosimus   *99*
The Princess Who Always Had an Answer   *103*
The Boat That Sailed on Both Land and Sea   *105*
The Liar   *110*
Ash Dummy Chops Down the Oak and Becomes the King's
    Son-in-Law   *112*
The Princess with the Louse Skin   *116*

Sheepskin Boy   *118*
The Princess Who Danced with a Troll Every Night   *123*
Stuck on a Goose   *127*
The King's Hares   *128*
Prince Greenbeard   *132*

Tales of Heroes and Heroines   *143*

The Three Swords   *145*
The Peasant Girl in the Floating Rock   *156*
Manasse and Cecilia   *157*
The Princess in the Earthen Cave   *160*
The Silver Dress, the Gold Dress, and the Diamond
    Dress   *168*
The Boy in the Birch-Bark Basket   *173*
The Castle East of the Sun and West of the Wind in
    the Promised Land   *176*
Prince Vilius   *185*
The Three Sons Who Each Had a Foal, a Puppy,
    and a Sword   *195*
The Twelve Kidnapped Princesses   *197*
The Tale of White Bear   *203*
Little Rose and Big Briar   *208*

Metamorphoses   *219*

The Serpent Prince   *221*
The Widow's Son   *228*
Gray Cape   *231*
The Animal Husbands   *234*
Prince Faithful   *239*
The Rats in the Juniper Bush   *248*

Tales of Men and Women   253

Like a Cold Wind in Warm Weather   255
The Quick-Learning Girl   255
The Girl Who Gave a Knight a Kiss Out of Necessity   257
The Fussy Fiancé   260
Pär and Bengta   261
Who's Got the Dumbest Husband   263
Geska   264
The Stingy Farmer   266
The Man and Woman Who Changed Jobs   267
The Contrary Old Woman (legend)   270
The Tale of a Suitor (legend)   270
The Hunter and the *Skogsrå* (legend)   271
The Woman in the Hole (legend)   273
The Man Who Married the *Mara* (legend)   274
The Hidden Key (legend)   275

Moral Tales   277

His Just Reward   279
Master Pär and Rag Jan's Boy   280
The Girl in the Robbers' Den   291
Funteliten and His Mother   293
The Girl Who Stepped on the Bread   298
A Tale of Two Beggars   298
The Filthy-Rich Student   299
The Bad Stepmother   303
The Tale of the Copper Pot   304
The Two Chests   305
Godfather Death   309
The Bear and the Woman   312
The Boy, the Old Woman, and the Neighbor (legend)   313
The Salt Mill (legend)   314
Old Nick and the Widow (legend)   317
The Lazy Boy and the Industrious Girl (legend)   318

The Parson's Wife Who Had No Shadow (legend)   *319*
The Despised Rake (legend)   *320*
The Tale of the Sculptor's Beautiful Wife (legend)   *320*
The Big Turnip (legend)   *322*

Parsons, the Good Lord, and the Evil One   *325*

"Yet a Little While, and the World Seeth Me No More"   *327*
The Devil and the Tailor   *327*
Kitta Gray   *328*
The Pregnant Parson   *330*
Forging with Sand   *333*
The Parson, the Sexton, and the Devil   *333*
The Sermon About Nothing   *336*
Sven Fearless   *336*
The Tale of the Parson and the Sexton   *339*
The Farmer Who Sold His Soul to the Devil (legend)   *341*
The Night-Blind Parson (legend)   *341*
The Burning Lake (legend)   *346*
The Bishop's Visit (legend)   *346*
One More Schnapps (legend)   *347*
The Hare in the Treetop (legend)   *348*
Exchange Heads with the Devil (legend)   *348*

Tall Tales, Superstitions, and Jingles   *351*

The Mountain in the Forest   *353*
The Old Lady's Cat   *354*
The Snake Cookers   *354*
The Goat Who Wouldn't Go Home   *355*
"Eat the Bread Too!"   *356*
The Little Old Woman   *357*
The Three Lying Old Women   *358*
The Biggest Stable and the Biggest Pot   *358*
The Black Cow, the Pot, and the Cheese   *358*

Boots for the Son in America   359
That Was the End of the Tale   360

Notes   361

Bibliography   377

The Illustrators   381

Permissions Acknowledgments   383

Acknowledgments

Collecting, editing, and translating folktales for a volume of this magnitude could not have been done without a great deal of help along the way. We are deeply grateful to the many people and organizations that showed enough interest in this project to offer their time, support, and expertise.

We were fortunate to receive financial support for our research from a number of distinguished institutions. These include the Swedish Institute, the New York State Council on the Arts (through the New York Foundation for the Arts), the Research Foundation of the City University of New York, the John Anson Kittredge Educational Foundation, and the Långmanska kulturfonden in Stockholm. We'd especially like to thank Elisabeth Hall, formerly of the Swedish Institute, for her enthusiasm, professionalism, photographic memory, and her hospitality during our visits to Stockholm. Marna Feldt and John Walldén of the Swedish Institute in New York were also immensely helpful. We'd like to thank Lynda Hansen of the New York Foundation for the Arts, and the late Gregory Kolovakos of the New York State Council on the Arts, whose dedication to the art of translation was legendary. Barbara Bralver of Lehman College, CUNY, guided our many grant applications with an able hand.

A number of experts in the field of Scandinavian folklore were kind enough to share their expertise with us. Professor Torborg Lundell (University of California, Santa Barbara) offered support at many stages of the project, read the manuscript and gave us useful criticism, and passed on to us one of her favorite tales, "The Two Chests." *Swedish Legends and Folktales* by Professor John Lindow (University of California, Berkeley) was an inspiration and an invaluable source of background material, particularly in the writing of the Introduction. Åsa Nyman of the Institute of Dialect and Folklore Research in Uppsala (ULMA) answered numerous queries, gave expert advice, and put her staff at our disposal. Bodil Nildin-Wall of the Institute of Folklore in Gothenburg (DAG) was hospitable and helpful during our visit to the Gothenburg archives, and took the time to answer many questions. We are indebted to Anders Salomonsson of the Institute of European Ethnology and Folklore in Lund (LUF), and especially to Ulla Pihl, who was prompt, thorough, and unflappable, even when bombarded by all sorts of questions. Thanks also to the staff of the Nordic Museum, Stockholm, and to Helena Järvinen of the Library of the Finnish Literature Society, Department of Ethnology, Helsinki, for supplying hundreds of pages from the Liungman anthology.

The first glimmers of research on this project began during a year our family spent in Helsinki. Marianne Bargum and Marja-Leena Rautalin of the Information Center for Finnish Literature guided us to libraries and archives, and Charlotte Enderlein of Albert Bonniers Bokförlag (Stockholm) supplied us with publishers' addresses and illustration sources.

We have many friends who lovingly contributed moral, editorial, and emotional support during the long gestation period of this book. Thanks to Nancy Garrity for the weaving terms in "The Quick-Learning Girl," to Beverly Lieberman for long lunches and hand-holding, to Meme Black for her sharp-tongued intelligence, and to Lillian Fisher for confidence building and maintenance. Tom Engelhardt's brilliance carried us through the writing of the Introduction, and his thoughtful advice helped us clarify our separate responsibilities and limits.

Finally, our thanks to Pantheon editors, past and present: to André Schiffrin, for having the confidence in us to offer us this project; to Shelley Wanger; to Yoji Yamaguchi, for his patience and levelheadedness; and especially to Wendy Wolf, whose enthusiasm and encouragement were the driving force behind this book.

Lone Thygesen Blecher

George Blecher

New York, 1993

Introduction

My mother's father was a carpenter of modest means living at the edge of a forest on an island called Bornholm, in the middle of the Baltic Sea. Although Bornholm belongs to the Kingdom of Denmark, it is actually far closer to Sweden than to Denmark.

Like many a fairy-tale princess, my mother felt trapped on the lonely island. Her family couldn't provide for her, and in her farm and forest community, schooling lasted only four years, although she was allowed to repeat the last year three times because she was so eager to learn.

When she finished school, she had to go away to serve as a maid on a large farm where, the story goes, a baby had been smothered to death by heat and blankets not so many years before. Besides having to do heavy physical work, my mother, who was small for seventeen and very pretty, was preyed upon by the farmhands and treated cruelly by the farm couple. In a burst of courage and daring that folktale heroes seem to have more of than the rest of us, she left one night and boarded a large ferry headed for Copenhagen, stowing away among the lifeboats. In Copenhagen, when she tried to leave the ship with the other passengers, she was detained, but the crew took pity on her and helped her find the home of her aunt and uncle. Later she married a schoolteacher and became a kindergarten teacher herself. They had three daughters, who would listen spellbound to her tales of hardship and her heroic quest into the unknown. She'd escaped a terrible fate and had been rewarded accordingly: she'd gotten her prince (my schoolteacher father) and a fortune (an education and a profession)—living proof that folktales are the stuff of real life.

Our summers, in turn, were spent back on my mother's island, and there my sisters and I developed an affinity for the natural world, and for the farmers and solitary woodsmen who lived scattered through it. They were people not very different from the Swedes of a hundred or more years ago who populate this collection of folktales.

In fact, the similarities between my mother's Bornholm and Sweden are numerous. The dialect spoken on Bornholm is close to Swedish and very different from the rural dialects spoken in the rest of Denmark—indeed, other Danes used to call the Bornholmers "half-Swedes." During the great rural famines of the nineteenth century, many poor peasants from southern Sweden came to Bornholm for work, so the present population is, to some extent, a mixture of Swedes and Danes. Even the natural topography of Bornholm might be seen as a microcosm of Sweden. In the North are tall, dramatic, craggy rock formations, and then the land gradually slopes down to gently rolling sandy beaches in the South. In between is fertile farmland, and in the center, until violent storms destroyed large sections in the 1950s, stood large pine and deciduous forests dotted with lakes and meadows.

Every summer for my first fifteen years I roamed the dark forests of Bornholm in the company of my island cousins. We built fern and moss huts, dressed ourselves in costumes made of flowers and leaves, and explored the island, especially the ruins of a medieval castle surrounded by a moat. After dark the forest was transformed into a landscape of shadows and sounds: every moss-covered boulder became a troll; the mist on the ponds turned into the steam from the swamp woman's brew; wood sprites and elves scurried at the edge of our vision; and the wind and animal sounds added an eerie music. We were brave—or rather we goaded each other to acts of bravery and danger—and we had many ways of keeping our spirits up.

We sang and told each other stories—half-legends, half-gossip, half-made-up, half-true. They were stories of the strange people who inhabited our community on Bornholm, such as Mor-Hanna, who we were sure was a witch because she dressed in rags and walked bent over a gnarled cane, who lived in a house that stank of cats, and who yelled at us when we ventured too close. There was our cousin who went berserk at times and ripped up whole potato fields, and our recluse great-aunt who spent her time making strange rock gardens and whispering to herself. There were the family stories of what happened to this aunt after she'd run away with the "wrong" man, and that uncle whose house burned down; bawdy tales of the maid from the inn who always seemed to end up in the wrong bed; and, most important, ghost and graveyard stories informed by horror stories we'd read or seen at the movies. In this way we did our best to terrify and comfort each other by turns—until we finally made it to the footbridge across the brook, the first sign of home and safety.

This was as close as I got to Sweden in my childhood, but it left me with a sense of kinship for and closeness to the rural Swedish

world that gave birth to most of the tales in this book. Since my childhood I've traveled often through the Swedish forest and lake country, where nature can be threatening, even overwhelming, and moss-covered boulders, dark pine forests, and misty lakes almost demand that humans fill them with creatures of the imagination.

At the time when most of these tales were collected, Swedish villages were few and far between, and farms were widely scattered. In the North, Lapps roamed the highlands and mountains near the polar circle with their reindeer herds, mingling only infrequently with the Swedish settlers of the far northern provinces. These settlers in turn eked out a meager living in the mountains, where the soil was poor and only the owners of the mines and lumber mills prospered.

From north to south, Sweden is about 970 miles long, and the landscape changes from the extreme of its dramatic, mountainous northern half through heavily forested land dotted with lakes in the central part; southern Sweden is primarily low, rolling farmland. Though pockets of industry developed in Sweden rather early, the large majority of Swedes—who lived mainly in southern and central Sweden—supported themselves by farming, fishing, and forestry. Farms were usually self-sufficient, and the important crops were grains like rye, wheat, barley, and oats and various kinds of tubers, such as potatoes, beets, and turnips. In the North, cattle were taken up into the highlands to graze, which meant that members of the household, often young girls and boys, would spend whole summers in the mountains alone. In general, it was common for people to spend long periods of time alone in nature in connection with several different tasks: fishing, charcoal-burning, logging, and hunting. Possibly because of this history, solitary communing with nature for lengthy periods has remained a vital and common need for the Swedes. Whereas it used to be something done out of necessity, today it is considered an important and respectable pursuit to leave the city and spend time alone in nature, soaking up the restorative *ensamhet* (solitude, rather than loneliness) inherent in the forces of nature and one's own company.

This is the kind of world in which people tell each other tales. After a long day of hard work the farm population would gather after the evening meal, one person rocking a baby to sleep, another filling and smoking his pipe, still others sewing, mending, or knitting, while everyone's attention would be turned to the person who was blessed with the gift of tale-telling. While tired bodies rested, minds and imaginations came alive. In the world of the tales all wishes could be fulfilled and all dreams come true: honesty and true grit were rewarded, falseness and cowardliness punished. In a time of meager book learning among the rural population, these tales passed down within families were the vessels of art, culture, dreams. Aside from Bible stories, the tales country people told each other were some of the only ways for them to feed their minds, spirits, and hearts.

When one speaks of a "Swedish folktale," one doesn't necessarily mean that it originated in Sweden, merely that it was recorded there. Sweden, in fact, has many characteristics in common with other northern European cultures, so it is always a difficult job to determine a tale's origins and the paths it has traveled. Unlike the legend (*sägn* in Swedish), the same folktale (or *saga*) can usually be found in many different countries, with each adding its own variations. In this book we have chosen to focus mainly on the folktale, including legends only when we felt that the story hovered on the often blurry border between the two categories, or when exclusion would have meant a scarcity of tales about certain supernatural beasts and creatures that

appear primarily in legends. In the words of Jacob Grimm, the distinction between the two groups is relative: "The wonder-tale is more poetic, the legend more historic."

The main difference between the folktale and the legend is that the latter is meant to be believed. Shorter and less complex than the tale—usually consisting of only one episode and its consequences—the legend takes place in the quotidian world, often with references to real places. While the supernatural elements in a tale are meant to be taken as part of the general fantasy, in the legend they are assumed to have really happened. On the other hand, the tale is told as entertainment, not to be believed. Often the narrative is structured formulaically—for example, the triple repetition in which the hero must perform a certain task three times before the action can continue. In order to help the reader separate tales from legends, we have put the legends at the end of each section, and indicated them as such in the notes. One of our major reasons for focusing mainly on the tale is that a few excellent volumes of *sägner* already exist in English translation, while Swedish *sagor* are sparsely represented in English.

Not surprisingly, a large number of the tales in this book deal with creatures of the imagination—giants, trolls, *tomtar* (household spirits), *skogsrå* (forest spirits), *näck* (water spirits), *marar* (nightmare hags), and others. Clearly they filled a need on the part of the rural population to explain the inexplicable, to deal with the fears and horrors of everyday life, and to name the unknown. Undoubtedly, they went a long way toward dealing with the innate mistrust of any stranger who happened to come along, and supplied an excuse to keep one's distance. But they were also images of inner demons, of wishes and feelings too confusing to express and of a need for excitement and mystery amid a rather hard and tedious life. Most of all, they indicated a sense that nature was alive and full of unpredictable wonders and horrors.

In both the popular and scholarly traditions, giants (*jättar* in Swedish) are considered the oldest of the supernatural beings. Like the Greek Titans, they were believed to have lived on earth before humans, and in some versions to have been driven away by either Thor's lightning bolt or the onset of Christianity. Tales about the giants emphasize their stupidity and how, in spite of their great size and strength, they could be outsmarted by clever humans, who usually took ruthless advantage of them.

In form, not size, trolls were akin to both giants and humans. They were thought to live social lives very similar to those of human beings, working in houses and stables, celebrating births and weddings. There are even tales about trolls and humans sharing things or doing favors for each other. Still, in the Swedish folk tradition, trolls were blamed when something went wrong; at the very least, they were the prime suspects when something was stolen. Abnormal or deformed children were also blamed on trolls or thought to be troll changelings, and peasants might try to make the troll "mother" take back her child by treating it badly, beating it, or in some instances putting it in a lit oven or throwing it on the garbage heap. Kidnapping (*bergtagning*, literally "to be taken into the mountain") was also attributed to trolls, and if a person wandered lost and hungry in the forest, the danger of being taken in by trolls was great. (Clearly, somebody lost in the forest for days might begin to see trolls behind every rock.)

Contrary to the image we have of trolls today (the heavyset, fuzzy-haired, grotesque but rather cute creatures imagined by illustrators and the modern toy industry), they were thought by people of earlier times to look very much like darker and uglier humans, whom one didn't know or trust and who lived outside the Christian community. In fact, Christianity was thought to be the strongest weapon in the fight against all otherworldly elements, and so when someone was lost in the forest, villagers would ring the church bell loudly, hoping to scare away any ungodly creatures.

Just as familiar as the trolls in popular Scandinavian beliefs were those domesticated household spirits called *tomtar*. *Tomtar* were small, gray-clad figures, perhaps with red stocking caps (like Christmas elves), who might sometimes be spied in dark corners of stables and haylofts. They were considered a sort of folk conscience, and, as the caretakers of livestock, they offered assurance that life would be conducted in a proper manner on the farm. In return for the prosperity and harmony they brought to the household, they expected to be fed a bowl of porridge at regular intervals and to be treated with respect.

Another important group of creatures were the solitary *rå: skogsrå* (forest spirits), *sjörå* (lake or sea spirits), *bergrå* (mountain spirits), each associated with a particular part of nature. (The term *rå*, from the Swedish *at råda*, means "to rule over something"—in this case a certain part of the natural world.) The *rå* were almost always female, and it was their aim to seduce lonely men away from society into their sexual clutches by their irresistible beauty. In return for their sexual prowess, the men would be given luck by the *rå* in their different pursuits. The *rå* often had odd, animal-like physical characteristics such as a tail or a hole where their backs were supposed to be, and, if caught unawares, might be seen in their grotesque true form. More than likely, the long periods alone fishing, hunting, or charcoal-burning in the forest made men prone to erotic wishful thinking.

A similar solitary creature with a dangerously erotic aspect was the *näck*. This male creature would rule over a certain body of water; aided by his virtuoso violin playing, he would lure men or women to their death in his watery kingdom. When sighted in the shape of a horse, he was known as a *bäckahäst*, or brook horse.

Among other supernatural creatures who often appeared in Swedish lore were *marar* (nightmare hags), nameless ghosts and the "walking dead," witches, God and Satan—and, less often, werewolves, elves, and various animals such as ravens, snakes, and dragons with magical characteristics. Taken all together, these creatures evoke the complex inner life of people living close to the land, who in many respects felt dwarfed by and helpless before the natural forces surrounding them.

As we prepared this book, it became clear to us that few cultures had engaged in such a concerted effort to collect and document their folkloric past, and our goal became the compilation of a comprehensive and lively anthology that included tales from as many of the important collectors and as broad a geographical base as possible. This meant searching through not only the numerous published collections of tales, but also the voluminous—and largely unpublished—material stored in archives at the universities of Gothenburg, Lund, and Uppsala, and at the Nordic Museum in Stockholm. We have tried to choose as many different tale types as possible from among those most widely represented in Sweden to give the reader a sense of both the broad range of tales available and the richness of the collective unconscious from which they sprang.

Until the beginning of the nineteenth century the European intellectual community did not take folktales seriously as a legitimate cultural product. However, the publication of the Grimm Brothers' *Kinder- und Hausmärchen* in 1812 marked the beginning of an entirely new attitude toward the common "folk" and their culture. Napoleon had raged through Europe, and all the countries touched by his wars were in need of strengthening their national self-image. In the case of Sweden, national pride was smarting from the recent loss of Finland, but contrary to Finland and Norway—in which the folklore movement became a means of defining these nations' very identities—Sweden's identity had not been as profoundly threatened. Nevertheless, interest in collecting and preserving the rich tradition of folk narratives and beliefs was awakened at this time, and intellectuals proceeded to carry out the important early groundwork of collecting in various parts of the country; in 1873, with the founding of the Nordic Museum, folklore collecting in Sweden became systematized.

The modern study of Swedish folklore can be said to have started with Gunnar Olof Hyltén-Cavallius (1818–1889). A native of Värend in Småland, early in his career he teamed up with George Stephens, an English antiquarian and scholar of Nordic philology and folklore, to collaborate on what became Sweden's first important published collection of folktales, *Svenska Folk-Sagor och Äfventyr* (Swedish Folk and Fairy Tales) of 1844–1849. Influenced by the work of the Brothers Grimm, Hyltén-Cavallius and Stephens also used as models contemporary collections of tales by Asbjørnsen and Moe in Norway and Christian Molbech in Denmark. In conscious opposition to the literary reworkings of folktales by earlier collectors, they left the narrative content of their material unchanged. However, they did rework the style of the tales, resulting in a somewhat stilted prose that borrowed excessively from the style of medieval ballads, which they felt conveyed the "romantic" spirit better than the homey style of most of the original tellers. Apparently, they were wrong, at least as far as the public was concerned; their folktale collection was a commercial failure. Nonetheless, the tales in the Hyltén-Cavallius–Stephens books formed the foundation on which all further Swedish tale collections were built.

Although they did a great deal of their own fieldwork, Hyltén-Cavallius and Stephens employed several other people to collect and record tales for them, including Hyltén-Cavallius's father, Dean Carl Fredrik Cavallius; the painter Sven Sederström; folksong specialists Arvid August Afzelius and Adolph Ivar Arwidsson; and the author Carl von Zeipel. However, in a category by himself was Michael Jonasson Wallander (1778–1860), generally known as Mickel i Långhult—informant, collector, living archive of Swedish folk materials.

As a young man, Mickel had drifted restlessly around his native southwest Småland, working on various farms and in local market towns selling his wooden spinning-wheel handicrafts. In 1817 he married a farm widow but soon discovered that he had no practical farming talents and completely mismanaged her farm. In fact, he seems to have spent most of his time socializing in a nearby village, where he delighted everyone with his lively sense of humor and talents as a raconteur. As he was the only one in the area who could write well and he kept an extensive diary, he was useful to the farmers in noting down and storing a wealth of local information. However, his penchant for drinking and his less than dependable behavior left him destitute, and he ended up in a small cottage on what had previously been his own farm, taken care of by an old woman known as "Hora-Anna" (Whore Anna).

Prompted by a friend of Dean Cavallius's, Mickel spent much time in his later years writing down all the folktales, local legends, and folk beliefs his remarkable memory could recall. These were passed on to Hyltén-Cavallius, who proceeded to polish them in his own style. However, many of Mickel's original manuscripts were preserved, and from these posterity has been able to enjoy his unique voice. Several of Mickel's tales are included here, displaying his irony, his talent for dialogue, and his infectious humor.

A contemporary of Hyltén-Cavallius was Baron Nils Gabriel Djurklou (1829–1904), who did most of his collecting in his native Närke. Although critical of Hyltén-Cavallius's reworking of folktale material, Djurklou did much the same thing—rewriting the tales, first into "standard" Swedish and later into the lively Närke dialect. The products are humorous and, in some cases, small literary masterpieces, though by no means the original words of his informants. Djurklou was also the founder of Föreningen för Närkes folkspråk och fornminnen (approximately, Society for the Preservation of the Local Dialect and Antiquities of Närke). Since then, many societies modeled on Djurklou's have been established all over Sweden.

August Bondeson (1854–1906), highly respected for his sensitive collections of folk narrative, worked primarily in Halland and Dalsland in southwest Sweden. Although he began under the influence of Djurklou's editing principles, he later changed to a more precise rendering of the tale texts, becoming the first collector who not only recorded the tales but also supplied a full description of the contextual setting, something modern collecting takes for granted. The author Eva Wigström (1832–1901), from Skåne in the south of Sweden, was another important early collector. In an effort to protect her informants' anonymity, she created fictional personae, which to some degree detracted from the scholarly value of the tales she recorded. However, the size and quality of her collection place it among the most important in the country.

On the island of Gotland off the eastern coast of Sweden, Per Arvid Säve (1811–1897) gathered a treasure of local lore and tales. Some of his most important informants were his own sisters and aunts and, above all, his mother's cousin, Engel Lisa Kahl. He describes "Aunt Engel Lisa" as a "childlike soul with a bottomless treasure of tales and pranks which she took pleasure in telling and performing for the children." It is interesting to note that in this educated middle-class home, the telling of folktales was entertainment for children, while in its original rural setting it was primarily for adults; only a few tales, such as animal tales, were specifically directed at children.

The most important collection of tales from northern Sweden was by Olof Petter Pettersson (1859–1944), born in the county of Wilhelmina in southern Lappland. His folkloristic activity lasted a good fifty years, stretching from a time when folk narrative was still a living part of the rural communities to years when its importance gradually diminished. As Pettersson had an extraordinary memory, many of his tales were simply those he remembered from his own childhood, but he also had a network of informants and was faithful to his material.

By the beginning of this century the study of folklore had entered the Swedish university, becoming an academic subject in 1912 when Carl Wilhelm von Sydow (1878–1952) became lecturer and later professor of folklore at the University of Lund. Among Von Sydow's achievements were his pioneering work in the theory of folklore classification and the development of an internationally accepted folkloristic terminology. Because folktale material was being collected in a more efficient manner by students and official "recorders" all around the country, a series of archives were established in the universities of Uppsala, Lund, and Gothenburg, and in the Nordic Museum in Stockholm. The last extensive single effort at folktale collecting was by Waldemar Liungman (1883–1978) in the 1920s when, through advertisements in the press, he gathered an impressive body of tales that he later supplemented with tales from a variety of other sources and published in *Sveriges Samtliga Folksagor* (1949–1950).

At present an awesome amount of material is available to the folklore researcher, and Sweden's archives are among the most highly organized and thorough in the world.

To select the tales for this book we used several criteria. Aside from including as many different collectors as possible, and making sure that we represented all parts of Sweden, we wanted to cover the tale types that had a large number of variants as well as the ones that were unique to Sweden. But, of course, the single most important criterion was to find *interesting* tales—whether charming, dramatic, humorous, bawdy, or romantic.

Swedish Folktales and Legends is loosely organized according to the Aarne-Thompson type catalogue,* beginning with animal tales, then going on to tales of trolls, giants, ghosts, and other supernatural creatures. These are followed by a section of humorous tales about dunces and knaves, and then by several sections of "wonder-tales": tales about courting a princess, others about heroes and heroines, a third group about change and metamorphosis. After these come a more earthy section about relations between men and women, another about fate and morality, and a third that includes comic tales of parsons, God, and the Devil. We end with a short section of lies, formula tales, superstitions, and whimsical tales impossible to categorize. As already mentioned, we have included several legends at the end of each section and in an appendix have written brief notes about each tale.

The illustrations for the book were gathered from classic volumes of Swedish folktales. Most of the major Swedish illustrators of folk and children's literature of the first half of this century are repre-

---

* For explanation of the Aarne-Thompson type catalogue, see page 361.

sented, many of whom—including John Bauer, Elsa Beskow, and Einar Norelius—shaped the fantasy life of generations of Scandinavians. Thanks to them, all Scandinavians know "for a fact" what trolls, *tomtar*, and giants look like, and can spot a supernatural creature behind every rock or tree in the forest.

These illustrators were part of a revolution in Swedish children's literature. During the latter part of the nineteenth century a group of public-school teachers began to voice criticism of the tame, sentimental "vacation" stories and nursery tales of the time aimed almost exclusively at the children of the privileged classes. Inspired by the populist movements of the turn of the century, teachers, writers, artists, and publishers developed new material that would also appeal to the children of farmers and workers, a literature that dealt with new subjects like the pleasures of hard work and which dared to depict children as more adventurous and independent. For inspiration many of them returned to the national folklore heritage, which by then was beginning to be organized and available in various locations around the country. A Golden Age of quality children's literature ensued, which has lasted to the present day—Astrid Lindgren's *Pippi Longstocking* is only one of an impressive list of Swedish children's classics.

I want to end by mentioning that my mother who ran away from her native island now lives happily next to another forest in Denmark where she, like her mother before her, makes forays to pick berries and mushrooms; and that my children have the pleasure each summer of hearing her stories, eating her country food, and experiencing the connection to a life that is still quite close to nature and the lore of the past.

And now, to quote the storyteller "Old Greta" from Wilhelmina County in Southern Lappland: "Gather round, children, and put your feet up on the bench or else the troll will come and bite you!"

Lone Thygesen Blecher
1993

"Small Birds Can Kill Too!"

ANIMAL TALES

Small Birds Can Kill Too!

Once there was a farmer who was so stingy that he wouldn't even let a small bird eat its fill. The bird got angry and flew away, but one day when the farmer was ploughing his field, it came back and alighted on the horn of one of the farmer's oxen. It started to peck at the ox, saying, "I'll peck a hole in it, I'll peck a hole in it!"

The farmer picked up a rock and threw it at the bird, but killed his ox instead. Then the bird alighted on the horn of the other ox and started calling out and pecking in the same way. The farmer got even angrier, and threw another rock at the bird. Now he'd killed his other ox!

When he got home, he wanted to wash away his anger with a glass of beer, but the bird was sitting before him on the beer barrel. The farmer asked his wife to go fetch him a sledgehammer, and with it he smashed not the bird but the barrel, and all the beer ran out.

Later, when the farmer was about to eat dinner, there sat the bird on the edge of the butter pitcher, covered with butter. The farmer grabbed the rascal and was about to kill it, but first he wanted to lick off the butter. The bird slipped right into the farmer's stomach, and that was the end of that cheapskate of a farmer.

The Rooster Wins the Race

The black grouse and the rooster had an argument about who would have the privilege of becoming the farm bird. They decided to have a race; whoever reached the farm first would be the farm's official bird.

The black grouse flew a lot faster, and the rooster began to worry that he'd lose. So he called out, "Hey, Brother Grouse, what's that white thing underneath your tail?"

When the black grouse stopped to look, the rooster had time to overtake him, and that was why the grouse became a bird of the forest.

The Fox, the Bear, and the Honeycomb

A bear and a fox were living together. One day they came upon a large honeycomb, and the bear said, "Let's save it for the fall so that we'll have something to eat."

The fox agreed.

But that night when they went to sleep, the fox woke up and began to pound the ground with his tail. Finally, the bear woke up and asked, "What's all that pounding about? You'd better go see what it is!"

The fox got up, and later, when he came back, the bear asked him, "So what was it?"

"It was my oldest brother, who came to invite me to the birth of his child," answered the fox.

"What are they going to name the child?" asked the bear.

"The Beginning," answered the fox.

The next night the same thing happened.

"Now *you* go see what it is!" said the fox.

"No, *you* go!" said the bear.

So the fox went, and when he returned the bear asked, "What was it?"

"It was my second brother, who came to invite me to celebrate the birth of his child," answered the fox.

"What will they name the child, then?"

"The Middle," answered the fox.

The third night the pounding started again, and the bear woke up.

"Now it's your turn to get up and see what it is," said the fox.

"No, I'm so heavy and clumsy. You go!" said the bear.

So the fox went, and when he came back a while later, the bear asked, "What was it this time?"

"It was my youngest brother inviting me to come celebrate the birth of his child."

"And what will they name the child?"

"Licked Clean," answered the fox.

"That sounds strange," said the bear. "I hope you haven't been eating the honey!"

When they went to check the honeycomb, the bear saw that it

was empty, and got so angry that he decided to kill the fox the first chance he got.

How the Bear Got His Stubby Tail

One winter a man drove around the countryside selling fish. He was riding through a big forest when he came upon Mickel Fox out looking for something to eat. In no time the fox caught a whiff of the fish, and since he hadn't eaten anything fresh for a long time, his mouth started watering. As quiet as a louse he hopped onto the wagon and started feasting off the herring and roach and all the other good things. The fishmonger drove along without suspecting a thing, and the fox was as careful as he could be. But once, when he bit into a fish head, it made a little crunching sound, and the man heard it. He turned around to see what kind of company he'd picked up, and when he saw the fox, he grabbed the reins and gave him a swat. The fox rolled off the wagon and into the road, where he lay stretched out, dead to the world.

Now I'm not sure if in those days there was a reward for shooting foxes, but a fox skin is always good to have, so the man jumped off, threw the fox back into the wagon, and drove off.

But after Mickel Fox had been lying still for a little while, he woke up and looked around. "I'm no quitter," he thought, and started tossing fish off the wagon one after another. The fishmonger didn't notice a thing. He just sat there thinking about business— wondering how much money he'd make, and if he'd have any trouble selling his fish. Finally, when only a few fish were left on the wagon, the fox thought that now might be the time to jump off. So he did, and the fishmonger went on his merry way.

The fox had quite a job gathering up the fat fish that were lying all over the road. But when he was done, Mickel sat down by his pile and had himself a real feast. Just then, however, a bear happened to be loping by. When he smelled the fish, he lumbered right up to the fox and asked, "Where did you get all that fish, Mickel?"

"Well," answered the fox, "I caught them with my tail."

"I could do that too," the bear decided.

"Why not?" answered the fox, and proceeded to describe down to the last detail exactly how he'd done it. He'd simply gone out onto the ice, stuck his tail through a hole, and when the fish had started biting pulled them in. The bear was relieved that there was nothing more to it, and he wanted to go right off to the lake.

"Now, now, just hold your horses!" called the fox. "You haven't heard the whole story yet. When a fish starts to bite, make sure that you don't pull your tail up right away, or else he might let go. Give him time to get a really good hold and *then* yank as fast as you can."

Thanking the fox for the good advice, the bear slouched away toward the shore to do exactly what the fox had told him. When he'd held his tail in the water a good while, it felt to him as though a fish were biting, which made him very happy. But since the fox had warned him against pulling up too soon, he sat there a good while longer. Finally, it felt like the fish was holding on tight, and he pulled up as hard as he could. Ow, did it hurt! When the bear turned around to look for the fish, a piece of his tail was stuck in the ice!

Since that day, the bear has had a stubby tail.

The Fox and the Rowanberries

A bear was eating rowanberries when a fox came by to visit. The bear asked, "Brother, would you like some rowanberries to eat?"

"No," answered the fox, "they're too sour."

"They're not that sour," said the bear.

"Then let me taste," said the fox.

"Very well," said the bear, and he bent the rowanberry tree down to the ground, saying, "Now bite hard into the branch over there!" When the fox had sunk his teeth in, the bear asked, "Do you have a good grip on it?"

"Yes," said the fox. The bear let go of the tree and the fox flew up into the air, yelling, "Please, dear friend, help me down!"

"All you have to do is let go," said the bear. "I'll catch you!"

The fox let go of the branch, fell to the ground, and was knocked senseless. Then the bear told him, "Now I've finally paid you back for the time you fooled me into losing my tail!"

"They're Sour," Said the Fox

The fox was standing under a rowanberry tree looking up at the berries without being able to reach them. He asked the magpie for a few, but she wouldn't get him any. So he said:

> "It's all the same to me;
> They're too sour anyway.
> But if my old mother had a few,
> She'd be pleased to eat them, I'm sure."

The Fox and the Crane
Invite Each Other to Dinner

One day the fox invited the crane home for dinner, but he did it only to be mean and to make fun of her. He prepared a tasty soup and poured it into a shallow tin bowl. The crane couldn't get at the soup: all she could manage was to wet the outermost tip of her beak. The fox kept urging her to eat and asking her why she didn't like the food—and finally she had to go home hungry.

Of course, the crane couldn't stand having the fox make a fool of her, so she invited him to her house to get even. The fox couldn't decide whether to go or not, but finally his curiosity got the better of him. The crane had made a soup with pieces of meat and dumplings, but she served it in a jar with an opening so narrow that the fox couldn't get anything but his nose into it—and barely even that. The crane, however, could stick her beak right down to the bottom and fish out pieces of meat and dumpling, while the fox could only sniff.

"Is something wrong with my food?" asked the crane. "You're not eating! I do hope you're not the type who needs encouragement. Well, then, I guess I'll have to eat it myself." And the crane began to eat, while all the fox could do was drool.

When the crane was full, she said, "Never let it be said of me that my guests went home hungry." And this time she found a bowl for the fox so that he could eat some too.

Why the Hare Has a Cleft Lip

One day the fox, who is very proud of his great tail, met the scared little hare and began to make fun of him.

"You poor wretch, you couldn't frighten a flea! But everyone respects me for my grand tail."

So they walked on, and the hare felt more and more miserable about what the fox had said. They came to a farmyard, and while crossing it the hare happened to hop right into the middle of a flock of sheep. The sheep scattered in all directions, and out of the hare burst such a tremendous laugh that his lip split open. That would show the fox that the little hare could frighten not one but many! Since that day, the hare has had a cleft lip.

Another time the fox said to the hare, "You're so neat and dapper, you should stay with the womenfolk!"

Of course the fox knew that it was bad luck for women to see the hare's cleft lip: if a pregnant woman looks into the face of a hare, her child will be born with a harelip. That's why hunters always cut the hare's head in such a way that women can't see the hare's mouth.

If It Were Summer . . .

In the wintertime when it's cold, the hare says to himself, "This summer I'll be sure to build me a house."

But when summertime and warm weather come around, he forgets all about it. He just hops around, saying happily, "A bush is enough for me! A bush is enough for me!"

The Wolf and the Fox

One night the wolf and the fox were walking along together. They made a bet that whoever saw the sun shine first that morning would get a fat sheep.

Both of them went up to the top of a hill. To the east was a great wide plain, and to the west were tall mountains.

The wolf sat down facing east where the sun usually rises, but the fox looked to the west.

Suddenly, the fox yelled, "Will you look at that!"

The first rays of the sun were shining on the tops of the western mountains, and so the fox was the one who got the fat sheep.

The Wolf Who Wanted to Become Stronger

Once, while a farmer was ploughing his field, a wolf came up to him and asked, "Why is it that your oxen are so strong?"

"Because they're gelded," said the farmer.

"If I were gelded, would I be just as strong?"

"You'd be even stronger."

"Then geld me," said the wolf. "But what if it won't heal?"

"Oh, it'll heal in eight days," said the farmer.

"Well, if it hasn't healed in that time, I'll come and geld *you*!"

Without further discussion, the man gelded the wolf. Each day the farmer went out ploughing, but on the eighth day he decided not to leave his home. His old woman wanted to know why, so he told her about his agreement with the wolf.

"Is that all?" said the old woman. "I'll go plough instead of you.

Just give me your pants, and you'll see something you won't forget!"
And she went off to the fields to plough.

Late in the morning, the wolf came limping along, dragging his hind legs.

"You promised that it would heal in eight days, but it still hurts. So it's my turn to geld you! I want you to feel how I'm suffering!"

"Pooh," said the old woman. "I gelded myself as soon as I got home, and it hasn't healed either."

"I'd like to see that," said the wolf.

"All right," said the old woman, unbuttoning her pants and lying spread-legged on the field so the wolf could take a look.

"Oh, goodness, that's much worse than mine," he said. "I'd better go find some healing leaves to put on that. Just lie still."

The wolf limped off. Along the way he met a hare, to whom he said, "There's a farmer back there who's gelded himself, and I'm looking for some healing leaves. Meanwhile, you fan the wound with your paw so that the flies won't get to it."

So that's what the hare did. He sat there fanning with his paw, but the old woman let fly a thundering fart. The hare got so frightened that he jumped high into the air and ran away. Along the way he met the wolf, who asked him how things were going, and the hare told him: "Very badly. Now another hole's opened up below the first, and it smelled so bad that I had to leave."

"If it's that bad, I'm not going back either," said the wolf, and he never did.

The Billy Goat and the Wolf

One day the billy goat stood drinking and studying his reflection in the water. When he noticed his horns, he said to himself, "I don't need to be afraid of the wolf! I never knew I had such big horns!"

But the wolf was lying in wait behind him. He said, "What was that you just said?"

Very frightened, the billy goat turned around and answered, "Oh, don't mind me! One talks so much nonsense when one is drinking!"

Hold the Wolf by the Tail

Once two *knallar** were out walking. They happened to see a hole in the ground, which they realized had to be a lair of some kind. They were both curious, so one of them crept down the hole while the other stood watch outside. It so happened that just at that moment, the she-wolf came home; for it was a wolf lair they'd come upon. Naturally, the peddler who was standing outside got worried about his friend, so when the she-wolf tried to crawl inside, he grabbed hold of her tail and held on. Because of the wolf, it grew dark inside the lair, and the peddler who was inside started shouting, "Who's that blocking the light?"

"If the tail breaks, you'll find out soon enough," called the other.

And that was the end of the story. What happened to them and whether or not the tail held, I have no idea.

* *Knallar:* peddlers from Västergötland in southwest Sweden. These men were often regarded as little more than scoundrels, but they were also instrumental in the transmission of folktales. They are often thought of as fools, particularly by the people of the neighboring provinces of Småland and Skåne, in the tradition of the Fools of Chelm, the Molbo stories of Denmark, etc.

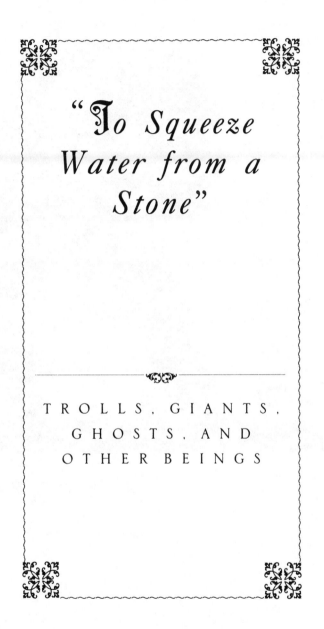

"To Squeeze Water from a Stone"

TROLLS, GIANTS,
GHOSTS, AND
OTHER BEINGS

To Squeeze Water from a Stone

Once an old woman was making cheese. She asked her servant boy to go to the forest to chop some wood, and when he came back she'd give him some of it. The boy agreed to go, but he wanted the cheese first.

So she gave it to him, and off he went. Soon he spied a giant, so he bent down and picked up a rock from the ground.

"What are you eating?" asked the giant when they met. The boy told him that it was cheese, and when the giant asked for a piece, the boy gave him the rock instead. The giant gnawed at it and tried to eat it, but ventured that it was an awfully hard, dry piece of cheese.

"Not to me it isn't," said the boy, and he squeezed his piece of cheese till the whey dripped from it. The giant thought that was well done—he himself couldn't have done it—and he said that he thought the boy must be very strong.

"Yes, I believe I'm stronger than you," said the boy. The giant asked if he'd like to be his servant, and the boy said he would if the pay was good.

"If you stay for a year, you'll get as much money as you can carry," said the giant.

They went off to the giant's cave in a nearby mountain. There the giant introduced him to his wife, telling her that he'd hired the boy as his servant.

"Very good, very good," she said. "Now both of you can go to the spring and fetch me a tub of water."

It was a terribly big tub, so the giant stuck a big pole through its handles to carry it more easily. The boy asked the giant to walk first, since he didn't know the way to the spring, and this way he got the giant to hold the pole so close to the midpoint that the boy could sit on it, and the giant carried both him and the tub to the spring. When they'd filled it up, the boy told the giant to walk ahead as well, for it was a bit heavier to carry at the back: this way he got a ride going home too. After they'd put down their burden, the giant said he could tell that he was getting old. He couldn't do as much as he used to; in the old days he could carry the tub home all by himself, and it hadn't seemed even half as heavy as it did now.

The next day the boy was to go out ploughing. The giant was supposed to join him, but he changed his mind and told the boy to go alone and put the oxen back inside when he'd finished. But the boy couldn't figure out how to do that: there was no door in the house where the giant kept the oxen, for he would just pick up the house and place it over them. Of course, the boy couldn't do this, so he killed the oxen instead, chopped them up into little pieces, and threw the pieces in through a little hole. When the giant came by, he asked if the boy had put away the oxen.

"Oh, yes!" he said. "But first I split them up." When the giant saw that the boy had killed his oxen, he was beside himself!

The next day they had to thresh the grain. Both the boy and the giant went to the barn and spread the grain, and the giant brought out flails so big that the boy had never seen their like. He could barely manage to swing them at all. The giant, however, went ahead and pounded so hard that the barn resounded, while the boy merely stirred up the hay so that it swirled to the ceiling.

"This is how you do it," he said to the giant, but no matter how hard he beat, the giant still couldn't make the hay float up that way. When the boy finally got tired, he said that the flails were too small. This made the giant so mad that he went to his old woman and complained.

"Everything I do is bad! I can't do anything right!" he said. The old woman advised him to get rid of the boy.

"I'll roast him in the oven," she said. "And you can invite all your friends." That the giant liked, and he set off immediately to invite his friends to the feast.

By the time the boy came inside, the old woman had fired up the oven, and she asked him to sit on a baker's peel* and take a look inside. But the boy had been listening outside when they were talking, so he knew that he should be careful.

"I don't know exactly what you mean," he said. "You'd better show me first." So the old crone crept up on the peel to show him how to sit, and at just that moment the boy pushed her into the oven

---

* A baker's peel is a shovel-like implement used for putting bread into an oven or taking it out.

and roasted her. Then he put her on the table and climbed up above the doorway, where he placed several large rocks.

A while later a group of giants came inside. They didn't want to start the feast until the old lady joined them, so they sat there for quite a while, waiting. When she still hadn't come, they took a peek at the roast, and saw that the old crone was lying there instead of the boy.

"The boy's cooked her!" they yelled, and rushed out into the kitchen to catch him. But as they entered, the boy threw a rock at each one's head, and they all died.

Afterward, he took all the giant's money and became a very rich man.

The Girl Who Wouldn't Spin

Once there was a widow whose daughter was so full of her own thoughts and daydreams that the spinning wheel always stood idle by her knee, and no matter how much her mother complained, it didn't help a bit.

Finally, her mother got so annoyed at always seeing the spinning wheel stand idle that one fine day she picked up both wheel and daughter and put them on the cottage roof. She told her daughter that she could sit there and spin gold out of mud and straw as much as she pleased, for all the yarn that they'd ever see on *her* wheel.

Surrounded by mosquitoes and sad thoughts, the girl sat there in the sun looking out into the road, with the blasted spinning wheel by her knee. Just then the young king of the country happened to be riding past their farm. When he saw the girl with her spinning wheel on the roof, he stopped and asked what was going on.

"She's spinning gold out of mud and straw," answered her mother.

Taking her at her word, the king immediately ordered the girl to come down off the roof. When he saw how beautiful she was, he told her that she could spin in his royal castle, and if she really could spin gold out of mud and straw, he would take her for his queen.

The girl didn't dare say a word, for she couldn't seem to get away from that spinning wheel, and so she went along to the castle without a protest. The king gave her a fine room, a spinning wheel, and plenty of mud and straw, and now she was supposed to spin gold for him and good fortune for herself. But this was easier said than done, and the girl cried her eyes out when she was left alone.

She sat like this far into the night, brooding about her fate, when suddenly in front of her appeared an ugly little troll. "Don't cry, my beauty!" said the troll. "I'll teach you how to spin gold from mud and straw, if you'll agree to certain . . . conditions."

"And what are they?" she asked.

"If you can't tell me my name within three days, you'll have to come along with me and be my bride," said the troll.

"I'll cross that bridge when I get to it," she thought to herself, and didn't waste any time agreeing to the troll's conditions. He gave her a pair of gloves, which, when she put them on, helped her to spin the purest gold out of mud and straw.

On the first and second day she spun one skein of gold after another, which the king thought was just fine. On the morning of the third day she was still spinning, but now with a trembling heart, for she still didn't know the troll's name, and the king had become very dear to her.

The king, however, was as pleased as could be, for he thought the young spinning girl from the poor farm even lovelier than all the

gold she had spun. It was still too early in the day to pay her a visit, so he went for a walk in the forest while she sat in her room worrying how to free herself from the troll.

Around noon the king came to see her, wanting to talk about their marriage. But the girl couldn't speak. She just looked sad, and the king thought that he'd better tell her something to amuse her. So he told about his walk in the forest. "And as I was walking along," he said, "I spied a tiny, ugly old troll, hopping and skipping around a juniper tree, singing:

> 'Today I'll grind my malt,
> Tomorrow I'll celebrate my wedding.
> In her room the maiden sits howling,
> For she doesn't know my name.
> My name is Titteliture,
> Titteliture is my name!'

Did you ever hear anything so funny?" asked the king.

"Titteliture? I'm free! You've saved me from the troll!" cried the girl, and she hugged the king and kissed him smack on the mouth. When the troll heard this, he got so furious that he exploded.

The king celebrated his wedding with the girl who hadn't wanted to spin, but who'd spun both gold and a queen's crown for herself.

The Boy Who Worked for the Giant

Once there was a tenant farmer who had three sons. The oldest one went to town looking for work. As he was walking down the road, he met the mountain giant, who asked him where he was headed. Well, he said, he was out looking for work.

"Maybe you'd like to work for me," said the giant.

"Sure," said the boy. "Why not?"

They agreed that the boy would serve the giant until the nightingale sang, and that the first one to get angry would have his back slashed and salt sprinkled in the wound as punishment.

The next morning the boy had to go out to plough. The giant

had a dog named Hops; when Hops came home, the boy could come home too. But Hops just lay in the field all day long without moving. After a whole day of ploughing with nothing to eat, the boy got tired and finally went home.

"It's not fair," he complained. "I work all day long and I get nothing to eat!"

"You're not angry, are you?" said the giant.

'Well," said the boy, "you can't help getting angry working all day without a morsel to eat!"

So the giant grabbed him, cut up his back, and sprinkled salt in the wounds. When the boy got home to his parents, he was in terrible pain.

Then the second son said, "Well, I guess it's my turn now to go to town and find work."

Soon he too met up with the same giant. But he didn't fare any better than the first, and returned home in terrible pain.

Now the third son said, "I guess *I'll* have to go to town and work. We can't all stay at home, and you two aren't too bright, anyway."

"You?" said the father. "If your brothers couldn't get work, what makes you think you can?"

The fact is that they'd always called the youngest boy Ashboy. He was the baby and had always stayed home with his mother, playing in the ashes.

When he met the giant, the giant asked him where he was headed.

"To town to find work," said the boy.

"Don't you want to work for me?" said the giant.

"Sure, why not?"

The boy agreed to work for the giant until the nightingale sang, and whoever got angry first would have his back slashed and salt sprinkled in the wound. He too had to go out ploughing with Hops; when the dog came home, the boy could too. Soon it was dinnertime. Since the boy had been ploughing all afternoon, he was very hungry. He drove down to a nearby inn, sold both horses, and bought food and aquavit. Later, when he came home, the giant asked, "Where are the horses?"

"I got hungry," he said. "So I went to the innkeeper, sold them, and bought some food. You're not angry, are you, Pop?"

"No," said the giant, "but it's too bad about my horses." He just couldn't allow himself to get angry.

Later the giant and his wife were invited to a party. The giant told the boy, "Tomorrow you're to stay home. You have to bake bread from these three barrels of flour, and brew a barrel of malt with plenty of hops in it. Then you have to lay a goat bridge* across the swamp, and then come to meet us. The old lady doesn't see too well, so you've got to lead her home. And you might as well cast an eye on me too now and then."

Early that morning, the boy got up and prepared for baking. He baked and fried and put the loaves out to cool on the floor. Then he brewed a barrel of malt, and when he saw Hops he grabbed him and threw him into the barrel. Then he went ahead and slaughtered all the giant's goats, including a big buck. He turned them on their backs with their legs sticking up, and the buck he placed in the middle of the bridge, legs and horns straight up in the air. He cut out all their eyes and put them into his pockets. Then he went off to the party.

Inside, they were sitting around a table having a merry old time partying and drinking. The boy took a few goat eyes and threw them in the giant's face.

"Aha!" said the giant. "So there you are."

After the boy had been standing there awhile, he started to get bored, and threw a few more goat eyes at the giant.

"Ah yes!" said the giant. "If you just wait a moment longer, we'll be ready to go."

After the boy had waited a moment longer, he took a whole fistful of eyes and threw them in the giant's face.

"Well, well," he said. "Now we're almost ready; I think we'll leave soon."

Finally the giant stood up, and they started home, with the boy leading the old woman. When they'd walked along for a while, they came to the goat bridge.

"Better hold on tight to those poles," the boy said.

* In boggy or swampy grazing areas, farmers often lay down planks for goats and sheep to cross. In this case the boy takes his assignment literally and makes the goats themselves into a bridge.

He was talking about the goat legs. When they got to the middle of the bridge, he said, "Just grab this, then you can stand and rest a little while."

She grabbed the horns of the big buck.

"Oh!" said the old woman. "I think I'm holding the big buck's horns." But she couldn't see.

Then the giant came.

"What's going on? Have you killed my goats?"

"Yes," said the boy. "I couldn't make a goat bridge without them, could I? So I killed them all and put them there as a bridge. They're nice to walk on! You're not angry about that, are you, Pop?"

"No," said the giant.

When they got home, the giant asked, "Did you bake the way I ordered you to?"

"Oh, yes," said the boy.

"Did you brew too?"

"Yes, Pop. Come here and taste!"

The giant took the ladle and was about to taste the drink.

"Go all the way to the bottom," said the boy.

The giant's ladle came up full of big bones.

"God help me!" he said. "I think these bones belong to Hops!"

"Yes, you told me to put plenty of hops in there, so I put in Hops too to make the drink really good. You're not angry about that, are you, Pop?"

"No," he said. "I'm not."

He simply couldn't get angry!

"Now we have to go to sleep," said the giant.

The boy pretended to go to the barn where he slept, but he went around to the window to hear what they were saying.

"What are we going to do about this fellow?" said the giant. "He'll finish off everything we own. When he's asleep, why don't we go down and kill him with the big sledgehammer?"

When the boy heard this, he took a big bunch of straw, put it in his bed, and covered it well. Later that night came the giant and his old woman.

"Are you asleep?" they said to the boy.

No answer.

"Yes, he's asleep," said the old woman.

The giant went up and hit him with the sledgehammer. There was no sound.

"I got him," said the giant. "It's nice and quiet."

Then they went back to their house to sleep.

Early that morning the boy came in.

"Did you sleep well last night?" asked the giant.

"Oh, yes, but in the middle of the night something pricked me in the head. Maybe it was a flea or something."

The next night the giant said to his old woman, "We can't kill him that way. We'll have to burn him up instead!"

This time too the boy was listening, and he took a rock and put it in his bed. Later that night the giant and the old woman came along with a lantern and a red-hot iron bar. Again, everything was nice and quiet. But the next morning the boy walked in.

"Did you sleep well last night?" the giant asked him.

"Yes, but in the middle of the night something felt sort of warm. But it soon passed."

The next night the giant said to his old woman, "We can't burn him *or* kill him. I don't know what to do!"

The boy was listening by the window.

The giant continued: "Go and climb up into the great big tree by the cliff and sing like the nightingale. That way we'll be rid of him, for then he'll have finished his service."

But the boy heard this too. He got a saw and sawed the tree so that he could chop it down with two or three strokes of the ax.

Early next morning the giant said, "You can go home now. Today the nightingale sang."

"That nightingale I'd like to see!" said the boy, and when he got to the tree he took his ax and chopped two or three times until the tree and the old woman fell. Then he went back to the giant.

"No, there was no nightingale in that tree. It was just an old lady sitting up there chirping. But I finished her off. I chopped down the tree, and with it that chirping old lady."

"That does it!" said the giant. "Now you've gone and killed Mom!"

"Well, you're not angry about that, are you, Pop?"

"No," said the giant.

He didn't dare lose his temper.

"Well, I suppose you'd better stay here," the giant said. "You can cook and clean, and we can live together."

"Sure," said the boy, "that suits me just fine."

The giant was old, and his eyes were giving him trouble.

"My father had the same problem," said the boy. "When his eyes started hurting, he got something to put in them, and it helped. He probably still has some of it at home."

"Well, hurry on home and get some," said the giant.

So the boy took off. In town he bought a few pounds of lead.

"The cream is cold," he said to the giant. "We'll have to heat it up."

"Does it hurt a lot when it's in the eyes?"

"Yes," said the boy. "Father said that it hurt a lot, but it was over soon."

"Well, if it hurts a lot and I get angry, twelve men won't be able to hold me down."

"Well," said the boy, "it does hurt quite a bit."

"Then drive those big iron stakes into the ground and hammer them deep. I'll lie down, and you can chain me by the arms and legs."

This the boy did. He drove the stakes down as far as he could, and shackled the giant with chains. Then he melted the lead.

"Open your eyes as wide as you can," he said, "so I can get in as much as possible."

The boy filled both his eyes with molten lead. The giant shot up, pulled the stakes out of the ground, and ripped the chains off.

"Now you're in for it!" he said to the boy, angry enough to kill him.

Because he couldn't see, he ran around groping for him, but he couldn't catch him. Finally, the giant sat down in the doorway.

"You'll starve to death!" he said to the boy.

The giant owned a great big stud ram, which the boy was good friends with. This ram liked to go inside the house, and at just that instant it walked under the giant's arm. "Oh, my ram!" said the giant, stroking its back, and the boy petted the ram too when it came inside. Then he killed it, took its skin, and pulled it over his body. On all fours the boy walked under the giant's arm, and the giant patted him saying, "Oh, my poor ram!"

In and out of the house the boy walked, making off with the

giant's gold and silver. Every time he walked past, the giant patted him and shouted, "Oh, my poor ram!"

After hitching one of the horses to a wagon, the boy loaded up all the gold and silver, and when he was ready to leave, he said, "Good-bye, Pop! I've slaughtered your big ram. It's lying on the floor. Now you can eat it up!"

And the boy left. Now he was a very rich man.

Little Hans

A young man named Nils was on his way home one night, when he happened to pass a graveyard where he saw two spirits fighting wildly.

"What's going on here?" Nils asked the spirit who'd fared the worse.

"Well, while I was alive, I owed him six stiver,* which I couldn't pay back before my death. That's why he won't give me any peace in my grave."

Nils took out his little purse and paid the six stiver to the other spirit, whereupon both ghosts disappeared.

A few days later Nils was planning to go out into the world to seek his fortune. First he went to his mother's grave to ask her blessing. When he stood up after kneeling beside the grave, he found that a young man his own age was standing next to him. The youth asked Nils if he could come along, as he too was going out to seek his fortune; he said that his name was Little Hans. Nils agreed gladly, and so they went on their way together. Whenever they needed something, it was Little Hans who managed to get it; they didn't lack for a thing.

After walking for a long time they finally arrived at a town where all the houses were draped in black. They went into an inn and inquired why the town was in mourning.

"You must have come a long way," said the innkeeper, "since

---

* A stiver is an old copper coin, worth approximately one cent.

you don't know about the unhappiness that has befallen us. The king's only daughter has been put under a spell by an evil wizard, and the king is in such deep mourning that he ordered all houses to be covered in black. The princess is gloriously beautiful, and many princes have proposed to her. But they must solve three riddles before they can have her hand. If they don't answer these riddles correctly, the princess has their heads cut off and their bodies hung up in her garden. By now, it's full of bodies, but the princess likes to stroll there among her admirers. The king is brokenhearted, and has asked everyone to pray for the poor princess and all the unhappy souls."

"Nils, you must propose to the princess," said Little Hans. "I'll help you, but first come with me."

He turned around and headed toward a big forest on the outskirts of the town. For a long time they walked around in the forest looking for something, and finally arrived at a deep pit, at the bottom of which lay a grizzled old man who couldn't climb out. Little Hans helped the old man out, and as a reward he received a gray cape, a sword, and a pair of wings. Whoever put on the cape would become invisible, and everything he touched with the sword would stick to it. The wings could take one anywhere one wished.

The two friends arrived at the castle, which looked gloomy and foreboding covered in black from top to bottom. Little Hans put the cape on to make himself invisible, while Nils went to tell the king that he intended to propose to the princess. This made the king and all the court very sad, and they tried to talk him out of it. But the princess just laughed and smiled happily at her new suitor.

The first riddle that Nils had to solve for the next day was to figure out what the princess was thinking about. He was taken to a small room where he could sit and ponder all night long. Little Hans, however, followed the princess into her room.

That evening the princess opened the window, put on a pair of wings, and said, "Up to the Brocken!" *

Little Hans put on his own wings and flew after her. As they flew,

---

* The Brocken is a mountain in northern Germany where, according to northern folklore, witches assembled for hedonistic rites.

he struck the princess with his sword, so that she shouted several times, "Ouch, what terrible weather we're having!"

Finally, they arrived at the Brocken. The princess entered the mountain, followed by Little Hans. Inside, it was teeming with horrible trolls who looked like cabbage heads on broomsticks. On a throne sat a disgusting old troll who was their leader.

"Welcome, princess," said the troll. "Any more victims coming up?"

"Yes," she said, and asked him for something to think about the next day.

"Think about this," said the troll, giving her a silver spoon.

The princess flew back to the castle, with Little Hans following behind. When she returned to her room, she went to put the spoon into her chest, but Little Hans held out his sword and touched it so that it stuck to the blade.

Little Hans brought the spoon to Nils, and the next morning when the princess asked him what she'd been thinking about, Nils showed her the spoon. The princess's face turned as white as linen, but the king and the court rejoiced over what had happened. The king decreed that the town be draped in white as a sign that the suitor had solved the first riddle.

The next evening the princess again put on her wings to fly to the Brocken, and Little Hans followed behind. This time he struck her so hard with the sword that she shouted many times, "Ouch, ouch, what awful weather we're having tonight!"

When the princess arrived she was greeted warmly by the troll, who this time gave her a gold ring to think about. He wished her better luck, and she went on her way. When she was above the ocean, she threw the ring down so that no one would get it. But quick as lightning Little Hans put out his sword and caught it; and when he got home, he gave it to Nils.

The next morning when Nils gave the princess the ring, she turned white as chalk and fell off her chair. But the king was so delighted that he decreed for the whole town to be draped in red.

That evening when the princess and Little Hans were on their way to the Brocken again, he beat her so hard with the sword that she cried out, "Ouch, ouch, ouch, such weather we're having tonight!"

The troll asked the princess if the suitor had solved the second riddle. When the princess answered that he had, the troll said, "This time, think about my head. Nobody will be able to guess that. But just in case, I'll follow you out to see if anyone's been listening."

The troll followed the princess to the door and stuck out his disgusting head. At just that moment Little Hans made sure to chop off his head, which stuck to the sword. The princess hadn't noticed a thing. Off she flew, with Little Hans following behind.

The next morning when the princess asked Nils what she'd been thinking about, he took out a large bundle and opened it. The troll's head rolled out onto the floor! And when the princess saw it, she fell down in a dead faint.

Everyone felt that the princess must be punished for all the evil she'd done, and Little Hans suggested that if she were to be put in boiling water and then whipped for three days with hazel sticks, the evil spirits would be sure to leave her.

And it was true. After she'd suffered this terrible punishment, she became a good and decent person again, and was so kind and friendly that everyone loved and respected her. She married Nils, who also got half the kingdom in the bargain.

One day Little Hans came to bid them goodbye, saying that he wanted to be on his way. The king asked him to stay at court as his advisor, and Little Hans thanked him for the honor but said that he couldn't stay any longer. He told them that he was the dead man whom Nils had helped at the graveyard by paying his debt. Now he wanted to return to his grave.

When the old king died, Nils and the princess became king and queen, and they ruled long and happily together.

Onen in the Mountain

Once there was a farmer who had three sons. His fields were right next to the fields of Onen in the Mountain; only a stream separated them. It was a good thing for the farmer that the stream was there, for trolls can't cross running water, and he didn't think too highly of Onen.

One day the farmer told his sons to go over to Onen's, propose to his daughters, and at the same time take Onen's blunderbuss and kill the rooster that woke him every morning when he went out to work in the fields. The boys went on their way, but when they came to the mountain, Onen was gone. Onen's wife, an obliging sort of woman, let them sleep overnight in the attic where the daughters slept. Early in the morning Perkel, the youngest of the boys, got up and found the blunderbuss that killed everything it touched. First he killed the rooster and then all three girls. Then he woke his brothers up, and they all hurried home.

Soon afterward Onen returned. Since he was tired, he fell asleep immediately and slept until the sun was high in the sky. He asked his wife why the rooster hadn't woken him up as usual, but all she knew was that the farmer's sons had come in the evening to propose to their daughters, and they were still up in the attic. When Onen went to check, the first thing that he saw was the vigilant rooster with his legs in the air. In bed lay all three girls, dead. Enraged, Onen rushed down to the stream, where he spied Perkel standing on the other side.

"How do you do, Perkel!"

"How do *you* do, Pop!"

"Are you the one who stole my blunderbuss, killed my rooster, and murdered my daughters?"

"Yes, Pop, I'm the one!"

"Will you be back again?"

"Yes, Pop, that I will!" And the rascal just walked calmly away.

Onen, who couldn't cross the stream, had to turn back home. "You just wait," he thought. "When you come back, you'll get what's coming to you!"

Now it happened that Onen was the owner of a pair of golden sheets that the farmer coveted, and one day he told Perkel about them. Perkel said that he could probably get his hands on them if only he could have a bit of dissolved yeast. That evening, at dusk, he snuck up to the mountain and into the troll's bedroom, concealing himself under the bed.

During the night, after Onen and his wife had fallen asleep, Perkel slipped out and poured the yeast between them. A while later Onen woke up.

"Ma, you've disgraced yourself!"

"No, Pa, you have!"

"No, I tell you, it's you!"

"It's not so terrible, Little Papa, it really isn't!" the old woman said, and she took off the sheets and brought them outside to dry on the ground.

Onen was so sleepy that he quickly dozed off again. Perkel chose just the right moment to slip out of his hiding place. He quickly snatched up the sheets and ran back home.

In the morning when the old woman went out to take in the sheets, they were gone. "Oh, no, Little Papa, that bad Perkel has been at it again!"

Onen rushed outside. When he got to the edge of the stream, he saw Perkel on the other side, standing calmly as if nothing had happened.

"How do you do, Perkel!"

"How do *you* do, Pop!"

"Are you the one who killed my rooster, stole my blunderbuss, murdered my daughters, and took my golden sheets?"

"Yes, Pop, I'm the one!"

"Will you be back again?"

"One more time, Little Pop!"

One late fall evening the farmer and his sons were returning from the forest. It was dark, and they kept stumbling over rocks and roots. But Onen's mountain was lit up as bright as moonlight. "Wouldn't it be wonderful to have a lantern like Onen's, a moon of the purest gold?" said the farmer. "Then we wouldn't have to stumble about in the dark."

Perkel started wondering how to get his hands on Onen's wonderful lantern. Before long he got an idea. He filled his knapsack with salt, and one evening climbed to the top of the mountain. Through a hole he could look down and watch the old woman stirring the porridge pot. Stealthily, he grabbed a handful of salt and let it fall into the pot, but the old woman's eyes were so dim that she didn't see a thing.

At dinnertime Onen came home. Hungrily he took a big spoonful of porridge.

"Phooey!" said he, spitting it out. "Too much salt!"

"It's not so bad, Little Papa, not so bad at all!" the old woman said. "I haven't even salted it yet, but I can go to the well to get some water to thin it."

Taking the golden moon-lantern down from the wall, she went outside. But when she put it down to draw water, Perkel was right there waiting. First he pushed her headfirst into the well, then snatched the lantern and raced off. After Onen had waited a while, he started to get impatient. He found her down in the well and the lantern gone, and on the other side of the stream Perkel was lighting his way with the golden moon.

"How do you do, Perkel!"

"How do *you* do, Pop!"

"Are you the one who killed my rooster, stole my blunderbuss, murdered my daughters, took my golden sheets, killed my wife, and stole my golden moon?"

"Yes, Pop, I'm the one!"

"Will you come back again?"

"Yes, Pop, one more time!"

By now Onen had only one treasure left—a horse in a stable locked with twelve strong locks. But even this was more than Perkel thought he should have, so he collected as many keys as he could, and one night after much effort he managed to get the horse out of the stable. But as he was about to mount up, the horse started whinnying and stomping, and Onen came rushing out. Finally he'd caught the boy, and he wasn't likely to give him up easily.

At first Onen put him on a diet of nuts and cream until he grew good and fat. Then Onen went to invite his friends for a feast. The troll's old mother stayed home to prepare the feast and make sure that Perkel was well roasted. She fired the oven seven times hotter than usual, and then went to get the boy. When she told him to sit down on the paddle, Perkel pretended to be so dumb that he fell off every time he tried; finally, the old woman had to show him herself. No sooner had she gotten on than Perkel grabbed the paddle handle, pushed the old woman into the oven, and closed the hatch. Afterward, he took a sheaf of straw, wrapped the old woman's clothes around it, and put it in the bed. Then he went to the stable, took out the horse, and rode home.

A while later Onen came back. At first he wondered why everything was in a mess, but when he saw the old woman in bed he figured that she'd gotten tired and had lain down to take a nap. But after some time had passed and she still hadn't moved, he shook her. The sheaf of hay fell apart. That was when he realized that Perkel had been up to his old tricks again. He ran to the oven and opened the hatch: there sat old grandma cooked to a crisp. In the stable the horse was gone, and on the other side of the stream Perkel was swaggering about.

"How do you do, Perkel!"

"How do *you* do, Pop!"

"Are you the one who killed my rooster, stole my blunderbuss, murdered my daughters, took my golden sheets, stole my gold moon, killed my wife, stole my horse, and roasted my old mother to a crisp?"

"Yes, Pop, I'm the one!" Perkel said.

That made Onen so angry that he burst!

The Gullible Troll

Once a troll decided to take over a field that belonged to a farmer. After much discussion they agreed to share the crop between them.

When seeding time came, the farmer asked the troll which part of the crop he wanted, the top or the bottom. "The bottom," answered the troll. When the crafty farmer heard this, he seeded the field with wheat, so that at harvest time he'd get the grain while the troll would get nothing but straw. The next year the troll chose the top. This time the farmer sowed turnips, and fooled his partner again.

Tired of a field that gave such bad results, the troll agreed to risk his part in a bet: whoever could mow the fastest would get the whole field to himself. The day before the competition the farmer sprinkled iron rods in among the grass that his opponent was to cut. When the competition began, the troll mowed and mowed, but he didn't get very far, for he was constantly meeting obstacles that he took to be an unusually hard kind of sorrel. Soon his scythe was so dull and chipped that he had to stop and take a break. But custom demands that one man cannot sharpen his scythe without the other one joining him. So the troll turned to the farmer, who was way ahead of him, and asked him in a despairing voice, "Aren't you going to stop soon and sharpen your scythe?" "Me?" answered the farmer with feigned surprise. "Oh, no, not yet. Ask me again around noontime, then we'll see."

"No thanks," the exhausted troll answered, "I'd rather give up right now."

As he spoke, the troll disappeared. As a reward for his cleverness, the farmer got to keep his field in peace.

The Clever Boy

Once there was a boy who worked for a giant. It was a very hard job. The giant had a great big ox that made a horrible mess, and the boy had constantly to sweep out after the ox, and he still couldn't keep the place clean. The giant was always bawling him out.

One day when he'd worked especially hard, the boy got a bright idea. He took a cork and pushed it into the ox's rear end. In the morning the giant came to inspect the barn, and found everything nice and clean, but he couldn't understand why the ox was so fat, or why it wouldn't eat.

"Perhaps you'd better take a look, Pop," said the boy.

"Perhaps I should," answered the giant, and started his examination. When he got to the tail, he lifted it up, causing the cork to fly out of the ox's behind. It hit the giant right in the temple so hard that he died on the spot and was buried under the manure.

The boy took over everything the giant owned and lived there happily for the rest of his days.

The Bäckahäst

ometimes a creature called the *näck** appears as a white horse. Whoever is quick enough to pull out a few hairs from his tail—if he adds these horsehairs to the hairs in his fiddle bow—may become an excellent musician. But if he wants to become a master musician, equal to the *näck* himself on the fiddle, he must get one of the *näck*'s own violins, which are not easy to come by. Extraordinary measures are needed.

An old fiddler in Norrbyås County† said that he learned his art in the following way. After cutting his left "nameless finger"‡ and collecting the drops of blood on a scrap of linen, he took his fiddle late one Thursday evening to a brook that ran north–south. When he reached the brook, he sat down on a rock and pulled the bow across the strings a few times. A big black pig came toward him. This was not the vision he'd expected, so he immediately hurried home.

The next Thursday evening he returned to the brook. This time he saw a black dog. As the dog wasn't what he'd wished to see either, he went home once again without succeeding in his quest.

Finally, on the third Thursday evening, the *bäckahäst* came. His coat was a dazzling white, and he galloped so fast that sparks flew from his hooves. Stopping in front of the fiddler, he snorted fiercely. The fiddler was frightened, but when he saw a violin on the horse's back, he regained his courage. Walking up to the *bäckahäst*, he took the violin and replaced it with his own and the scrap of linen; he also made sure to pull out a few hairs from the horse's tail. These he fastened to his bow, and from that moment on he could play the fiddle better than anyone in the entire county.

But there was something odd about his playing. A soldier at Hidingsta Field§ told this story:

---

* *Näck:* water spirit. When the *näck* takes the form of a horse, as in this tale, he is called the *bäckahäst*, or brook horse. The word *näck* is related to Greek, Sanskrit, and Old Irish verbs meaning "to wash." It is well attested among older Germanic languages and shows association with water monsters.

† Norrbyås County is in the district of Närke.

‡ I.e., his ring finger.

§ Hidingsta Field is in Norrbyås County in the district of Närke.

One evening, after attending a party that lasted several days, the fiddler—who was quite drunk—came to visit the soldier. The soldier invited him to sit down, and after some small talk they started discussing the fiddler's skills on the violin. The soldier praised him to the skies.

"Well, I do know a thing or two about the fiddle," said the fiddler. "But if you could hear me when I really get going, you'd be amazed. It's probably better for us both if you don't."

"What could be so dangerous about that?" asked the soldier. "Why don't you just tune up and give us one of your best reels? It would be a great pleasure for all of us."

"Very well, have it your way," said the musician, placing the violin on his back. In this peculiar position he began to play.

The notes he brought forth had a curious power: not only the soldier's children, but tables, chairs, and even the chopping block in the corner by the stove began to move with the music. The music grew wilder and wilder and faster and faster, and so did the dancing. When even the newly acquired Dalecarlian clock* started to dance, the soldier was terrified. He asked the fiddler to stop, but he kept playing faster and faster. In desperation the soldier rushed up to him and grabbed his arm so that the bow was pulled away from the strings.

The fiddler collapsed on the floor like an empty sack, and lay there for a while, dead to the world. The soldier and his wife helped him onto the sofa, and little by little he revived. He grabbed the soldier's hand.

"Thanks for your help," he said. "If you hadn't taken the bow from the strings, it would have ended badly. The *strömkarl*† himself was playing; all I did was supply the arms. If you hadn't helped me, he'd have played the death reel on me. He was just getting warmed up when you saved me."

The fiddler took his leave and went on his way, but the soldier's wife threw some burning embers after him, and the soldier nailed a broken scythe up above the door.‡

* A clock from Dalarna, or Dalecarlia, a province in northern Sweden. These grandfather clocks are internationally known for their distinctive painted and carved designs.

† *Strömkarl:* "water man," another term for the *bäckahäst* and the *näck*.

‡ Throwing burning embers and nailing a broken scythe above the door were common methods to ward off evil.

"When it comes to the tricks and snares of trolls and the Evil One, one can never be too careful," said the soldier.

The Skogsrå *at Lapptjärns Mountain*

Anders Hansson tended his charcoal stacks deep in the great forest on Lapptjärns Mountain. Silent and gloomy, the forest surrounded the stacks and the little cabin. But Hansson was not the timid sort; he'd met the *skogsrå** many times, and he hadn't run even a single step when it threatened to chase him.

Still, he couldn't get any peace. Every night when he wanted to go to bed, a big *skogsrå* would come along and plant itself in the cabin doorway. Its mouth was so big that it reached from the doorstep to the top of the door frame, and it would scream, "What's your name? Have you ever seen such a big mouth? What's your name? Look what a big mouth!"

Hansson said that his name was Myself. He didn't want to tell his real name to a troll; that might cause trouble. Night after night the disgusting *skogsrå* returned and stood there in the doorway, shouting, "What's your name? Have you ever seen such a big mouth?"

For a long time Hansson considered what he could do to drive away the horrible *skogsrå*. Not that he was frightened—not a bit! But he wasn't getting any sleep. So one night when the *skogsrå* stood there gaping again, he flung a full pot of boiling tar right into its open mouth. You should have seen what a ruckus that made! The *skogsrå* started dancing around so that everything in its way went flying, and it screamed with all its might, "Myself has burned me! Myself has burned me!"

"Did you burn yourself? Then it's your own fault! Did you burn yourself? Then it's your own fault!" came the answer from all corners of the forest.

And from that day on, Anders Hansson never saw the *skogsrå* again.

---

* *Skogsrå*: forest spirit; see Introduction, page xxi.

To Catch Smoke

s everyone knows, a district like Västergötland has a lot of old superstitions. From my mother's father, who was born the twenty-third of March, 1826, I heard the following tale about *tomtar:* *

In Wadsbo, on quite a large farm, lived a farmer who was considered by everyone to be very rich and mysterious. His farm was big, but what most mystified the people of the area was that, although he lived all alone, he did all the work by himself. In fact, he was often further along in his chores than his neighbors, many of whom had both farmhands and servant girls. Everyone speculated back and forth, but no one could solve the riddle.

Years passed, and the farmer's wealth grew. He cultivated his fields, built new roads, broke stones, and cleared land. No one ever saw anyone but him working there. But actually the farmer had had no peace, neither night nor day; the *tomtar*, who did nearly all the work on his farm, were always nagging him to give them more. According to legend, *tomtar* can't stand being idle, and they were making this farmer quite dizzy in the head.

Just when he didn't know what else to give them, it occurred to him that the road to town went around a large, almost bottomless swamp; here the *tomtar* would have their work cut out for them.

One morning the farmer brought them to the swamp and showed them where he wanted to build the road. He walked along marking the way, but it was so difficult to find his footing that, so the story goes, the *tomtar* built the road as fast as he could walk. Every time he got stuck in the mud and sludge, the *tomtar* would catch up with him and a bump would appear, and when he moved at a faster pace, the road would sink. When he'd struggled his way across the whole swamp to firm ground, he turned around and was astonished to see that the whole road had been completed.

Now what was he going to do with all these *tomtar?* He didn't have any more work for them, and without work they'd give him no peace. In his despair, he sat down on a rock and lit his pipe. Suddenly, he had an idea. As he blew out a cloud of smoke, he called to

---

* *Tomtar:* household spirits; see Introduction, page xxi.

the *tomtar* to collect the smoke and bring it back to him. They all ran off to do as he bid, but the task proved impossible even for them, and legend has it that after seven years only one lonely *tomte* returned to the farmer. This *tomte* had managed to collect a little bit of the smoke, which he'd kept in a quill.*

During all the years the *tomtar* were gone, the farmer couldn't find farm workers to help him, for everyone assumed that he'd been associating with evil spirits.

The road spoken of in this story is in Wadsbo, more precisely between Rambotorp and Åsbotorp,† and to this day is called the Tomte Road. The surface of the road was later smoothed out a bit, but the original Tomte Road remains on top of the ridge. If one is to

---

* Translation uncertain from the dialect term *fjäderspinne, fjäderpenna*, or *fjäder-spänne.*

† Wadsbo, Rambotorp, and Åsbotorp are all villages in the district of Västergötland.

judge it by its bumpiness, it looks as if the legend might be true. I myself have walked it several times, and I could see with my own eyes how it was made.

The Tale of the Troll Woman

Once there was a troll woman who lived in a mountain not far from Vadstena.* One day she went flying off to visit another troll woman in Omberg. On her way she spied a farmer's wife sitting by the side of the road. She flew down, sat next to her, and helped pick lice from her hair. Suddenly, they heard thunder.

"What was that?" the troll woman asked.

"Just the foals pawing at the stall," the farmer's wife said.

A little later there was a new thunderclap.

"What was that?" the troll woman asked.

"Some people driving across the bridge," the farmer's wife said.

But the farmer's wife could feel that the troll had put her hand under the belt that she always wore around her waist. Quickly she unbuttoned it. Just then there was another clap of thunder. Now the troll woman got up, very angry, and said to the sky, "You could have told me ahead of time that you were out in your wagon!" †

She took a firm grip on the woman's belt and flew up in the air. The belt followed along, but the farmer's wife stayed where she was, and the troll had to turn around and fly back toward Vadstena. Before she got home, the lightning struck her. She crashed to the ground but didn't die; instead, she swelled up until she was huge. This was how a farm boy found her as he came walking by. He went home, found a gold ring that had been through three weddings, and cast it into a bullet. With that he shot the troll.

Her skeleton can still be seen today in the Vadstena church.

* Vadstena and Omberg are towns in Östergötland, in southeast Sweden.

† This presumably refers to Thor, whose wagon creates thunder, and who in this tale protects the farmer's wife from being abducted by the troll.

The Tale of Speke

Once there was a man named Speke who killed his wife by hammering a six-inch spike into her head. Then he died and was buried, but many years later they had to dig up the graves. He hadn't decayed—he was a slimy mass that they took and put in the church chapel.

At the parsonage was a cook who wasn't afraid of the dark. They asked her if she'd go and fetch Speke at twelve o'clock midnight and bring him to the kitchen: if she'd do it, she'd get a dress. So she did. She went and brought Speke to the kitchen, but when she lifted up a pot and said "In the name of Jesus" (that's what they always said when they put the pots on or took them off the stove), Speke sneered and leered. Finally, she got fed up with him. They said that they'd give her another dress if she'd carry him back at the same time of night, and she said that she would.

When she picked him up, the slimy mass grabbed her, saying, "Go to my wife's grave and ask if she forgives me. Don't leave till you get an answer!" The cook went, and she got this answer: "If God forgives, I can forgive too." When she came back, she told this to Speke. Later he decayed in one night.

The Gypsy Girl and her Dead Fiancé

Once there were a gypsy boy and a gypsy girl who loved each other. They belonged to different clans, both of which were large and wealthy. They were constantly in each other's company; the boy was beautiful and so was the girl—beauty they didn't lack!

Whatever happened or didn't happen, one lovely day the boy's father goes to the father of the girl and proposes on behalf of his son. His offering is quite handsome; no small amount of gold does he put up for her. But the girl's father says no. He has other plans for his daughter.

The boy's father walks home in a sour mood. For his son's sake, however, he makes one more attempt, and even another. He adds

more and more ducats to the offer. But the girl's father is immovable.
He will not let the wedding bells ring for his daughter and this gypsy's
son. And there it stands.

Mischtó!* The clans part and go their separate ways. Days pass—
months—even years. Whatever happened or didn't happen, one evening the young gypsy comes riding to the girl on a gorgeous white
horse. He's dressed magnificently. Truly, he's a man one could fall
in love with. He speaks with his woman; not many words are needed.
They run off together.

He puts her in the saddle in front of him. They ride. It is night.
Dark. The man says nothing. He just rides and rides. How long they
ride, I don't know, so I can't tell you. Finally, he stops his horse.
And where are they? In the graveyard.

"Oh, my love, do you live here?" says the girl.

"Yes."

He leads her to an open grave, takes her hand, and says, "Now
come to our home!"

"Yes, my dear, go ahead of me and receive my clothes. I can't
enter your house dressed as I am now."

And what happens? The dead one is willing. He reaches his hand

---

* *Mischtó:* Rómani exclamation meaning "good," "well," "all right."

out of the grave to take his beloved's clothes. Garment after garment she takes off, ripping each one into thin strips which she gives him, one by one. Time crawls by. It is midnight. It won't be dawn for a long time. Strip after strip she hands to the dead man. Thinner and thinner she makes them. She's torn up the *dikló,** the apron, the dress. Alas, the hand wants more, more . . . What can she give him? Soon she is naked. She offers her earrings. One by one. And now . . . ? Oh, the pearls! She's got the pearls! She takes them off. One by one, she pulls off her pearls and gives them to the dead one. Isn't there light in the sky? Seven pearls left . . . five . . . four . . . three . . . The hand waves for more, more . . . Then the rooster crows, singing out his morning call! The grave shuts, shuts on the outstretched hand, which is waving for more . . .

Naked, the girl runs to the bell tower. She rushes up the stairs, grabs the rope, and pulls. The bells chime. The people wake up. What's going on? Is there a fire? They get up and rush to the bell tower.

"Who's ringing?"

"Oh, it's only I, a woman!"

"So come down!"

"For the love of God and Man, I can't. I'm naked. What happened is this, dear friends . . . " And she tells them.

"Woman, if you're telling a lie, your punishment will be severe. This is a serious matter."

"Go to the gypsy's grave! His hand may still be seen. In the name of merciful Christ, hurry!"

And they search and find the grave with the hand sticking out of the ground.

They dig up the dead one, and make a large pyre. On that he is burned. He will trouble no one again.

So the story goes, dear friends. This is what happened once, according to the elders.

* *Dikló:* the multicolored headdress of the married gypsy woman. It is a great shame for a married woman to show herself without her *dikló,* which tells us that the girl is now married.

Hobergsgubben

There was to be a christening at the home of the neighbors of a troll called Hobergsgubben,* and so the hosts thought that they'd better invite him. As a neighbor he was fine, but as a guest he ate far too much, and so they weren't too eager to have him at the christening. Still, they sent their boy off with the invitation.

"Will there be music?" asked Hobergsgubben.

* The name Hobergsgubben refers to a medieval belief that trolls lived in the *höjbergs*—tall hills or mountains—and that humans had better stay friends with them.

"Yes, Saint Peter will be playing, and Saint Michael will play the drums," answered the boy.

Hobergsgubben had misgivings about both of them, especially Saint Michael, since the day he'd thrown his drumstick* after Hobergsgubben and knocked off one of his thighbones.

"This party won't be much fun," thought Hobergsgubben. But he thanked them for inviting him, and he asked if it was customary to give a christening gift.

"Yes, those who want to be honorable usually give one," answered the boy.

Hobergsgubben took the boy into his treasure trove and gave him a sack to hold while he shoveled gold into it.

"Will anyone give more than that?" he asked the boy.

"Yes, those who want to be honorable usually give more," he answered.

So he added another shovelful.

"Will anyone give more than that?" Hobergsgubben asked again.

"Yes, those who want to be honorable usually give more," answered the boy.

So Hobergsgubben added another shovelful, and asked, "Will anyone give more than *that* as a christening gift?"

By now the boy didn't think he could carry any more gold, so he said that he'd never ever seen a grander christening gift. When he returned home with his sack, he was praised to the skies for his cleverness and cunning.

The Trolls and the Bear

When I was thirteen or fourteen years old, I served as a shepherd's boy on Bornholm.† It was in Klemensker County,

---

* Saint Michael was considered the celestial drummer, or thunder-maker. In other versions of this tale, Thor is the drummer. "Throwing the drumstick" refers to Saint Michael's striking the troll with lightning.

† Bornholm is an island belonging to Denmark, situated just south of Sweden, to which poor Swedish peasants sometimes went to find work (see Introduction, pages xv–xvi).

close to Rønne, on the west side of the island. The farm where I served was called Bear's Farm. The owner of the farm told me how the farm got its name:

In the old days there were always trolls around the farm. One day a man came with a tame bear and asked if he could sleep there.

"Perhaps this isn't the best place," said the farmer. "We get a lot of trolls around here."

"That suits us just fine," the man said.

It was close to Christmas when he came. That night at twelve o'clock, the trolls arrived, driving their wagon right into the central courtyard. They got out, walked into the kitchen, and started frying and broiling. One of the trolls was so big and fat that they had to carry him in. Later they came into the dining hall, where the man was lying on a bench by the stove, smoking his pipe. He'd tied the bear by one leg to the cast-iron stove. The trolls asked for the man's pipe, but he wouldn't give it to them, for that would have given them power over him. Then they wanted to lie on the bench by the stove, but he wouldn't let them do that either. So they set food on the table, and when they were ready, they asked the man if he'd eat with them, but no, he wouldn't. They threw bones to the bear, but he wouldn't eat them either. Finally, after the trolls had sat themselves at the table, the man let the bear loose, and he attacked the trolls. They ran to the door, but the fat one had to be dragged, and the bear nipped his behind. Though they left everything behind on the table, they managed to take along the kitchen things.

That morning the farmer asked how the man had managed during the night.

"I collected a few things last night," said the man with the bear, pointing to the table: everything was made of gold or silver.

"Will they come back?" asked the farmer.

"Yes, most likely, but whoever starts a job must finish it."

A while later the trolls did come back, this time around two o'clock in the morning. Again the man lay smoking his pipe on the bench by the stove. This time he'd put the bear by the door, and now the bear attacked the trolls as they entered.

"How did it go last night?" asked the farmer the next morning.

"Well enough, but now they've sent for the head troll of the whole countryside. He's so big that he can eat Pussy and me in one bite."

The man cooked up a pot of tar, mixed in some explosives, and boiled it for seven hours until the pot turned a glowing red. That night the trolls came back.

"It's smoky in here tonight," said the head troll. "Did you ever see such a big mouth?" And he gaped until one lip lay on the doorstep and the other reached the top of the doorway. "I'll take Pussy and you in one bite," he said.

"Did you ever taste this kind of porridge before?" said the man, throwing the pot of tar into the troll's mouth.

That morning the farmer asked if they had come back again.

"Yes they did," said the man. "And if they ever return and ask if the big cat is still here, tell them yes."

About half a score years later, the farm boys were watering the cows one day in a pond near the farm. It was a few days before Christmas. As they were getting ready to drive the cows back inside, one of them saw a small red boy waving at him, saying that he wanted to talk to him.

"No, I don't have time," said the boy. "I have to tie up the cows."

"Come on, I need to talk to you," the red boy said again. "Do you still have that mad cat?"

The boy didn't know what he meant, but then he remembered the bear and said, "Yes, we still have it, but it's had kittens, so now we have seven of them."

"Oh, save us from that mad cat!" yelled the red boy, and he disappeared.

Later the farm boy came back inside and told the farmer what had happened; he was so pleased that he gave that clever boy a big reward.

After that, the trolls never came back to Bear's Farm.

The Giant's Toy

People don't talk so much about giants, but they believe in them all the same. Here's one story that I've heard, not read, about them.

Before the Lapps came to the *fjäll*,* it was ruled by giants. One day when the giant woman was outside, she came upon a curious thing. She put it in her scarf, intending to cook it and eat it up. But first she wanted to show it to the giant, who was away. So she put it down and let it run around inside the mountain wherever it wanted. That was the first Lapp. As he was running around, he found an ax that wasn't too big for him to lift. He carefully waited for the giant as he crept through the long tunnel into the mountain, and he hit him on the head and killed him. After a while the giant woman came crawling from the opposite direction to see what was going on, and she too got a blow from the ax. Since then the Lapps have been the sole masters of the *fjäll*.

* *Fjäll:* a highland area in northern Sweden.

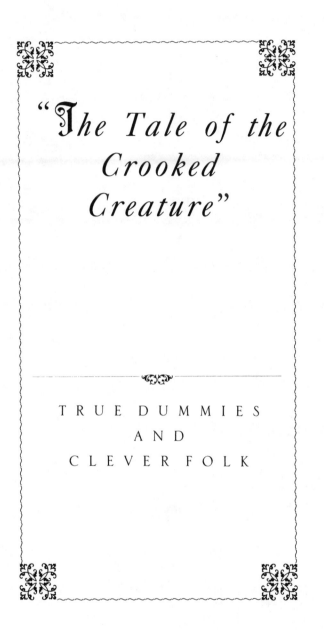

"The Tale of the Crooked Creature"

TRUE DUMMIES
AND
CLEVER FOLK

The Tale of the Crooked Creature

I can't tell you exactly when this story took place, but it's enough to say that once upon a time a Göing* was driving north on the plains with a wagonload of hops. He'd been gone for only a few days when he ran out of feed for his horse. But he wasn't worried; when he came to a clover field, he got off his wagon, took his sickle, and cut himself some fodder.

At that moment the local field guard† came along, and the Göing got scared and drove off, leaving the sickle behind. When the guard saw that sickle, he thought it must be some kind of strange animal, for, you see, the plains people don't have sickles, and he'd never seen one before. He ran off to blow the village horn, and when all the villagers had gathered around, he said, "It seems that some kind of crooked creature has come to our fields, and he's already eaten up some of the grass."

At first the men stood around thinking, but then they each grabbed a staff and went off to the field. There they found the dangerous creature lying asleep—they could tell it was sleeping because it didn't move at all. One of the very bravest stepped up and struck the crooked creature with his staff as hard as he could. But the creature jumped up and fastened itself around the alderman's neck. When the townspeople saw this, they rushed forward and started to pull it off, for they thought—and you can understand why—that it might hurt him. But they sliced off the alderman's head, and that was the end of him and the story as well.

---

* A Göing is someone from Göinge County in the northern highlands of Skåne in southern Sweden.

† In the past, a so-called *vångagömmare*—approximately, "field guard"—was appointed in certain Skåne towns to watch over the fields of the village to make sure that neither animals nor humans did them any harm.

Wise Klara

Once there was a king who had three daughters, the youngest of whom was named Klara. One day the king had to go away to war. To protect his daughters from all harm, he built a tall tower for them in the forest. Since the tower had no doors, the princesses had to be hoisted up, and when they were all well inside, he gave each of them a wreath.

"If your wreaths are still fresh and green when I return, I'll know that no one got in to see you and that no misfortune befell you," said the king.

When he left, the three princesses cried. But they soon recovered and started looking around. The tower was very beautifully outfitted, and they started eating the lovely food that had been left for them. But after some time they grew bored. All day long they sat by the window, hoping that someone would walk past.

One day a prince from a neighboring country was taking a walk beneath the tower. Immediately, the two eldest princesses started to talk and joke with him, and he came back every day to talk with them. After some time had passed, he asked if he could come up to visit. The two eldest princesses wanted to throw down a rope ladder, but the youngest, whom they called Wise Klara, advised them not to disobey their father.

One day shortly afterward, a poor old beggar came walking by the

tower. Since it was raining and a cold wind was blowing, he begged the princesses to let him come up. Wise Klara urged them not to, but the sisters let the poor old man into the tower anyway. No sooner had he entered, however, than he threw off his broad cape, and there stood the young prince. The princesses were very surprised to see him, but he just laughed with delight over the trick he'd played on them. All day long the two eldest princesses played games with the prince, but Wise Klara was angry about how he'd fooled them.

When evening came, the prince didn't want to go home, and asked if he could sleep over for the night. But it was cramped in the tower, so the oldest princess had to give him her bed and sleep with her sister. The next evening he still didn't want to leave, so he lay in the middle princess's bed. But on the third night he wanted to lie in Wise Klara's bed. She wasn't pleased with the idea of giving her beautiful bed to the prince, and she decided to take revenge. After she loosened a few floorboards, she took away the base of the bed; when the prince lay down, he crashed right through the hole, landing on the ground under the tower.

Wise Klara stood by the window, laughing. He had to limp shame-facedly home.

After some more time had passed, the princesses began to wish for some of the good food that they knew was in the prince's castle. They begged Klara, who was so clever, to get it for them. At first she refused, but finally she let herself be convinced, and, disguised as a kitchen boy, she went off to the prince's castle to seek work. She got it, for a great feast was being prepared in the castle. As the food was about to be served to the prince and his guests, the chief cook went out for a moment to give an order to the footmen. Wise Klara quickly stuffed her pockets with as much food as she could. Then she turned over all the pots and pans, threw water on the hearth, and wrote on the table with a piece of coal: "Wise Klara was here!" Then she ran off to her sisters with the food.

When the chief cook came back to the kitchen and saw what Wise Klara had done, he was terribly upset. The whole party was ruined, and he ran crying to the prince to tell him what had happened. When the prince came down to the kitchen and saw what was written on the table, he knew who'd done the mischief.

After a while the princesses began to wish that they had some of the good wine in the prince's castle. Wise Klara had to go off again. This time she arrived at the castle dressed as a serving boy and asked for work; since the prince was about to give a great drinking party, she was allowed to help out. When no one was looking, she stole the key to the wine cellar. There she poured wine into a bottle for her sisters and pulled out all the stoppers of the wine barrels. Then she wrote on a barrel: "Wise Klara was here!"

When the prince found out about it, he ordered anyone who came to the castle to be arrested; that way he'd finally catch Wise Klara.

The older princesses weren't satisfied with what they'd gotten, so a little later Wise Klara was sent to fetch some fruit for them from the prince's garden. Barely had she gotten into the garden before the head gardener grabbed her. The prince was sent for, and he gloated happily as he came down to the garden. He wanted to punish her himself, so he ordered that no one be allowed to enter the garden no matter how much she yelled and screamed. But he was alone with her for hardly a moment before she threw a rope around him and tied him to a tree! Then she took his stick and beat him so thoroughly that he screamed for mercy. But no one dared countermand his order and go into the garden, and when the courtiers finally got up their courage and ran to his aid, Wise Klara had disappeared, leaving the prince lying battered and senseless by the tree.

Finally, the king was due to come back from the war, and the princesses took out their wreaths to look at them. The wreaths of the two eldest were withered and yellow, but Wise Klara's was fresh and green.

"That's what you get for being disobedient to our father, and for letting the prince into the tower," said Wise Klara.

Her sisters wailed and whined and begged Wise Klara to help them, which she finally promised to do. So when the king asked to see the wreaths, the princesses lined up in a row with Wise Klara in front. After she'd shown her wreath, she snuck it behind her back to the next sister, who showed it to her father and in turn passed it on to the eldest sister.

The king was very pleased. He let the princesses out of the tower and arranged a grand party for them. Since the prince had recovered from the beating that he'd gotten from Wise Klara, he came too. But now he hated the older princesses for being disobedient to their father, and talked only to Wise Klara. It didn't take long before he was so in love with the wise, beautiful girl that he proposed. But Wise Klara didn't want him, and it was only after her father insisted that she consented.

After the wedding, the prince told his bride that he'd forgive all the tricks that she'd played on him if she'd manage to protect herself from his revenge on their wedding night. Wise Klara, who little by little had grown fond of the prince, said that she could protect herself quite well. She went out, got a pig, trussed up its legs, and put it in her bed under the covers.

That evening when they were preparing to go to bed, Wise Klara hid behind a door while the prince sneaked up to the bed and started hitting it as hard as he could. The pig screamed so pitifully that Wise Klara jumped out and begged him to stop!

After that the prince never again tried to get revenge on his Klara, and they lived happily together. The prince became king and Wise Klara his queen, and they were both much beloved by their people.

The Stupid Boy Who Didn't Know About Women

Once upon a time like any other time, there was a rich farmer who had only one boy, and this boy happened to be a dummy. Even though he was almost grown up, he didn't want to have anything to do with the ladies. But his old man thought up a plan: he sent the boy to town with a couple of old oxen to sell, and he told him, "When you get to town, be sure that they pay you *ligghos** for the oxen."

When the boy got to town with the oxen, a butcher came up to him and asked, "What do you want for those oxen?"

"I want some *ligghos*," said the boy.

"I see," said the butcher. "Bring them into the yard, and I'll see that you get some."

The boy led the oxen into the yard and tied them up, and then

---

* *Ligghos = ligga hos = ligga med* = lie with, sleep with.

the butcher invited him inside and gave him delicious food to eat. The boy ate as much as he could, and then some.

Then the butcher asked him, "Do you think you got enough *ligghos* for the oxen?"

"Oh, yes," said the boy, "those were really good *ligghos*!"

When the boy returned home, his old man asked him if he'd gotten *ligghos* for the oxen.

"Oh, yes," he said, "I got some really good *ligghos*, and I want some more right away!"

This cheered the old man up. He ran and found the girl he wanted his son to marry, and he persuaded him that if he married her, he'd get all the *ligghos* he wanted. Naturally, the boy married her on the spot, but they were barely through the ceremony before the boy began to cry for *ligghos*, and he got so insistent that they had to make up the bed immediately. They told him to lie down next to his bride.

"No," said the boy, "I want *ligghos* on the table."

They brought the bedding from the bed and started to arrange it on the table, telling the boy and his bride to do it on the table if that was how they wanted it.

"No," said the groom, "I can't eat *her*, can I?"

So finally they put food on the table, and when the finest dishes were served, the groom said, "Now that's *ligghos*!"

Finally, the old man understood what the boy meant when he said *ligghos*. How everything worked out later on nobody knows, but at least the old man was happy: he'd married off his son.

Counting the Stars in Heaven

Once there was a boy who was asked by the king if he could count the stars in Heaven. The boy took a piece of paper and a needle and poked so many holes in the paper that it was impossible to fit in another one. Then he handed the paper to the king and said, "When Your Majesty has counted all these holes, then I'll count the stars."

That got him out of that problem.

Then the king asked him if he could count all the drops of water in the ocean. "That's easy," said the boy. "But first Your Majesty must shut off the water in all the lakes, and streams, and rivulets, and the rain from the sky." Of course, that was impossible, so he got out of that one too.

Later the king asked if the boy could tell him when the first minute of eternity had passed.

The boy said, "In the Mediterranean Ocean stands a large diamond mountain. Every hundred years a bird comes and strokes the mountain with its beak. When the mountain is worn down, the first minute of eternity will have passed."

So he got around that one as well, and I believe that he won some sort of special reward for the answers to these questions, but I don't remember what it was.

Fools

Eleven *knallar** were walking through a field of rye. The rye was ripe and moving like waves in the wind, which made them think they were in the Red Sea. When they came out on the other side, they wanted to count heads to see if any among them had drowned. All of them counted, but they forgot to count themselves, so they never got more than ten no matter how they tried. Then they met a farmer and explained their problem to him. He showed them a soft cowpat, and told them to stick their noses in it; that way they'd be able to see how many they were. After they did this, they saw that they were eleven.

* *Knallar:* peddlers; see note, page 12.

The Princess of Catburg

nce there was a poor peasant couple who were always fighting with each other. All they had was a boy and a girl and a cow and a cat.

After the woman had cooked porridge one day, neither the husband nor the wife wanted to lick the whisk; they both wanted to scrape the pot. The man grabbed the pot and the woman the whisk, and they started chasing each other. Up the mountains and down the valleys they ran, away from children and cow and cat.

They never came back, so the children had to decide how to divide their inheritance. Since all it consisted of was the cat and the cow, one of them would get the cat and the other the cow. The boy wanted the cow, but the girl didn't want the cat. However, the cat said to the girl, "Won't you please take me? You won't be sorry."

So the girl took the cat, and off they went, the girl with the cat and the boy with the cow. After walking for a while the cat said to the girl, "Come along with me right now!" She did as he said, and they walked and they walked until they came to a great castle. There the cat told the girl to strip stark naked, crawl into a tree, and keep her mouth shut. This the girl did, while the cat went inside the castle.

"How do you do?" said the cat when he was inside. "There's a naked princess in a tree out there. She's been attacked by robbers and they've stripped all her clothes off. I demand that you dress her in the finest clothes you have, for she's very highborn. If you do this, you'll be handsomely rewarded, but if you don't, I'll tear you to pieces."

Frightened, they immediately dressed her in the finest clothes they had and brought her inside the castle. That evening the cat told them, "Now get a bed ready for her. And it must be the very finest you have, for she's a very important person."

The people in the castle wondered if she was really as highborn as the cat would have them believe. To test this, they decided to put peas in her bed to see if she felt anything—she would, of course, if she were really as high and mighty as the cat insisted. But the cat overheard them, and he told the peasant girl what to say when they

asked her in the morning how she'd slept: "Well," she'd say, "I didn't sleep so well, actually. I felt something hard under me. No, I sleep much better at home in Catburg!"

In the morning all went as the cat had said. The girl answered just the way he'd instructed her, and they decided that she must be very highborn. But they still wanted to test her one more time. This time they sprinkled grains of rice instead of peas under her down mattress. Again the cat found out what they intended to do, and he told the girl how to answer when they asked how she'd slept. In the morning she said exactly what the cat had taught her: "Thank you, I slept somewhat better, but I still felt something hard under me. I sleep better at home in Catburg." Now the entire castle was convinced that she was of very high birth.

This peasant girl was very beautiful, and the crown prince was so delighted with her that he soon proposed to her, and she accepted.

One day a little later when the princess and the crown prince sat playing together, she started laughing quite uncontrollably. She'd seen the old man and woman—her parents, that is—running by. The old man was still running in front with the pot, and the old woman behind him with the whisk. She found this so funny that she couldn't stop laughing. The prince asked what she was laughing at. "I'm laughing because my home at Catburg is built on gold pillars instead of the clay pillars you have here," she said. But the prince, who'd

heard so many tales of the wonders of Catburg, was curious to see it. "If it's so beautiful at Catburg, it's there we must go."

Now of course the girl was very unhappy, since she didn't have any castle at all, but the cat comforted her and promised to take care of everything. She and the crown prince prepared for the long journey.

The cat ran ahead of them, and soon he came to a large field where many men and women were busy cutting and raking. The cat said to the field workers, "In a little while a prince and princess will drive by. When the prince asks who owns this field, tell them it belongs to the princess of Catburg. If you do this, you'll be handsomely rewarded, but if you don't, I'll tear you to pieces." The people promised to do as the cat had told them. And so when the prince heard that his princess owned such a large field, he knew for sure that she was rich.

By now they'd traveled so far that they had to find shelter for the night. While the prince, and the princess of Catburg, were sleeping, the cat found a fine castle for the peasant girl.

As it happened, a giant lived in a big castle nearby. During the night the giant went out hunting, and the cat snuck into the castle and prepared it for their arrival. Later, to make sure that the giant wouldn't be able to get in—well, the cat shat into the keyhole.

Then, toward morning before the sun came up, the giant came home. Of course he couldn't get the key in the keyhole. He started to shout for them to open the door, but the cat stood inside and laughed, saying that if the giant would only calm down a little the cat would tell him the story of his life.

"At first they kneaded me, and then they baked me," the cat kept repeating. But the giant grew madder and madder. He roared for them to let him into his castle. Finally, when the cat saw that the sun was coming up, he called out to the giant, "Hey, take a look at that pretty maiden!" The giant turned around. When he looked at the sun, he burst and died.

The cat got some people to drag him away and made sure to take the key that was in the giant's hand. He opened the door and then went to fetch his masters and lead them to Catburg.

The prince and the princess and the cat lived happily for the rest of their lives in the beautiful castle of Catburg.

Pretend to Eat, Pretend to Work

Many years ago there lived a farmer who was so miserly that he couldn't make himself eat more than one meal a day. Naturally, the farmhand who helped him didn't get fed any more often than the man of the house himself, and it was obvious that he sure wasn't getting any fatter.

Strangely enough, this farmer didn't have a bad reputation in town. He had more money at the bottom of his chest than the parson himself, and the fact that he was stingy didn't bother people, since he didn't take anything from anyone. But it was surprising that anybody would work for him, since he'd let neither himself nor anyone else eat his fill more than once a day. Probably, no one could really imagine how bad it was until he'd taken a job there and tried it for himself. Also, the farmer wasn't too stingy with his wages, and when it came to the work itself, it wasn't all that bad.

One time he got himself a boy who was mighty clever, and who nagged his master to give him more to eat. In the middle of the busiest harvest season, when the farmer and his boy were out cutting the oat field around evening mealtime, the farmer saw the parson coming down the road. All the harvest folk in town were sitting on the ground with their food sacks, but the farmer and his boy were still working away. The farmer was ashamed, as you can imagine; he didn't want to show the parson that he was so stingy that he had no supper for himself and his boy. So he said to the boy, "Let's sit down and pretend to be eating while the Holy Father walks by."

During this time the boy made sure to unbind the scythe blade from the handle without his master noticing. When the parson had gotten a good ways past them, the farmer said to his boy, "Back to work now, and hurry so we can make up the work the parson prevented us from doing!"

The boy jumped up. In a jiffy he started cutting and swinging the scythe so roughly that the farmer in front of him feared that he might cut the back of his legs. He told the boy to be careful, and when they got to the end of the field, he turned around and saw that the boy's cut was untouched; the boy had simply walked along waving the empty handle.

Of course, the farmer was furious; he asked him what sort of nonsense that was. But the boy wasn't a bashful type. He answered his master right to his face: "If we pretend to eat, then we can pretend to work too!"

Now the farmer realized that the boy couldn't be treated in any old way, and from that day on he fed him as much as the other farmers in town fed their hired hands.

Lazy Masse

Once there was a woman who had a son named Masse. He was called Lazy Masse because he was lazy and dumb and never did anything but lie by the hearth and sleep. One day after his mother had scolded him more than usual, she sent him out to sell butter.

"Offer it to the first person you meet," she said. "And if you can't get the money right away, ask if you can come and get it tomorrow."

Masse went on his way, determined to get rid of the butter as fast as he could so that he could get back to the hearth again.

The first thing he came upon was a milestone. He walked right up to it, lifted his cap, and asked politely if the gentleman would like to buy some butter. Then he remembered that his mother had told him to let the buyer taste the butter, so he smeared it on the stone, which was hot from the sun. When the butter started melting and running off, the boy said, "Aha, I can see that you like it. Do I get the money now, or should I come back tomorrow?

"I see," he said when he got no answer. "Then I suppose that I'd better come back tomorrow."

When he got home, his mother shouted at him, "So how did it go? Did you get rid of the butter?"

"I certainly did. He ate till it dripped down his beard," said Masse.

"Did you get any money?"

"No, but I'll get it tomorrow," answered the boy.

The next day Masse went off to get his money for the butter. When he got to the milestone, he bowed deeply and asked the gentleman to please give him his money. When he got no answer, he bowed again and again, even more deeply, for his mother had told him to be very polite. But if he still got no money, said she, he should resort to violence.

After he'd bowed and scraped for a long time, he finally got mad, and started complaining and cursing. When that didn't work—and he didn't dare come home without the money—he took a stick and started beating the milestone. After a while the upper part fell down, and a bunch of silver coins rolled out. Someone must have put them there to hide them, and then forgotten all about them.

Masse carefully picked up all the coins and apologized profusely for being so disrespectful. Then he took off his cap, bowed again, and went home.

His mother's eyes bulged when the boy came home with so much money, but when she asked Masse to explain, he couldn't. Since he'd done so well, she let him go out again the next time she'd churned enough butter to sell. This time she told Masse to go straight to the parsonage and, if he saw the dear pastor himself, to speak directly to him.

"But how will I know if it's the dear pastor himself," Masse asked, "since I've never seen him?"

"Well," answered his mother, "the dear pastor is always dressed in black, and he wears a white collar around his neck."

Masse walked off. When he got to the parsonage, he met a big black dog wearing a white collar. Masse bowed low and asked if the dear pastor would like to buy some butter. To make it easier for dear pastor to taste the butter, he put the bucket down in front of the dog. It was gone in a moment, and Masse asked if he would get his money now or tomorrow. When there was no reply, he said, "Very well, I understand. I'll come back tomorrow."

The next day when he arrived at the parsonage, the dog—who now recognized the boy—came eagerly to greet him. Masse bowed and asked to be paid for the butter. But when the dog realized that he wasn't about to get any treat, he started growling and barking.

"Aha," said Masse, "yesterday when you got the butter, dear pastor was nice and friendly, but now that I'm asking for money, you insult me!"

Masse and the dog stood arguing with each other for a good long time. Finally, Masse got so mad that he took the dog and threw him

onto his back, saying that he'd carry him to the county magistrate, who'd be sure to make him pay.

While Masse was walking down the road with the dog on his back, scolding and quarreling, a carriage came along at a leisurely pace and pulled up next to him. An old man sitting in the carriage said to his traveling companion, "What on earth is that boy doing? Let's stop and find out!"

He told the driver to stop, and he called Masse over to the carriage. The old gentleman asked him what he was angry about.

"Yesterday I went to the parsonage to sell butter," said Masse, "and I met the dear pastor himself. That's him right here, by the way. He ate up all my butter right on the spot, and promised that I'd get my money today. But when I came back, all I got was scolding and rudeness instead of money, so now I'm taking him to the county magistrate. *He'll* be sure to give me justice."

The old gentleman started laughing so hard that a large boil burst. He'd been on his way to see a doctor about it, but now, thanks to Masse, he felt hale and hearty. The old gentleman wanted to reward the boy in some way, but as he was leery of giving money to such a fool, he asked him first to let go of the "dear pastor" and then show him the way to his home.

Masse jogged along, with the carriage following behind. The old gentleman gave Masse's mother as much money as his trip to town would have cost, but begged her never to send Masse out on his own again.

Now the boy could lie by the hearth in peace and quiet. With the money he'd found in the milestone and the sum the old gentleman had given them, they had enough to live well all their days, and to eat their butter themselves.

Big Tomma and Heikin Pieti

As a very young man, Heikin Pieti worked for a stingy old Lapp called Big Tomma. He had to work both night and day guarding Tomma's reindeer herd. For wages, all he got were two reindeer a year.

After he'd been with Tomma for five years, he decided to move away and start his own life. But it happened that Tomma had a beautiful daughter the same age as Heikin Pieti, and Pieti wanted to take her along with him and marry her.

The day before the move Pieti went up to Tomma to tell him what he'd decided. Tomma got raging mad, and when he heard that Pieti intended to marry his daughter, he threatened to take back the reindeer he'd given him. When that threat didn't work, he decided to kill him.

There was no time to spare. Pieti and his daughter might run off any moment when his back was turned. So, after the argument, Big Tomma went straight to a *häbbre** took out a big flour sack, and headed toward Pieti's tent where Pieti lay sleeping, unaware of Tomma's evil intentions.

Tomma crept up to Pieti, who was very small, and carefully, without even waking him, stuffed him into the sack. Then Tomma put the sack on his back and headed toward the beach to throw it into the lake. On his way, however, he passed his own tent, where his old lady was brewing coffee at that late hour. Tomma couldn't stand that, so, leaving the sack outside, he went into the tent and started bawling her out.

His daughter Inga, Pieti's fiancée, had been following behind her father, unable to come to Pieti's aid. After her father had gone inside the tent, she quickly ran and woke Pieti in the sack. At first he didn't know what was going on, but when she told him of the danger he was in, he woke up quickly. Together they ran to the *häbbre* and took out a dead reindeer calf that hadn't been skinned yet. They brought it back to the sack and put it in instead of Pieti, then placed the sack in the same position as Tomma had left it. Then they quickly hid behind some trees where they'd be able to watch Tomma.

When Tomma had argued for a long while with his wife and had drunk a few cups of coffee, he went out to finish the job of drowning Pieti. Throwing the sack with the calf onto his back, he hurried toward the lake, where he flung it into the water with all his might. Then he went back to his tent, and fell dead asleep.

Meanwhile, Pieti had packed his bag and baggage. He took a rein-

* *Häbbre:* a Lappish storehouse built on stilts.

deer bullock from the forest, loaded it with all his things, and said goodbye to Inga, urging her to say nothing to the old man. Then he went off toward his new life, leaving both reindeer and Inga behind.

After ten years, fate willed that Pieti and Tomma would meet again. It happened in the forest not far from Tomma's camp. Now Tomma was very old and could barely manage to tend his reindeer, while Pieti was in his prime. When they met, Pieti was herding a large flock of reindeer that he'd managed to gather together during the ten years. Seeing Pieti and his large flock, Tomma almost fainted, but when Pieti came up to him and took his hand in a friendly manner, he collected himself enough to ask how Pieti had gotten out of the water and assembled such a large herd.

"After you threw me in the lake," Pieti answered, "a mermaid in a castle down at the bottom graciously took me in. I lived like a king. But one soon tires of the good life, and after two years I came up onto land and started my old Lapp life again. So I'd have something to live on, she gave me these five hundred reindeer."

Tomma was very superstitious, and believed in mermaids and such. He asked Pieti to throw him down to the mermaid so that he might spend his last days with her. Pieti didn't need to be asked more than once. He threw Tomma right into the lake and happily trotted off to Tomma's camp, where he found Inga, still unmarried, waiting for him.

After a few days they went to the nearest town and had the banns posted. Then they lived happily together with their large reindeer herds.

Only the birds know how true this Heikin Pieti tale is, but according to old Lapp custom, one must always believe everything that the Lapps say.

For Long Springday

Once there was a stingy woman who had an only daughter. Whenever the girl asked her mother for one of her favorite foods, she answered, "You have no sense or reason! We have to save that for Long Springday!" What she meant was that they had to save the food until spring, when the days grew longer and more food would be eaten.

Now there was an especially long spit of sausage that made the girl's mouth water. But when she asked her mother for it, she got the usual answer: "You have no sense or reason! We have to save that for Long Springday."

It happened that a vagabond heard them talking, and he made sure to stop by when the woman was away.

"What's your name?" the girl asked.

"Long Springday," he answered.

"Then you're the one who gets all our sausage."

"That's right. Go right ahead and fry up a couple of links for me. The rest I'll take along in a bag," he said.

The girl did as he said, and when he'd eaten his fill, the vagabond said, "I've actually been sent here to give you some sense and reason."

"How do you do that?" wondered the girl.

"Well, just lie down, and I'll show you."

She did as she was told. He lay down on top of her.

"Can you feel the reason going into you?" asked the vagabond.

"Yes," the girl whispered. "But what about sense? Where is that?"

"That's the sack that's slapping you between your legs," answered the tramp.

When he was all done, he took off with their sausage and a lot of other food that they'd saved for Long Springday.

When the woman returned, she immediately noticed that the sausage was gone, and wondered what the girl had done with it.

"Well, Long Springday's been here to get it," answered the girl.

"You have no sense or reason!" said her mother.

"Oh yes I do," answered the girl. "He gave me both. Reason he stuck way up inside my body, and he kept slapping me on the thighs with a sack of sense."

The Students and the Eclipse of the Moon

It happened once, ages and ages ago—long before people in the country had ever heard of an almanac—that two students went out walking into the countryside. They had gone so far that they couldn't get back home before dark, so they had to ask for lodging on a farm. But at the time farmers were very suspicious of anyone they didn't know, so no one would give them a roof over their heads for the night.

One of the students began to despair, but his friend comforted him, saying, "At the next farm our luck is sure to change."

It wasn't long before they came to a large farm. It was brightly lit up, for they were having a carding party, which meant that there were a good number of womenfolk gathered there to help the people of the farm with the wool carding.

"Here," the students said, "we should have some luck."

They knocked, and the master himself came to the door.

"May we please have lodging for the night?" they asked.

"No!" answered the farmer, and was just about to shut the door when one of the students stuck his foot in the jamb so that the door couldn't shut. The farmer allowed them to come inside to sit down and rest.

After the conversation had grown a bit lively, one of the students insisted that he could darken the moon: he knew perfectly well that there'd be an eclipse of the moon that evening. As the time drew near, he asked the farmer for a bucket of tar and a brush. A ladder was placed against the roof, and the student climbed up and pretended, as the surface of the moon began to darken, to paint it with the tar brush until the entire moon was dark. The poor, frightened folk who were looking on with horror began to cry that their moon was ruined forever and they'd never again be able to enjoy the moonshine.

Then the student offered to clean up the moon again in exchange for good lodging and meals. He was given a water pail and a clean brush, and the cleaning started the same way as the darkening, until the surface of the moon was bright again. Though the people were pleased and happy that their moon had regained its luster, they were terrified of these wizards, and gave them the very best the farm had to offer of food and drink, and the best places to sleep for the night.

The Numbskull Who Thought
He Married a Man

A daughter of a rich farmer took a fancy to the farm's servant boy, but the girl's father didn't want him for a son-in-law. He'd picked out another fellow for her—one who was frightfully rich, or splendid, as they say.

The girl had to obey her father, the way it usually goes in such stories, although she did so reluctantly. But there was nothing to be done, and so they held a tremendous wedding party.

When the boy danced the first dance with the bride—for he was at the wedding, of course—they agreed to play a nasty joke on the groom.

That night, after the bride and groom and guests had gone to bed, the boy snuck upstairs to the attic bridal chamber and said to the groom, "The foreman wants to talk to you!"

In only his nightshirt the groom went to see the foreman, and the foreman, who was in on the joke, said, "All I want you to do is let the cattle sniff your shirt. That means good luck for them and the whole farm."

The gullible groom believed him and did as he asked, and the foreman could hardly hold back his laughter when he saw him walking around letting all the livestock smell his shirt.

When the groom had left the bridal chamber, the bride said to the boy, "Come lie here in bed!" The boy did as she said, while she got up and hid underneath the bed.

When the groom returned, he was furious to see that his bride had turned into a man. He ran downstairs and woke his father-in-law, screaming, "You miserable country yokel! You've married me to a man!"

But the farmer just laughed, which made the son-in-law even madder.

"I'm telling you, you've married me to a man! Come and take a look!" he yelled. And so the farmer went along with him. But by the time they got to the attic room, the bride was lying in bed just as before, and the boy was underneath.

The farmer scoffed, "You're a liar! The girl is right there in bed, you blockhead!"

The bride laughed, and so did the boy—but not so that anyone could hear him—and the groom was humiliated, which was no wonder.

Tälje Fools

One day a ship arrived in the harbor of a small town called Tälje.* Aboard the ship was a cat, an animal that the Tälje folk had never seen before. They were so taken with the cat's beauty that they persuaded the captain to sell it to them, which he did for a pretty penny. Triumphantly, they carried the cat off to the Town Hall, where everyone crowded around to see it. Suddenly, someone remembered that they'd forgotten to ask what the cat ate, so they all rushed down to the beach where the ship was sailing off, and yelled after it to find out what to feed the cat.

"Milk!" someone from the ship shouted through a horn. But the Tälje folk couldn't hear. They thought he'd said "Folk!"

Now they got very frightened. The cat would have to be killed, they decided. But no one dared enter the Town Hall to grab him, though all the citizens of the town were soon standing outside with every weapon they could find.

Finally, someone got the bright idea to set fire to the Town Hall. The horrible animal would be killed without fail, and the damage to their Town Hall wouldn't be anything compared to the lives that would be saved. No sooner said than done: they started burning down the Town Hall! When smoke started to reach the room where the cat was, it jumped up into the attic, and from there through an opening in the roof onto the roof of another house. The Tälje folk were horror-struck; they lit a fire to that house too! And so it went from house to house until the cat finally was able to jump down into the street and run off to the forest. You can imagine the predicament of the poor

* Tälje refers to the town of Södertälje outside Stockholm. In earlier times the people of Södertälje, or Tälje folk, were the target of ridicule from the Stockholmers, in the tradition of the Fools of Chelm or the Molbo stories in Denmark.

Tälje folk: their town had burned down, and everyone was still afraid that the cat would attack them!

After a while, however, they calmed down and decided to rebuild their town, starting with the Town Hall. After all the logs had been cut and trimmed, they had to be brought to the building site. But since the town was in a valley, they carried each log down a long, steep hill. As they were carrying the last one down, they got so tired that the log dropped to the ground and rolled all the way down the hill.

"Well, haven't we been dumb!" they said. "Why didn't we think of that sooner? But it's not too late." And so they carried all the logs back up again and let them roll downhill, one after another.

Then they started building. But the paymaster always ended up short one paycheck. He'd forgotten to count himself when he totaled up the number of workers, but on payday he always made sure to pay himself first. Finally, they decided that anyone who worked on the Town Hall had to stick his nose into the clay at the edge of a big puddle on the square; then the paymaster would put the money into each of the holes. That was the way it was done as long as the work continued.

Now it happened one day that a lobster crawled up out of the water onto the beach. All the Tälje folk immediately gathered around and started speculating about what kind of creature it might be. Finally, they agreed that it had to be a tailor from abroad because he was holding a pair of scissors in each hand. Because the town had recently finished rebuilding the Town Hall and the Tälje folk thought it would be proper for all of their officials to wear new inauguration uniforms, they decided to seize the moment and have them designed in a truly modern style. Placing a piece of homespun fabric in front of the foreigner, they humbly asked him to cut the patterns for them. Crawling backward across the cloth, the lobster seemed to be making cutting motions with his claws, which they judged to be scissors. Very carefully the town tailors followed with a piece of chalk his every twist and turn, and when he crawled off the cloth, they started cutting along the chalk line. Later, when the pieces were to be put together, it was a terrible mess: no matter how they assembled them, they couldn't come up with anything that looked like clothing.

Finally, they realized that the foreigner had been pulling their leg, and they condemned him to death. They decided to drown him because, being a foreigner, he couldn't be buried in their hallowed ground. And so, with great solemnity—and bitterly lamented by all the pious women of the town—the lobster was taken out to sea in a boat and thrown into the water, a well-deserved punishment to him and a warning to others who dared make fun of the people of Tälje.

For a while the Tälje folk lived in peace until the day came when the mayor decided to find out why they were all so poor. After much deliberation he concluded that it was because all their money went to buy salt from foreigners.

"Why then," someone said, "couldn't we grow our own salt? That way the money would stay in the country. Before long we'll be just as wealthy as we now are poor!"

Everyone loved that idea. They pooled their money, bought a field, and seeded it with a couple of barrels of salt. That fall, all the grass on the field was harvested, and they started to thresh it. But even though they worked so hard that they were completely exhausted, there wasn't any salt to be had. They sat down and started to think the problem over. Finally someone suggested that the birds had probably eaten up all the salt. Everyone thought that this was likely, so they decided that next year they would appoint a worker to stand guard and chase the birds away.

Again they pooled their resources and bought a few more barrels

of salt. But even though the field was guarded day and night, they got no more salt than the year before.

The poor Tälje folk were at their wits' end, but the mayor, who was a wise fellow, didn't let them lose courage. After pondering long and hard over the problem, he finally decided that the only possible reason for their failure was that the guard had probably crushed the salt plants with his feet.

A reward was offered to whoever could prevent the birds from eating the salt and stop the guard from crushing the plants. For a long time the problem went unsolved, until one day a clever head suggested that they pay someone to carry the guard who chased the birds away. This brilliant individual got the reward!

The Thief's Three Masterpieces

Once there was a poor tenant farmer who had three sons, just like the farmers in other stories.

The farmer's little plot of land was on the estate of the county governor.

One year the harvest was so poor that the old man couldn't support his sons anymore and had to send them out to earn their living on their own.

He decided to appeal to His Lordship, the county governor. With great humility he begged the count to grant permits of safe conduct for the three boys, who were going off into the big world. The county governor granted him his request, and gave him signed permits sealed with his own personal seal.

At first the three boys traveled together. They visited many towns and cities before they had any luck. After many weeks they came to a town, where the oldest was taken on as a shoemaker's apprentice and the middle one as an apprentice to a tailor.

The youngest didn't know yet what profession he wanted to pursue, so he went to an inn to have a drink or two. There he struck up a conversation with a few disreputable characters who happened to be sitting next to him. They asked him what sort of fellow he was and what kind of work he could do.

He answered them politely: "We're three sons whose old father can't support us anymore. My older brothers are apprenticed for six years to a shoemaker and a tailor. Here you see the permit that I was given by His Lordship the county governor. It gives me permission to look for work wherever I like."

"That's more freedom than we'll ever have. Why don't you come along with us? We'll feed you, and whatever you earn is yours to keep."

And that's the way it happened.

The youngest son went along with these bad fellows, and in due course became an accomplished thief. He earned quite a lot of money during the six years he was apprenticed to them in this fine craft.

When the time came for all three brothers to finish their training period, each in his own profession, they decided to visit their old father and see if he was still alive. The shoemaker had grown into a fine, presentable, well-dressed man, and the other two brothers had done equally well, and were highly thought of in their fields. The shoemaker and the tailor bought a horse and a sled, and traveled together. The thief stole a horse and sled with bells, and traveled by himself like a true gentleman. They drove right past the county governor's manor and down to their old father's cottage.

At first their father didn't recognize them, for they'd all grown during those six years. After they greeted him and he could see that they really were his sons, he said, "Welcome home, my dear children! As you can see, I'm very old and weak."

At that moment His Lordship's servant came by to find out who the gentlemen were who hadn't stopped to call on his master.

"You can tell His Lordship that these are my sons to whom he gave permits of safe conduct six years ago, and who have come home to me again."

After telling his master who the gentlemen were, the servant was sent straight back again to invite them to dinner that same day. They thanked him and promised to come in a little while. An hour later they were treated to a fine dinner, and they thanked His Lordship humbly for both the meal and the honorable treatment they'd received at his hands six years before.

The count asked them where they'd been these six years, and the eldest one replied. "I learned the shoemaker's trade. And now I humbly beseech Your Lordship to be kind enough to sign my apprenticeship certificate."

"Everyone needs shoes, even I," said the count. "I'll make sure to read through your papers and sign them.

"And you," he said to the middle son, "what profession have you pursued? Did you also learn shoemaking?"

"No, Your Lordship, I learned the tailor's trade. Like my brother, I humbly request that Your Lordship read the apprenticeship certificate that my master has given me."

"I'll do it during the Christmas holidays," said the count. "I assume you'll be staying at home with your father for a while, now that you've traveled so far."

He turned to the youngest son. "It's quite extraordinary how much you've grown, and how ruddy and fine you look! You were so little and scrawny and skinny and pale when you lived here with your father. And now you're as fat and solid as a log, and you look mighty clever as well. What kind of craft have you?"

"I've learned to steal," answered the youngest, "and I humbly request that Your Lordship sign my certificate right away so I can go back and practice my craft."

At this His Lordship gave a slight smile.

"You don't really mean that, do you?"

"Yes," answered the thief, "it's the God's own truth. I don't have time to stay around with my father, like these two layabouts."

"Well," answered the gracious count, "you'll have your certificate signed by and by. But first you must give me three proofs of your skills."

"And what might they be?" asked the thief.

"Tonight, you must steal all twelve horses from my stables."

"Done!" said the thief.

He had his job cut out for him, but wise men know their own tricks.

The county governor ordered his twelve stable hands each to guard one horse for the night. The thief went into town and bought two pitchers of schnapps and a pint of a good sleeping potion. He put the mixture into pint bottles, made himself a beggar's bag filled with good food, and waited until the night was so cold and snowy that you couldn't see your own hand. Disguising himself as an old beggar woman, he went to the stables after everyone in town had gone to sleep.

When he came to the stable door, he knocked and begged the stable hands to take pity on a beggar woman and let her in for the night; otherwise, she'd have to sleep in the street and freeze to death.

"There're twelve of us," thought the boys. "Isn't that enough to deal with one old woman?"

"Yes," said one of them. "Watch my horse and I'll let her in. She's a human being like the rest of us."

He got down from his horse, opened the door, and let the old woman in. Then he immediately locked it again and went back to his horse, which stood fully saddled and outfitted with carbine pistols and all the ammunition anyone could use. The old woman sat down by the stove. It was nice and warm, and she started scraping the snow from her clogs, while blessing the merciful young men who'd taken her in out of the cold.

After she'd sat there warming up, she began to search through her bag to see what she'd managed to beg that day for Christmas Eve. She took out a piece of bread and a little piece of meat, and started gnawing on them. Then she took herself a little drink, went up to the boys, and poured a taste for each and every one of them. She meant well, for they'd saved her from lying outside in the cold night. And the boys thanked her for the refreshment that warmed their insides.

Then they said, "In the chaff room you'll find some hay. Old mother can take it and put it next to the stove for a bed. You'll find some horse blankets to put under and over yourself so you won't be cold tonight."

She thanked them, saying that on such a long night she'd be happy to sleep as long as she could. Then she gave them all another drink and said, "I feel so sorry for you poor fellows who have to sit out there in the cold. You'll catch your death!"

And she gave them another sip, until some fell asleep on their horses and others tumbled off into the stalls.

Suddenly this old lady became strong and alert. She loosened the

saddle straps and lifted off both saddle and man. Then she put out the fire.

The thief left with all twelve horses in tow; he'd won the first round.

In the morning His Lordship came down to the stables to greet his faithful servants and see how things were going.

"Well, good morning! How did you boys manage?"

"Quite well, Your Lordship."

"I fear that you won't think the same when you're all awake. Where are my horses?"

One of them answered, "We let them out to be watered, Your Lordship."

But the count replied, "It looks to me like the only drinking was done by you! Look how groggy you all are, you scoundrels. I can't imagine that you were much more alert last night!"

When the sun came up, the thief returned all twelve horses and asked His Lordship to sign his apprenticeship papers.

"No," he answered, "not until you've passed the second test. Tonight you must steal all the silver from the table in the upper hall, as well as my wife's nightgown and the ring on her finger."

Now the thief really had his work cut out for him!

The count brought his silver up to the hall and placed it on a table. He collected all the guns on the farm and put them in the hall too. When evening came, he went upstairs to guard the silver himself.

The thief took a long ladder and placed it against the wall near a window in the same hall where the count was waiting. Then he went to get the corpse of a prisoner who'd been hanged eight days before on a gallows outside town. He climbed the ladder and held the dead man before the window. When the count saw him, he grabbed a gun and shot right through the window. The thief dropped the prisoner, and the frozen, rigid body rattled down the wall.

"Thank goodness!" thought the count. "Now I'm rid of that scoundrel."

He extinguished all six candles and went downstairs to his wife's bedchamber. The countess asked, "Was that you shooting?"

"Yes," he answered. "Now I'm free of that rascal, and I can sleep in peace."

"Like the Devil, you can," said the countess. "When the servants find him lying there in front of our window, there'll be a great fuss all over town. Put a rope around his neck, drag him outside town, and throw him into a ditch. That way people will believe that he was drunk and had an accident."

"You have a point there," said the count.

He got up, got dressed, and put on his big fur coat, and with rope in hand went off to drag the thief away.

At just that moment the thief entered the room and said to the countess, "My dear, I'm afraid you must give me your nightgown and your ring to bury him with; otherwise, we might have his nasty ghost haunting us for the holidays."

"You have a point there," said the countess, sitting up in bed. In the dark she pulled off her nightgown and her ring and handed them over, for she thought that he was His Lordship, her dear husband.

The thief rushed to the hall, gathered up all the silver in a sack, and took a gun to defend himself if he happened to run into the count. Now he had won the second round!

At that moment His Lordship returned from disposing of the corpse. He found the countess lying naked in bed.

"Why are you lying there without your nightgown?"

"You know why! You came back yourself and asked for my nightgown and ring to bury the thief with, so he wouldn't haunt us during the Christmas holidays."

"Damn! That thief has been at it again!"

Later that morning the thief came back with the silver, the nightgown, and the ring, and returned them all to the count. Again he implored His Lordship to sign his permit of safe conduct and apprenticeship papers.

"No," said he. "This very Christmas Eve night you must bring our old parson and all his money here. Then you'll get your permit and permission to steal as much as you like—as long as you leave me be."

"Very well," said the thief. "It will be as you say."

Now the thief had to figure out how to pull off this difficult feat. First he went and bought ten pounds of thin wax candles; then he went down to the fish market and bought two bushels of crabs. Later, at dusk, he put all the crabs on the church altar and the pulpit railing as well as on all the benches; then he cut the candles into pieces and put them between the crabs' claws. He stole a horse and tied lots of bells to it, then rode up to the church and stopped by the sexton's garden gate. There he tied the horse firmly and placed a wad of hay so far in front of him that he couldn't reach it. Then the thief walked into the church, lighted all the candle pieces, and waited for the Christmas Eve service.

The sexton finally woke up, dizzy in the head from some early celebrating, and looked at his clock. It had stopped. Then he looked out the window and saw that the church was lit up and the bells were ringing. He thought he'd overslept, so he dressed hastily and hurried to the church.

When the thief heard him step onto the church porch, he began to chant these words: "Whoever gives me all his money, he shall follow me to Paradise alive."

When the sexton heard these rapturous words from the strange priest, he thought to himself, "It must be our old ancestors preaching!"

Quickly he ran off to find the old parson, and said, "I think Saint Peter is preaching to us in the church. He's making a wonderful offer to us old dry sticks."

"Is that so? What is he saying?"

"Well," said the sexton, "he's saying that whoever gives him all his money will get to follow him to Paradise alive. I want to do it!"

"So do I," said the parson.

So he hurried off and got all his money except four riksdaler* which he put into the bottom of a sock for his old mother.

When the thief heard that both the parson and the sexton were in the church vestibule, he started to chant again: "Whoever gives me all, all, yes, all his money, he shall follow me alive to Paradise tonight."

"That must be the all-knowing Peter," said the parson. "Run back home to Mother for the four riksdaler in the sock! He says, 'All your money'!"

---

* The riksdaler was a Swedish monetary unit that served as the basic unit from the sixteenth century to 1878.

The sexton ran off, and brought back the four riksdaler.

When they were inside the church, the thief began to speak: "Welcome, ye faithful servants of the Lord of Zion! I have come to lead you back to Him."

The thief put the decrepit old parson in a big empty sack, tied him to his sled, and rode off to His Lordship the county governor. The parson kept hitting his head on the hard, bumpy road, and he started to curse.

"Haven't you always taught us sinners that the road is long and the gate is narrow?" asked the thief.

"Yes, at least that's what it says in the handbook."

When they got to the count's chicken coop, the chickens and geese began to cackle.

"Now I can tell," said the parson, "that we don't have far to go. I hear the old saints rejoicing for my soul!"

The thief put the bundle of money under his arm and the sack on his back, and went in to see His Lordship.

Now he'd finally completed all three tasks. All his papers were signed, and the count gave him full authority to steal—from other people.

By now, however, the thief wasn't sure that he cared for the work anymore; in these hard times he didn't think it was worth all the trouble!

The Girl and the Calf's Eyes

Once there was a girl who wasn't quite right in the head. One day a suitor was expected to call on her at her mother's farm. Her mother told her to make sure to lower her eyes and look demure.

"But once in a while you *can* cast him an eye," said the mother.

The day the suitor arrived, the daughter was busily cleaning out the innards of a newly slaughtered calf. Remembering her mother's advice, she lowered her eyes most of the time, but all of a sudden she picked up a calf's eye and cast it at the suitor!

The King, the Headsman, and the Twelve Robbers

It is a common belief among the peasantry that the executioner, or headsman, is entitled to the title, honor, and privileges of state assessor, as soon as he has properly chopped off fifty heads.

During the reign of King Charles—some say Charles XII, but it probably was Charles IX*—there was to be a great execution in Östgötland;† and since only fancy folk and great men were being put to death, the king himself went down there to see that everything was done correctly. The executioner in Stockholm was given the task of carrying out the punishment; however, since he had hardly more standing than his apprentice—the so-called butcher boy—has nowadays, he had to walk and run all the way. In order to get to Östgötland, he had to walk across Kolmorden,‡ which was always filled with robbers, although they—like *skogsrå*,§ giants, and trolls—aren't seen much nowadays.

As evening approached, he sat down by the side of the road. He saw some blue smoke rising among the trees, and, curious to find out what this might mean, he stumbled on a hatch door in the ground, which was so well covered with sod that one could hardly see it. Soon the hatch was lifted, and an old crone stuck out her sooty face. When she saw him standing there, she said, "What do you think you're doing? Hurry away if you value your life! The robbers will be back soon, and if they see you, you'll never hear the cuckoo again."

This was not something you'd want to hear more than once, and though the headsman was hardly timid, he quickly turned back the way he'd come. As he was a very wise fellow, he scratched with his broad ax blade on the trees so that he'd be able to find the place

---

* King Charles XII reigned from 1682 to 1718, and Charles IX from 1550 to 1611.

† Östgötland or Östergötland is a province in southeast Sweden.

‡ Kolmorden is a sparsely populated, forested highland area between the southern part of the district of Södermanland and the northeastern part of Östergötland.

§ *Skogsrå*: forest spirit; see Introduction, page xxi.

again. Even though his task right now was to settle accounts with lords and barons and other fine gentlemen, he had a burning desire to make the acquaintance of these robbers, and to see just how firmly their heads were attached to their bodies.

After he'd completed the job down in Östgötland, and had chopped off heads until his arms were about to fall off, he went to the king to collect his wages. He told of his adventure in the forest, and the king, who was a clever and brave gentleman, decided to go with the headsman to meet these robbers. Because the headsman was strong and resolute, the king felt that he needed no one else to help him.

Disguised as beggars, they went on their way, and when they got to the headsman's marks on the trees, they sat down by the side of the road. At dusk the robbers, all twelve of them, came sneaking along. They approached the king and headsman and asked what they wanted. The headsman answered that they were a couple of poor, homeless vagabonds who'd stopped to rest by the side of the road because they were tired and hungry. Very well, said the robbers, but that would do them little good, for they were about to die.

"Merciful sir," said the headsman in a pitiful voice, "although our lives are hardly worth living, it would be a pleasure, just once, to eat ourselves really full—even if it is our last meal."

The leader of the robbers laughed and granted them this favor. They wouldn't be the first to whom he'd served a last meal.

They all went along to the robbers' den, which turned out to be a large underground room with a long table in the middle and benches all around. Standing by the stove was the sooty old crone, who was cooking food and heating wine that was later poured into chalices. The two beggars stayed by the door, which was securely locked and bolted.

After the robbers had eaten and drunk, the two beggars were allowed to approach the table. A large platter of meat and a goblet of hot wine were set before each of them, and they were told to eat quickly. They grabbed the steaming goblets, but instead of emptying them, they threw them into the eyes of the robbers, blinding them, then grabbed their swords and in no time cut down all twelve.

In the cave was much gold and silver; this the king gave to the headsman and the old crone to share, but he still didn't feel that the headsman had been properly rewarded.

"Tell me what you want," he said, "and it shall be granted."

What the headsman really wanted was a title that would prevent other people from shunning him. So the king gave him the title of assessor, which could be passed on to his successors as soon as they chopped off fifty heads. The new assessor became a very rich man. Splitting up the robbers' treasure proved to be no problem, because after the old crone had washed the soot from her face, she turned out to be neither old nor ugly, and she became his wife.

Twelve Men in the Forest

In olden days there were said to be many highwaymen in the forest up here in the mountains, and the shepherd girls and boys were always terribly afraid of them. Anytime they heard someone shouting in the forest in a rough voice, they immediately thought that highwaymen were afoot.

Once there was a girl who was tending the sheep in a faraway meadow. This particular girl could play the goat horn so well that the people back in the village could understand exactly what she wanted to say. One day they heard her blowing the horn. This is what she was saying:

> "Tuss, tuss, tussle in the horn.
> Twelve men are in the forest.
> The little dog they have hanged.
> The great ox they have thrashed.
> The bell cow they have drained.
> And now they will rape me
> And take me far away from here."

When the men in the village understood what the girl was saying, they hurried up to the meadow, and when the highwaymen saw them coming, they fled into the forest and were never seen again.

The Wise Daughter

J heard my old grandfather tell this story:

Once, a long time ago, there was a great famine in the country. Since there wasn't enough food to go around, people started killing old people and eating them. But in this country lived a woman who was said to be of noble birth and was famed for her wisdom. This woman didn't like the sacrifice of the old people, and one day she dared to tell her father what she thought. He got very angry, and when the king of the country heard what she'd said, he summoned her to see him. But she was not to come on foot, nor by wagon, nor on horseback, nor by boat. She was not to be dressed, not to be naked, not to come during the day and not at night, not during the new moon, and not when the moon was waxing or waning.

So she hitched two young men to a sled and let a ram walk next to it. Then she put one leg in the sled and the other over the ram; she came the third day before Christmas, at dusk and during a full moon. For clothes, all she wore was a fish net.

Bellman Stories

O ne day King Gustav III of Sweden* lost his way when he was out riding. After quite a while he came upon a small cottage. His horse stuck its head in through the open window, and the king shouted, "Is anyone home?"

"Half a man and a horse's head," answered a boy sitting by the stove.

"And where's your father?"

"Out looking for something he doesn't want to find."

"And your mother?"

* King Gustav III reigned 1772–1792.

"Doing the neighbor woman a favor that she can't return."

"And your sister?"

"Sitting crying over last year's happiness."

"Now listen," said the king, "just what sort of nonsense is this? That you're half a man I can see for myself, and that the horse's head is inside the cottage I can see as well. But what do you mean by saying your father is out looking for something he doesn't want to find?"

"What's so hard about that? He's out checking the fence for holes, and the fewer he finds the happier he'll be."

The king laughed and looked appreciatively at the boy.

"But what about your mother? What's she doing? How can she do a favor for the neighbor's wife that she can never return?"

"The neighbor's wife has just died," said the boy, "and Mother is washing the body."

"And your sister who's crying about last year's happiness. What's that about?"

"Isn't it obvious? Last year my sister had a sweetheart, and she was as happy as a lark. This year she's got no one and sits crying all day long, rocking the baby."

The clever boy, who was none other than Bellman himself, pleased the king so well that he made him his court jester.*

This turned out to be a wise choice, for the king held him in high esteem for his ready wit and cleverness.

One day the king invited Bellman to dine with him at a royal banquet; to honor him he placed him on his left. This annoyed the other courtiers, who thought it beneath their station to sit at table with a common man such as Bellman.† Therefore, the courtier sitting on the king's right side boxed his neighbor's ear and told him, "Pass it on!"

The slap was passed from one man to the next all around the table until finally Bellman received a proper boxing too. The intention was that he would have to slap the king, and it was obvious what the outcome of that would be. However, Bellman got up and said:

"Whenever my father to the fence did come,
He hurried up and turned around!"

And he returned the ear boxing with such a smack that the hall rang out with its sound.

One day Bellman was strolling in the castle garden with some ladies-in-waiting. After a while he was seized with the most urgent need to empty his bowels. So he went aside and did what he needed to do. Then he placed his hat over his load and called out, "Ladies! Come along! Come along! I've caught a bird. Come quick and see it!"

* Carl Michael Bellman (1740–1795), troubadour, singer, wit, is perhaps the greatest poet Sweden has produced. Unfortunately, his poems are untranslatable, and there is little written about him in English. However, a good introduction to Bellman and his times is *The Life and Songs of Carl Michael Bellman* by Paul Britten Austin (Allhem Publishers, Malmö, and American-Scandinavian Foundation, New York, 1967). The term "court jester" is not applicable to the real Bellman, who served as the king's songwriter and troubadour.

† Although Bellman was of common birth, his father was an educated civil servant and his maternal grandfather a minister from the province of Dalarna.

And the ladies in their fancy crinolines came running.

"What is it, Bellman? What did you catch?"

"Well, I seem to have caught a bird. I've got it right here under my hat. Now help me so it won't get away. Make a circle, and when I pick up the hat, grab it as quickly as you can!"

And the beautiful ladies did as he said, and what they got all over their hands we can all well imagine.

One little countess was quite beside herself. She wouldn't even look at her finger, but cried and shouted, "Oh, please take the finger away! Take it away! Chop it off! I can't bear the sight of it!"

"Very well, my dear lady!" said Bellman. "I'll do as you ask. But to make it easier, please stick your finger through this hole in the fence, and I'll go to the other side and chop it off."

The little countess did as he said. Bellman picked up a stick and hit the finger with a resounding whack.

"Ow!" screamed the lady, and she withdrew her finger and stuck it in her mouth!

"Twigmouthius, Cowbellowantus, Perchnosimus"

OR,

HOW TO WIN
THE PRINCESS

Twigmouthius, Cowbellowantus, Perchnosimus

nce there was a king who was so terribly learned that ordinary people couldn't comprehend him at all, and he didn't understand them either. He found seven wise men who were able to interpret his wisdom for the common people, and, in turn, translate what they said into language lofty enough for the king to comprehend.

The king had no son, but he did have a daughter, and in order for her to be happily married and the kingdom ruled in a properly learned fashion, he issued a proclamation that whoever was learned enough to make the king and his wise men speechless would get the princess and half the kingdom. But whoever tried and failed would lose his head for having dared exchange words with the king.

This was no child's play, of course, but the princess was incredibly fair and beautiful. The king didn't keep her locked away either; princes, counts, barons, priests, doctors, and scholars from all corners of the world arrived, and as soon as they caught a glimpse of her, they wanted to try their luck. But no matter how learned they were, their learning never reached any farther than their shoulders: every one of them lost his head.

Far at the other end of the kingdom lived a farmer who had a son. This boy was no fool: he was quick to catch on and quick both to think and talk, and he was afraid of nothing. When the parson read the king's proclamation aloud in church, the boy decided to try his luck. Nothing ventured, nothing gained, he thought, and he went to the parson and said that if he would study with him at night, the boy would work for him for free in the daytime.

"Whoever's going to wrangle with them had better be able to do more than chew bread," said the parson.

"That's for sure," said the boy. "But I'll give it a try, I will."

Of course, the parson thought that it was hopeless, but to get such a good worker for just the price of his meals made it hard to say no, and he did as the boy wished.

As time passed, however, the boy became thoroughly bored with studying.

"Who wants to sit here studying and losing the little bit of sense

one already has?" he thought. "And it won't do any good either, for when luck is with you, both ox and cow have calves, but if your luck is bad, you won't get a calf from anything." He threw his book against the wall and went on his way.

As the boy walked along, he came to a large forest whose trees and bushes were so entangled that he could barely get through. While he was pushing ahead, he thought about what he'd say when he got to the castle, and how to use the learning he'd gotten from the priest. Suddenly, a branch struck him across the mouth so hard that his teeth jumped up and down.

"That's a Twigmouthius, that is," he thought.

A little later he came to a meadow, where a cow stood bellowing so fiercely that he nearly lost his hearing.

"That's a Cowbellowantus, that is," he thought.

Soon he came to a stream. As there was neither bridge nor plank across the stream, he had to put his clothes on his head and swim across. While he was swimming, a perch came along and bit his nose.

"That's a Perchnosimus, that is," he thought.

Finally, he arrived at the royal castle. Things didn't look very pleasant there: human heads had been set on long stakes, and they grinned so horribly that one could almost get scared of them. Luckily, the boy wasn't that type.

"God's peace to you!" he said, tipping his hat. "There you sit laughing at me, and it's very possible that I'll be joining you before nighttime and helping you grin at the others. But if I make it through alive, I promise that you won't sit there much longer."

Then he stepped up and knocked on the gate.

The guard came out and asked him what he wanted.

"I'm here to propose to the princess," said the boy.

"You?" said the guard. "You certainly look the type, don't you! Are you completely crazy? We've had princes and counts and barons, and priests and doctors and scholars, and every one has lost his head. What makes you think you'll do any better?"

"None of your business, sir," said the boy. "Just open the door, and you'll see someone who's afraid of nothing."

But the guard wouldn't let him in.

"Do as I say," said the boy, "or don't blame me for the consequences."

But no, the guard still wouldn't obey.

So the boy grabbed him by the collar and smashed him against the wall. Then he walked in to meet the king, who was sitting in his great hall with his seven wise men all around him. They had long faces and were so skinny and frail that they looked like scarecrows. Hanging their heads, they sat there staring at the floor, lost in thought.

One of them finally looked up and spoke to the boy in ordinary, everyday language, "What kind of fish are *you?*"

"A suitor," said the boy.

"And do *you* want to propose to the princess?"

"That's the way it looks to me," said the boy.

"We've had princes and counts and barons, and priests and doctors and scholars, and all of them have left here without their heads. Better turn around and make for the hills while you still have yours," said the wise man.

"Don't you worry about that. Worry about what you yourselves might have between *your* shoulders," said the boy. "If you tend to your business, I'll tend to mine. Why don't you first tell me how you got to be so wise, for I can't say that you look especially wise to me."

The wise man started running off a long list of reasons why he was so wise, and when he was through, the second one started and then the third and so on and on until they got to the seventh. The boy didn't understand a word of it, but he didn't lose heart; he just nodded as if he understood.

When the last one finished, he asked, "So, do you understand now why we are so wise?"

"Well," said the boy, "I knew how to babble and chatter just like that when I lay in my cradle and walked in a halter. But since you're such lovers of learning, I'll give *you* a question, and it won't be a long one either. Twigmouthius, Cowbellowantus, Perchnosimus: can you tell me what they are?"

All the wise men craned their necks and strained their ears. They put on their glasses and started frantically looking through all their books.

But while they were reading and cogitating, the boy stuck his hands in his pockets, looking so carefree and unconcerned that they had to wonder about that too—how he who was so young could be so learned and still look exactly like normal people.

"Well, how are you doing?" said the boy after some moments. "Can't all your learning give me an answer to such a simple question?"

Looking up at the ceiling and down at the floor and sideways at the walls, the wise men pondered and cogitated some more.

But give him an answer they couldn't—not even the king, who was much more learned than all the others put together. Finally, they had to give up. So the boy got the princess and half the kingdom, and there he ruled in his own way: if it wasn't any better, at least it wasn't any worse than the king did with all his learning.

The Princess Who Always Had an Answer

Once there was a king whose only daughter had an answer for everything between heaven and earth. Naturally, such a princess couldn't marry just anybody; if she was to have a husband, he had to be even cleverer than she.

The king proclaimed in every land and nation that whoever was wise enough to put the princess at a loss for words would marry her and become king when he died. Many suitors signed up immediately, for the princess was so beautiful that no one was her equal, and her father's kingdom was so large that there was none larger on this side of the moon.

When the princess saw how many suitors she had, she decided that the ones who didn't succeed should have their heads cut off right away. In that way, she figured, most of them wouldn't try at all, and she'd be left in peace to read her big books, which she thought were much more fun than sitting around answering stupid questions.

But this isn't at all what happened. Although the suitors were worried about their heads, the princess was so beautiful and her father's wealth so tempting that they couldn't stop trying to win her and the kingdom. For many, many days the princess had a terrible job being smarter than all her suitors, and the executioner had just as big a job cutting off their heads.

Finally, there came a poor shepherd who had headed for the

castle immediately when he'd heard of the princess and how to win her.

While he was walking along wondering what questions to ask her, he saw a dead magpie lying on the road.

"I'll bring that along," he thought. "You never know when it'll come in handy."

A little later he saw an old willow fence-strap, which some farm-hand had lost while building fences.

"I'll bring that along too," thought the boy. "I might find a use for it."

After walking a little farther, he found a wedge lost by a wood-cutter on his way home from work.

"Why not take that along too?" the boy said to himself. "You never know what it might be good for."

Finally, just as the spires of the king's castle came into view, he found a pair of crooked ram's horns.

"I'll take these along as well," he thought. "As long as I've picked up all this other old junk, it can't hurt to take these ram's horns, too."

And so he tucked away the magpie and the fence-strap, the wedge and the ram's horns.

Before long, he was standing in the vestibule to the princess's chamber, waiting for the princess to sit on her throne so that he could ask her questions that would put her at a loss for words. After a long while a courtier came and opened the door, and the boy walked straight up to the princess on her throne.

"So, what is it you want to ask me?" said the princess, yawning.

The boy, who'd never seen a princess in his life, stood with his mouth open in amazement, stunned by how beautiful and elegant she was.

"Well," she said, "if you've already lost your voice, then maybe you'd better lose your head!"

And the princess waved to her chief executioner.

But now the boy regained the power of speech.

"How terribly hot it is in here!" he said.

"Ha-ha," laughed the princess, "it's much hotter up my behind!"

"I see," said the boy, "then perhaps I might be allowed to cook this magpie up there so I can have a bite to eat before I lose my head?"

And he pulled out his dead magpie and held it up before the princess.

The princess was almost speechless, but then she recovered. "You may do that," she said, "but you're not going to be able to get it up there."

"Oh, yes," he said, "I'll manage as long as I have this wedge to help me."

And he pulled out the old wedge he'd found on the road and showed it to the princess.

She grew very embarrassed and hardly knew what to say, but finally replied, "That'll burst my little butt!"

"Oh, no," the boy said. "If that's the only problem, then I know what to do. We'll just wrap this around your butt; then it'll hold."

And he took out the old willow strap he'd found on the road.

Now the princess couldn't manage to say a word. She sat there completely silent and embarrassed, and thought for all she was worth.

"You speak in such a crooked way that it makes my head spin," she said.

"Yes, you and I can speak both straight and crooked," the boy said. "But any more crooked than this you'll never be!"

And he took out one of the ram's horns that he'd found on the road.

But now the princess jumped up.

"Well, I never saw anything like it!" she yelled.

"Aha," said the boy, "then you'd better see this!"

And he brought out the other ram's horn and showed it to her. That shut her up, and never again did she try to sound wiser than her husband, for of course she married the boy who had put her at a loss for words.

The Boat That Sailed on Both Land and Sea

A boy was building a boat by the edge of the sea when along came an old woman and asked him what he was planning to do with it. "Well," he answered, "this boat can sail over both land and sea."

"Not that boat," she said. "But because you're a clever boy and my godson, I'll give you one which *can* sail over land and sea."

The next time the boy came down to the shore, a boat was waiting at the edge of the water. He realized that this boat was a christening gift.

A rumor was going around the kingdom that the king was very ill, and that whoever could cure him would marry the princess and become king after he died. The boy made up his mind to try his luck, so he went down to his boat and decided to sail to the royal castle to find out what he needed to do to cure the king and claim the princess for his wife.

The moment he got in the boat, the old woman was suddenly standing there next to him, wishing him good luck on his journey. She encouraged him to bring along all the people he met along the way, for they might be of use to him. Then he sat down, and the boat started sailing across the land.

At the side of the road was a man with pieces of lead bound to his feet. The boy stopped the boat and asked him about it, and the man answered, "In order to walk normally I have to bind these pieces of lead to my feet. Otherwise I'll run too fast; I can run to the end of the world in ten minutes, I can!"

"Why don't you come along with me?" said the boy. And the man did.

When they'd gone along for a while, they met a man with his finger up one of his nostrils. The boy stopped the boat and asked why he was doing this. The man answered, "If I were to breathe through both nostrils, houses and forests would be blown away."

"Why don't you come along with me?" said the boy. And the man did.

Then they met a man who had tied a rope around a whole forest. The boy stopped and asked why he'd done this, and the man answered, "My master is building a house, and I'm supposed to bring home trees for him to use, but I'd rather bring home the whole forest at one time." The boy said, "Why don't you come along with me?"

When they'd sailed a while longer, they met a hunter with a

bandage over one eye. The boy stopped and asked, "Why do you have a bandage on one eye?" The man answered, "With two eyes, I can see and shoot much too far; one eye is enough for me." And the boy said, "Why don't you come along with me?"

When they'd gone a while longer, they met a man lying with his ear to the ground. The boy stopped and asked why he was doing this. The man answered, "I can hear the grass grow, and if I don't keep one ear to the ground, I can hear all the way around the world." The boy said, "Why don't you come along with me?"

When they'd gone a bit farther, they met a man who had a feed bag on his behind. The boy stopped and asked what that was all about. "Well," said the man, "I have to have a feed bag there, otherwise I'll shit all over the place." "Well, why don't you come along with me?"

By now they'd reached the castle. The boy went inside and stated his business. The king, the princess, and the entire court were all gathered in the throne room, and when he asked what he had to do to win the princess, the king and the entire court burst out laughing. Many had already tried and failed.

Then the king said, "For a long time I've been suffering from a stomach ailment. The only thing that will help is the Water of Life, which can be found in a spring at the end of the world. If you can get me that drink and cure me of my illness, you'll have the princess for your wife—on the condition that you get it for me in ten minutes." The boy was given a bottle and sent on his way.

He went down to his boat and said to the man with the pieces of lead on his feet: "Take the lead pieces off, run to the end of the world, and fill this bottle with the Water of Life. Then run back as fast as you can." The man did as the boy ordered, and soon he was out of sight.

After nine minutes he still hadn't come back, so the boy told the hunter to take the bandage off his eye and find out where he was. The hunter saw him lying right next to the spring under a tree, but he couldn't tell if he was alive or dead. Then the boy told the man who could hear the grass growing to find out whether he was breathing. He listened and heard the messenger snoring, so the boy ordered the hunter to shoot into the tree above the sleeping man so that some fruit would fall and wake him. Putting his rifle to his shoulder, the hunter shot down an apple that fell on the face of the sleeping man, who jumped up, grabbed the bottle that was lying next to him, and was home in half a minute.

The boy brought the bottle to the king with half a minute to spare. The king drank from the water and was immediately cured.

Now the boy claimed his princess, but since the king was totally well again, he didn't want to stand by his word. "You can't have the princess for your wife," he said, "until you fulfill another condition. You must bring back a chest in which the king of the neighboring kingdom keeps the gold he stole from me the last time we were at war!"

When he realized that the king wasn't going to keep his word, the boy was downcast, but he thought to himself, "Well, I might as well try." So he took his men on board and steered across the sea to the land of the neighboring king. The castle was by the sea, and the boy entered by himself. He was greeted kindly, but when he asked for the treasure chest, the king was amazed and said that he needed to think it over.

The next day the boy returned and was told that the king had conferred with his ministers, who'd advised him not to give back the chest—and that is the answer the boy received. So he returned to his boat and thought up a plan.

The man who had a bandage covering one eye took it off and could see that the chest was in a castle vault. The hunter agreed to shoot through the keyhole to open the lock, and the man who was very strong promised to carry the chest home. They all decided that they would steal it at night when everyone was asleep.

That night the hunter put the rifle to his chin and shot. The man who heard so well listened and heard that the lock and the door were open, and that everything was ready. Then the strong man and the man who could run fast went up to the castle and brought the chest back to the boat.

As they were hurrying back to the boat, an alarm sounded; the guard had discovered that the door to the treasure vault had been opened. A search was organized for the stranger, who everyone thought must be the thief. When the boy had made sure that the treasure and all his men were aboard, he set sail. But the king pursued him with his fleet, and was close to catching him when the man with his finger up his nostril blew so hard that the king's ships were blown back to where they came from.

After the seas calmed, the king set out after the thief again, and this time he almost caught up with him. Now the boy and his men were in a fix, and they nearly got caught, but the man with a feed bag on his behind took it off, and the king's ships all got stuck in the muck.

The boy brought all the men back to where he'd found them. He himself went to the king and handed over the treasure, and this time the king had to keep his word. Since he was very greedy, he figured that he couldn't have a better son-in-law, so he lived on the money that the boy had given him, and the boy and the princess took over the kingdom. No one dared go against a king whose boat could sail across land and sea.

The Liar

Once there was a princess who'd got it into her head that the only man she could take for a husband was someone who'd lie so baldly that it would make her furious.

Naturally, the king wanted to see his daughter married, so he issued a proclamation throughout the whole country, and soon liars began arriving at court as numerous as the birds in the sky. But all of them lied and lied until they were all lied out without getting any answer from the princess except, "Well, it *could* be true!"

In that country lived a farmer's son, and when he heard of the challenge, he thought to himself, "I'll be damned if I can't make up lies that would make a princess furious!"

Not that he'd ever applied himself to that art before. Perhaps he just felt so energetic and fresh to the task that he dared take it on. He went to the king's castle, where the princess invited him to walk in the garden.

"Tell me about your parents," she said.

"My father was a windmill and my mother an old filly. They had three children together: one was never born, another never saw the light of day, and the third one was me," he answered.

"That may be," said the princess. "But look what big cabbages my father has!"

"Oh, they're nothing compared to *my* father's cabbages. Once fifteen horseback riders took shelter from the rain beneath one leaf. I went and poked a hole in the leaf, and they all drowned in the waterfall," said he.

"That may be, but what do you think of my father's new stable?"

"Not bad! But *my* father built one so tall that one day when the thatcher dropped his ax, a magpie had time to build a nest and lay eggs and hatch babies before the ax reached the ground. And the house was so long that if the cow mated with the bull in the doorway, the calf would be running by her side by the time she'd gotten halfway to her stall."

"Well, that may be. But take a look at my father's cows," said the princess.

"Yes, he's got a lot. But *my* father has a herd so big that when we make cheese, we have to pour the milk into a dried-up lake."

"How do you get the milk to curdle?" she asked.

"Oh, we just take some horses and tie rennet* around their legs, and then we let them out into the milk," said the boy.

"I see, but how do you manage to knead the cheese later?" asked the princess.

"That's as easy as pie. We have an old mare that we let stomp around in it. One time the mare foaled in the cheese, and when the foal came out of the dry rind, I walked in. After I'd walked around for a bit, I saw a fellow with a pair of pants made of alder wood. He stood there chopping down twigs, while two wagon wheels played ball with each other. One of the wheels bumped into me. 'Sorry!' I said. 'I've forgotten to pick rocks for you.'

"A little while later I met a man carrying a bundle of fish. I traded him the cheese rind for the fish. But then I came upon another man carrying a bundle of thatching straw, and I traded the fish for it. Later I climbed up to Heaven on the thatching straw and saw the sun sitting and spinning and the moon reeling yarn, while Saint Peter was separating the wheat from the chaff. When I'd seen what I wanted to see,

* Rennet is the lining membrane of a cow's stomach, used to curdle milk for making cheese.

I took a fistful of husks from Saint Peter and wound them into a rope, and hoisted myself a good way down. When the rope stopped, I scratched my back and caught hold of a fine louse, which I skinned. I cut the skin into strips, tied them to the rope, and hoisted myself down a few more miles. When the rope stopped again, I took another louse from my back and made another rope, but when that stopped, I had no more of the little buggers on my back. There was nothing to do but let go. I dropped three thousand feet up the ass of a dog, and there sat your father and my father, drinking and competing about who was the better farter, but your father lost and borrowed money from my father—"

"That's a lie!" the princess shouted, getting furious.

"That's what I was after!" he answered. And now the princess became sweet again, and she admitted that he'd won her as only a true liar could.

Soon afterward, the king made a great wedding feast for them, but I got there too late to go to the party.

Ash Dummy Chops Down the Oak and Becomes the King's Son-in-Law

Once there was a tenant farmer who was so poor that he lacked most everything. Still, he was lucky enough to have a wife and three boys.

The two eldest were a couple of strapping fellows, but the third seemed to do nothing but lend truth to the adage that there must be "a troll in every brood." Because he sat most of the time by the hearth helping his old mother scrape pots and pans, and sometimes stirred the ashes and drew pictures with the poker or his fingers, his brothers called him Ash Dummy. But his mother loved him and called him her darling, for she thought that in the future when the other boys were off working at the castle, this boy would stay home and close her eyes when she died.

And that's the way it was. Everyone was content, each in his own way: the older boys went their way, and the old woman and Ash Dummy went theirs, but the farmer himself no one really paid attention to, which is often the way it goes in this world.

As it happened, the castle wasn't terribly far away, and the family heard many stories about what was going on there. They heard that an oak had grown up right outside the king's window and that it was so big and leafy not a beam of sunlight could get through. The oak seemed like a punishment for their sins, and the king wanted it chopped down; but no one was able to, for the more one chopped, the fatter it got. Since it seemed that no one could cut down that oak, the king finally declared that whoever cut it down would become his son-in-law. That was all very well and fine, you might think, and whether anyone tried his luck, I can't say, but probably quite a few did.

Now it occurred to those two boys, Ash Dummy's brothers, to give it a try. So one lovely day the eldest told his old mother to rustle up some pancakes and a few provisions for the trip and to bake some sourdough rolls for his food pack, for he was going a-courting. His middle brother stayed home, but he thought he'd take Ash Dummy along to carry his backpack; besides, he might come in handy.

Off they went, one who had business to do, and Ash Dummy, who just—so his brother thought—had come along for the ride. They had to walk through a stretch of forest, and as they were walking, they suddenly heard some chopping. It sounded quite a bit like a woodpecker, but also like the faint sound of an ax.

"Go take a look," the brother told Ash Dummy.

He went in among the bushes and saw an ax chopping, but no one was holding the handle!

"What the devil is going on here?" said Ash Dummy.

"Well," said the ax, "I've been waiting many years for you. Come take me, and I'll make you happy."

Ash Dummy took the ax and brought it to his brother.

"What do you want with such a worthless ax? Take a look at mine. This is a real ax!"

"I'm sure you're right," said Ash Dummy, "but it might come in handy if I live long enough and keep my health."

After a while they arrived at the castle. The eldest brother announced that he'd like to try to chop down the oak and win the princess.

"Go right ahead," they said, "but if you don't succeed, you'll fare very badly."

"Nothing ventured, nothing gained," he answered. "At least I can't do worse than badly."

They showed him the oak and he started to chop, but no matter how big and strong he was, and no matter what a fine ax he had, he got nowhere; the more he chopped, the thicker the oak grew, although the chips flew to heaven. Finally, there was nothing for him to do but give up and go home.

"Oh no you don't, my fine fellow," they said. "You don't get away that easy. We want to have some words with you."

And someone walked right up to him, cut off both his ears, and threw them into the nearby lake. To this day that lake is called Earless.

"Damn, that hurt!" said the brother, but it was no use complaining now; he might lose his nose as well. With Ash Dummy at his heels, he hurried home, trailed by his misery.

The brother who was next in line got very excited about trying his luck. And why not? The pancakes, the provisions, and the sourdough rolls were still untouched. So he dressed in his best, picked up his shiny ax, and went on his way, with Ash Dummy toddling close behind just like the last time. This time they took a different route, across a field, and as they walked along, they suddenly saw a spade digging away and throwing dirt high above the treetops.

"I want to take a look," said Ash Dummy, but his brother had other things on his mind. When Ash Dummy got to the field, he said, "What the devil is going on? A spade but no man?"

"I've been waiting for you for years," said the spade. "If you take me along with you, I'll make you as happy as a clam."

"That sounds good," said Ash Dummy, and picked up the spade and left.

"What do you want with such an awful spade?" the brother said.

But Ash Dummy answered, "It'll come in handy sometime, assuming we live to see that day."

Soon they arrived at the castle. Ash Dummy stayed back, but his brother went inside and announced his intention of cutting down the oak and winning the princess.

"If you're man enough, it'll go well," they said. "But if you're not, you'll fare badly."

"Fare badly, fare well, go as it will," he said. "If I don't try, I'll never know."

And he started chopping. The ax was sharp and shiny, and the man who held the handle was in fine shape, but though he chopped until the chips flew over the rooftops, the oak tree just grew thicker with every stroke. He chopped and chopped until he grew tired, and he was just about to leave when a fellow seized him by the scruff of the neck and said, "Oh no, my friend, we must have a little talk." He took out a shiny knife, cut off both his ears, and threw them into the lake called Earless.

"Now you can go," said he. The second brother gathered up his belongings, and, grateful to have his nose left, he and Ash Dummy hurried home. Whether or not Ash Dummy watched his brothers getting their ears cut off, I really don't know, but both of them brought their misfortune home with them to their parents, that's for sure.

Be that as it may, it occurred to Ash Dummy that since the pancakes and sourdough rolls still hadn't been eaten, it was his turn to go to the castle and try his luck. His mother didn't object; she thought that if her baby proved cleverer than his brothers, it would serve them right.

"Go right ahead, my dear boy," she said, giving him a small lump of butter to spread on the cold pancakes and a ball of cheese to carry in his pocket. "I'm sure you can carry your own food bundle and ax," she said.

So off Ash Dummy went, while his mother stood watching him. His brothers had been cocky and finely dressed, their axes shiny and their noses stuck in the air, but Ash Dummy had to go in his everyday clothes: that was all he had—that, and the little ax he'd found in the forest, and the spade that seemed to have been given to him by Our Lord Himself. "It's sure to be useful for something," he thought.

He decided to take a different route from his brothers—the long way. So what, he thought, nothing's too far for a pig in a pea field. He walked through a forest and arrived at a stream, or a river, that he couldn't cross without getting wet. As he stood there wondering what to do, the river said to him, "Follow me to my source. Then you'll know what to do."

After walking a good long way, he found at the source of the stream a nut and in it a hole, out of which poured all the water.

"Very peculiar," said Ash Dummy.

But then the nut spoke: "I've been lying here waiting for you for years, so just plug up the hole and take me along with you. I'll make you happy."

He plugged up the hole, put the nut in his pocket, and ran off happily. Before long he arrived at the castle and told them that he too was ready to take on the challenge. "Go right ahead and try," said the castle guards, though they thought it was ridiculous. "Let's see what kind of man you are."

Ash Dummy picked up his little ax. When he started chopping at the oak, it was like cutting the cheese and pancakes in his bundle. After a few strokes the oak fell to the ground—lock, stock, and barrel.

It wasn't going to be quite so easy to win the princess. The king insisted that now he had to dig a well full of fresh water right by her window. So he took out the spade that he'd found in the field, and soon the well was done. Where was the water? Oh, yes, he removed the plug in the nut and threw it into the well. Soon it was filled with water.

"What do you say to that?" said Ash Dummy.

"I'll give you a new coat and dress you like a gentleman," said the king. In a few moments the old Ash Dummy was gone. In his place was a handsome fellow—the king's future son-in-law.

The Princess with the Louse Skin

One day a tenant farmer found a louse under his shirt collar, probably the kind of louse with an ace of spades on its back. He didn't want to kill it, so he put it into a wooden clog and fed it. It grew and grew until finally there was no more room in the clog, so he made for it a little house something like a doghouse.

One day the king happened to be passing by. He saw the animal and asked to buy it. This was arranged, and the next day he sent a couple of his guards to bring it to the castle. I don't know exactly what happened, but the guards probably didn't fancy walking on the road with a large louse, so they may have been a bit rough on it when it wouldn't walk fast enough, and finally they beat it until it died. After skinning it, they brought it to the king, saying that it had died along the way. The king had a belt made from the skin, which he gave to the princess, and later he announced that anyone who could guess what the princess's belt was made of would have her for a wife and inherit the kingdom after him.

Suitors came from all corners of the country, but none guessed correctly—counts and barons and princes and poor folk all tried their luck.

Now it happened that a farmer had three sons, and they too wanted to try. But the youngest couldn't go with them, because he was a bit backward and they were ashamed. So he walked by himself. After walking a whole day, he got hungry and sat down by the roadside to eat. Soon a mouse came along and started nibbling at his cheese, and when the boy had eaten his fill, he let her stay in his food bag. The next day when he was eating, a dung beetle came along and sat in his butter dish, and it was allowed to stay too. On the third day an ant joined them.

Finally, the boy came to the king's castle. It was the day before Guessing Day. He walked into the great hall, and when he opened his food bag, the animals crept out and said in one voice: "Say 'louse skin,' say 'louse skin'!" The mouse hid in a hole and the ant in another, and the dung beetle crawled up onto the windowsill.

The next day the hall filled with people. Everyone shouted out the names of different kinds of skin, but no one said the right one. Finally the boy shouted, "Louse skin!" which no one had said before. The king was just about to admit that it was the right answer, when a count, who'd heard what the boy said, shouted "Louse skin" too. The king thought that the count was a finer fellow than the boy, so he said that they'd both gotten the right answer, and now they had to find a way of deciding between them. They decided that the princess would sleep between them, and whomever she was facing when she woke up was the man she would marry. She preferred the count, so she decided to make sure that it was he.

After the three had gone to bed, the princess turned her back on the boy, but in a little while the dung beetle came along and crawled up into the count's behind, and dug there until it smelled and stank. The princess had to turn over and face the boy, and when the king came in the morning to judge, it was the boy she was closest to.

But now the princess wanted to do the test over again, to which the king had no objections. The count got a pair of sturdy leather pants, and they went to bed again. That night the mouse bit a hole in the pants and the dung beetle went to work again, so the next morning the princess was again facing the boy, and there's no denying that he and she had started to make friends.

But now the king decided that the three had to sleep together one more night. The count had a metal plate put on the hole in his pants and a plug in his behind. This, he thought, would make it impossible for them to get at him. Sure enough, it wasn't easy, and they didn't manage until just before daybreak, when the ant crawled into the count's nose and bit him. That made him sneeze so hard that the plug shot out of his behind, knocking away the metal plate. This time, the king had no choice but to let the boy have the princess.

Sheepskin Boy

Once there was a farmer who had three sons. The youngest was usually called Sheepskin Boy because he always wore a sheepskin coat, and his job was to tend the sheep in the woods. He also carried a ram's horn, which he blew on to gather the sheep.

One day Sheepskin Boy and his flock came to a mountain in the woods, on top of which sat a troll making pots.

"Won't you exchange your ram's horn for my fiddle?" asked the troll, showing him a fiddle lying at his side. "It's a remarkable one. You can make anyone dance as long as you like."

"It'd be nice to own that fiddle," thought the boy, and so he traded his ram's horn for it.

The boy played for the sheep, and they danced just as long as he played.

He and his flock walked farther on, and finally came to a green

meadow next to a mountain. There he let his sheep graze. Before long another troll came out of the mountain, angry because the boy had let his flock eat the grass on his meadow.

"Just wait," said the boy. "I'll make you dance." And the boy played his fiddle, and the troll started to dance. The boy didn't stop until the troll had danced himself to death.

Walking through a gate in the mountain, the boy entered a great hall. He looked for something to eat, but found only a small box on a stone table in which lay a whistle. The boy blew it and there appeared another troll, who said his name was Lunkentus. He asked what the king desired.

"I'm not your king," said the boy.

"Yes, since you've killed my king, now you're king in his place."

And for the first time in his life, the boy was given enough food to really eat his fill.

"I don't suppose," asked the troll, "that you've heard that the princess of this country is sitting up there on the Glass Mountain with a golden apple in her hand? And that anyone who can ride up the side of the mountain three times will get both her and the golden apple, and become king of the country?"

No, the boy hadn't heard.

"If you want to ride up the mountain, just do as I say. Don't tell anyone; just come back tomorrow. You can keep the whistle, and every time you blow on it, I'll come to help you."

With his sheep the boy walked back home, where everyone was

talking about the princess on the Glass Mountain. His brothers said that they were going to try their luck.

"Can't I try too?" begged Sheepskin Boy.

"You haven't the proper clothes. And you can't ride up the side of any mountain. Go back to the woods and tend your sheep!"

The next day Sheepskin Boy trudged off to the woods with his flock. When he arrived at the mountain, he blew his whistle, and instantly the troll appeared. The boy said he wanted to ride up that Glass Mountain, and the troll gave him clothes and a suit of armor made of copper. All the fittings on the horse's bridle were copper too. In addition, he was given a little bottle filled with a potion, and enough copper coins to fill his pockets.

"When you get to the mountain," said Lunkentus, "ask someone to hold your horse while you go aside and drink from the bottle. Give the copper coins to the groom holding your horse. You mustn't stay on top of the mountain or accept the golden apple."

When the boy arrived, he saw his father and his brothers. The brothers had tried to ride up but had failed; as a matter of fact, they'd hurt themselves and their horses.

Sheepskin Boy asked his father to hold his horse. Then he walked aside, drank from the bottle, and gave the copper coins to his father. Afterward, he rode up the mountain, sending splinters of glass flying, and rode back down immediately. He came back to Lunkentus, exchanged the copper suit for his sheepskin coat and linen pants, and started for home.

At home everyone was talking about the unsuccessful rides, and about the foreign prince dressed in copper who'd ridden up the mountain. Sheepskin Boy pretended to know nothing about it; he merely asked if he could try next time. "But you have no clothes! You can't ride up the mountain!" was the answer he received.

The next day Sheepskin Boy went back to the woods, where he met Lunkentus.

Now he was given silver armor and silver coins; and when he arrived at the mountain, his father and brothers had once again failed. Everyone wondered who the distinguished prince might be. The father held the horse while the "prince" went aside and drank from the bottle. He gave the silver coins to his groom and proceeded to ride right up the mountain and right back down again. Then he went

back to Lunkentus, changed his clothes, and toward evening came home with his flock.

At home they were all talking about the rides up the Glass Mountain. The same prince who'd ridden the first time had appeared in silver armor, and he'd completed the ride; everyone wondered if he could do it a third time.

The brothers wanted to try a third time too, and Sheepskin Boy pleaded with them to take him along. But they just made fun of his sheepskin coat and linen pants, and the next day he returned to the woods with his sheep.

This time the troll gave him gold coins and a suit of gold armor. Next to the Glass Mountain were standing his father and brothers, displeased that they'd failed a third time. While his father held his horse, the boy drank from the bottle; he gave his father the gold coins and rode straight up the Glass Mountain. The princess and her courtiers wanted him to stay and tell them who he was, but he rode off. In his haste, however, he dropped one of his gold shoes, which the princess picked up.

The princess tried to find out who owned the shoe. Many people tried it on, but it fit no one; the person who came closest was a distinguished nobleman.

Sheepskin Boy insisted that he try on the shoe too. He was greatly ridiculed, but he didn't care and soon he was on his way to the castle dressed in his sheepskin coat and linen pants. The shoe fit him like a glove. He blew his whistle, and immediately Lunkentus appeared with the golden armor and the golden apple. The wedding was celebrated with much pomp and ceremony.

Back in Sheepskin Boy's house, they were wondering why he hadn't returned. At the same time, he suggested to the princess that they go visit his family. "Whatever I do, don't get angry with me," he said. "Just pretend that nothing unusual is happening." And he put on his old clothes and went home ahead of the others.

When he arrived, they scolded him for having been gone so long. "I've been working in the king's kitchen and haven't been able to come before. Now the king, the princess, and the whole court are coming here to visit."

"But what will we do?" wailed the boy's mother. "We have nothing to offer the king!"

"Give them potatoes and pan drippings," said the boy. "The king loves nothing better."

"But who will serve them?"

"I will," answered the boy. "I'm used to it."

The king, the princess, and the whole court arrived. Everyone sat down at the table, and the Sheepskin Boy carried out the dishes. He gave two potatoes to each person, saying, "These are for you, and that's all you get."

When he returned to the kitchen, his mother yanked his hair hard for being so cheeky. But as he was about to serve the drippings, he pretended to stumble, and he dropped the whole pan in the princess's lap. His father grabbed him by the collar, pulled him outside, and locked him in the pigsty.

That night the princess was to sleep in a room in the attic. During the night the boy broke out of the pigsty, got a ladder, and climbed up to her. She opened the window and let him in.

In the morning the boy's father came to wake the princess, and found the boy in her bed. The old man stood in the doorway motioning with his arms, whispering, "Get away, get away!"

"No," answered the boy. "It's so nice here; this is where I'll stay."

At that moment the princess woke up and started to laugh. And she told Sheepskin Boy's parents and brothers that he was her husband. The boy went outside and whistled for Lunkentus, who brought clothes and a horse and carriage.

When the old king died, Sheepskin Boy became the king of the land.

The Princess Who Danced with a Troll Every Night

Once there was a princess who had to dance with an evil troll every night until she danced out seven pairs of shoes. Her father the king promised the kingdom and the princess's hand to anyone who could break the spell.

A boy heard of this and decided to try his luck. But before he got to the castle, he had to walk through a big forest full of thieves. After he'd walked for a while, he heard them coming, so he threw himself on the ground and placed his hat over a rock. Soon the thieves arrived.

"What are you doing there?" one of them asked.

"Hush, hush!" said the boy. "I have a bird under my hat that lays golden eggs, but I can't pick it up before daybreak."

"What do you want for that bird?" asked the thief.

"I'm not going to sell it," said the boy. "But if you'll show me the way out of the forest, perhaps you can have it for free."

"We've placed three balls in the forest which show the way out. If you follow them, you'll find it."

"Then I'll go," said the boy. "But whatever you do, don't touch the hat until the sun comes up, or you'll have no golden eggs."

The thieves did as the boy told them, never suspecting that he was fooling them.

When the boy had walked for a while, he found the first ball. "I'll take it along," he thought. Then he walked on until he found the second ball, which he also brought along, and when he came to the third, he took that one as well. By then he was out of the forest with all three balls in his pocket. "They may come in handy," he thought.

After he'd walked a very long way, he arrived at a large mountain, on top of which two giants were fighting.

"What are you fighting about?" asked the boy.

"We've inherited a pair of seven-league boots from our grandfather. Whoever is stronger will get them."

"The first one to catch the ball gets the boots!" shouted the boy, and threw one of his balls off the steepest side of the mountain. The giants jumped after it as fast as they could, and the boy pulled on the boots and strode away seven leagues.

A little while later he came to another mountain where two more giants were fighting.

"What are you fighting about?" asked the boy.

"Oh," said one of the giants, "our grandfather has left us a cape that makes you invisible when you put it on. Whoever is stronger will get it."

The boy took his second ball and threw it off the steepest side of the mountain, shouting, "The first one to catch the ball gets the cape!" And while the giants jumped to get the ball, the boy put on the cape. He took one seven-league stride and was gone.

Now he found himself on yet another mountain on which two more giants were fighting.

"What are *you* fighting about?" asked the boy.

"Well, we've inherited a lantern from our grandfather with which we can see all the paths of the trolls. Whoever is stronger gets the lantern."

"The first one to catch the ball gets the lantern!" shouted the boy, and threw his third ball off the mountain. The giants jumped for all they were worth. But the boy took the lantern, and off he went seven leagues at a stride, invisible and knowing all the paths of the trolls. "Now perhaps I can try to free the princess," he thought.

He took a few more long strides and arrived at the castle.

"I'm here to break the troll's spell," said the boy when the king asked him what had brought him there. "But I'll have to sleep in the same room as the princess."

At first the king wouldn't hear of it. But finally he agreed, and that evening the boy bedded down in the princess's chamber. He pretended to be asleep as a trapdoor opened in the floor and a troll said, "Is he asleep?"

"Yes, he is," said the princess.

"Then let's go," said the troll, and they were gone.

The boy picked up his lantern and looked around the room. He opened the trapdoor and saw a tall ladder, which he climbed down, but he couldn't see the princess or the troll.

As he walked along, he came to a large garden in which the trees and fruit were made of silver. He picked a silver apple and a silver leaf and put them in his knapsack. In a while he saw another garden in which everything was gold. He took a gold apple and a gold leaf and put them into his knapsack.

When he held up his lantern, he could see a large lake, and on the lake the troll was rowing the princess in a boat. "How will I get across the lake?" thought the boy, but then he took one very long stride and just managed to make it across.

Now he was at the troll's castle, but it would still be a while before the troll arrived with the princess, for they had a long way to row. "I'll go inside for a bit," thought the boy, and he did. No one was in sight. First he came to a great hall where tables were set. "I wonder what kind of food this troll has," thought the boy. The dishes were piled with fried worms and pieces of frogs. He went into the next hall and saw seven pairs of clogs. In a third hall was a floor made of spikes, and the boy understood that the princess had to dance out all seven pairs of clogs on the spiked floor with the troll each night.

Soon the troll and the princess arrived. The boy went outside and sat on a bench, but the troll couldn't see him because he was invisible.

Nevertheless, the troll yelled, "I smell the blood of a Christian!"

"Yes, you do," said the boy to himself.

"Come inside and eat," said the troll to the princess.

They went inside, followed by the boy. He stood right behind the princess's chair, and each time she raised a forkful of food to her mouth, he pushed her arm so that the pieces fell under the table.

"Don't you want any food?" said the troll. "If not, we'll go in and dance."

When they'd gone, the boy took the pieces of worm and frog and whatever else was on the table, and put them into his knapsack. Then he went back to the castle, crawled up through the trapdoor, and lay down to sleep. The princess had just gotten home in the morning when the king came in.

"Well, have you released the princess from the troll's spell?" asked the king.

The boy began to tell his story, but the princess screamed, "He's lying! Throw him out!"

The boy took out his knapsack and showed the silver and gold apples, and the pieces of worm and frog. The spell was finally broken: no longer did she have to return to the troll's castle each night to dance. The king was so overjoyed that he gave the boy both his kingdom and the princess.

Stuck on a Goose

A king once promised that whoever could make his daughter laugh would get her and half the kingdom.

A boy heard of this offer. One day he went fishing and caught a pike, which he put into a bucket. Because it splashed around in the funniest way, he headed for the castle to show it off.

On his way he met an old woman. "Where are you going, my boy?" she said.

"I'm going to show the princess this pike to make her laugh. If she does, I'll get half the kingdom," said he.

"Why don't you take this golden goose," said the old woman, "and I'll take your pike. If someone pets her, just say, 'You can't pluck the feathers, but if you want to come along, hang on.' "

The boy agreed to the exchange, and after a while he met another old woman. "That's a wonderful goose you have there," she said.

"If you want to pet her, you can, but you can't pluck any feathers," the boy said. When the old woman petted the goose, he added, "If you want to come along, hang on!" Immediately, the old woman stuck to the goose and had to follow along to the castle.

When they passed the blacksmith's, he and his apprentices were standing outside shoeing a horse. "Take a look at that old woman chasing a goose. Why don't you run over and kick her in the butt!" said the blacksmith. The apprentice ran over, but just as he was about to kick, the boy yelled, "Hang on!" And the poor apprentice had to run after them, kicking the old woman's behind.

When his master saw the apprentice running along, he ran after him with a pair of tongs. With these he grabbed the apprentice, but the boy yelled, "Hang on!" And now he too had to run along behind them.

Finally they arrived at the castle, where the princess was sitting looking out the window. When she saw the boy with his goose, the old woman with the apprentice hopping on one leg, and the blacksmith, she started laughing.

"Oh, you'll have to laugh harder than that," thought the boy.

Then he ran past the kitchen. A cook was standing in the doorway with a porridge ladle in her hand. She chased after them and hit the blacksmith on the back. "Hang on!" the boy yelled, and took another turn around the yard. When the princess saw the cook chasing the others with the porridge ladle on the blacksmith's back, she almost died laughing.

And the king gave his daughter to the boy.

The King's Hares

A king and queen's only daughter had so many suitors that they simply didn't know what to do with them. As strange as it sounds, the king and queen weren't really very eager to see her married; they'd rather have kept her for themselves. Finally, the king issued a proclamation that anyone who could guard the king's three hundred hares for three days could have the princess. However, if he didn't succeed, he'd have one strip of skin cut from his back and one from his stomach.

In that particular country lived a farmer who had three sons. The two oldest were vain and haughty and despised their equals, especially their youngest brother. When they heard of the king's offer, the eldest one immediately decided to go off to try his luck. Their father gave his permission because he thought that the clever boy might very well manage to become the king's son-in-law. He outfitted him as best he could, and the boy set off for the king's castle.

Passing through a forest, he met a poor old woman who greeted him kindly and asked where he was going.

"None of your business, old hag!" he answered.

"Well, what do you know," she said. "If you'd been a bit more civil, I could have given you some good advice and shown you the way!"

But he said that he knew the way by himself and didn't need any advice.

He arrived at the castle without further incident, and was told the conditions of the test: if he could guard the hares and bring all three hundred of them back to the castle at night, he could claim his princess. But if a single one was missing, he knew the punishment that awaited him.

The boy agreed to these conditions, and the king ordered all the hares to be let loose. They had barely touched the ground before they each ran in a different direction. No matter how the boy scurried all day long about the forest, by evening he didn't return with even a single hare. The king had a strip of skin cut from his back and one from his stomach, and then let him go.

Naturally, when his eldest son returned home in this condition, his father figured that this would be the end of their dreams about marrying the princess.

But he was wrong. His second son thought that if his brother had just acted a little more sensibly, he'd still have the skin on his back and stomach, and the princess as well. He wanted to try his luck, and wouldn't change his mind no matter how much his father tried to talk him out of it. Since there was nothing to be done, the father outfitted this son as best he could, too. But he didn't fare any better than the eldest: he was disrespectful to the poor old woman he met in the forest, the king's hares ran away from him, and he finally returned to his father's farm in just as poor shape as his brother.

Now the youngest brother got up from the hearth, where he'd been lying in the ashes, and said that it was his turn to try guarding the king's hares. The old man took this very badly, for although he didn't think very much of his youngest son, he still felt that he could get some use out of him while his older brothers' wounds were healing, and so he wanted to keep him at home. But the boy insisted on going; since his father wouldn't outfit him at all, he left as he was, with nothing but a little bundle of food in his hand.

When he arrived at the forest, he met the same old woman who had greeted his brothers.

"How do you do, dear mother!" said the boy.

"I thank you for that! You're a kind soul to greet a poor, wretched old woman," she answered.

"Oh, I greet everyone I meet," said the boy. "But if you're not used to common decency, you must be hungry as well. Let's find some place where there aren't too many ants, and sit down and share my sack of food."

The woman was happy to do this. They sat down, and when the boy saw that his food sack wouldn't be enough to silence her hunger, he promised to save a little for her from his meals when he started working for the king. She asked him what he was planning to do, and he answered that he was going to try to guard the king's hares.

"For that you're going to need a good whistle," the old woman said, and she gave him a whistle, telling him that all he had to do was blow in it when he wanted to gather the hares. Not only would the three hundred come to him, but one extra for each day he remained on guard. The boy thanked her, and promised to give her more food if she'd come and find him in the forest.

The old woman went on her way, and the boy walked to the king's castle. There, just like his brothers, he received permission to attempt to guard the hares. Before he left, he took a look at the princess, and she took a look at him too. She wished in her heart that he'd be able to guard the hares better than all the others.

He was given a sack of food, but he made sure to put aside a large part of it for the old woman. The king ordered all the hares to be released, and immediately they ran in all directions.

"Go ahead and run off!" thought the boy. "Sooner or later you'll dance to my whistle!"

Then he followed after them to the forest at a leisurely pace. The old woman met him, got her food, and told him what he should do if someone came to visit him.

As noon was approaching, a boy came riding along on an ass. He reined in the animal next to the shepherd boy and asked if he could buy a hare; he was willing to pay anything for it.

"They're only for sale at one price—two hugs from the buyer!" answered the shepherd. He saw perfectly well that the boy who wanted to buy the hare was none other than the princess herself, who had disguised herself to test him. She said that there wasn't any point in two boys hugging each other, and she'd much rather pay hard cash. But the boy held firm to his price. She hadn't gotten far with her hare before the boy blew his whistle, and it hopped out of the princess's basket. She didn't notice it, however, until she arrived at the castle and was about to show the hare to her father. Oddly enough, she didn't seem very sorry that the hare was gone.

That evening the boy blew his whistle, and all the hares gathered around him. He drove them back in a flock to the castle, and when the king counted them, there was actually one too many.

"In this world everything should increase if it's any good," said the boy.

The next day the princess again came out to the forest dressed like a boy. But the shepherd recognized her, and their dealings were the same as before. The hare she bought ran away from her, and in the evening the boy had two hares too many. The princess couldn't help smiling, but the king was annoyed at the shepherd boy's luck, and thought that tomorrow he himself would trick him into selling at least a few hares.

Toward noon on the third day, the king arrived, dressed like an ugly old crone and riding an old white mare. He asked to buy two hares. The shepherd recognized him and answered that the hares could only be bought at one price—three kisses by the old lady under the horse's tail.

"Well, why not?" thought the king. "It's obvious that he doesn't recognize me, and no one else will see me do it." He kissed the place that he was supposed to kiss, got the hares, and rode home. But when he got back to the castle, the hares had again disappeared from the basket, and that night the boy had three hares too many!

When the boy asked for his rightful reward, the king didn't want to give him the princess until he completed one more task—to fill a whole barrel with Truth.

"That's not hard," said the boy.

The barrel was placed in the grandest hall of the castle, and the king, the princess, and the entire court sat down to see if the shepherd boy could fill it with Truth.

"On the first day," he began, "when I had to guard the king's hares, a strange boy came riding on an ass to see me. He bought a hare from me for two hugs. But that boy, he was really the princess. Isn't that the truth?"

"Yes," answered the princess.

"Then into the barrel it goes!

"The second day that same boy came back and bought a hare from me for the same price as the day before. Isn't that the truth?" the boy asked.

"Yes," answered the princess.

"Then into the barrel with that; it's getting full!

"And on the third day," he continued, "an ugly old crone on a miserable old white mare came—"

"No, stop it!" the king blustered. "The barrel was full a long time ago!"

Of course, he didn't want his whole court to find out where he'd kissed his old mare. And so the young man and the princess were allowed to have each other.

And there they built their house, there they patched their shoes, and there they're still dancing around in their clogs.

Prince Greenbeard

*O*nce there was a princess who was very particular about her suitors. Several princes asked for her hand, but she sent them all away, for she was so fine-mannered that the slightest thing offended her. She was really very, very fussy.

Finally, however, a prince came along who won her heart, and she decided to marry him. He visited her court often, and grew to be very well liked by everyone. Sometimes, of course, the princess thought that he too fell short of her standards, but she liked him well enough to ignore it.

One day even his luck ran out. For dinner that evening they had a dish with stewed vegetables, and the prince happened to spill a little on his chin, which got caught in his goatee. This was enough to extinguish the hot flame of love that burned in the princess's heart.

From that moment on, she couldn't bear the sight of him. In vain everyone tried to convince her to change her mind.

"Do you really think," she said proudly, "that I could love a creature who behaved so badly? From now on he shall be called Greenbeard!"

These words wounded the prince deeply, and he decided to take his revenge. He left the court and went home.

Two years passed. Then the prince decided that it was time to return to the princess and try to win her—or at least to shame some of the pride out of her. But there was no point in going back as a prince; he knew that things would go as badly as the last time. So he disguised himself as a poor stranger looking for work. He shaved off his beard and changed his appearance as much as he could. When he arrived at the castle, he asked to speak to the king. This request was granted, and soon he was standing before His Royal Highness.

"What can I do for you, my boy?" said the king in a friendly manner.

"Your Most Gracious Majesty, please forgive a foreigner for asking most humbly to be admitted into Your Majesty's service as a stableboy. I promise that I will perform my tasks faithfully and honestly."

At first the king refused, saying that he already had too many servants. But the prince offered to serve at very low wages, and finally the king called his stablemaster to him.

"Let this stranger have two of my worst horses. That'll test his mettle.

"What's your name?" continued the king, turning to the stranger, whose features he thought he recognized.

"Per Greenbeard," answered the prince, bowing deeply.

"Per Greenbeard?" said the king, surprised.

At that moment the princess entered the room and looked sharply at the stranger. She whispered to her father, "Don't you think this man resembles the prince who was here two years ago?"

"He even has the name you gave him before he left," said the king.

But neither really suspected that it was the very same Greenbeard who was standing before them.

When Greenbeard was leaving, the king patted his shoulder:

"Now make sure you behave and do your work well. If you do, I'll give you a better post later on."

Greenbeard bowed humbly and left.

He began working with the worst horses in all the king's stables. But through his diligence and faithful care, they soon became the best horses the king owned; better horses had rarely been seen.

Before long the king wanted to promote Greenbeard to assistant stablemaster. He thanked the king for the honor, but declined; instead, he asked the king to be gracious enough to grant him another wish.

"Very well. What might that be?"

"Would Your Majesty be gracious enough to give me a bit of earth in the royal garden? There I could plant flowers to adorn the garden."

"That can be done, my boy."

"And there is one thing more that I hope Your Majesty will not deny me."

"And what might that be?"

"That I am the only one who is allowed to make decisions about my flowers, and that no one, whoever he may be, may take a single one without my permission."

The king gave his permission for this too.

Greenbeard left the stable and started working in the garden. Before long, myriads of flowers were growing there. Not only were they more beautiful than the other flowers in the garden, but they were also so different one from the other that no one had ever seen their like.

Greenbeard was extremely particular about his flowers. Not a single human being was allowed to beg or buy any—not even the princess, who came to Greenbeard and offered him money. To make sure that no one stole them, he posted a guard over them day and night, and the guards had to swear on everything they held dear to guard them well. He also asked for a small hothouse where he could grow the loveliest flowers all winter long.

Around New Year's the king held a great celebration. It was his golden anniversary as well as his fortieth year as king, and all the most important gentlemen in the realm were invited. There would be a grand ball, and all the ladies competed over who would be the most beautifully dressed.

Everyone wanted Greenbeard's flowers to decorate her clothes. All the court ladies begged him in vain. They offered him money or anything else he wanted—but nothing worked. The princess herself went to Greenbeard and entreated him to give her flowers, but she fared no better. Finally, she complained to the king, and asked him to order Greenbeard to give her the flowers. But it was impossible; he'd given Greenbeard his word.

"And I cannot take back my promise. A king's word is law."

Soon the day of the party drew near, when all the ladies would gather in the beautifully decorated ballroom. The princess decided to make one last attempt to get Greenbeard's flowers.

"My dear Greenbeard," she said, "won't you please give me some? Look, here's a handful of gold coins for just a few!"

"No," he said seriously and firmly. "I wouldn't part with a single flower even if Your Highness gave me a whole hatful of money. But I might give some flowers to my gracious princess if she granted me one small wish. If you agree, I'll give you the most beautiful flowers in my whole hothouse."

"Whatever might that be?" she exclaimed happily. "I'll be happy to promise you anything you want, as long as it's possible. Tell me!"

"One evening, after the party is over, I'd like permission to lie on the inside threshold of your bedroom. Isn't that a simple request?"

The princess thought this over for a long while. Finally, she said, "It is, but it's impossible for me to grant. How would you get past the guard? And if you were found, it would mean great unhappiness for both of us."

Greenbeard assured her that he'd be able to get in and out without being seen.

"If that's really true," she answered, "then your wish shall be granted, even though it's risky."

Greenbeard picked some of his most beautiful flowers. Before he gave them to her he said, "I must ask of you one more wish, my lovely, gracious princess. You must not give a single one of these flowers to anyone else. If you break your promise, things will go badly for you."

"Don't worry, I promise to keep my promise," said the princess. And she took the flowers and went happily on her way.

The other ladies were shocked that Greenbeard had given the

princess the flowers while they'd gotten nothing. They renewed their pleas to him, but he was immovable.

When the princess arrived at the ball adorned with Greenbeard's flowers, everyone was dazzled by her beauty, and all the guests from around the realm wanted to know where she'd gotten the wonderful flowers.

"I have a foreign gardener who has planted them in my garden. He's built a hothouse there, too," said the king.

Everyone wanted to see and speak with the unusual gardener, and perhaps get a flower from him.

"Well, I don't think you'll have much luck," said the king. "He never gives them away."

"How very strange!" they all said.

The king, the queen, the princess, and all their guests went down to the hothouse where Greenbeard was working. He was very surprised to see this elegant party, and bowed deeply. Although they admired and praised his wonderful flowers, Greenbeard didn't give them a single one; displeased, all the guests went on their way.

Now the princess had to fulfill her end of the bargain. It wasn't easy for Greenbeard to sneak into her bedroom, but one evening, while the royal family were eating their meal, he managed it and hid under her bed.

After the princess had gone to sleep, he crept out from his hiding place. At first the princess was so frightened that she almost screamed, but Greenbeard calmed her down. He went to the door and lay down by the threshold. But it wasn't long before he began to moan and groan, saying how cold he was. The princess worried that someone might hear him.

"Dear Greenbeard," she asked, "please be quiet. What if someone heard you? We'd both be very unhappy."

For a while he was quiet, but then he started again, complaining louder and louder until finally the princess had to let him sleep at the foot of her bed. Soon he renewed his moans and groans until the princess let him have a piece of her blanket. Then he grew quiet and soon he was sleeping peacefully. As the sun was rising, he snuck away.

Shortly afterward the princess heard her chambermaid telling one of the queen's ladies-in-waiting that someone definitely had been in

the princess's chamber. When she'd cleaned there, she'd found a lump of dirt that someone must have brought in on his shoes; the princess *never* had dirty feet! Frightened, the princess hurried to Greenbeard in the garden.

"We're both done for," she said, crying.

"Done for?" he cried, pretending to be frightened. "What's wrong, my gracious princess? I trust I haven't somehow offended the king?"

"No, but my chambermaid discovered that you've been inside my chamber!"

"Then death awaits both of us," Greenbeard said in feigned despair. "But be of good cheer. If you go along with me, I know how to save us both," he added in a calmer tone of voice.

"But how? You can easily save yourself by fleeing, but how can you save me?"

"Don't worry, just follow my advice. All will go well."

"I'll do anything you say, as long as you save me," said the princess.

"Very well then, we must both flee. My parents are fairly rich. They own a small farm. We can go there, and no one will ever find us. I know a shortcut to the border. Soon we'll be safe."

Now of course Greenbeard could have told her who he was, for the princess was so scared that she'd surely have forgiven him for anything he'd done. But first he wanted to rid her heart of pride.

The next night they went on their way. Now the proud princess felt what it was like to be a poor wanderer, and she learned to be happy with whatever she got. Often she was on the brink of despair, but her faithful Greenbeard took tender care of her. However, he also made sure to take a longer route than necessary so that she'd have a real chance to experience the difficulties of the road. After several months they arrived in Greenbeard's country, where the princess gave birth to a little son.

Finally, they came to the estate where Greenbeard's father lived. It was a large, beautiful estate a few miles from the capital; it was here that the royal family usually spent their summers.

Greenbeard sat down in the grass and started speaking to the princess, who was so exhausted after all their troubles that she cared about nothing anymore.

"My dear, gracious princess," he said, "not far from here lies the royal castle. Why don't you rest here while I go and ask permission to build a hut in the park. Afterward, perhaps I can get some work at the farm so that we won't have to go begging anymore."

There was joy in the court at Greenbeard's return. No one had known where he'd been; they'd all thought that he was dead and that they'd never see him again. Greenbeard told his father all his adventures, in particular how he'd dealt with the princess.

"Tomorrow I'll bring her here. I'll tell her that she must help out with the baking and other chores. On punishment of death I forbid anyone to speak to her—to ask where she comes from or pay any attention to what she does."

All day long the princess sat waiting for Greenbeard. When evening fell and he hadn't come back, she started to wonder if he'd return.

"Perhaps he's abandoned me! Oh, woe is me! Perhaps he doesn't love me any longer. He's deserted me and left me on my own! It would have been better for me to die than to suffer like this!" said the princess to herself, tears pouring down her cheeks. If she hadn't had her little child to take care of, she would probably have taken her own life—she was that unhappy.

The sun had already disappeared behind the mountains. All the songbirds who had been singing for the princess fell silent when Greenbeard returned, dressed in his gardener's clothes. When he saw the abandoned princess rocking their hungry little son in her lap, tears came to his eyes. Though he tried to hide it, his love for her and the child overcame him, and, crying, he fell to his knees and buried his face in her lap.

"Here I am, back again. Forgive me for staying away so long, gracious princess! It wasn't my intention; I was detained at the castle. Please don't be sad. Soon you'll be happy again. I've been promised that we can stay at the castle, where you must help with the baking. Soon the prince's wedding will be celebrated, so go as early as you can. I'll stay with our child and take care of him. I'll also build us a beautiful hut where we can stay for a few days. After the wedding, we can move to the castle."

By now the princess had calmed down, and they ate the food that Greenbeard had brought along. They made a bed under a tree and slept well until the birds woke them in the morning.

The princess awoke in a slightly better mood than that of the previous day. Greenbeard told her what to do when she arrived at the castle: they agreed to say that they were married and act as if they were man and wife.

"My dear friend," said Greenbeard, "when you make all that good bread dough, won't you take a few lumps and hide it away for me? I'll have to spend all day here without anything to eat."

"Oh, my dear," said the princess, "how can I do that without someone seeing me? And what would happen to me if I were discovered?"

"If you're careful and don't do anything foolish, no one will see you. Just put aside a little lump of dough as you're working."

She promised to do her best.

But the princess was very worried when she went off to the castle; it was the first time she'd had to work for a living, and she didn't really know how to go about it.

When she saw the castle that reminded her of her own home and previous life, she wanted to turn back. To think that she, so celebrated and admired as a princess, would be received like a vagabond! Though deeply wounded, she gathered her courage and continued on. When she arrived, she was received more kindly than she'd expected: no one criticized her, although it was obvious that she wasn't used to working. When no one was looking, she took a few lumps of dough and stuck them into her pocket.

Meanwhile, Greenbeard left his little son with a nursemaid and took a different road to his home. There he changed his clothes and his appearance as best he could.

He went down to the kitchen and said to the princess, "Are you Greenbeard's wife?"

"Yes, I am," she sighed deeply.

"Don't feel bad about that, little friend. Greenbeard will soon get a fine position."

At these words, her face lit up.

"And what a clever wife Greenbeard has," the prince said, grabbing her around the waist. Then he felt something lumpy in her pocket and took out the dough; the princess got so upset that she almost fainted with fear. When the prince saw how hard this was for her, he regretted that he'd talked her into it. With tears streaming down her face, she begged his forgiveness and asked to be allowed to leave immediately. But the court ladies detained her for a while, trying to comfort her.

Greenbeard hurried ahead to the large, fine hut he'd had built. When the princess returned, he was sitting with the baby on his knee. At once she told him all that had happened.

"You speak as though the prince likes you! I don't believe it," said Greenbeard.

"Yes, it's true," she assured him. "I'll never go again to the castle to work, that I can tell you. You'll just have to try to support me somehow."

He promised her that she wouldn't have to work anymore, and that from that day on he'd support her.

The next day Greenbeard went to the castle, and the princess and the child stayed at the hut. At sunset Greenbeard returned.

"I've got interesting news," he said.

"What has happened?"

"As you know, the prince is to be married tomorrow, and it can't be postponed because so many guests from all over the kingdom have already arrived. But the princess still has not arrived, and they need someone in her place at the wedding. He's chosen you!"

The princess couldn't believe her ears.

"How can the prince want me," she said, "when there are so many court ladies to choose among?"

But Greenbeard assured her that it was true, and that she had to hurry there early the next day.

When morning came, he worked hard to persuade her to go to the castle. She was ashamed of what had happened, and it embarrassed her to pretend to be a princess, when once she'd been so mighty and rich. But finally she gave in, and was surprised to see the great respect that everyone paid her.

Greenbeard had hurriedly dressed in his royal clothes to receive his wife-to-be. After she too was dressed in beautiful clothes, she got into the royal carriage and sat down beside him.

As they rode past the hut, the prince ordered his men to set fire to it. (The little boy had been brought to the castle, and the only thing that was left was a pair of Greenbeard's pants.) When the princess saw the hut burning, she shouted, "Oh no, Greenbeard's pants are on fire!"

The prince couldn't control himself any longer. He took her into his arms and said tearfully, "It is I who proposed to you four years ago, and whom you despised because I spilled some greens on my chin. To avenge my terrible hurt, I made you go through these trials. Now I've had my revenge, and your suffering is over. I beg your forgiveness for what I've done."

"Oh, my dear friend," said the princess, crying with happiness, "is it really true? I forgive you gladly. Because of my terrible pride I don't deserve any better. I thought I was the noblest and best on earth, but now I've seen how sin punishes the sinner."

At the castle there was great rejoicing when Greenbeard married his princess, but in the princess's homeland there was great mourning. In vain they searched for her everywhere. Finally, they gave up, convinced that Greenbeard had stolen her away.

One day a stranger arrived at court, bringing a letter from Prince Greenbeard, as he was still called, and his wife. In the letter Greenbeard begged forgiveness for having stolen the princess away, and told everything that had happened. He invited the king and his family to visit so that they could see the princess and the young prince.

One can understand how surprised and pleased the king and his entire court were at this news. The king didn't rest until he saw his lost daughter again, and words cannot describe their joy when they were reunited.

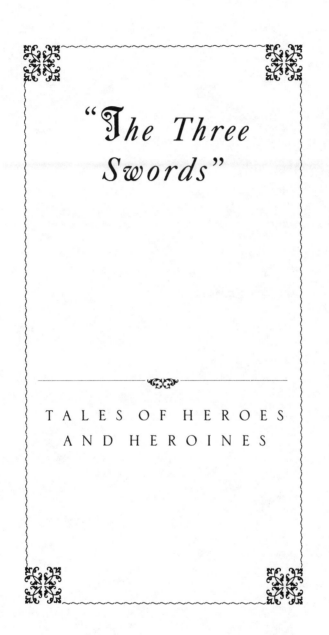

"The Three Swords"

TALES OF HEROES AND HEROINES

The Three Swords

Once there was a blacksmith like many other blacksmiths. This is how all stories begin.

One spring when he'd finished sowing his field, he planned to go into the forest to chop wood and build a charcoal stack.

After he'd eaten his breakfast and was ready to leave, he said to his wife, "Don't forget to bring food for me! You'll find me by the round grove of trees."

When it was getting close to nine o'clock, his wife came along with his food. While he ate, she sat down to rest, as usual; after he finished, she would bring the crock home with her so that she could use it again, for they were newly wed and poor.

After he'd eaten, as he prepared to take his usual nap, his wife invited him to lie by her.

After they'd slept awhile, the wife got up and started to walk away, taking his ax with her.

"What do you want with my ax?" asked the blacksmith. "We have four more at home in the shed."

But the woman just walked away without answering.

The man was surprised, but then he thought, "Well, I suppose she'll leave the ax by some tree or bush where I can find it again when I walk home tonight." And he went back to the work of piling wood for his charcoal stack.

After a short while, along came another woman who looked like the blacksmith's wife, with a midday meal for her husband.

"Don't you want to stop to eat your meal?" she asked. "The day's already far along."

Very surprised, he answered, "Eat now? What do you mean?"

"Well," answered the wife, "I know I'm late, but it's not because I've been idle. I've been baking and churning so you could have fresh bread and butter."

Now the blacksmith was even more perplexed, but he kept quiet and pretended that nothing had happened, and sat down to eat as much as he could swallow.

About seven years later it happened that this same blacksmith was standing by the chopping block chopping firewood for the night when along came a boy carrying an ax on his arm.

"What's wrong with your ax?" asked the smith. "Does she need fixing or sharpening?"

When the boy didn't answer, the blacksmith took the ax and looked it over very carefully. Then he said, "There's nothing wrong with it, but I'll be damned if this isn't *my* ax!"

"If it's your ax," said the boy, "you're my father."

The blacksmith had to acknowledge him as his son just as he'd recognized his ax, and, very worried, he went inside and told his wife that a boy had come along whom he wanted to take on as a helper. She said that there were quite enough people already in the household, but after much pleading he convinced her, and the boy was brought into the cottage and given food and clothing, and every day he went with his father to the smithy.

Time passed. The boy was clever, willing, and enormously strong, for he was half-Christian and half-troll, but he also had such an appetite that his father didn't see how he could feed him. So one day the smith went to the king's castle and asked the cook if he'd like a kitchen helper.

"Yes," the cook answered, "I just happen to need one. Send him along right away."

"If my son lives in the castle," thought the blacksmith happily, "maybe he'll get enough to eat."

When the boy heard that he'd been taken into the king's service, he said, "Dear Father, make me three swords: one that weighs three pounds, one that weighs six pounds, and one that weighs twelve pounds. Also, get me three linen coats, one for each sword. If you do as I ask, I promise you that one day I'll be so rich that you'll never have to work again."

It wasn't easy for the poor blacksmith to collect as much iron and steel as he needed in so short a time. But because he feared the boy's enormous strength, he didn't dare go against his wishes. After the three swords had been made just as the boy had specified, the third weighed only eleven pounds; one pound of iron had melted away when it was being tempered. This made the boy angry, and he said, "If you weren't my own father, I'd test your handiwork on your own neck! Now I'm not sure I'll be able to defend myself with it!"

His son's anger frightened the blacksmith even more, and he didn't reply. But he thought, "The sword should be heavy enough for you, even if you are strong. I know how much trouble it gave me just carrying it from the hearth to the anvil!"

The boy took the three swords and the three linen coats and hid them under a rock. Then he went with his father to the castle and started his service with the cook, just as he'd been promised.

It so happened that the king who ruled over the country had been out on a war expedition. On his way home, a great storm had come up, and everyone thought that the ship and everyone on it would perish. But the fierce, terrible storm had been caused by three sea trolls, who wouldn't let the king ashore before he promised each of his three beautiful daughters to them.

When the king arrived home, he issued a proclamation throughout the land that whoever could save the three princesses would get one of them for a wife, as well as half the kingdom—and the other half when he died. But no one among the king's many men dared to fight the three terrible sea trolls—except for a tailor, who acted brave and said he'd do everything in his power to defend the princesses.

When the time came for the princesses to be given to the sea trolls, there was great mourning throughout the kingdom. The eldest princess was brought down to the shore with all her retinue following behind. She sat down on the sand and burst into tears. But the brave tailor forgot all his big promises and climbed into a nearby pine tree.

Meanwhile, the boy went to his master and asked to go to town to have a little fun, and this the cook agreed to. The boy ran back home, took out the three-pound sword, pulled the linen coat over his clothes, called his little dog, and walked down to the seashore. When he got to where the princess was sitting, he greeted her in a courteous manner and asked why she was sitting there so sadly.

The princess answered, "My father, who was caught in a storm at sea, has promised me to a terrible sea troll. He's coming to get me any minute. Oh, I'm so miserable!"

"But is there no man or champion in all your father's kingdom who can save you?" asked the boy.

"Yes," answered the princess, "there's a tailor up there in that pine tree. He promised to save me!"

The boy smiled slightly and said, "I wouldn't put too much faith in a champion like that. But if you'll pick the lice out of my hair while I take a nap, I'll save you!" He said to his dog, "Little Faithful, stand guard over us!"

Then he put his head in the princess's lap, and she picked through his hair while the tailor sat silently in the pine tree, watching them. But as the boy slept in her lap, the princess pulled a red silk thread out of her singlet and secretly threaded it into his long hair.

At that moment a loud rumbling came from the sea. The waves rolled all the way up the beach, and out of the depths came a big, ferocious monster with three heads. The troll's dog was as big as a year-old bull calf.

"Where is the princess who was promised to me?" asked the troll.

"She's sitting right here," answered the boy. "But you'd better come closer so that we can talk it over."

"Are you making fun of me, you little ragamuffin?" said the troll.

"No, but I've come to fight you for the princess."

"Very well," answered the sea troll. "Shall we let our dogs fight each other first?"

"That suits me if it suits you."

So the boy and the sea troll set their dogs on each other; a furious fight ensued, but finally Little Faithful, the boy's dog, bit the troll dog in the neck until its blood poured out in the sand. Then the boy said, "Now you see how poorly your dog has fared. And you will fare no better!"

He went up to the troll, drew his three-pound sword, and slashed so hard that all of the troll's three heads fell into the sea.

"I've been saved!" cried the princess joyfully.

She asked the strange boy to go home with her to the castle to be rewarded for the great deed he had done for her, the king, and the whole kingdom. But he declined, saying that his help had been a small and paltry thing, not even worth talking about. Then he grabbed some pearls and jewels that the sea troll had been wearing, bid the princess a fond farewell, and hurried away.

The brave tailor was still sitting in the top of the pine tree. But now that the danger had passed, he quickly climbed down, drew his sword, and forced the princess to swear that he and no one else had saved her. Together they went off to the castle, and, as you can imagine, there was great rejoicing when the princess returned. Immediately, the king ordered a great feast to be prepared, and the tailor was seated next to the king and hailed as the greatest warrior in the land.

The next day the middle princess was to be given to the sea troll, and the court mourned as loudly as before. But since the brave tailor had saved the eldest, many believed that he could save her sister as well.

The young princess was taken down to the sea, accompanied by the entire court. When they arrived, she sat down on the beach and cried bitterly, her tears falling on the white sand. The tailor just crept up into the pine tree again and hid among its branches.

Meanwhile, the boy went to his master and said, "Dear master, please let me go into town and have a little fun. Yesterday I barely had enough time to look around."

The cook answered, "If the tailor succeeds in killing the second troll, there'll be an even bigger feast than yesterday's, and I'm alone to do the cooking. That vat over there holds eighteen tubsful of water, and I won't have anyone to help me bring in a single bucket."

The boy asked his master if he'd let him go after he filled the vat. Thinking to himself that it would be evening before anyone could fill up a vat that big, the cook agreed. But the boy just picked up the huge vat, ran to the well, and filled it so full that the water overflowed. He also took some beautiful pearls out of his pocket and gave

them to his master. Now that the cook had seen the boy's enormous strength, he said, "Go in peace, but don't take too long!"

The boy hurried home to get the six-pound sword. He pulled the linen coat over his everyday clothes, called for his dog, and headed again for the sea.

When he got to the spot where the princess was sitting on the beach crying, the tailor in the treetop was overjoyed to see him. But the boy didn't let on that he saw the tailor. He just greeted the princess in a friendly manner: "Most honorable princess, why are you sitting here so sad and lonely?"

"My father was caught in a terrible storm at sea and promised me to a sea troll," she answered. "Now I'm afraid he'll come any minute to take me away. Oh, I'm so unhappy!"

"Isn't there anyone who can save you from the troll?" asked the boy.

"Well, there's a tailor up there in that pine tree. He's promised to save me just as he saved my sister."

The boy smiled again and said, "I wouldn't count on him if I were you. But if you'll pick a few lice out of my hair while I rest, I'll save you." He called to his dog: "Little Faithful, stand guard over us!"

Then he put his head in the princess's lap and she picked the lice out of his hair while the tailor sat in the pine tree looking on. The princess pulled a black silk thread out of her cape and threaded it into the boy's long hair.

At that moment Little Faithful began to bark, and there was a loud rumbling from the sea, the waves reared up onto the beach, and out came a huge, ugly, six-headed sea troll. The troll's dog was as big as a two-year-old ox.

"Where is the princess who was promised to me?" asked the troll.

"She's sitting right here," answered the boy. "But you'd better come closer so we can talk it over!"

Then the troll said, "Do you mean to say that you want to fight me, you little dustbin?"

"That's what I'm here for," answered the boy.

"Yesterday you killed my brother, but today I'll make an end of you. But first let's let our dogs fight."

"That suits me," said the boy.

They set their dogs on each other, and in the end Little Faithful bit the troll dog's neck until its blood poured out and it lay dead on the sand.

Swinging his six-pound sword, the boy chopped away at the troll until all six heads rolled into the sea.

The princess was overjoyed, and she asked the strange boy to come with her to the castle to be rewarded for his great deed. But he thanked her humbly and, taking his leave, went on his way.

Now that all danger had passed, the tailor, who'd been sitting in the pine tree more dead than alive, quickly climbed down. He drew his sword and forced the princess to swear that he'd saved her. Fearing for her life, she agreed, and the tailor and she went to the castle, where they were received with great joy. A feast was prepared, even more sumptuous than the previous one, and the tailor sat next to the king and was treated with great honor and respect.

On the third day the youngest princess was to be taken to the sea troll. Now there was even greater mourning than ever before—not only in the royal castle, but all around the kingdom, for everyone loved the little princess for her beauty and gentleness. Many put their faith in the brave tailor, but the princess herself couldn't be comforted; as she sat on the beach waiting for the sea troll, she cried bitter tears. The tailor forgot all about his big promises, and once again crept up into the tall pine.

Meanwhile, the boy went to his master and said, "Please, dear master, let me go to town and have some fun one last time! I promise it will be some time before I ask again."

Since the cook remembered the boy's incredible strength and generosity, he couldn't refuse such a small favor. Thanking him humbly, the boy took some golden jewelry out of his pocket and gave it to his master, and the cook thanked him for this great present.

Then the boy ran off to fetch the third sword, which weighed only eleven pounds. When he swung it in his hand and felt how light it was, his anger came back to him and he said to the blacksmith, "If you weren't my father, I'd let you have a taste of this yourself! Now fate has to decide if I return."

He fastened the sword at his side, pulled the linen coat over his everyday clothes, called for his dog, and walked off toward the sea.

When he arrived where the little princess sat crying, the tailor sighed with relief, but the boy pretended not to notice him. He walked up to the princess and greeted her humbly, saying, "Honorable princess, why do you sit there so sadly?"

The princess answered, "My father has promised me to a sea troll, and I'm scared that he's coming to take me. I'm so miserable!"

The boy's heart was moved, for he'd never seen such a beautiful maiden before.

"Isn't there anyone in your father's kingdom who can save you?" he asked.

"There's a tailor up there in that pine tree. He's promised to save me, just as he saved both my sisters."

But the boy smiled a third time and said, "He's not worth much! But if you'll pick the lice out of my hair for a while, I'll risk my life for you."

"I'd be glad to do that," said the princess, for she'd already fallen in love with the handsome, dashing boy.

The boy called out to his dog: "Little Faithful, stand guard over us!"

He put his head in the princess's lap and had a good nap while she deloused him. But when the princess noticed the threads her sisters had braided into the boy's hair, she thought it very strange. She pulled a silken thread out of her cape and tied it to the boy's hair in the same manner.

At that moment Faithful began to bark, and a loud roar came from the sea.

"Time to get up, beautiful princess," said the boy. "Give me your apron. It may come in handy."

She did as he asked, and he cut it into twelve pieces.

Now there was a terrible rumbling, the waves came crashing high up onto dry land, and an incredibly huge monster of a sea troll appeared. He had twelve ugly heads, and his dog was as big as the biggest bull!

"Where is the princess who was promised me?"

"She's right here," said the boy. "But you'd better come a little closer so we can talk."

Then the troll said, "I suppose you expect to kill me, you little worm, just like you killed my brothers."

"That's why I'm here."

"Just wait!" said the troll. "You've met your match today. But first we'll let our dogs fight."

"Suits me," said the boy.

The dogs started a furious fight, which came to an abrupt end when the troll dog grabbed the boy's dog with his teeth and swallowed him in one bite. That was the end of Little Faithful, and it seemed a bad omen. But the boy wasn't frightened: he stepped forward and swung his sword so hard that all of the troll's twelve heads fell into the sea. But then something strange happened: as soon as one head had been chopped off and had rolled into the water, it came to life again and jumped right back onto the troll's neck.

When the boy saw this, he called, "Noble princess, please put a piece of your apron on the neck as soon as I chop off the head; otherwise, it'll come right back to life."

When the boy chopped another head off, the princess did as he'd told her. He slashed again, and again a head fell off, and the princess put another piece of her apron on the neck. And so on until the boy had chopped off seven of the heads.

Then the troll begged for mercy, saying, "Put up your sword! If I can go my way, I'll leave the princess in peace."

But the boy was angry and he answered, "Now that I've beaten you, you won't get away alive!"

He swung his sword so hard that one head after another fell to the ground, and the princess was always there to put a piece of her apron on the wound. They didn't stop until he'd cut off all twelve heads, and that was the end of the sea troll. All this time the tailor had sat in the tree, too scared to move.

Now that the battle was over, the princess exclaimed joyfully, "I've been saved!"

And she thanked the boy for his help and begged him to come home and receive the honor and reward he deserved. But he refused again, saying that he didn't deserve any thanks for such a small, paltry thing. Humbly he said his farewell and went on his way.

Now the tailor climbed down again, drew his sword, and threatened to kill the princess if she didn't swear that he'd saved her from the sea troll. The princess didn't like this, for she'd come to care very much for the boy. But she didn't dare go against his wishes, and together they walked to the royal castle. Brokenhearted, she said very little as the tailor strode by her side, gesturing grandly with his arms.

The king was overjoyed; he'd never thought that he'd see his youngest daughter alive again. His whole court greeted them and showed them every honor. One cannot even begin to describe the rejoicing that went on now that all three princesses had been saved, and the story of the brave tailor spread across the whole kingdom.

When it was time for the celebration to begin, there was no food on the tables, and the king sent his youngest daughter to the kitchen to ask why. The cook replied that his kitchen helper had been away, and that he'd had to prepare all the food himself. As the princess was returning with this message, she passed the kitchen boy. She thought it peculiar that he turned away from her, and when she looked at him more closely, she recognized her brave hero. Happily, she ran to tell her sisters what she'd discovered.

While the princesses were talking together, the king came along and heard what they were saying. Greatly surprised, he demanded that they tell him everything exactly as it had happened. So the youngest princess spoke for all of them, telling everything from beginning to end, with her sisters nodding in agreement. The king was furious at the tailor's deceit, but also very glad to be able to reward the true hero. He sent a message for the kitchen boy to come to him immediately.

All the king's servants were amazed, but the boy didn't want to go. "How can I go before the king?" he said. "I'm only a poor boy with no clothes to wear."

The messenger answered that if he knew what was good for him, he'd better obey the king's request.

So, bravely holding his head high, he strode into the hall where the king sat with all his guests, and the tailor at his right hand. When the tailor saw the boy who'd saved the princesses, he turned all colors. The king asked in a loud voice, "Are you the one who saved my three daughters?"

"Everyone says that it wasn't I but the tailor who saved them," said the boy boldly.

"No!" cried the princesses all together. "You were the one who saved us, and there are the three silk threads that we threaded into your hair while you were asleep in our laps!"

Each of the princesses ran up to the boy and embraced him, and each found her silken thread in his long hair. Now everyone could see that the princesses had told the truth.

"Since you're the one who saved the princesses," said the king, "you deserve the reward. I'll give you my youngest daughter and half my kingdom."

All through the castle there was great rejoicing, and the wedding was celebrated soon thereafter. The brave tailor snuck away from the celebration, and no one has seen nor heard from him since.

The Peasant Girl in the Floating Rock

Once there was a peasant whose wife gave birth to a little girl. They all lived happily together for several years, but then the wife fell very ill, and after a short while passed away. Her husband mourned her bitterly, but he married again after a year. The new wife didn't like her stepdaughter, and treated her so poorly that the little girl, in her longing for her mother and in despair over her fate, decided to throw herself into the sea.

As she sat on the beach lost in thought, something resembling a green rock floated up to her on the water. She was very surprised by this curiosity, and wondered what the floating object could be.

The rock came closer and closer, finally stopping right before her. It opened up, and two beautiful young maidens stepped out.

"How do you do, my girl! Why are you sitting there brooding?" one of them said.

She told the sad story of how she'd been treated so badly by her evil stepmother, and said that she wanted to throw herself into the sea.

"You mustn't do that! Even though we are both princesses, we too wanted to throw ourselves into the sea to free ourselves of our stepmother's cruelty. A kind mermaid gave us this strange home instead. Come along with us, and you'll be as happy as we are."

Thanking them warmly for this offer, the peasant girl stepped inside the rock. She'd never seen anything so gloriously beautiful in her whole life.

As soon as she entered, the rock began to move again. It floated and floated across the wide sea for days and months, and finally came to rest in front of a royal fortress.

The king happened to be sitting by the shore, and was very surprised when he saw the floating rock. He ordered his men to carry it carefully into the dining hall for all his guests to admire.

But the poor girls in the rock were hungry! Since they didn't know what else to do, they quickly snatched something from the royal table while the servant went to tell the guests that dinner was served.

When the king and his court noticed that the food had been touched, they were surprised and shocked. At first they thought that the dogs had been stealing, but even after they tied them up before the meals, the food robberies continued. Then they posted a guard in the hall, hidden in an old clock in the corner.

As he sat there peering through the clock glass, he soon found the explanation to the mystery, and told the king about the beautiful girls in the rock, and what they were doing. The king walked around the rock several times, but couldn't find an opening. So he shouted, "If anyone's inside, open up immediately! Otherwise I'll smash you into a thousand pieces."

The poor girls were very frightened, but there was no helping it: they had to open up. The entire court, which had just gathered for mealtime, was absolutely amazed to see three girls step out of the rock. They'd never seen such wonderfully beautiful young girls before, and above all they admired the peasant girl, who beamed with youth and beauty.

Instantly the king fell head over heels in love with her, and before long asked for her hand. The two princesses got the king's two brothers for husbands. In this way their misery was exchanged for joy and happiness, and never again did they have any wish to throw themselves into the sea.

The wonderful rock was kept in the royal fortress and passed down from generation to generation. It is said to be there even today.

Manasse and Cecilia

Two young merchants living in the same town were very good friends. When their wives got pregnant, they agreed that if one had a son and the other a daughter, one day the two children would have each other. And that's how it happened. One had a boy and the other a girl; the boy was named Manasse and the girl Cecilia. Sometime later Manasse's father died, and, because he was deeply in debt, his widow became destitute. Cecilia's father, who was rich, took in Manasse, and made him his shop clerk. Meanwhile, the children grew, as did the love between them.

When Cecilia's father saw this, he regretted the promise he'd made, and the first chance he got, he tried to get Manasse out of his house. He had sailor's clothes made for him so that he could be put on a ship to Constantinople, and he gave the captain secret orders either to put him to death or set him ashore on some uninhabited island. Manasse and Cecilia were terribly unhappy, but there was nothing to be done. Secretly, Cecilia gave him a little money, and then he took his rifle and sailed off.

It was a long journey. A terrible storm came up, and the ship was stranded on a reef.

The captain said to Manasse, "It's your fault we're stranded here. You bring us bad luck. Go ashore immediately, and then you can go your own way."

Manasse was miserable, but he had to obey. So he took his rifle and went ashore on the uninhabited island, where he survived by hunting. One day a lion came running with a small child in its mouth; Manasse took aim and shot the lion. Immediately afterward, a woman came running, screaming and calling for her child.

Manasse answered, "There lies the lion, and here's your child."

Delighted, she gave him a bottle of water which could heal all ills, and which would be of great use to him and to others. "Now go down to your ship again. It's exactly where you left it. Sail off, and good luck to you," she said.

He really did find the ship in the same place, but now it was infested by a terrible plague. The first mate had died and two others were dying. Manasse gave the sick ones some drops, and they got well immediately.

As soon as Manasse got on board, the ship floated free of the reef. Surprised and frightened, the captain didn't dare deny him passage, and they arrived safely at Constantinople, where the emperor's daughter had been suffering from leprosy for seven years and had been abandoned by all the doctors. The emperor had just announced that whoever could cure her would get her hand in marriage and rule the country after him. Manasse asked to try his cure on the princess. He rubbed her fingers with the drops, and the sores disappeared immediately.

Meanwhile, Manasse's ship sailed off; the captain was pleased to be rid of him. When the captain arrived home, he told them that Manasse had jumped ship. Cecilia was very sad to hear this, but her father was delighted.

In Constantinople the princess's health was improving daily, and Manasse was allowed to care for her alone. The healing water in the bottle never diminished, and after a month the princess could get up. At court they considered Manasse a prince, and after six months the princess's sores had healed completely.

Now Manasse wanted to go home, for he still thought constantly of his Cecilia. The emperor offered him the princess and the kingdom after he died, but Manasse confessed that before he was born he'd been betrothed to another girl, whom he loved dearly. So the emperor gave him a small kingdom for himself and his descendants, and a fleet of twenty ships.

He sailed home, and before long anchored outside the town where Cecilia lived. A salute was fired and answered from the fortress. That evening Manasse, dressed in his old sailor's clothes, went ashore after giving orders for his men to come and get him the next day at an agreed-upon signal.

He went to see his poor mother, and asked her about Cecilia. She told him that the next evening Cecilia was to marry a rich merchant against her will, and then she went to Cecilia and told her that Manasse had come home. Cecilia rushed to meet Manasse, who, as far as anyone could tell, was still poor. Her father and her fiancé quickly noticed that Cecilia was missing, and they discovered her just at the moment when she and Manasse were falling into each other's arms. Her fiancé walked up to them and spit at them, and that was the end of their wedding plans!

The next morning Manasse and Cecilia walked down to the dock. When he gave the signal, a grand sloop headed in toward land. Together, they went aboard, and Manasse disappeared into the ship to change into his princely attire. When Cecilia came down a little later, she didn't recognize him. But Manasse couldn't hold back his tears for long.

"I'm your faithful Manasse," he said. "And this entire fleet and a whole kingdom belong to you and me."

Manasse ordered his men to shoot at Cecilia's father's house—first with blanks and then, if necessary, with real bullets—and to order her parents and former fiancé to come aboard if they didn't want the prince to destroy their whole town. When the parents arrived, Cecilia and Manasse received them respectfully, but the fiancé was put into slavery for having spit at them.

Afterward, a noble wedding was celebrated on board the ship, with pomp and ceremony and both salvos and rockets. Later Manasse and Cecilia claimed their kingdom and lived with great joy and happiness for many years.

The Princess in the Earthen Cave

A long, long time ago there was a king whose only daughter was so beautiful and gentle that she won everyone's heart. When she grew up, many princes and courtiers came to propose to her, among them a prince who was both handsome and brave. Before long they fell in love and decided to get married.

Meanwhile, war had broken out, and enemies forced their way into the princess's country. As her father hadn't an army strong enough to defeat them, he arranged for an earthen cave to be built in the forest where he could hide his daughter until the end of the war. The princess and her handmaiden were lavishly supplied by the king with food and drink. They were also given a dog to keep them company, and a rooster to help them tell the difference between day and night. Then the king, with the young prince at his side, readied himself for war.

When the young people said goodbye to each other, they were both terribly downcast. The princess said, "Something tells me that we may not meet again soon. So make me this oath: Never marry anyone who cannot wash the spots from this cloth, and complete this weaving."

With these words she gave her betrothed a cloth and a piece of weaving that was artfully woven of gold and silk. The prince took them both and said that he'd never forget what his beloved had said. Then he went away.

When the armies met, there was a violent battle. Luck was against the king, and after a brave struggle he fell. The young prince had to return to his own country, and the enemies burned and ravaged until everything was one great desert. The castle itself was leveled, and no one knew if the princess was alive or dead.

Meanwhile, the princess and her handmaiden had been sitting in their earthen cave, sewing and waiting for the king to come for them. But seven years passed without word from anyone. By then the food had been eaten and they'd had to kill the rooster, and from then on they couldn't tell day from night. Shortly afterward, the princess's handmaiden died of sadness and hunger, and now the princess was completely alone in the dark cave. In her great distress, she finally took a knife and began to chop at the roof. She worked early and late without rest, and at last made a hole in the wall. On the third day she stepped out of the cave where she'd been sitting for so many years.

Dressed in her maid's clothes, the princess called for her dog and started wandering through the deserted landscape. After walking far

and wide without seeing a soul, she spied smoke rising through the trees, and before long came upon an old man burning charcoal. She asked him for a little food, and while she worked for him in return, he told her of the king's death and the enemy's devastation of the country. Now the princess realized that she was completely alone.

After some time had passed and the charcoal stack had turned to coal, the old man said that he didn't need the princess's help anymore. He advised her to seek work at the castle; they'd probably have work better suited for her, he said. So again she set out on her journey, and after some days arrived at a large lake. Sadly, she sat down on the beach, wondering how to get across. At that moment a wolf came running out of the forest, and said:

"Give me your dog,
And I'll help you across land and sea!"

It was terribly painful for the princess to part with her dog, but she didn't dare disobey. When the wolf had eaten his fill, he said:

"Sit down on my back,
And you'll travel safe and sound."

The princess got on the wolf's back, and he carried her across the lake to the other shore. There stood a beautiful castle, which belonged to the princess's fiancé from long ago.

While the princess and her handmaiden had been in the cave, the young prince's father had died, and he'd become king of his country. The years had passed, and he'd stayed unmarried until finally his courtiers begged him to search for a queen. Now that seven years had elapsed and he'd still heard nothing from her, he thought that she must be dead. So he'd let it be known that whoever could wash the princess's cloth and finish the weaving would become his queen.

Maidens arrived from east and west, but no one could fulfill the requirements. Among those who tried was a highborn maiden to whom the princess appealed for work when she arrived at the castle. Calling herself Åsa, the princess was taken on by the noble lady as a handmaiden; no one at the castle knew who she really was.

When it was the noble lady's turn to complete the weaving, it went just as it had for the others: she couldn't make heads nor tails of it. One day when she wasn't in the room, the disguised princess sat down in the weaving chair and wove a long piece. When the noble lady came back, she saw that the weaving had grown, and she wondered who'd helped her. At first the princess wouldn't say, but finally she admitted the truth. The lady was overjoyed, and of course sent the princess back to the weaving chair to weave more fabric.

Soon the rumor traveled all over the castle that the noble lady had succeeded in adding to the unusual weaving. The king himself began talking of marriage, and often went to the lady's chambers to see how the work was proceeding. But whenever he arrived, the weaving chair was empty. Thinking that this was strange, he asked the noble lady about it.

"My Lord, I am too shy to work when you're watching," answered the lady cunningly.

The king was satisfied with this answer, and it wasn't long before the weaving was ready.

The second task was to wash the king's cloth, which the lady didn't do any better than the others; the more she washed, the darker the spot grew. But one day the princess sat down and started washing, and soon the spot grew smaller. When the lady saw it, she was highly pleased; the princess finally had to admit that she was the one who'd washed it, and the lady ordered her to complete the task.

Rumors spread all over the castle that the noble lady was washing the king's cloth. Again there was talk of a wedding, and the king himself came down to the lady's chambers often to see how she was progressing. But as soon as he arrived, all work stopped. Again, he asked why.

"My king, I cannot wash the cloth with golden rings on my fingers," she answered shrewdly.

Again the king accepted her answer, and it wasn't long before the cloth was clean. The lady had fulfilled the king's requirements.

Now there was great rejoicing throughout the kingdom, and preparations for the wedding began. On the wedding day itself, the lady took sick and couldn't ride to the church. Secretly she asked her maid to go in her place, which the princess promised to do. She dressed as a bride, with golden rings on her fingers, and was put on a beautiful horse. No one knew that she was riding in her mistress's place.

As the princess sat on her horse, her face pale, the heavy gold crown on her head and her veil pulled down, the wedding procession started on its way. Beside her rode the young king, unaware of what she was thinking and feeling. When they'd traveled for a while, they arrived at a bridge. Legend had it that if a bride of common birth rode over this bridge, it would collapse. The princess said:

"Stay, stay, broad bridge!
Two true royal children are riding across."

"What are you saying, my beloved?" asked the king.
"Nothing special," answered the bride. "I'm just speaking to Åsa, my handmaiden."
They rode along farther and arrived at the castle where the princess's father had been king. Weeds were growing through the rubble. The princess said:

"Here thistle and thorn grow,
Where before gold was piled in every corner.
Here all belongs to cattle and swine,
Where I used to pour mead and wine."

"What are you saying, my beloved?" asked the king.
"Oh, nothing special," answered the bride. "I was just speaking to Åsa, my handmaiden."
They continued till they came to a lovely linden tree, and the princess said:

"Are you still here, my old linden?
Here where I exchanged rings with my beloved."

"What are you saying?" asked the king again.
But the bride answered as before: "Nothing special. I was just speaking to Åsa, my handmaiden."
They kept riding, and right afterward a couple of doves flew past. The princess spoke:

"There you fly with your mate;
Tonight I'll lose my dearest friend."

"What are you saying, my betrothed?" asked the king.
"Oh, nothing. I was just talking to Åsa, my handmaiden."
Before long, they heard the cuckoo calling. Then the princess
said:

"The cuckoo calls in the tall pines.
Back home the bride is foaling in the stall."

"What are you saying, my dearest?" asked the king.
But the princess answered him exactly as before.
Now the wedding entourage started through the dark forest near
the old earthen cave. The king rode up to his young bride and asked
her to tell him a story to pass the time. The princess sighed deeply
and said:

"For seven years I sat underground,
There I forgot tales and riddles.
Evil befell me,
Coal I burned.
Evil I suffered,
The wolf I rode.
Today I travel instead of my young mistress."

"What are you saying, my beloved?" asked the king again, feeling
strangely ill at ease.
"Nothing special," answered the princess. "I was just speaking
to Åsa, my handmaiden."
Now they arrived at the church where the ceremony was to take
place. The princess said:

"Here I was baptized Rose and Star,
Now I'm just Åsa, my handmaiden's name."

The wedding entourage entered the church with pomp and ceremony: first came the musicians, followed by the bridal courtiers and

knights, and finally the bride with her maidens of honor. The young couple were seated on the bridal bench and married with all the splendor befitting a royal couple. All thought that the noble lady had married the king.

After the sermon had been read and the king had exchanged rings with the princess, he took out a silver belt and buckled it around her waist; this belt had a lock that was so complicated that no one but the king could open it. Then everyone returned to the castle, where they ate and drank, danced and played games. But the princess hurried back to her lady's chambers and exchanged clothes with her mistress so that no one would notice that she'd stood as bride in her place.

Later that evening, as the king was speaking to his bride, he said, "Tell me, dear friend, what was it you said when we were crossing the bridge?"

The lady's face turned red. Finally, she recovered herself and said, "I've forgotten, but I'll ask Åsa, my handmaiden."

The bride went off to her maid and asked her what she'd said. Then she went back to the king. "Yes, now I remember:

Stay, stay, broad bridge!
Two true royal children are riding across."

"Why did you say that?" asked the king. But his bride couldn't answer.

After a while the king asked again, "Tell me, dear friend, what was it you said when we passed the old castle? I'd really like to know."

Again the lady grew very embarrassed, but soon recovered and went to her maid to ask her. When she came back to the king, she said, "Now I remember. I said:

Here thistle and thorn grow,
Where before gold was piled in every corner.
Here all belongs to cattle and swine,
Where I used to pour mead and wine."

"Why did you say that?" asked the king, but his bride was silent. Again some time passed, and the king asked, "Tell me, dear friend, what was it you said when we rode past the linden? I'd really like to know."

But the bride wouldn't answer him. She had to ask Åsa, her handmaiden. When she came back, she answered: "Yes, now I remember. I said:

Are you still here, my old linden?
Here where I exchanged rings with my beloved."

"Why did you say that?" the king asked, but the bride didn't answer. Now the king was in a great quandary: why couldn't she tell him anything without first speaking to Åsa, her handmaiden?

That evening when they were going to bed, the king asked, "Tell me, dear friend, where is the belt that I gave you in church?"

"The belt?" asked the bride, turning pale. But then she recovered. "Oh, I gave that to Åsa, my handmaiden."

The maid was sent for, and when she came, she was wearing the belt around her waist.

After the king showed them that only he could open the lock, the lady got up and stormed out of the castle. But now the king recognized his true bride, who told him everything that had happened since they'd been parted. There was great rejoicing among the wedding guests, and the king felt that finally they'd been well rewarded for all their sorrows.

The king got his princess, and everyone celebrated the reunion of the couple who'd waited so long for each other. After that I left.

The Silver Dress, the Gold Dress, and the Diamond Dress

Once upon a time there was a king whose queen was much older than he. This queen had a daughter whose beauty was unequaled, and with each passing day she grew even more beautiful. When the queen died, the king wanted to marry her daughter, but the princess didn't want to marry him. The king fell more and more in love. Every day he begged and implored her to become his bride, and finally the poor girl saw no way out but to run away. One night she left, dressed in coarse, simple clothes, and with only a small bundle under her arm. All went well, and a few days later she crossed the border into the neighboring kingdom.

One day as she was walking through a great forest, she met an old man with a big, bushy beard. He stopped and asked, "Who are you, my child?"

The princess didn't answer.

"You needn't be afraid of me," said the old man. "Even if I can't help you, I promise I won't harm you either."

When she heard the kindness in the old man's voice, the princess felt calmer, and believed that he wouldn't hurt her. She told him who she was and why she'd run away. The old man praised her courage and resourcefulness.

"If you follow my advice," he continued, "everything will be all right. Six miles from here is the royal family's summer palace. Go there and ask for a job as a scullery maid. I'm sure they'll give it to you. If you ever need help, take this staff and walk over to the mountain near the palace. Hit the side of the mountain with the staff and cry, 'Wee folk, give me what I want, and do as I ask!' and your wish will be granted immediately."

The princess thanked him humbly for this precious gift and went on her way.

Toward evening she arrived at the palace, walked into the kitchen, and asked to be hired as a scullery maid.

"You look a bit small," said the cook, "but I guess we can use you as a chambermaid. You can sleep over there in the corner."

The next day she started her service. Soon she was very well liked for her kindness and helpfulness. One day the prince rang for her.

"He probably wants his bathwater," said the cook to the princess. "Take this water basin up to him. And hurry!"

The princess took it and ran up the stairs to the prince's chambers. But when she opened the door and saw how handsome he was, she was so surprised and delighted that she dropped the precious water basin on the floor.

"Frightfully clumsy girl, that one," thought the prince.

The next day he rang again.

"He wants his towel," said the cook. "Take this and run right up with it."

The princess took the towel and ran. But just like the previous time she was so captivated by the prince's looks that she stood in the doorway staring at him.

"Why are you standing there gaping?" asked the prince. "Give me the towel!"

But instead of politely handing it to him, she threw it in his face!

"What a horrid creature!" thought the prince, and forbade the other servants to send her up with anything ever again.

That night the princess couldn't close her eyes; she just lay in bed fretting about what she'd done. By being so distracted, she'd insulted the prince whom she now loved dearly. And he never wanted to set eyes on her again! But then she remembered the old man's staff, and thought that the time would soon come when it might prove helpful.

One Sunday morning she overheard the cooks discussing how much they wanted to go to church; they worked every day in the kitchen, and never got to hear God's word.

"Go ahead to church, all of you," said the princess. "I'll make the food by myself."

"Hardly likely," said the chief cook. "But you might as well give it a try. If worse comes to worst, we'll eat a cold meal for dinner."

And they went away.

No sooner were they out of sight than the princess took her staff and ran off to the mountain.

"Wee folk, get me a silver dress with shoes and a hooded cape to match!" she cried.

Instantly, she was dressed in a dress of shining silver so beautiful that no queen had ever seen its equal. Then she wished for a silver carriage with six black horses in silver harnesses, and a coachman and footman dressed in silver livery. She asked the wee folk to prepare a delicious dinner at the palace and told the coachman to take her to church and wait for her outside.

When she arrived, everyone was so spellbound by her beauty that they almost forgot to enter the church. Light as a breeze, the princess tiptoed up the aisle and sat down among the royal ladies. The king, the queen, and the entire congregation sat in silent amazement, staring at the unknown woman. Never had they seen such a lovely young maiden with such magnificent clothes. The priest kept losing his place, and the young prince couldn't keep his eyes off her. He was already head over heels in love.

While the congregation was singing the closing hymn, the princess hurried out, jumped into the carriage, and cried:

"Light before me, darkness behind!
Let me fly quick as the wind!"

And she disappeared out of sight. When she arrived at the mountain, she changed into her own clothes, and by the time the court returned from church, she was sitting in her usual place by the stove, dressed in her old rags.

"Well, is all the food ready?" asked the chief cook when he returned.

"I hope so," she answered. "Take a look!"

"You've done a wonderful job," he said. "I almost couldn't have done better myself. And thanks to you, we saw something in church we'd never even dreamt of."

At the royal table all the talk was of the mysterious lady. The prince couldn't eat or drink; all he thought about was the beautiful stranger. That whole week he was ill with impatience, and when Sunday came, he ordered his footmen to stand guard by the church door and grab her if she tried to get away.

On Sunday morning the chief cook said to the chambermaid, "Won't you please stay home and prepare the dinner again so that we can go to church and see if the beautiful lady returns?"

"I'll be glad to," she answered.

Hardly had they left before the princess took her staff and ran off to the mountain. There she ordered the wee folk to prepare the dinner as before, and this time she wished for a golden dress with gold shoes, and a gold crown and a golden carriage drawn by six golden-yellow horses.

Everything went exactly as before. The prince fell even more deeply in love with the beautiful stranger. When the princess ran out the church doors, the prince's footmen tried to grab her. But they suddenly felt as though they were being beaten on their arms with sticks, and they had to let go of her. When the prince heard how they'd failed, he was furious, but when he saw the black-and-blue marks, he forgave them. Now he ordered them to spread tar on the doorstep of the church so that next Sunday the beautiful stranger would get stuck.

The meal was even more magnificent than the week before, and the chief cook received many compliments. He held his peace and accepted the undeserved praise.

Each day the prince grew sicker and sicker with longing, and could hardly wait until Sunday. This time the princess was dressed in a diamond-studded gown with a diamond crown on her head. Her carriage was made of sparkling crystal and was pulled by six snow-white horses. If there'd been amazement the previous Sundays, it was nothing compared to now: people could almost imagine that a fairy princess had come to visit them! Completely blinded by her magnificence, the prince suffered great pangs of love.

As they began the closing hymn, the princess got up and rushed toward the door. But when she walked across the threshold, one of her shoes stuck to the tar, and when she pulled up her foot, her shoe stayed behind. Because of this she was so delayed that when she arrived at the mountain, she didn't have time to change her clothes; she just threw her kitchen clothes over her diamond dress.

At the palace the little shoe was passed from hand to hand. Everyone marveled at its fine workmanship and the precious stones that studded it. But how were they to find the shoe's owner? Finally, the king and queen decided to invite all the girls of the kingdom to a great ball. When they arrived, each tried on the little shoe, but no one could fit it. A parrot, who was sitting in a cage in the window, called out time after time:

"Squeeze a heel and bend a toe.
To find the owner, to the kitchen go!"

He screeched this over and over again until someone paid attention.

"To find the owner, to the kitchen go!" said the prince. "What sort of nonsense is that? There's just that clumsy girl who drops water basins and throws towels in my face. I can't stand the sight of her!"

"Bring her anyway," said the king. "If nothing else, we'll have a good laugh."

The princess was called, and when she tried on the shoe, it fit perfectly.

"What small feet you have!" said the queen, raising the maid's dress a bit. Now all could see her diamond dress, and the prince rushed up and ripped off her rags. There she stood in all her magnificence, shining like the stars. The prince recognized her and fell happily at her feet.

"Finally I've found you, love of my heart. But who are you really?"

And the princess told them who she was and everything that she'd gone through.

Later a wedding was arranged, and they lived together happily for many, many years.

The Boy in the Birch-Bark Basket

A poor couple had a little boy whom they named Truls. Since they couldn't afford a baby-sitter, they brought him along whenever they went out in the fields to work. So that he wouldn't be cold, they wrapped him in a sheepskin, and his father made him a basket of birch bark. The neighbors called him Truls Birch-bark Basket.

One day, when the parents were out working, with Truls in his birch-bark basket at the edge of the field, they saw a huge eagle. They tried everything to scare off the eagle, but he took their little boy and flew away with him, far, far away to his aerie on top of a mountain, where he dropped the boy among his five eaglets. When the big eagle had flown away, the young ones tried to eat Truls up, but they didn't find it so easy. With his little chubby hands he punched them until they were so frightened that they didn't dare

touch him again. Later, however, when the two old eagles returned, it was Truls's turn to be frightened, and he crept as far in among the little eaglets as possible.

In this way time passed. He shared both joy and sorrow with his friends, ate raw meat just as they did, and grew up into a big strong boy. Soon the old eagles left the nest, but Truls and the five young ones stayed. The eagles flew out and got food for all of them, including Truls. In this way many years passed.

Now Truls decided that he and the eagles should go out to explore the world. He'd gone with them on many short trips, but now it was time for a long journey. So they flew off, and after a while they arrived at a great castle with a roof that shone in the sun. There they stopped to rest. Truls discovered a trapdoor on the roof, went down through it, and found that he'd entered a room full of clothes hanging on racks. He put on some real clothes, for his sheepskin had almost worn out.

On the stairs as he was leaving, Truls met a servant who thought that he was a foreign prince. Truls asked to see the king, but the servant told him that the king and queen were in deepest mourning, for their only daughter had been stolen away by a giant who lived in a nearby castle. He'd locked her up so that no one could get near her. His castle was surrounded by a wide, deep moat, and to make even more sure that no one could get across, the giant had surrounded the moat with a perpetually burning fire.

"I'll save the princess," said Truls. "Tell that to your king and queen. But five eagles are waiting on the roof for raw meat and water. After they're fed, we'll rescue the princess from the giant."

The eagles carried the boy to the giant's castle. The giant was so busy stoking his fires that he didn't notice that they'd landed on the roof.

Truls went searching for the princess. When he came to a locked door, he figured that that was where she must be, and when the princess realized that it was someone other than the giant who was knocking at the door, she was overjoyed.

Truls told her that he'd rescue her just as soon as he got water for his eagles. After he managed to pry open the door, he and the princess got water from a well, and the eagles took off with the boy and the princess on their backs. Just as they were leaving, the giant saw them and grabbed a big tree trunk to throw at them. But he lost his footing, and both he and the tree fell right into the flames. The fire flared up and the smoke almost suffocated the birds and the two people on their backs—still, they arrived happily at the princess's home, only a bit worse for wear.

The king and queen insisted that Truls and the princess marry immediately. Truls ruled the land with his father-in-law the king: everyone was relieved that now they were safe from the terrible giant, and wherever Truls went, the eagles followed.

But one day Truls and the princess went for a trip around the kingdom. As usual, his eagles flew with them, and as they were flying along, they suddenly heard a shot. One of the eagles fell down dead. Furious, Truls demanded that the man who'd shot one of his beloved eagles be brought to him.

"The prince must forgive me," said the man, "but I hate eagles. Once I had a little son, a clever little rascal whose name was Truls. He was our dearest possession. One day an eagle came and flew away with him. We've never seen him since. That's why it isn't strange that I kill every eagle I see."

"In that case," said Truls, "I must be your son. An eagle took me when I was little and brought me to his nest high up in the mountains. There I grew up together with my dear eagle brothers."

Truls's father and mother moved into the castle that had belonged to the giant; they were overjoyed that their Truls was alive, and that all had gone so well for him. When the old king died, Truls became king, and was honored and loved by all his people.

The Castle East of the Sun and West of the Wind in the Promised Land

Once there was a miller who ground grain all day long. Sometimes he found that grain was missing, but he had no idea where it was going, since the mill was always carefully locked when he was away. So he decided to find out. One day he locked all the doors and hid up under the roof of the mill to see what would happen.

After he'd been lying there for a while, three doves came fluttering in and looked around carefully. When they were sure that no one was watching, they landed, and they took off their plumage as if it were a garment. As soon as this was done, they changed into three beautiful ladies.

The ladies began to look around. There were several sorts of grain in the mill, which they put in their traveling bags. When they weren't looking, the miller went to where they'd left their plumage, and took a suit of feathers.

When the doves were ready to leave, they went back to where they'd left their plumage. Two of them pulled on their feather garments, but the clothes belonging to the third were gone. She was despondent; now she couldn't leave with the others!

After searching all through the mill, she finally saw the miller and said, "If you can tell me how to find my plumage again, I'll pay you."

"Now I know who's been stealing my grain," said the miller. "This isn't the first time it's happened. But if you'll promise to be my bride, I'll get your plumage for you."

"I will," said the maiden, "but only after you find out exactly where I live. All I can tell you is that it is on an estate east of the sun and west of the wind in the Promised Land."

The miller went to get the plumage and handed it to the beautiful maiden. Then she went on her way.

The miller mulled all this over a good long time. He longed to see her again, and so one day he prepared himself to go out and search for the place where she lived. A long time passed while he traveled through many different lands.

One day he came to a large forest. He wandered through it a long time until finally he came upon a poor, lonely cottage near the sea. An old troll woman lived there, and the miller told her that he was

searching for a castle east of the sun and west of the wind in the Promised Land. Had she ever heard of such a place?

"No, I haven't," said the old woman, "but I have power over all the fish in the great wide ocean, and I will gather them together. You can stay here until morning. Then I'll try to find out what you want to know."

When morning came, the old woman went outside carrying a large shepherd's pipe-whistle, and she blew so hard that it resounded through the forest all the way to the mountains. The fish swarmed together in great schools until the water began to run dry as far as the eye could see.

The woman said, "Listen, all you fish! Does anyone know how to find the castle east of the sun and west of the wind in the Promised Land?"

"No, we don't," they answered in a single voice.

"Well," said the woman, "that's all I can do. But I'll send you to my sister far away from here; she may be able to help."

He took his leave of the old woman, who'd filled his knapsack with several days' worth of supplies.

In a few days the miller arrived at the cottage of the old woman's sister. He went inside, greeted her kindly, conveyed her sister's greetings, and told her when last he'd seen her.

The old woman accepted his greetings quite solemnly. Then she gave him food and drink, and asked what had brought him on such a long journey.

"I'm searching for a castle east of the sun and west of the wind in the Promised Land. Your sister thought that you might know something about it."

"Oh, no," she answered. "But I have power over all the animals on earth, and I'll call them together and ask if any of them knows."

In the morning the old woman went outside carrying a horn, into which she blew so hard that the mountains trembled and the trees of the forest seemed to bend at the sharpness of the sound. Immediately, thousands of animals appeared, and soon the entire wilderness was swarming with them.

Now the woman asked, "Is there anyone in this great multitude who can tell how to find the castle east of the sun and west of the wind in the Promised Land?"

"No," answered the animals in a single voice.

"Well then," said the old woman, "I've done as much as I can. But I'll still try to help you. Far from here lives my sister who rules over all the birds of the sky. Go to her, give her my greetings, and tell her that I'm alive and well and have sent you to her."

After she'd filled his bag with enough food to last him a long journey, the miller thanked her respectfully and left.

A while later, when he'd found his way to the third old troll woman, he passed on the greetings from her sister and asked her if she knew anything about the castle east of the sun and west of the wind in the Promised Land.

"I've never heard of it myself," said the old woman, "but tomorrow I'll call together all the birds of the skies. Now refresh yourself and rest until morning; then we'll see what we can see."

When morning came, the old woman went outside very early and blew her pipe to assemble all the birds. Right away great flocks came flying, and landed on all the trees and branches as far as the eye could see.

When she thought that all were present, she shouted out, asking if any of them knew of the castle east of the sun and west of the wind in the Promised Land.

For a while there was silence, but then the birds answered individually, "We don't know."

Angry and disappointed, the old woman arranged her birds into groups and counted them all; an old eagle was missing, for she'd had a very long way to fly. The troll woman blew a signal in her pipe—quite a sharp one—but nothing happened. Impatiently, she waited some minutes more, but still nothing happened. Then she blew another signal, much sharper than the first, but still she saw nothing. She blew the third signal so sharply that the foundations of the mountains shook and the sound echoed in all the corners of the world.

Finally the eagle arrived, throwing itself before the old woman to beg her pardon.

"Where have you been so long?" she asked.

"I couldn't get here until now," said the eagle.

"Where do you live then?"

"In a castle east of the sun and west of the wind in the Promised Land."

"Very good, very good, that's just what I wanted to know. Carry this man unharmed to the place where you live. If you do this, you'll have my forgiveness for being so late. But remember to return as fast as you can with proof that you brought him there safely."

The eagle agreed, and they made ready to start. The miller thanked the old woman warmly, and, like her sisters, she supplied him with everything he needed for his journey. The eagle took him on her back and flew until she'd crossed the endless desert. Then they reached the ocean.

When she'd gotten a few miles out, the eagle pretended that she was tired and flew down so low that the miller's legs touched water. He shuddered, and then asked her, "Why did you do that?"

"Did I frighten you?"

"I might well be frightened when you act as if you're going to drown me."

"Well," said the eagle, "that was how frightened I was when the old witch blew her first signal for me."

She flew on a good ways before she started to dive so low that the miller was under water up to his armpits. This made him shudder even more, and he said, "What's all this about? Be careful or I won't give you any proof for the old woman."

"Were you frightened?" asked the eagle.

"I might well be when you act like you're trying to drown me."

"Well, that's how frightened I was when the old hag blew her second signal for me."

The eagle flew up high again, but gradually she swooped lower and lower until suddenly she dived so deep into the water that it was over the miller's head. He could barely hold on to the eagle's feathers, and this time he was really frightened—more so than the other times. And he was also very angry at the eagle for this rough treatment.

The eagle asked, "Now I suppose you were really frightened?"

"Yes, and if you do it again," he answered, "you'll drown the life out of me. You'd better listen for the old woman's signals! She might call you, and if you haven't anything to show her, you'll lose your life too."

The eagle flew higher and continued on her way.

One day she asked the miller, "Do you see anything?"

"I see something that looks like a twinkling star."

"Those are the gutters of the castle roof," said the eagle.

They went on for another day. Then she asked the miller, "Do you see anything?"

"Yes, I see something that looks like the moon rising."

"Those are the roofs of the houses," said the eagle.

On the third day the eagle asked, "Do you see anything?"

"Yes, it looks like many suns are rising."

"Then we're not far away," said the eagle.

That same evening they reached the castle. It looked more like a crystal mountain than a building.

When the eagle arrived, she landed in the midst of a large group of farm buildings. The miller dismounted and said, "Now can you tell me where the three princesses are?"

"I wouldn't think of it," said the eagle, "unless you give me the proof I deserve."

"Oh no you don't," said the miller. "First you must tell me where to find them."

The eagle feared the troll woman's anger, and she said to the miller, "On your right you'll see a great glass wall, and in the middle of this glass wall you'll see a silver door. Open it and walk in."

"Just wait here," answered the miller. "I want to see if it can be done." When the miller found the wall, he saw a key so big that he couldn't lift it. By the door stood a golden spear, but he didn't know what to make of it all, so he went back to the eagle.

"That key is so big I could crawl through its eye," he said. "I could never even turn it."

"I can't wait much longer," said the eagle. "I'm tired and hungry. Take the spear by the glass wall and stick it through the eye of the key. But first take the bottle hanging by the key and drink a few drops; it'll give you the strength to open the lock."

The miller hurried back, drank a few drops from the bottle, grabbed the spear, put it through the eye of the key, and turned. The door opened quite easily. Inside was a hallway, and on the right was a door that he unlocked with ease.

Inside, he found the three princesses whom he'd seen in the mill; and when his fiancée saw him, she threw herself into his arms.

"How did you get here?" she said.

"It wasn't easy, but now that I'm here, I hope that you'll fulfill the promise you made."

"I will," she said, "if you'll do exactly what I'm about to ask of you."

The miller hadn't forgotten that the eagle was waiting outside, so he hurried back with a piece of parchment, and he wrote a note and signed it, praising the eagle for everything she'd done. Then he wished her a good journey. The eagle flew off, and returned to the old woman with the miller's note.

"Everything's as it should be," said the old woman. "But don't think that I don't know how you mistreated him."

The eagle fell silent.

"Nevertheless, since you've done your work reasonably well, I suppose you have my forgiveness. You may go in peace."

The eagle flew off, and on the tenth day reached the castle where she'd brought the miller.

Even though the princess was enchanted, the miller had insisted that they be formally engaged according to the customs of that country. He went out walking one day with his fiancée, praising all the beauty around him.

"This is nothing compared to what it could be," exclaimed the princess. And when they arrived at a certain spot, she said, "I want you to chop off my head right here!"

"How could I do that when I love you from the bottom of my heart and know no peace except in your company?"

"Nevertheless, you must," answered the princess. "The spell will be broken only when a man loves and trusts me enough to put aside his love and take my life."

The miller pondered this a long while, and then thought, "Whatever happens must happen. My love for her is so great that I could never go against her wishes."

With that he took out the shining sword that he'd gotten from her armory, held her golden hair, and swung with all his might.

The instant that he struck the blow, a crash was heard so loud that it made the mountains tremble and the foundations of the castle shudder. The miller fell to the ground, unconscious. But what a sight met him when he woke up! Guards dressed in gold and silver with long feathers in their hats came up to him and greeted the brave man who'd saved them. For a thousand years everything had been as I've described, and now, instead of the glass mountain and the crystal boulders all around, there was a castle and town stretching for twenty-five miles into the country, as well as large formal gardens and many other wonders beyond description. The princess was standing before him, even more beautiful and wondrous than before. Taking his hand, she led him into the castle, and her two sisters came and thanked him solemnly for rescuing them. They too had become even more beautiful, and everything around them shone with joy and happiness.

Sometime later the miller began to think of his father and mother, and wished to share his pleasures with them. He also wanted to help them in their old age. So he asked the princess's permission to return home.

"That's impossible," she replied. "But since you've been so good and true, I'll try to help you."

She called a servant and went with them down to the stables. "Mount this steed," she said. "He'll take you over land and sea."

She gave the miller money and other provisions for the journey.

"Have a safe journey! But there is one condition that you must agree to first: never dismount for any reason at all. If you do, you'll never come back again."

This he promised to do, and went on his way.

And how they flew! Words can't even describe it! In three and a half days he was home, but because he couldn't get off his horse, he knocked on the wall of his parents' cottage until his mother came outside. He greeted her lovingly, and she thought what a great honor it was to receive him, for instead of his miller's clothes he wore a grand hat with a great plume of peacock feathers. She called for his old father, who fell halfway to the ground bowing before him. The miller motioned for him to rise, saying, "You mustn't do this, my father."

But his mother was just as humble; she bowed and scraped, welcoming him and bidding him come inside.

"That's impossible," he replied. "I don't dare, or I'll lose all that I now possess."

"You won't come into our cottage?" said his mother. "But you're just as much our son now as you were before. I can't believe my ears."

During their conversation the miller had taken out his purse and given them a goodly sum of money, enough to live on well for the rest of their days. But his mother held him by the arm and pulled him off his steed, saying to his father, "Bring it down to the shed"— for they had no stable.

At that moment the horse disappeared. Now the miller thought, "The promise I gave my fiancée is broken. And it's certain that I'll never be in her arms again!"

Mournfully he walked into his parents' cottage. They were even sadder, for now they realized that they'd been the cause of his misfortune.

At home the miller could find no peace of mind. So he left and wandered aimlessly in the forest. Finally, one day he sat down on a rock, and at that moment he heard something moving behind him. There stood his fiancée, who'd come to fetch him back. He threw himself into her arms, begging her forgiveness for what had happened.

"I'll forgive you," she replied, "though it has been difficult beyond words to find you. But my love for you urged me on. And because I knew that you didn't dismount willingly, I was given the power to take you back. Come, we have a long journey before us."

"But I must say goodbye to my father and mother," said the miller.

"You can do that later."

"But how can I do that if we leave?"

Nevertheless, they started on their journey and returned to the castle in a few days. There they were received with great joy by the princess's sisters, courtiers, and subjects. And a few days passed . . .

One day the princess said to the miller, "We'll celebrate our wedding in a fortnight." And she turned to her servants: "Begin the preparations for the wedding feast!"

On the morning of the wedding ceremony, the miller happened to wander into a room that he hadn't seen before. There sat his old father and mother, who'd been sent for by the princess. Rubbing his eyes, he stared at them in amazement. He thought that he'd been bewitched, because he'd never expected to see them there.

Then the princess walked in. She smiled at him and said, "Don't be startled. It really is your dear father and mother whom I've brought here without your knowledge."

Now it was time to go to the church and get married. The procession drove up, and the bride and groom boarded the carriages. The most distinguished citizens of the town—as well as all the princess's relatives—were present, and they accompanied the bride and groom to the altar.

When the ceremony was over, they returned to the castle with much delight and joy, though the music was properly solemn. Afterward, they lived together in great happiness.

Prince Vilius

Once there was a king who went off to war. On the way he and his men had to march through a big forest, and he got separated from his troops. All day long he rode until he began to look for a place where his horse could graze. Toward evening he came upon a small square meadow, in the middle of which was a white rock. The king sat down on the rock and let his horse eat the grass.

Later that night a little white bear came along. "How do you do, Your Majesty," he said.

"Peace be with you," said the king. "If you belong to the Devil then stay away from me, but if you belong to God I beg you to help me find my way home."

"I don't belong to the Devil or to God. I'm just a little white bear. But if you'll give me the first thing that Your Majesty comes upon when he arrives home, I will help you."

"I can't do that," said the king. "I have an only daughter, and she always meets me." The king thought, "Tomorrow is another long day, and surely I'll find my way."

All the next day the king tried but failed to find his way out of the forest. In the evening he looked again for the square meadow. When he found it, he was very happy, and sat down on the white rock; later that night the white bear came again to see him. They repeated the conversation of the night before.

Again the king rode all the next day, and in the evening he found the square meadow where his horse could graze. The white bear came again, and the conversation was repeated a third time. This time the king remembered that he had a little dog who sometimes came to meet him if his daughter was busy. And he thought, "Maybe I'll be lucky enough for the dog to meet me instead."

"Yes," he finally said to the bear. "You'll have whatever greets me when I get home."

The next morning the king set off, and this time he found his way. But when he arrived at his castle, it was his daughter who met him. "Oh, I'm so sorry that it's you who came to meet me," he said. "Tomorrow the white bear will take you away."

"Then that is how it must be," answered the princess. "What is important is that you have come home."

The next morning the white bear arrived with a fleet of ships. The king hadn't a proper pier, so the bear built one and placed a tall golden spire on either side with the king's name on one spire and his own on the other: PRINCE VILIUS. Then he sent for the king's daughter.

Now it happened that there was another maiden in the castle. It was decided to dress her like a princess and drive her to the pier in a fine carriage. But when she arrived, she wasn't allowed on Prince

Vilius's pier. "Send the real one," said the bear. "Only royalty may step onto this pier."

When the real princess was brought there, she was allowed to step onto the pier, and when she went aboard Prince Vilius's ship, the bear stood on his hind legs and held her with his front paws. Then they sailed off.

For many years the king had no word of his daughter. Then one day when he was out hunting he met the white bear, who told him that he was now the king's son-in-law; he and the princess had six human children.

"Be sure to give my daughter my love," said the king, "and tell her that I've remarried. She has a stepmother now. In case you forget, I'll give you this apple. Tonight when you go to sleep, the apple will roll out of your hands, and you'll remember."

That night when the bear came home, the apple rolled out of his hands.

"I've spoken to your father today," he said to the princess. "He's married again, and now you have a stepmother."

Since the princess hadn't had news of her father since she left, she was overjoyed. "Please let me go home and meet my stepmother," she pleaded.

"Wait till you've given birth to our seventh child; then we can go home properly." But the princess couldn't wait, and she begged the bear to let her go. Finally he did, but she had to be back by evening.

When she got home, her stepmother asked her if she'd seen her husband in human form yet. No, she'd never seen him as anything but a little white bear.

"I know that you are usually the first to go to sleep," said the stepmother. "I'll give you a bit of candle which you must keep hidden in your hand when you go to bed. Have him go to bed first, and when he's asleep, put your arm under his head. When you bend your arm, the candle will light, and when you straighten your arm, it will go out."

When the princess got home, she sat down to sew. The bear said, "What did you think of your new stepmother?"

"She's quite nice," she said.

"I hope you didn't get any bad ideas from her."

"Oh, no, she was just a nice old lady."

When evening came, he said, "Well, it's time you went to bed."

"Usually I go to bed first," she said, "but tonight, why don't you? I'm so busy with my sewing."

He went to bed and fell asleep right away. When the princess was lying in bed next to him, she put her arm under his head, and bent her arm to light the candle. He was so handsome that she couldn't bring herself to put out the candle. As she sat studying him, a drop of wax fell on him, and he woke up.

"I was sure that you'd gotten some bad ideas from your step-

mother," he said. "If only you'd waited till our seventh child was born, I would have been saved. We could have gone home to your father and stepmother as real people. Now, as soon as day breaks, I'll have to leave you and wander behind the sun and the earth where you'll never find me!"

And early that morning he left. After the princess had given birth to their seventh child, she started out on a journey to find him, her six children at her side and the seventh in her arms. After she'd walked a long way, she came to a little house.

"Good evening, dear mother," she said.

"Oh, thank you, gracious empress! I'm a hundred years old, but I've never been called 'dear mother' before. I'll give you as much mother love as I can; you shall have royal dishes to eat from and royal beds to sleep in, for I know you are searching for the white bear. But I don't believe you'll find him without a great deal of help."

Early the next morning the old woman got up and made breakfast for the princess and her children. Then she went out and blew into a shepherd's pipe. She ruled over many bears, and several of them came running. One old bear trailed behind. The old woman said, "You scoundrel, you rascal, why didn't you come with the others?"

"The others are young and I am old," he said, "and I have many hundreds of miles to run; my lair is down beyond your sister's cottage."

"Then go to the meadow and eat the best ox. Afterward, take the empress and her seven children to my sister, unharmed." She gave the princess a piece of an old frying pan, a piece of an old pot, and a piece of an old tablecloth. "These may come in handy sometime," she said.

They got up onto the bear's back and rode off. In the evening they arrived at the house of the second sister. She was two hundred years old, and when the princess called her "dear mother," she promised to help her. This old woman ruled over lions, and after breakfast she blew three times on her pipe. "You scoundrel, you rogue," she said to an old lion who arrived after the others, "why didn't you come with the others?"

"The others are young, and I am old. And I have many hundreds of miles to run; my lair is down beyond your sister's cottage."

"Then go down into the cellar and drain the biggest beer barrel.

Afterward, take the empress and her children to my sister's." She gave the princess a piece of a spinning wheel and a piece of an old yarn reel. "These may come in handy sometime," she said.

Now the princess and her children got up onto the lion's back and rode off. In the evening they arrived at the third sister's hut. She was three hundred years old, so old that she stood stirring the ashes with her nose. She promised to help the princess too, and they had the same conversation that she'd had with the second and first sisters. Then the old woman said, "There is one small problem. I'm expecting eleven robbers here tonight, and if they see you, they'll kill you and the children on the spot. But I'll give all of you a sleeping potion and put you outside. Then I'll cut your left pinky and put three drops of blood under the roof beams and three on the table."

So that's what she did, all of it. Later that night the robbers came home; their old leader came in before the others. "Phew!" he said, "Christian blood's been in this house!"

"Oh, yes, my dear, a big raven flew over our roof with a man's thigh in its beak, bleeding all over the place. If you don't believe me, take a look: there are three drops on the roofbeam and three on the table."

"All right, all right! Give me some food! I'm hungry and tired and want to go to sleep."

"Yes, my sweet," she said, "food you shall have."

Then they ate and the others went to sleep in different corners of the house, and the old man and the old woman got into bed. After a while the old woman began to dream. "Ha-ha-ha-ha-ha!" she laughed.

"What's the matter with you?"

"Oh, I was just thinking that the empress and her seven little children were riding on a lion. If you were home, would you give me permission to give them food?"

"If I saw them, I'd kill them on the spot. If she had obeyed him, the whole country would have been saved. But go back to sleep now, I'm tired."

"Yes, my sweet."

The old woman again pretended to be asleep. She began to dream. "Ha-ha-ha-ha-ha!"

"What's the matter with you now?"

"Is it far to the home of the white bear and Mrs. Sun?"

"Yes, but nobody knows the way better than our old gray falcon."

"Are there many obstacles on the way?"

"Yes, there are. After a while she'll see two red dragons fighting. She must ride straight between them saying, 'I can separate you, just as I can separate Prince Vilius and Mrs. Sun.' Later, she'll come to a big lake. Now if she had the kind of rocks that we have lying on our oven, and if she threw one into the lake, our old gray falcon could walk across with dry feet. But go to sleep! I'm tired."

"Oh, yes, my dear, I will."

After a while the old woman began to dream again. "Ha-ha-ha-ha-ha!"

"*Now* what's the matter with you?"

"Are there any other obstacles?" she said.

"She has to get there by this evening; there's going to be an engagement party at Mrs. Sun's."

"May I give them some food if you're not at home?"

"Yes, you may, but if I see them, I'll kill them on the spot!"

"Which way are you heading tomorrow?"

"South," said the old man.

"Which way should they go to get to Mrs. Sun's?"

"North," he said.

Early next morning the robbers left. The old woman woke up the children and the princess, and then went out to blow on her pipe. The falcons arrived, the old gray one a bit behind the others. "You scoundrel, you rogue," said the old woman, "why didn't you come with the others?"

"I'm old and have a long way to fly. My nest is all the way to Mrs. Sun's house."

"Well, now you must take the empress and her seven little children to Mrs. Sun." And she told the princess what she had to do during the journey, and gave her the stone.

After they had passed the dragons, they came to the lake and threw the rock in; now the falcon could walk across with dry feet. In the evening they arrived at Mrs. Sun's. The princess went inside and asked for shelter for the night. "Oh, no," said Mrs. Sun. "We're having an engagement party here, and you and your seven filthy little children can't stay in my fine rooms."

"Then couldn't we stay in your old chicken coop?"

"I suppose you could. But be off with you!"

When the princess entered the chicken coop, she put down the pieces of pot and old frying pan, and they became many pots and pans. Then she spread out the piece of tablecloth; it became a large, fine table covered with a cloth and all sorts of dishes filled with food. In another corner was a fine bed. She took out the pieces of spinning wheel and yarn reel, and they became a spinning wheel and a yarn reel, and she spun and wove gold for the inside and outside of the coop.

Early next morning when Mrs. Sun got up, the sun was shining brightly, but when she looked toward the chicken coop, she couldn't see it—it was even brighter than the sun! She went inside to speak with Prince Vilius: "My dear, exactly what kind of people arrived here last night?"

"I don't know," he answered. "Did anybody come here last night?"

"They wanted to come inside, but I wouldn't let them. So they asked to stay in the chicken coop. But now it is magnificent. Come take a look!"

Ever since the prince had arrived at Mrs. Sun's, he'd become a human being. Of course, he and the princess recognized each other, but they said nothing. She sat spinning gold to decorate the chicken coop.

"Can't I buy that spinning wheel from you?" asked Mrs. Sun.

"No, but you may have it if you let me sleep with your man tonight."

"That's a shameful request. I myself haven't been worthy of that honor."

But she wanted the spinning wheel so badly that in the end she agreed. Prince Vilius lay with the princess for one night. But Mrs. Sun had given him a sleeping potion, and he slept through the whole night; the princess couldn't speak with him at all. The next morning Mrs. Sun took the spinning wheel, but when she brought it back to her house, she couldn't make it work. So she went back

to the princess, who sat weaving gold for the inside and outside of the coop.

"Oh, you must let me buy that yarn reel!" said Mrs. Sun.

"Only if you let me sleep with your man tonight."

And Mrs. Sun agreed.

That evening Mrs. Sun went with the prince to the chicken coop. The princess had been to town that day and bought several packages of needles. Mrs. Sun gave him the sleeping potion, but this time he spilled it down between the bed and the wall. But Mrs. Sun sent along a man to guard him, and the guard overheard the princess telling the prince about all the hardships she'd suffered riding on the backs of the bear, the lion, and the falcon. Prince Vilius was silent, so she said, "If you don't answer, I'll prick you to death with these needles! You won't get out of here alive!"

"I hear what you're saying," he answered. "But you should have obeyed me!"

On their way back to Mrs. Sun's the next morning, the guard said to Prince Vilius, "Who was that person you lay with last night? She said that you had seven children together, and that she'd suffered great hardships riding on the backs of a bear, a lion, and a falcon."

"Don't say a word to anyone," said Prince Vilius.

When he met Mrs. Sun, he said, "We must celebrate our engagement party today."

"But we're not ready."

"It must be today or never," he said. So she agreed to do as he asked.

"And we must invite the people in the chicken coop," he said.

"Oh, no, we can't let them into our fine rooms, that woman and her seven filthy brats!"

"Then there'll be no wedding!"

Finally, she gave in. But she set up a table for the princess and her children in an adjoining room.

"They have to sit at our table," said Prince Vilius.

"But that will never do! Seven filthy monsters at our table!"

"At our table or nowhere!"

And she gave in.

The princess and her children were seated at the main table, with Mrs. Sun on the prince's right side and the princess on his left. While they were sitting eating, Prince Vilius turned to Mrs. Sun: "How do you think someone who separates good friends should be treated?"

Mrs. Sun thought that he was speaking about Prince Vilius and herself—that someone was trying to come between them. "They should be put into a barrel filled with spikes," said she, "and rolled downhill and uphill."

"Then that shall be your punishment!" said Prince Vilius.

They took Mrs. Sun, put her in a barrel full of spikes, and rolled her downhill and uphill. And that was the end of her.

The Three Sons Who Each Had a Foal, a Puppy, and a Sword

A farmer was told by a fortune-teller that his wife would bear him three sons. He also told him that his mare would bear three foals, his bitch three puppies, and his hen lay three eggs.

In his farmyard grew a tree, which the fortune-teller told him to look inside. There he would find three swords, one for each son, and he should give them each a foal and a puppy as well. When they grew up, he should send them out into the world to seek their fortune, one at a time, and each would take along one horse, one dog, and one sword. But the three eggs he was to save and watch over carefully. If a red spot appeared on any, it would mean that the one whose egg it was would be in danger. When one of the sons died, his egg would turn blood red.

The youngest son was the bravest, so he left first with his horse, his dog, and his sword. He arrived in a town where there was much suffering because a sea witch who lived in the ocean nearby lured people to her castle by keeping it lit up day and night.

When the boy arrived in town, he went to a hotel, or—well, it's so long ago, I don't know what they called it in those days. In the middle of the night he awoke and saw a bright, bright light. He got out of bed and stared at the castle in the ocean. Then he took his sword, his horse, and his dog and rode down to the beach. When he arrived, he saw a beautiful bridge leading to the castle, and he rode out onto it.

At the castle, he was met by a giant hag with seven heads who was carrying some pieces of straw. She said, "Put this straw on your horse, for he looks so dangerous that he might hurt me." He did as he was told, and the horse was transformed into a large granite boulder. She gave him a second piece of straw and said, "Put this straw on your dog; he looks so dangerous, he might bite me." And this he did too, being gullible and suspecting no evil. As he put the straw on the dog, it too was changed into a stone. Next she gave him drops to rub on the sword, and it too turned to stone. Then she grabbed the youngest son and put him into her troll prison. At home his egg turned red. They thought he was dead, which I suppose was true enough.

When the second son saw that the egg was red, he rode out exactly the same way as the first and got into the same trouble. The same things happened to him, and his egg turned red too.

Finally, the last son, who was the eldest, rode out to learn what had happened to his brothers, and he arrived at the same town and saw the shining castle. Now the horrible witch had raised the whole castle up above the surface of the water, bridge and all. When he got there, he told the witch that he didn't give a damn for her straws. Instead, he said, "Horse, fight this witch!" And the horse almost killed her with his hooves.

Then he told the dog to fight the witch, which he did until she was much the worse for wear. Then the boy demanded that she revive his brothers. "You're the one who took their lives!" he said.

And she did as she promised, and they really did come back alive, both of them.

Finally he said, "Sword, fight the witch!" And the sword chopped at her until all her heads were cut off.

Afterward, the three brothers rode back to town, where there was wild cheering and a big hullabaloo, for now everyone could see that the witch's castle had been destroyed. Later, the brothers went back home to their father, and that's the end of this story.

The Twelve Kidnapped Princesses

A very long time ago there ruled a king whose queen had given birth to two princesses. When she got pregnant again, she hoped that this time it would be a prince, so she asked a wise woman to tell her whether she'd have a boy or a girl.

The wise woman replied, "It'll be another princess, and after that you'll have nine princesses more. If you ever let any of them outside under the open sky before the youngest turns fifteen, a giant will come and take them all away."

"Stay with us until we see if you are right or wrong," said the king. But it happened exactly as the woman had said: twelve princesses in all.

The king began to think that if one thing were true, the other might be too, so he decided to guard the princesses carefully. He assigned them each a guard and gave the guards strict orders to be alert and vigilant.

One day the king had to go off to war, but first he spoke to his guards one more time, reminding them that the princesses were not allowed to go out until the youngest turned fifteen.

They promised to obey, and so they did, right up to the day before the youngest turned fifteen. But that day was so sunny and lovely, and the garden looked so inviting, that the princesses pleaded to go outside. At first the guards said no, but finally they relented and allowed them into the garden for just a moment. To be absolutely sure where they were, each guard held a princess by the hand. But as soon as they got outside, a cloudlike shape appeared and stole away all the princesses. As you can imagine, the guards were struck dumb with terror. Eleven of them ran away into the woods; only the twelfth stayed behind to tell the king what had happened. He soon let it be known in all the churches of the land that whoever found the princesses would have their hands in marriage.

In the neighboring kingdom, there lived a king with twelve sons. The youngest went to the father of the princesses and asked if he really meant what he'd said.

"Of course I do," said the king.

"Well then," said the prince, "we're twelve princes, and we intend to find them."

The king had a big ship outfitted with all the necessities, and the princes set out on their journey over the wild seas.

"Where are we going?" asked the captain.

"Wherever the wind takes us," replied the youngest prince.

When they'd sailed for a good while, their supplies began to run low. The youngest prince climbed up to the top of the mast to look around. He spied a great mountain far away in the south, and asked the captain to steer in that direction. When they arrived, the youngest prince wanted everyone to go ashore, but this his brothers refused to do. They told him that he could go alone if he wished, since this whole journey had been his idea.

So the youngest prince went ashore and walked along until he came to a big estate, and when he walked through the gates, he saw eleven beautiful mother-of-pearl stones in the courtyard. The prince entered a room with four silver doors, and then went straight into a room where a beautiful princess sat sewing.

When she saw the prince, she looked both happy and sad. "How did you happen to come here?" she said.

"I'm looking for twelve kidnapped princesses," he answered.

"I'm the youngest princess," she said. "The eleven mother-of-pearl stones in the courtyard are my sisters. But the big giant who kidnapped us will be coming home soon, and he'll kill you if he sees you."

"Can you protect me?" said the prince.

"Hide under the bed over there. And listen carefully to what he says."

A short while later the ground trembled with the approach of the giant. The princess quickly pricked her finger and let a few drops of blood fall on the floor.

"I smell a Christian!" said the giant.

"That's because I cut my finger," she answered.

The giant licked the blood and then asked for food. After he'd eaten, he lay down to sleep, and when he'd fallen asleep, the princess jabbed him in the side with her elbow.

"What is it?" he asked.

"I was imagining that someone came to take your life," she said.

"Oh, that'll never happen," said the giant, and went back to sleep.

A little while later, she jabbed his side harder.

"Now what is it?" said the giant.

"I was imagining even more clearly that someone was trying to kill you."

"No, that will never happen."

After he'd fallen asleep again, she jabbed him as hard as she could.

"What is it now? Can't you let me sleep in peace?"

"Well, now I'm absolutely sure that someone is trying to kill you," she said. "And it disturbs me greatly."

"There's nothing to worry about," he said. "Whoever intends to take my life will have to find my heart. And my heart lies in an egg, and the egg lies in a duck, and the duck lies in a well, and the well is in a big church, and that church is on an island, and that island is in the Sea of Blood." Now she let him sleep in peace. At daybreak the giant went out again.

"You heard for yourself that there's nothing to do," said the princess to the young prince.

"I'll give it a try anyway," said he. So the princess gave him three ducats and a small knife, and he went on his way.

That evening he arrived at a small cottage in the woods, where there lived an old woman with a nose so long that she could shut the door with it. But this old woman was good-natured, and as soon as she saw him, she said, "Aha, so a prince is coming this way! You've set yourself a hard task, and I can't be of much help to you, but farther into the forest lives my sister. Perhaps she can do more."

In the morning when he was leaving, she gave him a bird called Frost.

"It may come in handy along the way," said the old woman. "But when you return, I want him back."

Then the prince gave her a ducat and went on his way.

That evening he came to the second old woman. She had a nose so long that she could pick up the porridge pot with it.

"I see that you've been to my sister," she said. "Since she's helped you, I'll do something for you as well." And she gave him a bird called Softness.

"He's sure to come in handy," she said. "But when you return, I want him back. Farther into the forest lives my sister. She's wiser than I am, and can give better advice." The prince gave her a ducat as well, and went on his way.

That evening he arrived at the house of an old woman whose nose was so long that she could use it like a whip. She said to the prince, "Now you're almost at road's end, for over there is the sea. Since my sisters have helped you, I'll help you too. I'll give you a bird called Little Speedy, but I want him back when you return." The prince gave her his last ducat and departed.

When he arrived at the sea, at first he didn't know what to do. But then he thought, "I'll give Frost a try." So he called for the bird, and the sea froze so that he could walk across.

"Frost before me and Softness behind me," said he, and the ice thawed behind him as he walked.

When he reached the island, he saw the church before him. Inside, he found the cover of the well, and when he picked it up, the duck flew out.

"Get her, Little Speedy," said the prince, and Little Speedy flew after the duck and caught her. When the prince had her in his hand, he cut her open, took out the egg, and put it in his pocket. He returned the same way he'd come, gave back the birds, and thanked the old women.

When he got back to the princess, she asked him how he'd fared.

"Oh, pretty well, I guess," he said.

"Heaven help us all then, for here comes the giant. He'll kill you. Go away from here!"

"Oh, it's not as bad as all that," said the prince, and took the princess in his arms.

"No, don't touch me, then he'll kill me too!" said the princess. Just then the giant arrived.

"I smell the blood of a Christian!" he said. Then he noticed the prince. "Who are you? You're going to die this instant!"

"We'll see about that," answered the prince, squeezing the egg in his pocket. The giant fell to the floor, pleading loudly for his life.

"Then bring back the other princesses," said the prince, and the giant had to do as he was told. But when the princesses were no longer under the giant's spell, the prince squeezed the egg until it ran between his fingers, and the giant died anyway. Of course, the princesses were very happy, and each one tied a gold ring into the prince's hair.

When they'd taken everything along that they wanted, they all went down to the ship together, and the eleven princes were dazzled by the twelve beautiful princesses. But as they were about to set out to sea, the youngest princess saw that she'd forgotten her sewing box, and the youngest prince went to fetch it. Since the brothers wished to be rid of him and claim that they'd done everything themselves, they cast off the ropes, leaving the prince behind.

He didn't know what to do or how to get away, but as he walked along, he met a small, gray old man.

"Who are you?" asked the prince.

"Oh, I'm so old, so very old," answered the old man. "But if you kill me I'll help you." The prince didn't want to do that, but the old man told him that he couldn't die until a Christian killed him, and then explained that it was the greatest service he could do. Finally the prince agreed.

Then the old man gave him a box.

"This is a wishing box," he said. "If you like, you can get to the princess's castle in twelve hours, though it will take the others seven years. There you must take a job as a cook's helper, but keep your cap on until the time is right." When the old man finished speaking, the prince had to kill him as promised.

Then he wished himself to the castle—he was there before he knew it—and got a job in the kitchen. When seven years had passed, the princesses and the eleven princes returned, and as you can imagine, there was great rejoicing. All was made ready for their weddings.

The youngest princess decided that she wanted to scrub down everyone in the castle, and this she did. When no more people appeared, she asked if anyone was left.

"Well, there's still the cook's helper," said the king. "But let's leave him where he is."

"No, I want him right here," said the princess, and the boy was brought to her. But when she started to wash him, he threw his arms around her and kissed her. This cheekiness made the king absolutely furious, and he gave orders for the boy to be beheaded.

"But first I want to wash him," said the princess. And before she started, she took off his hat and saw the gold rings in his hair.

"Here's my true prince!" she shouted. "And here's my ring!" All the princesses recognized their own rings too.

"And your box is right here," said the prince, taking out the sewing box. They all realized that this was the prince who'd risked his life for them.

"Why didn't you speak of this before?" said the king.

"I wanted to see if they'd regret what they'd done," the prince answered, "but they didn't."

"What punishment do you wish for them?"

"Oh, well, they can each have a princess," he answered, "and then they can go home. But I'll take the youngest one, and the captain can have the ship and everything on board."

Everything was done as the youngest prince requested. A wedding feast was held, the likes of which had never been seen before or since. The young couple lived happily ever after, and when the old king died, they ruled the kingdom.

The Tale of White Bear

Once upon a time like any other time, there lived a king who had three sons. All three were tall and handsome, and the youngest—well, he was the handsomest. But the king was unhappy, for when his sons were born a soothsayer prophesied that they would all die violent deaths.

The young princes often rode out into the nearby forest to hunt. There they would stop at a small cottage where an old woman lived with a young, beautiful girl who was her distant relative. The old woman was stooped and ugly and a hundred years old, but she was wiser than most.

One day when the youngest prince, now turned twenty, and his brothers were out hunting in the forest, they stopped to greet their friends in the cottage. Later, the young girl remarked to the old woman how tall and handsome they all were.

"Yes," said the old woman, "but what good is that? Today, when they return to the king's castle, a big tree will blow down and kill the eldest. When the middle one comes into the stables, a horse will kick him to death. The youngest, he'll be kidnapped by White Bear."

The girl started to weep bitterly. "I can't save the two oldest," said the old woman finally, "but I will try to do what I can for the youngest."

It happened just as the woman had said. When the eldest prince entered the courtyard of the castle, a big tree fell down and killed him. When the middle prince went into the stables, an unruly horse tore loose and kicked him so badly that he died. The old king fell into deep mourning, and he placed a double guard around the bedroom of the youngest prince.

That night White Bear, the great forest troll, came to steal the youngest prince away, but the guards fought with him and knocked him about so badly that he ran away. During the day trolls have no power, but each night their strength doubles, so each night the number of guards had to be doubled, too.

After some time had passed, the king realized that his men couldn't continue these constant battles; many brave men had already lost their lives. The youngest prince would have to ride away and seek protection elsewhere. So he rode away through the forest, and around evening arrived at the cottage of the little old woman. There he asked for lodging for the night.

"I know what His Highness wants," said the old woman as he came to the door. "He wants me to protect him from White Bear." He was given a bed in an alcove, and went to sleep.

The old woman went out and called to her big dog: "Steel, go and kill a few oxen to give you strength. You must protect the prince from White Bear."

"Done!" barked the dog, and went on his way. During the night there was a terrible battle between the dog and the troll, but the dog was so strong from his good meal that he won, and at daybreak the troll went away.

When the prince awoke, the old woman said, "I cannot help you any longer. Get on your horse and ride first to the right, then to the left, then straight ahead, then right again, then left again, and then straight ahead. You will come to a small cottage where my two-hundred-year-old sister lives. Perhaps she can help you. You may also have my dog Steel for company." The woman wrote a letter for her sister on a piece of birch bark, and the prince rode away.

Toward evening he arrived at a small cottage, much smaller than the first one. The old woman was much smaller and more shrunken than her sister. When the prince gave her the letter, she said, "My sister has asked me to protect you from White Bear. I'll do as she asks."

She gave the prince some food and a bed in an alcove, where he went to sleep. The old woman called for her dog: "Iron, go with Steel and kill four oxen and eat them. Tonight you must protect the prince against White Bear."

"Done!" barked the dogs, and they were gone. At midnight the troll came. Now he was twice as strong, but the dogs won again, and at daybreak the troll had to flee.

When the prince awakened, the old woman handed him a letter written on a bit of birch bark and said, "I can't protect you any longer, but if you ride first to the right, then to the left, then straight ahead, then to the right again, then to the left, then straight ahead, you'll come to a small cottage. This is where my three-hundred-year-old sister lives. She's twice as wise as I am. Surely she'll be able to help you. And I'll let you borrow my dog Iron; he should help a bit." The prince thanked her and rode off with the dogs.

Toward evening he came to a cottage so small and low that he had to stoop to enter. The woman sitting inside was even smaller and more shrunken than the two before. After she'd read the letter, she squeaked in a high voice, "My sister asks me to protect you from White Bear tonight, and that I will do." The prince was given food and a bed in an alcove. The old woman limped to the stoop and called for her dog: "Lion, get Steel and Iron, and go kill six oxen and eat your fill. Tonight you must protect the prince from White Bear."

"Done!" barked the dog, and went on his way. At midnight the troll came. There was a ferocious battle. The troll was terribly strong, but the dogs were also strong from all the good food, and they overpowered the troll, who fled at dawn.

After the prince got dressed in the morning, the old woman said, "I can't help you anymore, but you may borrow my walking stick and my dog Lion. If you follow my advice, you will succeed. First ride to the right, then to the left, and then straight ahead, then to the right again, to the left, and then straight ahead until you come to a lake. In that lake is an island with a castle, but there is no boat and no bridge to the island. You must take my stick and strike the water saying, 'Bridge, lead me and my dogs, and water after me!' Then you'll get across to safety. White Bear doesn't dare go into the water, for his enemy the sea troll lives there, and they are old and constant enemies. But the prince must never be separated from his dogs; wherever the prince is, there must his dogs be also, and wherever the dogs are, there must he be as well!" The prince rode away, followed by his dogs.

At dusk they arrived at the lake that the old woman had described. The prince struck the water, saying, "Bridge, lead me and my dogs, and water after me!" They crossed over, and went up to the castle where a beautiful princess lived. The prince and princess took an immediate fancy to each other, and soon the prince asked for her hand in marriage.

Every day the prince would go hunting with his dogs while the princess took care of the house, and in this way they lived happily together. Even though the princess didn't especially like the big dogs sleeping in their bedroom, she accepted them because it was the prince's wish.

One day when the prince was away and the princess was standing on the shore, she spied a beautiful little white bear on the other side of the lake. Immediately, she wished that she could own it.

"Oh, sweet little bear, if only I could come to you," she said.

"So the princess can," he said with a voice as clear as a bell. "Just take the prince's stick by the head of his bed, strike the water, and say, 'Bridge, lead me, and water after me,' and the princess will get across." The princess did as he said, and soon she was at the bear's side.

"Oh, sweet little bear," she said, petting him, "if only I could bring you back home to the castle."

"That the princess can also do," said the bear. "Just take me in your arms, strike the water with the stick, and say, 'Bridge, lead me and my bear, and water after me,' and we'll both get across." The princess did as he said, and all went well.

By now it was almost evening. The prince would be back any moment.

"Where should I hide you, little bear?" asked the princess anxiously.

"Oh, just let me lie under the bed in the bedroom, but under no circumstances let the dogs in, for then I am lost."

Soon they heard the prince coming, and the princess ran to meet him. He embraced her, but she pleaded, "Please grant me my wish this one time. Don't let your dogs sleep with us tonight. They smell so bad."

"This wish cannot be granted," he said sadly. "Where I am, there must they be, and where they are, there must I be."

He opened the door, and the dogs rushed into the bedroom barking loudly. They crawled under the bed and dragged out the little bear, which they ripped at until he appeared dead. Afterward, the prince threw him on the garbage heap.

After the prince and princess had retired for the night, the princess couldn't sleep. She lay thinking of her beautiful little white bear, which was dead now. She wanted to look at him one last time, so she got up quietly, threw on some clothes, and went outside. But there was no bear to be seen; on the garbage heap lay a big, beautiful lump of gold shining in the moonlight. The princess wanted so much to possess it that she picked it up and put it in her bodice. When she came back to bed again, she had to climb over the prince, and she chanced to drop the lump of gold. It fell right onto his chest, piercing his heart and continuing out his back. Seeing that her husband was dead, the princess fled from the castle and hid in the woods. But the prince's faithful dogs lay down next to their master's bed and mourned for him.

After a while two little rats came out of their holes. The smallest one wanted to gnaw at the prince, but Steel struck her with his paw, and she fell down dead. Immediately, the other rat ran down the hole and returned with another, slightly larger rat with a little bottle tied around her neck. She started to rub the little dead rat with an ointment. Immediately, she revived.

Steel thought, "Perhaps the prince will revive if I rub him with that ointment."

So he took the bottle from the rat and started to rub it on the prince. Lo and behold, the prince opened his eyes! He realized that he couldn't stay on the island any longer, so he took his dogs and hurried down to the shore, holding the lump of gold in his hand. He struck the water with his stick and started walking across the bridge. When he came to the middle, he threw the lump of gold into the lake with all his might, and hurried on. In the water a horrible fight ensued between the sea troll and White Bear, but now the prince didn't have to be afraid any longer; he could return to his father's castle.

He came to the cottage of the three-hundred-year-old woman and told her his story. "It was I," the old woman said, "who wanted to gnaw at the prince and whom Steel killed with his paw." The prince gave Lion and the stick back, and thanked her for her help. Then he told the two-hundred-year-old woman his story.

"Oh, yes," she said, "it was I who ran to fetch the big rat when Steel killed the little one." He gave back Iron, and thanked her for all her help. Finally, he came to the hundred-year-old woman. The young girl was so happy to see him healthy and unharmed that she cried out for joy. The prince told of his journey, and the old woman said with a slight smile, "It was I who had the little bottle tied around my neck which my wise Steel took to rub the prince with."

For several days the prince rested in the cottage. During that time he fell so much in love with the young girl that he brought her home to his father's castle. Now that the prince had returned unharmed, there was great joy in the whole kingdom, and the old king had a wedding feast prepared for his son and the young girl. When the old king died, the prince became king.

And they built their home and patched their shoes and cooked their sausage skins in sap! And that's all I know.

Little Rose and Big Briar

Once there were a king and queen whose only daughter was named Little Rose. She was so beautiful and clever that everyone who saw her loved her. But one day the queen died, and the king took another wife. The new queen also had a daughter, but she was so haughty and ugly that everyone called her Big Briar.

The queen and Big Briar envied Little Rose and did everything in their power to hurt her. But she was always gentle and obedient, and did her chores willingly no matter how hard they were. This infuriated the queen even more; and the more Little Rose tried to please her, the crueler she became.

One day the queen and the two princesses were strolling in the castle garden. They overheard the gardener asking his boy to fetch an ax that had been left among the trees. When the queen heard this, she told Little Rose to get it. The head gardener cried out that that wasn't work for a princess, but the queen was determined to have her way.

When Little Rose came to the glade, she saw three white doves resting on the ax handle. The princess took some bread from her pocket, crumbled it in her hand, and scattered it before the doves.

"My poor little ones," she said in a kind voice, "please fly away from the ax because I must take it to my stepmother."

The doves ate the crumbs and gave up their perch willingly. But she hadn't taken more than a few steps away before the birds began discussing what reward they'd give her in return for her kindness.

The first dove said, "My gift is that she'll be twice as beautiful as she already is."

The second one said, "My gift is that her hair will turn a golden yellow."

"And my gift," said the third dove, "is that every time she smiles, a gold ring will fall out of her mouth."

Then the doves flew away.

When Little Rose returned, everyone was amazed at her beauty, her golden hair, and the gold rings that appeared every time she smiled.

Seething with envy, the queen called the head gardener and told him what he must do. Then she went for another walk in the palace gardens with her two daughters. When they passed the head gardener, they heard him say that he'd left his ax among the trees. The queen said that Big Briar should go get it, and even though the gardener protested, the queen had her way.

When Big Briar came to the glade, she too found three white doves sitting on the ax handle. The nasty girl got furious, and started throwing stones at them.

"Get away, you horrible things! Don't you sit there soiling the handle that I have to touch with my lily-white hands!"

At this the birds flew off, and Big Briar took the ax. But she hadn't gone far before the doves began to discuss how to punish the evil princess.

"My gift is that she'll become twice as ugly as she already is," said the first dove.

"My gift is that her hair will turn into a thorny bramble," said the second.

"And my gift," said the third dove, "is that a toad will jump out of her mouth every time she laughs."

When Big Briar returned, no one could bear to look at her horrible face, her hair that looked like a thorn bush, and the toads that jumped out of her mouth every time she laughed. The queen was very upset, and after that day she and her daughter hardly even smiled!

The stepmother couldn't look anymore at Little Rose without wanting to kill her. Secretly, she found a sea captain sailing to faraway lands, and promised him gold if he'd take the princess on board and cast her into the sea. The captain promised to do as she asked, but when the ship had gone far out to sea, there was a terrible storm and the ship sank; no one but Little Rose survived. She was carried on the waves to a green island in the middle of the sea, where she lived for a long, long time without seeing another human being. She lived on only wild berries and roots.

One day when Little Rose was wandering along the beach, she found the remains of a fawn that had been killed by wild animals. Since the meat was still fresh, she took the carcass and hung it on a branch that she stuck into the sand so that the birds could see it and eat from it. Then she lay down on the ground and slept. But she hadn't been asleep long before the sound of beautiful singing awakened her.

When she looked around, she saw that the bones had turned into a leafy linden tree and the skull into a little nightingale singing in the treetop. Each linden leaf chimed, and the notes blended together with the nightingale's song so beautifully that whoever heard it could believe that he'd gone to Heaven.

Now the princess didn't feel so lonely. Whenever she was sad, she went to the linden tree to be cheered up. But often she sat on the beach longing for her home across the sea.

One day she spied a proud ship under full sail. The captain was a young, handsome king. When they got close to the island and heard the beautiful music, the sailors thought the island must be enchanted and wanted to turn around. But their captain told them to wait until he found the source of the music, and he went ashore.

Underneath the linden tree sat a beautiful maiden with golden hair. He greeted her and asked if she ruled over the island, and Little Rose said that she did. Then he asked her if she was a mermaid or an ordinary human, and she said that she was a princess and told him

all the adventures she'd had and how the waves had carried her to the lonely island.

The king couldn't get over her beauty and bravery. Finally, he asked her if she'd be his queen, and she agreed. When they sailed away, Little Rose took along the nightingale and the green linden tree, and planted the tree by the castle.

The linden leaves played and the nightingale sang, giving pleasure to all who heard them.

After she'd been married for a while, Little Rose gave birth to a son. She thought of her aged father and sent him a letter telling him everything—except that his queen had been the cause of all her troubles. The letter warmed his old heart, and the hearts of his men— for they loved Little Rose too. But the queen and Big Briar were furious over Little Rose's luck, and they plotted to get rid of her.

The evil stepmother decided to visit Little Rose, who received her with great kindness. She didn't want to think of all the evil her stepmother had caused, and the stepmother herself acted very kindly and spoke many pretty words.

One evening the stepmother gave Little Rose a gold-embroidered silk chemise, which was enchanted. When Little Rose put it on, she instantly turned into a goose, which flew out of the window and threw itself into the sea. As Little Rose had shiny golden hair, so the goose had golden feathers. At that same moment the linden tree stopped playing, the nightingale fell silent, and the entire castle was plunged into sadness.

At night when the moon was shining and the king's fishermen went to empty their nets, they saw a beautiful, golden-feathered goose swimming on the waves. They thought that it must be some sort of special sign, but one night the goose swam up to one of their boats and greeted the fisherman, saying:

"Good evening! How are things at home in the royal castle?

Does my linden tree play?
Does my nightingale sing?
Does my little son cry?
Does my husband ever smile?"

When the fisherman recognized the young queen's voice, he answered sadly, "Things are bad at home in the royal castle.

Your linden tree does not play.
Your nightingale does not sing.
Your son cries both night and day,
And your husband never smiles."

At this the beautiful goose sighed with sadness. Then she said:

"Pity me,
I must roam the distant sea
And myself I'll never be!

Goodnight, fisherman! I'll return twice more, and never again!"

The bird disappeared, but the fisherman told the young king what he'd heard and seen.

The king promised a large reward for catching the goose. So they put their traps and snares in order and set out to sea.

When the moon rose, the golden goose came swimming again across the waves: "Good evening, fisherman! How are things at home in the royal castle?

Does my linden tree play?
Does my nightingale sing?
Does my little son cry?
Does my husband ever smile?"

The fisherman answered just like the first time, "Things are bad at home in the royal castle.

Your linden tree does not play.
Your nightingale does not sing.
Your little son cries both night and day,
And your husband never smiles."

Then the beautiful goose grew very sad and said:

"Pity me,
I must roam the distant sea
And myself I'll never be!

Goodnight, fisherman! I'll come back one more time and then never again."

As the goose turned to leave, the fishermen quickly threw their nets. She beat her wings and cried pitifully:

"Quickly let go, or forever hold tight!
Quickly let go, or forever hold tight!"

At that moment she turned first into snakes, then dragons, then other fierce animals. Fearing for their lives, the fishermen let go of the nets, and the bird escaped. But when the king heard what had happened, he told them not to be frightened by this optical illusion. He called for new and stronger nets to be made and forbade the fishermen on fear of death to allow the golden goose to escape again.

The third night, after the moon had risen, the king's fishermen rowed out to sea again. They waited a long time, but no golden goose appeared. Finally, they saw her coming across the waves. She greeted them as before:

"Good evening, fishermen! How are things at home in the royal castle?

Does my linden tree play?
Does my nightingale sing?
Does my little son cry?
Does my husband ever smile?"

The fishermen answered, "Things are bad at home in the royal castle.

Your linden tree does not play.
Your nightingale does not sing.
Your little son cries both night and day,
And your husband never smiles."

Then the beautiful goose sighed deeply and said:

"Pity me,
I must roam the distant sea
And myself I'll never be!

Goodnight, fishermen—now I'll never return."

As the goose was about to swim away, the fishermen threw their nets and held her tight. The bird beat her wings hard, screaming:

"Quickly let go, or forever hold tight!
Quickly let go, or forever hold tight!"

She changed into snakes, dragons, and monsters, but the fishermen feared the king's anger even more, and held tight. This time they managed to bring her home to the royal castle, where she was kept under careful guard. But the bird was sad and sullen and wouldn't speak, and the king's sadness grew.

Now it happened that a queer-looking old woman came to the castle asking to speak to the king. The guard answered, as he'd been told to, that the king was too unhappy to talk to anyone. But the woman insisted, and finally they brought her before him.

"Your Majesty," she said, "I've been told that your queen has been changed into a golden goose, and that you grieve both night and day. I've come to release her from her spell and give you back your wife, if in return you'll grant me a wish."

The king asked what her wish might be, and the woman said, "I live inside the mountain on the other side of the black river. I want you to build a stone wall around it so that your cattle will not come and disturb me when they're let out to pasture."

The king thought this a small favor to ask, and he promised to do it, although he doubted that she'd keep her end of the bargain.

Now the old woman described in great detail everything that Little Rose had suffered at her stepmother's hand. But the king found it hard to believe that the old queen had been so evil. Then the old woman asked to see the silk chemise that Little Rose had gotten from her stepmother. The old woman took it, went up to the goose, and pulled the chemise over her. Suddenly, the spell was lifted, and Little Rose stood before them in human form. At that moment the linden tree began to play and the nightingale to sing. The whole castle rejoiced, and the king kept his promise to the old woman, who everyone realized was a troll.

When Little Rose and the king visited her father, he seemed like a young man again, and everyone in his kingdom celebrated too. Only one person was unhappy; the queen realized that her deceit had been discovered and that her time had run out. When the old king learned how she'd made her stepdaughter suffer, he condemned her to death. But Little Rose begged for her life, and the king relented and ordered her to be locked in the prison tower as long as she lived. Big Briar was given the same punishment.

Then Little Rose and the young king returned to their own kingdom where the linden tree plays, the nightingale sings, the prince cries neither day nor night, and the king is always happy.

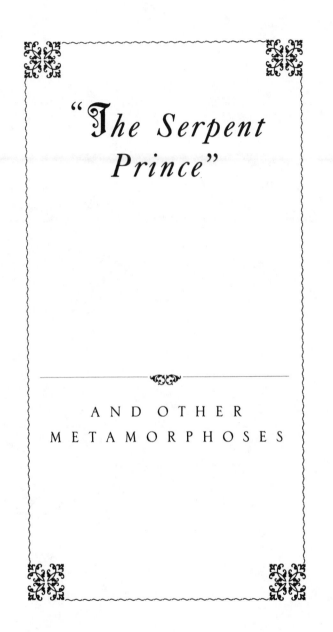

"The Serpent Prince"

AND OTHER METAMORPHOSES

The Serpent Prince

nce there were a king and queen who ruled happily over a large, rich kingdom. As the years passed, however, the king's heart grew heavy, for the queen did not bear him any children. Although the king didn't tell her of his sadness, she knew how it grieved him not to have an heir to the kingdom, and every day she wished fervently for a child.

One day a poor woman came to the castle, asking to speak to the queen. The queen's servants told her that they couldn't let such a poor beggar in to see their mistress, but the woman pleaded with them, saying that she wished to help the queen in her secret sorrow. They brought the queen this message, and she asked that the old one be brought before her.

The old woman said to the queen, "Your Highness, I know of your wish for a child. If you follow my advice, you shall have two."

The queen wondered how the old woman knew so much about her, but she promised to follow her advice.

"Bring a bathtub to your chamber and have it filled with water. After you have bathed, you'll find two red onions under the tub. Peel these very carefully and eat them; by and by, your fondest wish will be granted."

The queen did as the old woman told her. After she'd bathed, she found the two onions under the tub; they were the same size and looked exactly alike. The queen realized that the old woman was more than she appeared to be, and in her happiness she ate one of the onions, peel and all, before she remembered that they had to be well peeled. For the first one it was too late, but she peeled the other one thoroughly before eating it.

When the queen's time came, the first baby she gave birth to was a terrible serpent! No one saw it but the midwife, who, when she realized that the queen was giving birth to twins, threw the serpent out the window into the forest outside the castle. The second baby was the most beautiful little prince in all creation, and he was the only one shown to the king and queen.

There was great rejoicing in the castle and the whole kingdom over the birth of the beautiful prince, but no one knew that the older child was a serpent who lived in the wild forest. Time passed happily for the young prince until he turned twenty. Then his parents told him to travel to a neighboring kingdom to find a bride; they were getting on in years, and they dearly wished to see him married before going to their graves. The prince obeyed, and asked for horses to be hitched to his gilded carriage. But when he came to the first crossroads, a terrible serpent blocked his path.

"Where are you going?" asked the serpent in a frightening voice.

"That's no affair of yours. I'm the prince, and I go where I wish."

"Better turn back," said the serpent. "I know your errand, and you'll have no bride before I have a mate sleeping by my side."

The prince returned home and told the king and queen what had happened at the crossroads. They urged him to try again the next day, but the same thing happened; the terrible serpent blocked his way. The third time the prince tried to pass the crossroads, the incident was repeated; the serpent said in a threatening voice that before the prince got his bride, he, the serpent, would have a mate.

The king and queen could think of no better solution than to summon the serpent to the castle and help him find a mate. Since they believed that he'd settle for anyone at all, they decided to find a criminal or a slave to marry him. But when the serpent was given a criminal for a bride, the next morning she was found torn to pieces. The same thing happened each time the king and the queen found him a bride.

Soon this became known throughout the country. One woman in the kingdom greeted this news with great pleasure. This woman's husband had a beautiful daughter with his first wife, a daughter more beautiful than all other maidens, and so kind and good that she won everyone's heart. But his second wife, who'd been a widow, had a grown daughter who was ugly and cruel and who suffered by comparison with her lovely, kind stepsister. For years the stepmother bore a bitter grudge against her beautiful stepdaughter. When she heard there was a serpent in the king's castle that ripped apart all the maidens he was given, she went to the king and offered her stepdaughter for the serpent's bride. This gladdened the king's heart, and he asked that the young girl be brought to court.

When the messengers came to fetch her, she realized that her evil stepmother wanted her to die. All she asked was to be allowed one more night in her father's house. This she was granted, and she went straight to her mother's graveside. There she cried over her unhappy fate, and begged her mother to advise her in her hour of need. How long she lay crying, no one knows, but it's certain that she fell asleep and slept until dawn. Then she rose up, happy at heart, and began to search the field around her. She found three nuts that she hid carefully in her pocket.

"When I'm in great danger, I'll crack them one at a time," she said to herself. Then she left willingly with the king's messengers.

When they arrived at the castle, everyone grieved over the lovely maiden's sad fate. But she herself was full of hope. She asked the queen for a bridal chamber different from the one the serpent had had before. She also asked for a pot of strong lye to be placed over the fire, and three new scrubbing brushes. The bridal bed must be made up with all new bedding, she said, and she herself was to be dressed in seven layers of snow-white linen.

Later, when they were alone in the bridal chamber, the serpent ordered the maiden to undress.

"No, you undress first," she answered.

"None of the others asked that," said the serpent, surprised.

"I do," she replied.

He started twisting and turning, groaning and panting, and after a while pulled off his outermost layer of skin, which finally lay on the floor, terrible to behold. The bride took off one layer of snow-white

linen and threw it over the serpent's skin. Again he demanded that she undress, but she told him to undress first. With much pain and agony he pulled off one layer of skin after another, and on top of each layer the maiden threw one layer of her white linen until seven serpent skins and six snow-white layers of linen lay on the floor; the seventh layer she kept on. Now the serpent stood before her, a shapeless mass of bloody, dripping flesh. Using all her strength, she began to scrub him with the lye and brushes.

By the time she'd almost worn out the third scrubbing brush, there stood before her the handsomest youth in the world. He thanked her for saving him from his horrible enchantment, and told her that he was the king and queen's eldest son, and that it was he who would inherit the kingdom. He asked her if she would keep the promise she'd given as the serpent's bride, and share her life with him. This she agreed to gladly.

Each time the serpent had married one of the other maidens, a servant of the king had opened the door of the bridal chamber the next morning to see if the bride had survived. This morning he peeked in the door again, but was so amazed that he quickly shut the door and rushed to tell the king and queen of the strange sight: on the floor lay seven layers of serpent skin and six snow-white layers of linen. Next to these were three worn-out scrubbing brushes. And in the bed slept a handsome youth next to the lovely young maiden.

The king and queen were greatly perplexed. They had the old woman brought before them again, and she reminded the queen that she'd eaten the first onion with all its peels; that was why her firstborn was a serpent. Then they called for the midwife, who admitted that she'd thrown the serpent out the window into the forest. The king and queen embraced their firstborn and his young bride. They asked him to tell them of his sad life during the twenty years he'd lived in the forest, and they proclaimed throughout the kingdom that he was their eldest son and heir to their kingdom.

Soon the king and queen died, and the Serpent Prince became king.

It so happened that an enemy declared war on the Serpent King's kingdom, and since he realized that it might be at least three years before he returned to his land and his queen—and since he knew that she was expecting a child—he asked all the servants who stayed behind to take good care of her. In order for them to write privately to each other, he ordered two signet rings, one for himself and one for his young queen, and issued a command that only the queen be allowed to open a letter sealed with these seals. Then he said his farewells and rode off to war.

Meanwhile, the queen's evil stepmother was fuming over the success of her beautiful stepdaughter. Now that the king had gone off to war, this evil woman went to her stepdaughter, saying that she'd always believed her stepdaughter was destined for something great, and that it was she who'd arranged for her to become the prince's bride. The queen, whose goodness blinded her to the falseness of others, invited her stepmother to stay in the castle.

Shortly thereafter, the queen gave birth to two beautiful boys. After she wrote a letter to the king telling him the news, her stepmother asked permission to comb out her hair just as the queen's own mother had done when she was alive. The stepmother combed the queen's hair until she fell asleep; then she undid the signet ring hanging around her neck and exchanged the original letter for another, which said that the queen had given birth to two puppies!

When the king received this letter, he was much grieved, but he remembered that he himself had lived for twenty years as a serpent, and had been released from the enchantment by his young queen. So he wrote to his most trusted retainer, telling him to give the queen and the puppies the best possible care. But the stepmother intercepted this letter too, and wrote another which stated that the queen and the two little princes were to be burned at the stake. This she also sealed with the queen's own seal.

The retainer couldn't understand the king's order. Instead, he hid the queen and her boys away in the castle, saying that it was her husband's wish. Then he had a sheep and two lambs burned so that it would look like he'd carried out the king's command. The stepmother announced throughout the land that the queen was dead, adding that she had been an evil witch.

No one suspected that both the queen and her children hadn't been burned at the stake. However, when the time came for the Serpent King to return from war, the old retainer grew worried. He told the queen everything, showed her the king's letter, and begged her to leave the castle before the king returned.

So the queen and her two little sons fled into the wild forest. There they wandered a whole day without finding a single human dwelling, and soon they grew tired. A poor, miserable-looking man came along carrying some game. The queen was happy to see him, and asked if he knew where she and her little ones might find a roof over their heads for the night. He answered that he had a small, humble cottage in the woods where they could sleep. But he added that his life was completely separate from other humans: he owned nothing but the cottage, a horse, and a dog, and lived only by hunting.

The queen and her children slept in the hunter's cottage, and when she awoke in the morning he'd already gone out. She cleaned up and prepared the food, so that when he came home he found everything neat and clean; this seemed to give him some pleasure. Otherwise he spoke very little: all he said about himself was that his name was Per.

Later that day he rode out again, looking very unhappy. While he was away, the queen explored the cottage more closely and found a tub full of wet, bloody shirts. Though she wondered about this, she assumed that he must have gotten his linens bloody when he brought home his game. So she washed the shirts and hung them out to dry, without speaking of this to Per.

After some days she noticed that each time the mournful hunter came riding home, he took off a bloody shirt and put on a clean one. It was then that she realized that something other than game stained the man's shirts, and she gathered up her courage to ask him what it was.

At first he wouldn't say. But when she told him of her own fate, and how she'd saved the serpent, he said that as a young man he'd lived a dissolute life and had entered into a pact with the Devil. But before this pact had run out, he'd changed his evil ways and retired to the woods. Because of this the Devil had lost his power to claim him, but as long as he held the contract, he could force the hunter to meet him once a day in the forest where evil spirits whipped him until he bled.

The next day, the queen begged Per to stay and look after the princes; she'd meet the spirits in his place. He was horrified: not only would it cost her her life, he said, but it would also bring him even greater unhappiness. But she urged him to have courage, and made sure that she had the three nuts that she'd found by her mother's grave. Mounting Per's horse, she rode out into the forest.

Soon two evil spirits appeared, screaming, "Here come Per's horse and Per's dog, but Per himself isn't here!"

Then she heard at a distance a terrible voice asking her why she had come.

"I've come to take back Per's contract," answered the queen.

Among the evil spirits there arose a frightful clamor. The most terrible voice among them said, "Go home and tell Per that when he comes tomorrow he'll get twice as many lashes!"

But the queen picked up one of her nuts, cracked it, and turned her horse toward home. The trees started burning, and the evil spirits howled as if they were being whipped.

The second day the queen rode out again. This time the spirits didn't dare come quite so close, but they still wouldn't give her the contract. When she cracked her second nut, the whole forest behind her seemed to burst into flames. The evil spirits howled worse than the day before, but still wouldn't give back the contract.

Though the queen had only one nut left, she was willing to use it to save Per, and when she got close to the spirits' dwelling place, she cracked it. What happened to them she didn't see, but during the screaming and wild lamentation, the contract was handed to her at the end of a long branch. Happily, she rode back to the cottage and told Per what had happened. He'd been sitting in fear, but now his joy knew no bounds; finally he was free of the evil spirits forever.

Meanwhile, the Serpent King had arrived home. When he asked for the queen and the puppies, the servants were dismayed; they knew nothing of any puppies—the queen had given birth to two beautiful princes, but the king had ordered them to be burned at the stake. Now the king grew white with grief and rage, and called his retainer to him. The retainer showed him the stepmother's letter, and now everyone realized the great treachery that she had committed.

But he confessed that he'd spared the life of the queen and the princes; that they'd been kept hidden in the castle for three years; and that when the king had been expected home, they'd fled to the wild forest. This eased the king's sorrows, and he went into the forest to search for his queen and his children.

For a whole day the king wandered without seeing a single soul.

The next day was the same, but on the third day he arrived at the little cottage, went inside, and asked to rest awhile on the bench. The queen was so poorly dressed and downcast that the king didn't recognize her; neither did he think that the two boys dressed in coarse skins could be his sons. The queen recognized the king, but did not reveal herself.

The king lay down on the bench and soon fell asleep. But the bench was narrow, and while he slept, his arms hung down.

"My son, put your father's arm back up on the bench," the queen said to one of the princes. The boy picked up the king's arm, and then, as children do, flung it up hard.

This woke the king. He thought he might be in a robbers' den, but pretended that he was still asleep to learn exactly what kind of people they were. For a while he lay quietly, but when no one stirred, he let his arm slide off the bench again. Then he heard a woman say, "My son, put your father's arm back on the bench, but don't fling it the way your brother did!" He felt small hands gently gripping his arm. When he heard her voice, he recognized his queen, and he opened his eyes and looked at her and his children.

The king rose and clasped all three in his arms. Later, he brought them back to his castle, along with Per the hunter, his horse and dog. There was great rejoicing throughout the whole country. And the evil stepmother was burned at the stake.

The Serpent King lived a long and happy life with his queen; and I've heard tell that if they haven't died they're still alive.

The Widow's Son

Once there was a widow who was so poor that her only son had to leave home to earn his living. After he'd walked for quite a while, he met an old man who asked him where he was heading. The boy answered that his mother couldn't support both of them, so he was going to seek service in a household. The old man said that the boy could enter his service; since he was away most of the time, there wouldn't be much to do except to look after the house. The boy accepted his offer.

When he and the old man arrived home, the boy saw that the old man lived in a big mountain in the forest. After a few days the man told the boy that he was going away and said, "Promise me that you won't go any farther into the mountain than you've already gone. Don't enter any room you haven't been in before. If you do, I'll beat you within an inch of your life. I'll be away for a week."

The boy promised, and the old man left.

When the boy had been alone for a few days, he grew so curious that he couldn't help going into the next room. He didn't think that the old man would be able to tell that he'd been there. When he entered the room, he saw that it was empty except for a stick on a shelf. "Why is he so worried about that?" he wondered. But when the old man returned, he saw immediately that the boy had been in the room, and he gave him the thrashing he'd promised.

"If you go into the next room when I go away again, it will cost you your life," said the old man.

After a time he said that he was going away again, this time for fourteen days. The boy held himself back for a week, but then he forgot the old man's warning and went into the next room. All he found was a rock on a shelf above the door. When the old man returned, he beat him within an inch of his life, but the boy begged for mercy and was allowed to live. If he ever went into the next room, however, no prayers would save him: he would be sure to die.

Soon the old man went away again, this time for three weeks, and the boy waited fourteen days before going into the forbidden room. There he saw a bottle of water on a shelf, and in one corner a horse was tied up with a pot of ashes near his head and a bag of hay by his hind legs. The boy took the ashpot and replaced it with the haybag.

Then the horse said, "Since you've been so good to me, I'll help you. You're in the house of a troll. Take the stick, the rock, and the water bottle and get on my back. Otherwise, you're doomed."

The boy did all this, but then he noticed that his hair had turned to gold. When they'd ridden awhile, the horse asked if he saw anything behind them.

"Yes, a whole group of men are coming from far away," said the boy.

"Then throw the stick; the troll's coming with other trolls." The boy did this, and all at once a forest grew up that was so thick that the trolls had to turn back to get axes to chop their way through.

A little later the horse asked again if the boy saw anything. Yes, now it looked as though a whole county was behind them.

"Then he's brought many, many trolls. Throw the rock!"

Immediately, a mountain appeared that was so big that the trolls had to smash their way through. A little while later, the horse asked if he saw anything now. Yes, he saw a huge mass of men that looked like a whole army.

"Then he's brought *swarms* of trolls! Throw the water bottle, but be sure to throw it far away to the back of us so you don't spill anything on me," said the horse.

The boy did this, and immediately a large lake appeared. But because the boy had spilled a few drops on the horse, they had to swim before they came to dry land. The trolls swarmed into the lake, lay down, and began drinking, but there was so much water that they all burst.

"Now we're rid of them," said the horse.

Soon they stopped in a forest. The horse told the boy to go up to the king's castle and ask for work, but if he should ever need the horse, he should just come and get him.

After a while the king prepared to go to war, and the boy, who had found work in the castle, went to fetch the horse. When they got to the battlefield, the fight was going badly for the king, and he was preparing to flee. But the boy charged right into the enemy army and drove them away as fast as their legs could carry them. The king was so pleased that he promised him the princess and half the kingdom.

Now the boy took the horse home to the castle, put him in the stable, and gave him plenty to eat. But in the morning when he came down to the stables, the horse was standing there hanging his head dejectedly. Why wasn't he eating? asked the boy.

The horse answered, "Take your sword and chop off my head. I don't want to live anymore."

"No, I certainly won't," said the boy. "I'm going to give you your own stable and the best feed."

"If you won't cut my head off, I'll have to kill *you*," said the horse.

Turning his eyes away, the boy had no choice but to chop his head off. Suddenly there stood before him a stately prince, who thanked him for saving him. He had once been the prince of the neighboring kingdom, but a troll had transformed him into a horse.

"Now we'll be neighboring kings," he said to the boy, "and we'll never fight each other, will we?"

Gray Cape

Once a king who had three daughters went out hunting. After he and his retinue had been hunting all day long and shot a lot of game, they gathered in a royal lodge in the forest to have some refreshment. Unfortunately, they all had too much to drink, and carelessly went off to their homes, leaving the king behind.

Now the king was alone with only his coach driver for company. Even though the night was so dark that they could barely see the road, they started back home to the castle, and soon were lost in the forest.

Before long, an ugly troll came along and planted herself in front of the horses. All that could be seen of the troll was a horrible face and a gray cape. The horses were frozen to the spot.

The king got angry, and asked if the driver and the horses were also drunk.

"Noble master and king," answered the driver, "I'm afraid I can't do much about the present situation. If His Majesty pleases, there's a horrible troll blocking the horses' way, and I don't believe we'll get past her tonight."

The king stood up in the carriage and looked at the troll. He cursed her with a powerful oath, saying, "Evil troll, I bid you return to the Hell from which you've come."

But the troll just nodded at the king.

"If the king promises to give me the first thing that meets him when he returns, I'll give him leave to return home."

The king had a small bitch who he was sure would be the first to come to greet him. So, though he was very fond of her, he promised the troll and went on his way. However, his youngest daughter held her father very dear, and awaited his return impatiently. When she saw him coming, she rushed out to meet him at the gate, jumped into his arms, and kissed him.

Distressed and unhappy, the king said, "My beloved child, you've caused me great sorrow. You don't know that you've jumped into the arms of Hell!"

The king simply couldn't send away his dearest possession, so he sent his eldest daughter instead into the forest to Gray Cape. But the troll merely nodded at her, gave her a chain of gold, and asked her to return to her father.

Then he sent his second daughter into the forest to Gray Cape. But she too was given a gold chain and sent home to her father.

Now the king was despondent. He took his youngest daughter on his knee, kissed her a hundred times, and told her of his plight and his promise to the troll.

"It would give me great pleasure to save my father's life," said the princess.

So, with great sadness, the king sent her off to the forest.

When she arrived, she saw no one there, so she lay down to sleep and had an exceedingly lovely dream. She dreamt that she saw a prince who was wonderfully handsome, but who carried himself in a sad, sorrowful way.

When she woke up, Gray Cape was standing next to her. The troll greeted her very kindly, and brought her to a castle that was filled with beauty and wonders. She showed the princess all around and told her that all this was hers, but that there were no human beings to speak to, and even Gray Cape would only be present at meals. In the floor was a hatch that led to another room in the castle, but she was strictly forbidden to open it.

The princess looked at all the wonders of the castle, but soon got bored, since she had no one to talk to. Finally she thought of the forbidden hatch, and decided to wait until Gray Cape was gone to take a look at what was beneath it.

One day when she knew that the troll was far away, she tiptoed to the hatch and opened it. But she dropped it immediately, for do you know what she saw underneath? Gray Cape was standing there, although she'd just seen her leave. The princess went to the window and saw Gray Cape coming toward her.

Brazenly, Gray Cape walked up to her and said, "Tell me, princess, what did you see under the hatch?"

But she didn't dare tell. Instantly, the whole castle disappeared, and the princess was standing alone in the great, deserted forest.

Since she didn't know her way home, she began to wander aimlessly, and finally arrived at an unfamiliar castle. She was very tired, so she lay down and fell asleep in the king's garden.

When she awoke, the king was sitting by her side watching her attentively. Since he found her very beautiful, he asked her to be his wife—which she agreed to, because she had no one else to protect her. The king made immediate preparations for the wedding.

When they'd been together for a year, she gave birth to a prince. That night Gray Cape came to her, took the child away, and daubed blood around her mouth and on her fingers. Then she asked her, "Tell me, princess, what did you see under the hatch?"

But she didn't answer. And Gray Cape went away.

In the morning, when the king saw that she'd given birth but had no child, and also saw that there was blood around her mouth and on her fingers, he grew very sad. But he loved her so much that the next year she again gave birth to a prince.

Again Gray Cape came, took the child away from her, and daubed blood around her mouth and on her fingers. And again she asked, "Tell me, princess, what did you see under the hatch?"

But she didn't answer. Again Gray Cape disappeared.

This time the king grew even more unhappy that she had no child, but he still loved her so much because of her beauty that the next year she gave birth again, this time to a princess. And again Gray Cape took the child away, daubed blood around the queen's mouth and on her fingers, and asked, "Tell me, princess, what did you see under the hatch?"

Still she didn't answer, and Gray Cape went away.

This time the king grew very angry. He locked the queen away in a prison, accusing her of having eaten her children. She was condemned to be burned at the stake.

When the execution day came, crowds of people gathered in the courtyard. As the guards led her out of her cell and started to tie her to the stake, Gray Cape appeared and asked insolently, "Tell me, princess, what did you see under the hatch?"

Since she thought that she was going to die anyway, she said, "It was you I saw, you and your accursed gray cape—you whom I hate with all my heart and soul!"

The gray cape fell to the ground, and there stood a handsome prince just like the prince she'd seen in her dream when she first came to Gray Cape. In the presence of all, he begged her forgiveness for all the terrible things that he'd done to her, and asked her to accompany him to his castle.

The other king thought that this was more black magic, and he insisted that she be burned at the stake. But the prince took hold of her and, raising his shining sword, made his way through the crowd. He told her that he, not the other king, was her real husband, and that the children were really his and were waiting at his castle. He also told her that if she'd known of his terrible plight, she might not be so angry at him. Many years before, he'd gone to war in a foreign land, and on his way home had fallen asleep by a big river. When he awoke, a woman uglier than the ugliest ghost was sitting at his head. She told him that she was overcome with love for him and promised him many wonderful gifts.

" 'Go to Hell, old witch!' I told her. 'Do you think I can love and hate someone at the same time?'

"Then her face turned as green as venom, and she threw a gray cape over me, which almost made me senseless; and she put a curse on me that I wouldn't become human again until the princess I married and had three children with cursed me just as I'd cursed her!"

The princess was overjoyed to be with the handsome prince whom she'd secretly loved ever since she'd seen him in her dream.

They rode home to his castle and lived in great happiness until their deaths.

The Animal Husbands

An old man and an old woman lived in a big, big forest with their three daughters. Since Kari was the most beautiful name the old man knew, he called all three of them Kari. To tell them apart the eldest was called Big Kari, the next one Middle Kari, and the youngest Little Kari. When the girls grew up, the man and woman, who had barely enough to feed them, wanted to find them husbands so that they wouldn't starve. But this wasn't so easy, because no one ever came to the area where they lived except a lot of trolls.

Perhaps some nice troll wouldn't mind taking care of the girls and providing for them, thought the old man, and so one Thursday evening he went with Big Kari into the forest. They walked until they came to a crossroads where four roads met. The old man yelled as loud as he could, "Big Kari wants to get married!"

"I'll take her," answered a voice from one of the roads. A large bumblebee came flying and buzzed around Kari, humming, "Come with me!"

Kari wasn't particularly delighted with her bridegroom, but since he didn't look too dangerous, she went with him into the forest. Pleased, the old man walked home. Now he had one mouth less to feed.

The next Thursday evening he went with Middle Kari to the crossroads and shouted as he'd done before, "Middle Kari wants to get married!"

From the forest a bleating voice answered, "I'll take her!" Out of the woods came a large ram with enormous horns, who invited Kari to get on his back. She climbed up, held on to his wool, and off they went into the forest. The old man was delighted that it was turning out to be so easy to marry off his daughters.

Now it was Little Kari's turn, and the next Thursday evening he brought his youngest daughter to the crossroads.

"Little Kari wants to get married!" he shouted.

"I'll take her," came a cry from the air, and a white bird swooped low. It was a seagull, who looked so friendly and handsome that Kari was happy to go with him. And now all the old man's daughters were gone.

After some time had passed, the old man wanted to see how his daughters were doing. So he set off to learn what had become of them. He walked into the forest and followed the road to the left that Big Kari and the bumblebee had taken. When he'd walked a good while, he arrived at a cave in the earth, and when he saw a big bumblebee flying in through the entrance, he realized that he'd found the right place.

"Oh, Papa's coming!" shouted Big Kari, and they were both pleased that the bumblebee buzzed happily around the room. Kari wanted to give her father some refreshment, so she asked the bumblebee what it might be.

"Start cooking the porridge," said the bumblebee. "I'll take care of the drippings."

So Kari put the pot on the fire, and when the porridge was ready, she ladled it into a large dish. After it had cooled, the bumblebee alighted on the edge of the dish, and when he flew off again, it was full of the sweetest honey. Kari placed the dish in front of her father and invited him to eat. What a feast! He ate until he was about to burst. On his way home later, he was as pleased as could be. The bumblebee and Kari accompanied him part of the way, and as he left the bee said that soon the old man would hear some very good news about his sons-in-law. The old man was rather doubtful, but at least it was a good thing that Big Kari got such delicious food.

When he arrived home, the old man talked about what good porridge he'd been served and how delicious the honey was that his son-in-law had made. It hadn't looked at all difficult; if only he had some porridge, maybe he too could make honey. But his old woman thought differently, for he was hardly a bumblebee, and so they let it be.

After a while the old man decided to find Middle Kari and see how she was doing. He took the right-hand road that the ram had taken with her on his back, and finally he arrived at a small gray cottage. Outside on a green field a big fat ram was grazing, so he knew he'd found the right place, and he went inside. Inside sat Middle Kari spinning wool; she was so happy to see him!

"What can we offer my father to eat?" she asked.

"That'll be my problem," the ram bleated. "Just bring me a bowl." Kari went to get a large bowl, and she put it by the cottage wall. The ram backed away from the house, and then, rushing forward, he smashed his head against the wall so that the blood poured into the bowl. When he'd been bleeding for a while, he told Middle Kari, "There you are! Now take this and cook up a blood pudding for your father."

Kari put a pot on the fire, cooked up a big dish of blood pudding, and invited the old man to eat. This was not a dish the old man had every day, and he enjoyed it thoroughly.

"Poor you," he said to the ram. "You must have hurt yourself terribly."

"Oh, no," the ram answered, "it's nothing. We rams often fight and bash our heads together so that our horns fall off."

Well fed and taken care of, the old man went back home. The old woman sat sadly by the stove as the old man told her what good food he'd been given at Middle Kari's.

"Sure, you just go off and fatten yourself up," said the old woman, "while I have to sit here with the empty walls."

"Cheer up now," the old man said, "and bring me a bowl."

"What will you put in it?" she asked as she went to fetch a bowl. He placed the bowl on the floor, walked backward just as he'd seen the ram do, and smashed his head against the chimney beam so that he fainted and got a large bump on his forehead.

"Have your lost your senses?" the old woman asked, throwing a ladle of water over him. He had to stay in bed for several days.

When he got better, he decided to go and see how his youngest daughter was doing. This time he took the road straight ahead that the seagull and Little Kari had taken. After a long while he came to a little pond in the forest, and close to it was a cottage. On the steps of the cottage sat Little Kari with the white bird on her lap. She was stroking and kissing the seagull, whom she seemed very much in love with. After she whispered something to him, he raised himself up and asked the old man to follow him and said he would show him how he'd get their dinner. He flew up into a tree at the edge of the pond and sat for a while looking down into the water. Then he fluttered his wings, ruffled up his feathers, and made himself so bushy that he looked twice as big as before.

"Aren't I bushy now?" he said to the old man, who stood admiring his son-in-law.

"Yes, you're so bushy and marvelous that there's nothing like you," said the old man.

"Now watch how I get food for us!" Like an arrow the seagull dove down into the water. After a little while he came up with a large pike and asked the old man to hold it while he looked for another one. The old man got as much fish to eat as he could dream of—for him this was party food. As he was leaving, Kari told him that soon he and Mother would get distinguished visitors. When he got home, he explained that Little Kari had made the finest match of all the sisters. But best of all, he'd learned to fish in such an easy way that he wanted to show the old lady immediately. She went with him to the lake, where he looked for a birch tree with boughs stretching out above the water. He climbed up as high as he dared, stretched and preened himself, and asked, "Do I look proud and bushy?"

"You poor fool," she said, "what do you have to be proud of?"

"Just watch!" he said to the old woman, and jumped right into the lake; but even after his wife helped pull him out, he had no pike to show her. Sore and wet, the old man limped home, and in addition to everything else he caught a cold and had to stay in bed for several days.

A while later he wished to visit his daughters again, but now he couldn't find them. Their houses were deserted. The old woman and the old man grieved, and wondered where they could have gone. Then one day he walked outside his cottage and saw three fine carriages with coachmen and footmen heading straight for them. He yelled for the old woman to come outside. When the first carriage stopped, a splendid prince stepped out and offered his arm to a fine lady, shining with gold and jewels; it was Big Kari. In the second carriage he saw Middle Kari and an equally fine-looking prince. But out of the last carriage jumped the most beautiful princess with the youngest and handsomest prince. This was Little Kari, their youngest daughter, with the prince who once had been her white bird.

Now they learned what had happened. Nearby was a castle whose king had three handsome sons. One day when these sons had been out hunting in the forest, they were enchanted by an evil witch who lived there. But she made one condition: if, in the shape of a bumblebee, a ram, and a seagull, they could find young maidens who would share their homes, they would be freed from their spell. This had happened, thanks to the old man's bright idea of offering his daughters to anyone who would take them. There was great rejoicing in the castle as they prepared the weddings for the princes and the young maidens who'd saved them. From then on the old man and the old woman had an easy life, and the old man bragged mightily of having made such good matches for his daughters.

Prince Faithful

Once there were a king and a queen who had no children. Finally, after many years of wishing and praying, the queen gave birth to a son.

When the little prince was about to be baptized, men from all levels of society were invited to become his godfathers. Among them was a Dalecarlian,* who gave the prince a great mansion as a christening gift, but only on the condition that he stay away from the house until he turned fifteen.

The young prince grew up big and strong, and he was as good and beautiful as an angel. But none of the noblemen's sons who were his playmates could make him happy, for all he could think and dream about was his house, and he longed for his fifteenth birthday. Days and years passed—they were all long, but the last seemed like an eternity.

Finally, the longed-for day arrived, and the king took the prince's hand and led him into the house. In the first room was a grand fireplace, the vault of which rested on polished stone pillars, and all the walls from floor to ceiling were covered with gold and silver plates and shiny, beautiful copper bowls. Then they opened the door to the second room, which was even more magnificent. All the walls had silver hooks, and on each hook hung a golden saddle. In the middle of the room stood a magnificent horse with a gold harness, a scarlet blanket, and a blanket girth woven of silver.

Some days later the prince took his horse for a ride. As he rode along, he saw a pack of wolves fighting and tearing at each other.

"Separate them!" said the horse.

The prince did as the horse said, and pulled them apart.

"Thank you, dear Prince Faithful, for separating us. We will help you in return when you're in trouble," the wolves said.

The prince remounted his horse, mumbling to himself, "I don't intend to get into any trouble."

A little farther down the road the prince found his way blocked by giants fighting with each other.

---

* Perhaps because of the dark forests in Dalarna, or Dalecarlia (a province in central Sweden), many Swedes think of Dalecarlians as "wilder" and more hot-tempered than most.

"Prince Faithful, get off and separate them!" the horse said.

The prince did as the horse said, and pulled them apart.

"Thank you, dear Prince Faithful, for freeing us from each other. We'll help you in return when you're in trouble," said the giants.

When he'd been riding a little longer, he arrived at a big lake surrounded by tall mountains and forests. At the shore the forest opened into a green field, and the prince got off his horse, sat down, and looked out over the water. He picked up a long branch and tried to reach a few water lilies glistening white among the reeds. At that moment he spied a large pike, motionless, sunning herself right under the surface. Quickly, he grabbed the pike with both hands and lifted her squirming out of the water.

"Why are you bothering the pike?" asked the horse. "Put her back in the lake!"

The prince did as the horse said, and let go of the pike.

"Thank you, dear Prince Faithful, for letting me go," said the pike. "I'll help you when you're in trouble."

And she disappeared deep down to the bottom of the lake.

On the other side, at the head of a cove, the prince spied an immense castle that shone like pure gold in the sun.

"Get on my back. That's where we're going," said the horse.

Prince Faithful got on, and the horse plunged into the water and swam with him on his back straight out into the lake.

"When we get to that castle," said the horse, "you'll see a beautiful princess. After you've greeted her, she'll immediately ask you to go down to the stable to look after her horses. But don't do it, or you'll never get away again. Later you'll see her portrait painted on a small black wooden board, and she'll ask you to take it. But you mustn't do that, either."

"Strange advice you're giving me!" thought the prince.

But he'd hardly arrived at the castle and met the princess before she asked him to go down to the stables and look after her horses, exactly as his horse had predicted. The prince remembered what the horse had said, and declined.

"Why not?" asked the princess.

"My lovely princess," replied the prince, "since I can't stay for long, I don't want to be out of your company for an instant."

But when the princess brought him a small black board with her

image painted on it, the prince couldn't refuse it, so he accepted the painting and put it away. At that very instant he suddenly forgot that his father was a great king and that he was the heir to a large, powerful kingdom: all he could remember was his horse.

After a while he took leave of the princess and rode away. He rode and rode until he arrived at the castle of another king, far away, where he asked for work as one of the king's gardeners. But after some days the king began to wonder why he never saw his new gardener do anything but wander up and down the garden paths staring at a little picture that he had concealed in his pocket. The king sent for the prince to come to see him.

When Prince Faithful arrived, the king, who was terribly curious, demanded that the prince show him the little picture that he was always looking at instead of doing something useful. When the king saw it, he too was completely enchanted by it, and he asked the prince to bring the girl to him. Startled, Prince Faithful blurted out that he would. Now the king expected him to make good on his promise.

The prince didn't know what to do. "Perhaps the horse can help me," he thought.

So he went down to the stable and asked for the horse's advice. "I'd do anything not to lose her," he said, "but now I have to bring her to the king."

"Didn't I tell you to leave that picture alone?" said the horse. "I won't let you ride me, but I suppose there's no getting around doing what the king asks. At least hurry home so I won't have to starve!

"When you ask the princess to come with you, she'll ask you to play a game of golden dice; do this, but not with her dice, for you'll lose. Bring along your own dice; you'll win, and then she'll have to come with you."

The prince walked and walked for what seemed an endless distance until he arrived at the princess's castle. She was so happy to see him that she blushed, and immediately asked him if he'd play a game of golden dice. She took out her set of dice.

"No, I have my own," said Prince Faithful. "If I lose, I'll belong to you, and if you lose, you'll belong to me."

They played many, many games of golden dice, and Prince Faithful won every time.

The fact that the princess had to accompany him to the king seemed to make her terribly sad, and she wept bitter tears. But Prince Faithful asked her to hurry, for the horse's request not to let it starve to death weighed heavily on his mind. Finally, the princess came along, but not before she'd locked all her doors and taken along the keys. They went down to the lake and sailed across in a boat, but when they were in the middle, the princess threw her keys into the water. Then they walked the rest of the way to the king's castle.

The king was so taken with the princess that he couldn't say a word—she was that beautiful. He gave her her own chambers and ladies-in-waiting to help her comb out her hair.

Shortly afterward, the king proposed to her, but she said that she wouldn't be his bride until he sent for her bucks and does.

"Whom should I send for them?" asked the king.

"I don't care," she answered, "but they must be here before I marry you."

There was nothing for the king to do but to send for the gardener, whom he ordered to fetch the princess's bucks and does.

Prince Faithful didn't know what else to do but to go to his horse. The horse just kept eating in silence as he told his sad story. "How can I get all those animals to come with me?" he complained.

"You should have listened to me; then you wouldn't have had to walk. I won't let you ride on me, that's for sure," said the horse. "Why don't you search for those wolves that you separated, and ask them to help you bring the animals back?"

Prince Faithful started on his way. When he'd walked a good distance, he stopped and shouted at the top of his lungs for the wolves. From all directions they came running, and when they'd gathered around him, he asked them to help him lead the princess's bucks and does to the king's castle.

"It's a good thing that you finally got in trouble," answered the wolves. "Since you helped us, we'll drive your bucks and does to the king's castle, even though they'd make a delicious meal."

The wolves brought the princess's bucks and does, and Prince Faithful showed them to the king.

Now the king returned to the princess's chamber and slammed the door so hard that the walls shook.

"There are your bucks and does. *Now* will you be my bride?"

"No," said the princess, "not until my entire house is brought here."

"Hmm," thought the king, "I can't send the poor fellow all the way back again for the house."

But what else was he to do? So again he ordered his gardener to come up to the castle.

The gardener went back to his horse and asked what to do now.

"I don't want to lose the princess for anything in the world, but now I have to bring her house here too! How will I ever manage that?"

"It serves you right, Prince Faithful," answered the horse. "Didn't I tell you to leave that picture alone? You'll just have to walk—because I won't let you ride me—to the castle, and when you get there, call for your giants to come and help you. But be sure to hurry back before I starve!"

When Prince Faithful got to the castle, he shouted to the giants, asking them to help him carry the princess's castle to the king's castle.

"It's a good thing you got in trouble so that we can help you," said the giants. "If it hadn't been for you, we probably would have killed each other."

They grabbed hold of the crossbeams of the princess's castle and picked it up. The prince ran ahead and the giants followed, carrying the castle to the king as easily as young men carry a barrel of beer up to the attic.

After they'd arrived and put the castle down right in the yard, Prince Faithful pointed it out to the king. Again the king went to the princess's chamber and slammed the door so hard that the windows shattered and the whole castle shook.

"*Now* will you be my bride?" he said. "Look, the castle is here!"

"No," answered the princess, "the keys aren't here and without them I can't get into my house. Not until I have them in my hand will I be your bride."

"No one can find them," the king said, "but I have dwarves who are very clever. They'll make you some new keys."

"No," answered the princess.

"Bring hither my keys from the lake maiden's bosom.
Only then will I change my maiden name."

What was the king to do? Again he called for his new gardener, and the poor thing once again sought his horse's advice. He hardly dared ask again, for he was always getting scolded for being so disobedient; however, he really had no other choice.

So he went to the horse and said, "Things are worse than ever! Now I have to get the princess's keys which lie in the lake maiden's bosom. How will I ever get them?"

"If you'd listened to me and left the picture alone, you wouldn't have had to walk—for I won't let you ride me, that's for sure. But go off to the lake, and when you get there, ask the pike that you released to bring up the keys for you. But hurry back before I starve to death!"

Again Prince Faithful went on his way, and he walked and walked until he came to the lake where the princess had dropped her keys. He called for the pike, who came immediately.

"My dear pike," said the prince, "please help me get back my princess's keys, which she dropped in the middle of the lake."

"It's a good thing, Prince Faithful, that you got in trouble," said the pike, "for now I'll help you get your keys back."

In no time at all there was a flash like sunshine at the bottom of the lake, and the pike came up with the princess's bunch of golden keys between her sharp teeth.

When the prince returned to the castle, he brought the keys to the king, who was waiting impatiently for them. The king took them and entered the princess's chamber again, this time slamming the door so hard that the entire castle shook, sending an echo through the surrounding mountains. Even the mountain storms awoke, and began howling in the valleys and ravines.

"Now will you be my bride? Here you have your keys!" said the king.

"No," answered the princess.

> "Not until I get my medicine bottle,
> Standing in the old foundation
> Where, in bygone days,
> My house once stood."

The king's voice grew very stern, and he said:

> "If I don't get your consent then,
> Your *head* will rest on that foundation.

That will be all that's left
Where the house once stood."

Furious, the king returned to his chambers and demanded that his new gardener get him the medicine bottle.

Upset with all this endless running and fetching, Prince Faithful ran to his horse and asked, "Now, how am I supposed to find a bottle of drops in the foundation where the princess's castle used to be?"

"It serves you right, Prince Faithful! If you'd listened to me and left the picture alone, you wouldn't have had to walk, for I won't let you ride me, that's for sure. Now run off again, and take an empty bottle with you. When you get there, pull out the stopper. Lots of little birds will come flying, and each will leave a drop in the bottle. When it's full, put the stopper back and run back home again."

The prince did what the horse told him to do, but as he was putting the stopper back into the bottle, he spilled a few drops on a rock, and immediately a person appeared. As an experiment, he poured drops on more rocks, and from all of them more people appeared. They were such beautiful people that he couldn't stop himself from dropping drops on all the rocks he saw. When he finally returned home, he had nothing left.

"Well, now you've done yourself a greater harm than ever," said the horse when he heard this news. "But I'll take pity on you and let you ride me. Otherwise, I'm sure you'll pour out all the drops once again."

And off they went to the place where the castle had stood, and again the bottle was filled by the birds.

When Prince Faithful returned, he first put his horse into the stable and then went to see the king. When the king had the bottle in hand, he was very pleased, and he took it quickly to the princess's chambers. This time he slammed the door so hard that he woke up the thunder. Suddenly it was dark in the chamber, and right before his eyes the princess turned into many strange animals, each one shouting, "Summon the new gardener! He must die!"

The king was so frightened by all this bellowing and howling that he ran out, and quick as a flash called for the gardener.

"Where is my medicine bottle?" asked the princess.

"I gave it to the king as soon as I got back," answered the prince.

"Then you must die!" she said, and she yanked the bottle out of the king's hand, pulled a sword off the wall, and chopped off Prince Faithful's head. But at that same moment she dropped a few drops from the bottle into the flowing blood, and put the prince's head back on his body. He rose up again, alive, and more beautiful than ever. At that moment he forgot everything that had happened since he'd accepted the princess's portrait, and thought that only a short period of time had passed.

When the king saw how beautifully the gardener shone in the darkness, he opened the window shutters, which made the gardener shine even more brightly. At the same time a mighty thunderclap was heard, and the king fell to his knees and begged the princess to cut off his head too, and make him just as handsome as the gardener. Presto! she chopped his head off, but she didn't pour on any drops. And, quietly, Thor rode off with his life.

Suddenly the man from Dalarna who'd given the prince his mansion passed through the chamber, sighing, "Wait for me!"

"Oh, that I will surely do!" the princess said mockingly.

Then she turned to the prince: "My beloved Prince Faithful, the great wizard lying there was your godfather; he was the one who gave you the house and the horse. He thought that your curiosity would make you enter before you turned fifteen, and then I'd have had to become his queen, and you'd have been sentenced to death."

At that moment they heard whinnying outside. Prince Faithful knew that it was his beloved horse, and he unlocked the door. The horse walked in, stretched out his neck, and said, "Sister dear, please chop off my head!"

And the princess chopped off his head and dropped a few drops from her bottle into his blood. He was a human being, and a lovely prince at that—her brother!

All three agreed to celebrate Prince Faithful and the princess's wedding that very day. Later, Prince Faithful became king of the wizard's country, and the princess's brother became king of the kingdom in which Prince Faithful first met his beloved Mrs. Princess.

Later, rumor has it that the giants carried the castle back to where it belonged, the wolves kept the prince supplied with rabbit meat, and the pike caught fish for his cats. But by then I wasn't around anymore. So don't quote me.

The Rats in the Juniper Bush

Once there was a king who had three sons, all of whom he loved equally. Since he couldn't decide which one should inherit the kingdom when he died, he told each to take a horse and ride out in a different direction; whoever brought back the smallest dog would be king after him.

All three rode out to find small dogs, but the youngest prince sat on his horse dreaming of anything and everything, and let the horse wander where it pleased. After quite some time, the horse stopped, and when the prince looked around, he saw that he was on a large plain covered with juniper bushes; the horse had stopped by a very large bush, and wouldn't walk any farther.

Dismounting to take a look around, the prince noticed a staircase leading down into the ground under the juniper bush. He went down the stairs and came to an unlocked door, which opened into a very beautiful room. There were no human beings around, but after a while several rats came in and set two place settings and brought in silver dishes heaped with delicious food. Then a rat came in wearing a portrait around her neck. She greeted the prince and invited him to eat dinner with her. He thanked her and they sat down to eat.

The rat was very polite and friendly, and the prince had a lovely time for a while, but then he remembered that he was supposed to be searching for a small dog. He wanted to leave, but couldn't find the door, and the rat told him that he couldn't leave until the day when he and his brothers had promised to return to their father. This was very unfortunate, thought the prince, but there was nothing to do but stay.

When the time came for him to ride home, the rat said good-bye very graciously, giving him a large nut that she said his father should crack when he asked to see the prince's dog. So the prince had no choice but to ride home. When he arrived, his brothers had just arrived too, bringing with them the most beautiful little dogs. All he had was a big nut. But when he asked his father to crack it, lo and behold, a little dog hopped out; you can imagine how tiny it must have been. Naturally, the youngest prince was the winner.

Now the king said that he wanted them to try one more test:

whoever brought back the finest, most beautiful linen—long enough for a couple of sheets—would be king.

Each prince rode out in a different direction, but the youngest couldn't make his horse ride any other way than the first time, and soon he arrived again at the plain with the juniper bushes. Then he thought, "I'll go down and thank the rat for the dog but tell her straight off that I have to find a piece of linen, and that I have to look for it somewhere else." The rat received him happily, and asked him to make himself at home. He thanked her for the dog, but said that now he had to get a very fine piece of linen, so she must let him go. But the same thing happened: he couldn't find the door and had to stay until the day he was to return to his father. She took leave of him with great kindness and gave him another nut.

This time his brothers were there before him, with finely woven, beautiful cloth—while all he had was a nut. However, when the king cracked it, there was a cloth that was fine enough to fit inside!

Again the youngest son had won, but the king said, "We'll have one last test: whoever brings home the kindest and most beautiful fiancée will be king."

They rode out again, and again the horse of the youngest prince headed straight for the juniper bushes; the prince couldn't get him to go anywhere else. It stopped by the biggest juniper bush, and the prince went down to the rat and thanked her for the cloth, but begged her to let him go—after all, a fiancée was something that she couldn't provide. But the same thing happened: once he was inside, he couldn't find the door, and he had to stay. When the day came for the prince to leave, the rat told him that *she'd* be his fiancée. This made the prince even sadder, for he'd rather have returned without any fiancée at all than with a rat. But there was nothing he could do.

The rat harnessed eight large white rats to a carriage. Another rat drove the carriage and still another stood behind as footman, and off they went, with the prince riding next to them. Shortly before they arrived at the castle, they had to cross a stream. The prince rode across the bridge, but the rats drove right into the water. The prince was very distressed: he cared very much for the rat. But they didn't drown. Instead, they came out on the other bank, and now the white rats were eight beautiful horses, the driver and the footman were human beings dressed in grand livery, and inside the carriage sat the most beautiful princess. When they arrived, his was the most beautiful fiancée, and the king declared that the youngest prince would inherit the kingdom. But his fiancée said that this wasn't neccessary; she had a large kingdom of her own, and the king could give his to the other brothers.

After the weddings of all three princes, the youngest went home with his wife. When they came to the plain where the juniper bushes had been, he saw a large city, and instead of rats running everywhere, there were people walking in the streets. The big juniper bush had turned into a beautiful castle. Before he arrived, everything had been enchanted; and now the prince and his wife became king and queen and lived happily for many, many years.

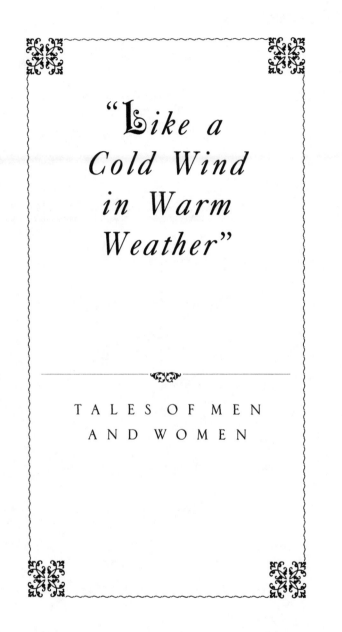

"Like a
Cold Wind
in Warm
Weather"

TALES OF MEN
AND WOMEN

Like a Cold Wind in Warm Weather

Once there were a man and a woman who lived very happily together. One day, however, the man got it into his head that his wife didn't like him as much as she had before, and he asked her, "Do you still care for me?"

"Yes," she answered.

"Yes, but how *much* do you care for me?"

"As much as a cold wind in warm weather."

The man didn't like that answer. "We can't be together anymore," he thought, and he packed his things and left.

As he was walking up a steep hill, it got so hot in the sun that his whole body was covered with sweat. When he got to the top of the hill a cold wind came along, and he thought that it cooled him so nicely.

Then he thought, "If she cares for me that much, I'll turn back." And after that they stayed together for the rest of their days.

The Quick-Learning Girl

Once a bachelor went courting. He visited a farm whose mistress had a daughter of her own as well as a stepdaughter, who was the prettier of the two. At least that's what all the suitors thought, and so the stepmother was always trying to show how useless the girl was in her work. For there were things that the poor girl had never been allowed to learn.

Since this suitor only had eyes for the stepdaughter, the mistress demanded that she go to the loom and weave five-harness cloth with five treadles,* something the girl had never tried before. You can imagine how miserable she was, for she liked the nice bachelor very much. So there she sat, stepping and treadling, treadling and step-

---

* On the old counterbalance looms the patterns are usually done in multiples of two; thus, the five-harness cloth in the story is an unusual pattern.

ping, but all she got out of it was "horses,"* and she wished herself seven leagues underground, she was so ashamed.

The suitor sat down next to her and looked at the cloth. Then he said, "My father had five horses, and when he wanted to groom them, he always started with the one farthest to the right, and then continued all the way down the line. Then he started with the first one again."

"I see," said the girl, and she did the same with the five loom treadles. Finally, she had no "horses" in her weaving anymore.

The suitor recognized that she was a clever girl, so he proposed to her and was accepted. They had a wedding at his farm that lasted eight days. That's where they live now, and that's where they mend their shoes and have children by the bushel; they sent me over here to tell you all about it.

* "Horses" are snags or broken threads in the weaving.

The Girl Who Gave a Knight a Kiss
Out of Necessity

Once there were some people who lived in a little house deep in the forest. They couldn't afford to keep a servant boy, but as luck would have it, they had a clever daughter who served as both girl and boy.

One time it happened that they had to take a sack of rye to be ground at the mill. They hoisted the bag onto the back of the horse, and the girl had to lead it there.

But when she'd gotten about halfway to the mill, the horse stumbled on a rock and the grain sack fell to the ground. She tried to hoist it back up on the horse, but it was too heavy and the horse wouldn't stand still.

While the girl stood there helplessly, a knight who was out hunting happened to pass by.

"Won't you please help me lift this sack up on the horse's back?" asked the girl when she saw the knight.

"Not unless you first give me a kiss," said the knight.

But the girl wouldn't do that; the sack could just lie there, she said to herself.

It was all the same to the knight, so he went on his way, and the girl was left standing there with her horse and sack.

But the knight liked her, for she was both beautiful and good, so he decided to test her again. He rode home, disguised himself in farmer's clothes, and at noontime came back to the girl in the forest.

"Good friend, won't you please help me put this sack of grain on the horse's back?" said the girl as soon as she saw the farmer.

"Not unless you first give me a kiss," said the farmer.

But the girl wouldn't do that; the sack would just have to lie there, she thought.

Well, that was all right with the farmer, and he went on his way. And the girl was left standing with her horse and her sack.

Now the knight thought even more highly of her, but he wanted to test her one more time. He went home, put on some old rags, smeared his face with soot, and slung a pack over his back so that he looked exactly like an old beggar. At sunset he came back to the girl in the forest.

"Dear old man, please help me put this sack back on the horse," said the girl when she saw the old beggar.

"Not unless you first give me a kiss," the old beggar said.

But the girl wouldn't do that. The sack could just lie there, she thought.

That was quite all right with the old beggar, and he started on his way.

The girl began to think that it would be pretty frightening to spend the whole night in the forest, so she made herself call him back and give him a kiss, no matter how much it embarrassed her.

In return, the old beggar helped her lift the sack onto the horse's back. Afterward the girl went her way and the old man went his.

But the knight couldn't forget the lovely girl. He thought about her night and day, and it wasn't long before he appeared in the forest at the house of the old man and woman and asked for their daughter's hand. They were so surprised to receive such an honor that they neither dared nor wanted to object. And the girl, for her part, didn't mind marrying the rich and handsome knight. So they celebrated the wedding, and they ate so much that no one needed to be ashamed, and the girl moved in with the knight, and they lived so well that a king couldn't have lived any better.

Even so, the girl wasn't always happy. The knight spent too much time hunting, and he brought his hunting cronies home with him to the castle time and again. As you might guess, they led quite a life: beer and wine flowed from the barrels, and cups were passed around without stopping, and every one of them wanted to be wilder than his fellow.

As soon as the knight had enough to drink, he too became loud and talkative, and then he usually said:

"I know a girl who gave a knight a kiss out of necessity."

His drinking companions thought this very funny, and they laughed and leered and stared at the mistress for a long time, and the knight laughed and leered as well. The knight's words made her feel very sad.

One day the mistress's old godmother came to the castle inquiring about how her goddaughter was doing. Oh, well, everything was quite all right, said the mistress. But the old woman could see that everything was not as it should be, and she asked what the matter was. At first the mistress wouldn't say, but the old woman kept on asking until she told her.

"Maybe we can do something about that," she said, for she knew more than other people, she did.

A while afterward the knight was out hunting. That day the forest seemed very strange, and the knight didn't recognize anything around him. Toward evening he wanted to ride home again, but he couldn't find his way. This was bad enough, of course, but even worse, he was getting very hungry; he hadn't eaten a crumb since morning. So he rode back and forth, back and forth, thinking that he'd find his way out, but it only grew wilder and darker around him. Finally, he spied a light and found his way to a little cottage. He got off the horse and went inside. There he saw an ugly old crone, who was setting a table with the most delicious-looking dishes.

"Splendid! Please allow me to buy a little food," the knight said very pleasantly.

"No," said the old crone, "I've no food for sale. But if you'll give me a kiss, you can have all you can eat."

"Ugh! Go to the Devil!" shouted the knight, and rushed out the door.

That was all right; the old crone didn't care one way or the other.

The knight jumped on his horse again. He'd rather forgo food forever than kiss an ugly, toothless old crone. He rode and rode until the sweat poured off him and the horse, but he just couldn't get anywhere but to that poor little cottage. By now it was midnight and hunger was gnawing at his insides, so he tried the old crone again.

"You must let me buy a little food!" the knight pleaded.

"No," said the old crone, "I've no food for sale. But if you'll give me a kiss, you can eat as much as you want."

"Let the Devil kiss an old witch!" shouted the knight, and he rushed out the door again.

Very well—it didn't matter to the old crone.

The knight roamed about until far into the second day, and now and then the smell of the good food found its way to him. But he couldn't find his way out of the forest, and no matter what he did, he never got anywhere but to that horrible cottage. Finally, he had to take another turn with the old crone.

"Listen here, mother, you simply must let me buy a little food!" the knight demanded.

"No," said the old crone again, "I've no food for sale. But if you'll give me a kiss, you can have all you want."

"Like hell I will!" screamed the knight, and was about to rush out the door again.

Oh, but that was quite all right with the old crone.

Then the knight stopped and made himself calm down. Certainly, it was hard to imagine kissing such an ugly old lady, but he couldn't let himself starve to death either. Besides, no one but he ever needed to find out, for the old crone didn't know him, and he himself certainly wasn't going to speak about it. So he closed his eyes and gave her a kiss. Then she gave him food, as much as he wanted, and he made sure to take his full payment for that kiss. As soon as he got back into the forest, he had no trouble at all finding his way home.

Before long, his hunting companions came to visit the knight again, and wine and beer flowed as generously as before. Finally, the knight became so jolly that he started up with his old line: "I know a girl who gave a kiss to a knight out of necessity." He laughed, and his companions laughed too.

"And I know a knight who gave a kiss to an ugly, toothless old crone just for some food," said the mistress.

Of course, it was her godmother who'd arranged the kiss, and she'd let the mistress know all about it.

Now there was even more laughing and shouting. But the knight only laughed and shouted a little, and thereafter no one ever spoke again of the girl who had to kiss a knight out of necessity.

The Fussy Fiancé

Once there was a man who left his fiancée after she happened to fart.

Later, when he passed by her house, he saw her outside searching through a pile of garbage. He asked her what she was looking for.

"I'm looking for a pin," she answered.

"You'll never be able to find it," he said.

"Well, I'm as likely to find a pin in a pile of garbage as you are to find a wife who never farts."

He considered this, and took her back.

Pär and Bengta

When Bengta married Pär, the silly girl thought that she'd been given another head in addition to the one she already had. She decided that she didn't have to use her own, for the man was supposed to be the woman's head.

In some ways Pär filled the bill. He ploughed his fields, and before year's end, Bengta had a baby boy in the cradle. But then came the first time for him to drive to town. Bengta asked him to buy her some sewing and darning needles, for his clothes were terribly worn out. This he promised to do, and she sat down to wait for his return. But when Pär came home and she asked him for the needles, he began to search through the straw in the wagon, for that's where he'd put them, like a fool.

"You should have stuck them into the band of your cap," said Bengta, patting her dear Pär.

The next time he went to town, he had to buy metal strips for a mash tub. But the dummy put the strips around his cap and would probably have gotten his head twisted off if Bengta hadn't pulled them off.

"Why didn't you just let the strips hang down behind the wagon?" said Bengta, kissing her dear Pär.

The third time he had to buy a side of pork. But when Bengta saw that it'd been trailing down behind the wagon all the way home and looked dirtier than a live pig, she began to wonder if she wouldn't be better off using her own head and keeping her new one for household things and other little trifles.

One morning she said to Pär, "Listen, Pär, today I'm going to town instead of you. All you have to do is churn the butter and make sure the cat doesn't get at it. Then fill the drinking barrel, make dough for baking, water the livestock, and take care of our boy. That's all, and that's not very much," said Bengta. Pär agreed.

As soon as she was out of the gate, Pär started churning, and although he muddled around with the churn pole terribly, he did manage to make some butter. Of course, he was very pleased with himself, but now he had to be sure to guard the butter from the cat, who jumped at everything she saw. At first Pär thought he'd sit on the lid of the churn, but then he remembered that he needed water for making dough, so he tied the churn to his back, picked up two buckets, and went to the well to draw water. But while he was doing that, the churn got loose and fell off his back, butter and all, right into the well.

In the midst of his misery and fear, Pär suddenly remembered that Bengta had told him to fill the drinking barrel. So he went to the brewing house, where he also found the kneading trough and the flour sacks. He started filling the barrel, and when it was full, he wanted to check if the stopper was secure, so he stood twisting it until the plug came out. At that very moment the cows started bellowing in the stable, and he rushed out, plug in hand, to water the livestock. But by the time he'd gotten them out of the stalls, he remembered the barrel and raced back to the brewing house. There the floor was one big puddle! This wouldn't do, so he emptied the flour sacks into the puddle to dry it out a little. But then the baby in the cottage started howling, and in the yard the cattle started butting each other. So he ran into the cottage, grabbed the baby out of the cradle, and tied him to a post so that he'd have his hands free to handle the unruly cows. All this took a good while, and when he came back to check on the boy, the life had run right out of him.

By now Pär didn't know what in the world to do, except to crawl into the oven and hide, for he was sure he'd be called to task when Bengta got home. So he just lay there in the oven, wishing himself seven miles up a dog's ass.

Meanwhile, Bengta returned from town. When she couldn't find her dear Pär, she started shouting, "Pär dear, where are you?"

"In the oven," he answered in a voice that sounded like a sick cat's.

"What's going on, Pär?"

"The butter's in the well, Bengta."

"Is that all, Pär? We could churn some more. Just come out here with me."

"The brew's all over the floor, Bengta."

"I can brew more, silly!"

"The flour's in the brew, Bengta."

"We can grind more rye, Pär. Just come out now!"

"The boy is dead, Bengta."

"That's very sad, Pär. But he was only our first one; we can have many more. Come out here now!"

Pär got up his courage, crept out, and went back to his usual chores, and both he and Bengta were satisfied. But one day when Pär was watering the bull, that awful creature attacked Pär, pulled his pants off, and turned him into a steer. And *then* Pär got a proper beating from Bengta!

Who's Got the Dumbest Husband

Once there were two women who had very stupid husbands. One day they made a bet to see which one of them was best at fooling her husband.

When one of the men was lying in bed feeling a little under the weather, his wife convinced him that he was dead. He was so dumb that he believed her, and he laid himself out so that he looked dead. His wife dressed him in burial clothes and put him in a coffin. Then she got everything ready and invited people to his funeral.

Among the funeral guests were the other woman and her dumb husband. When *this* husband had started to change his clothes for the funeral, his wife convinced him that he was already dressed! He believed her, and went along to the funeral in his birthday suit.

Afterward, they rode to the graveyard carrying the "corpse" to his grave while he lay in his coffin, peeking out. There was a small hole in the coffin, and through it he could see his neighbor walking stark naked in the funeral procession. After a while he couldn't hold out any longer, and he burst out laughing. One just can't bury a laughing corpse, so everyone had to walk back home again.

Geska

Once there was a girl called Geska, who was very rich but very stupid. A man married her anyway, figuring that wherever there's wealth, the rest will follow by and by.

One day he told her, "Go shear the sheep and tend to the wool so that we can make something warm and woolly."

Well, that was no problem. She sheared the sheep, but then she put the wool in the stove and burned it up.

"Now we've got something warm and woolly," said Geska to herself.

"How did you manage to finish so quickly?" the husband said. "The wool has to be spun and woven before you can make something warm and woolly."

"Oh," said Geska, "I just stuffed it in the oven and set fire to it. Believe me, it's warm in here!"

"Oh, you poor fool. God save me from you!" said the husband.

The next day he said, "Go and get butter at Mother's house and borrow a little salt too. Then hurry home again."

No problem. Geska got the butter and salt, but on the way home she had to walk across a swamp. The swamp was so dry from the sun that the earth was cracked, so she took all the butter and spread it into the cracks. When she crossed over a bridge, she saw a whole school of spawning roach. She threw the salt at the fish and hurried home.

Her husband said, "Did you get the butter?"

"Yes," said Geska, "I got three marks'* worth."

"Did you get the salt too?"

"Yes, I got a half-peck full."

---

* A mark is an old weight measure (1 mark = 425 g).

"Then where's the butter?" asked the husband.

"Well, when I crossed the swamp, there were so many cracks in the ground that were dying to be buttered that I gave them all I had. Believe me, there were still many that didn't get any."

"And where's the salt?" asked the husband.

"Well, when I was crossing the bridge there were so many fish in the stream that had water but no salt. So I threw them the salt, and believe me were they happy!"

"Oh, you poor fool! God save me from you!" said the husband.

The next day he said, "I want some white cabbage for dinner, so go fetch some bacon from the cellar and some cabbage from the garden. Then use one piece per head, and make sure it's enough for more than one meal."

Geska took all the bacon in the cellar and cut it into pieces. Then she cut off all the cabbage heads in the garden. Finally, she put one piece of bacon on each head of cabbage.

When her husband got home, he asked, "Is the cabbage ready?"

"Yes, come take a look in the garden. I put one piece on each head. I did it perfectly!"

"Oh, you poor fool! God save me from you!" said the husband.

Another day he said, "Tomorrow, go to town with one of the oxen. Get a hundred riksdaler* for him, or a deposit."

On the way Geska met a butcher.

"What do you want for that ox?" asked the butcher.

"A hundred riksdaler or a deposit," said Geska.

"Well, I'll give you a deposit," the butcher said, for he could see how it was with her. He told her to undress, and then he tarred and feathered her. Afterward, he let her go home, and he took the ox. When she got home, she looked awful.

"Where's the money for the ox?" asked the husband.

"I got a deposit," she said.

"Then where's the deposit?"

"Can't you tell, it's on me."

"Oh, you poor fool! God save me from you!" said the husband.

And then he said, "The king is planning to ride by here, and

* An old Swedish monetary unit; see note, page 87.

we're going over to the big oak by the road to watch for him. But first make certain that the doors are secure."

Geska lifted the doors off their hinges and tied a rope around them. Then she hung one on her front side and the other on her back side, and followed her husband to the great oak tree.

"Oh, you poor fool! God save me from you!" he said when he saw her. He made her climb up into the oak tree so that she wouldn't be seen, and he climbed up after her. Soon the royal party arrived and decided to have their picnic right there in the lovely clearing beneath the oak.

"Oh, no, I'm going to drop one of the doors," said Geska.

"Well, do it then," said the husband. And it came crashing down.

"Oh, no, I'm going to drop the other one too," said Geska.

"Well then, let it go!" And that one came crashing down too.

"What's all this?" said the royal party, getting frightened.

"Oh, no, now *I'm* going to fall," said Geska.

"Well then, go right ahead!" said her husband, and when the royal party looked up, down came Geska, all tarred and feathered. They thought it was the Devil himself, and they got up and ran away, leaving everything behind. Geska and her husband got to keep everything they'd left, so this time Geska hadn't been so stupid after all.

The Stingy Farmer

Once there was a farmer who was so stingy that he wouldn't even give his wife enough food to eat. When she realized this, she was careful never to eat when he was around. This satisfied the old man all right, but it so happened that one day he got quite sick. Now the woman didn't try to hide anything from her husband anymore. She ate her fill with him looking on.

The old man was beside himself. "I'll be ruined!" he thought. "She'll eat me out of house and home!" When he tried to speak, however, all that came out was "house and home." And so that's what he kept shouting. The old woman went to get her neighbors and told them that her old man was terribly sick, and that he wanted to make his will.

"He wants me to have house and home," she said.

"House and home," the old man kept moaning when the neighbors arrived.

"Yes, we hear you! Your wife will get your house and home," they said.

This made the old man so furious that he died right on the spot, and the old woman got his house and home, and everything else too.

The Man and Woman Who Changed Jobs

Once there was an old man, just like any other old man. This old man worked in the forest, chopping wood and burning charcoal, while his old woman stayed at home spinning, cooking, and taking care of the house. In this way their days passed one after another. But the old man always complained that he had to labor and toil all day long to support both of them while the old woman merely sat at home cooking porridge, eating, and enjoying herself. Even though the old woman told him that there was plenty to do at home as well and that the old man would be badly fed and clothed if she did not look after the house, the old man turned a deaf ear; he was convinced that he alone was pulling their entire load.

One day, after they'd bickered longer than usual, the old woman said, "Have it your way! Tomorrow we'll switch jobs. I'll go to the forest and cut wood for the fire, and you'll stay home and do my chores."

This suited the old man just fine. "I'll take good care of the house," he said. "But how you'll fare in the woods is another story."

Early the next morning the old woman said, "Don't forget to bake the bread, churn the butter, watch the cow, and cook the greens for dinner."

These were all mere trifles, thought the old man, and so they parted. The old woman took the old man's ax and went off to the forest while the old man began to build a fire under the oven and make the dough. When he thought it was ready, he began to bake it. But what sort of bread it was going to be was hard to say, for he forgot the yeast and put the loaves into the oven without first sweeping away the ashes.

The old man thought he'd managed the baking very well, and the thought of fresh bread awakened his appetite.

"Fresh bread is fine," he said to himself, "but if you have some bacon to go along with it, it tastes even better!"

So the next moment he went to the storehouse to fetch their last piece of bacon. But since the bacon was salty, he wanted something to drink with it. He put the bacon on the cellar steps and went downstairs.

Just as he was taking the plug out of the beer barrel, a dog came by and grabbed the bacon. The old man certainly didn't want to lose it, so he jumped up and ran off after the dog. But as he was running he discovered that he still had the plug in his hand, and he abandoned the bacon and ran back so that he could at least save the beer.

But it was too late. The barrel was empty and all the good beer had run out. This made him very unhappy, but he comforted himself with the thought that the old woman probably wasn't doing any better in the forest. Even if he had to do without bacon and beer, at least he still had the nice fresh-baked bread. With bread to eat, life is complete! as the saying goes.

But his comfort was short-lived. When he got inside the hut he found the bread burned to a crisp. Not a single bite was left for him to taste. It was a terrible state of affairs.

"This is no good at all," he moaned. "If only I'd let her stay at home! If I'm doing this badly, how might she be doing in the forest? By now she may have chopped off both arms and legs!"

But there was no time for thinking. The sun was already high in the sky, and he had to cook greens for dinner. For greens one must have something green, the old man said to himself, and as he couldn't find anything else green, he took the old woman's new homespun jacket, chopped it into little bits, and put the pieces in the pot.

He realized that he couldn't cook greens without water, but the spring was so far away. And besides, he also had to churn butter! How on earth was he going to manage it all?

"If I put the churn on my back and shake it while I'm running to the spring, it'll probably turn to butter by the time I get back," he thought.

And that is what he did. But in his haste he forgot to put the lid on, and when he bent to haul up the water bucket, the cream poured over his shoulders and head and down into the spring.

Disheartened, he returned with the soupy, creamy water.

Now he had to tend to the cow, and since he couldn't be both inside and outside at the same time, how was he going to manage? On top of the house's sod roof, the grass shone a bright green in the sunshine; *there* was a juicy pasture! He tied a long rope around the cow's neck and pulled her up onto the roof, then threw the other end of the rope down the chimney.

Feeling a little happier, he went back inside the cottage and tied the tether hanging down through the chimney around his own waist so that the cow wouldn't get away from him. Then he started blowing on the fire under the pot. But while he was occupied blowing, the cow fell off the roof and pulled him up into the chimney!

At that very moment the old woman came home with a big bundle of firewood on her back. When she saw the cow hanging alongside the cottage wall, she hurried as fast as she could and cut the rope. Then she went inside. There on the floor lay the old man, smoked, burned, and half suffocated.

"God preserve us!" she exclaimed. "Is this how you've been managing at home?"

The poor old man couldn't utter a word; he just moaned and groaned. But it didn't take the old woman long to see how he'd managed: the bacon was gone, the beer run out, the bread burned to coal. The cream was in the spring and her jacket chopped up in the pot. The cow was hanged and the old man himself badly bruised and burned.

What happened later is not hard to guess. The old woman was allowed to care for her house in peace and quiet while the old man went off to the forest. Never again was he heard to complain of his lot.

The Contrary Old Woman

Once there was an old woman who always did the opposite of what her old man wanted. One day when they were on their way to church, he wanted to go one way and she another.

Soon they came to a stream where the water level was so high that it reached all the way up to the planks of the bridge. The old man said that he wouldn't cross there. Oh, but that was just where the old woman wanted to cross. There was a railing, and the old man said that he certainly wasn't going to sit on it. But that was exactly where the old woman wanted to sit. Then the man said that if he did sit there, at least he would lean forward. So the old woman leaned backward. The man said that he surely wouldn't sit and rock on the railing, but that was just what the woman started to do. She fell backward into the stream, where she was taken by the current.

Now the old man was rid of her, which was what he'd wanted all along.

The Tale of a Suitor

This is a tale about a boy who was having trouble choosing a girl to take for his wife. He had to choose between two, so to test them one day he pretended to be sick and sent for each of them.

When the first one arrived, he said, "I'm sick, but I've been told that if I can have some of the dough sticking to your nails from the last time you baked, it will make me well."

The girl studied her nails carefully, but couldn't find what her fiancé wanted.

When the other girl came to visit, he repeated what he'd said to the first one, and the girl immediately started studying her nails. She had more luck—and she cleaned her nails and gave him the remedy that he claimed would cure him.

By this time he had no doubts about whom to choose: it was the first one, who'd washed and cleaned her hands properly.

The Hunter and the Skogsrå*

One day a hunter went out as usual to shoot birds in the forest. When he reached a large rock by the side of the road, he met a woman as lovely as the very finest maiden. She greeted him as though they were old friends. But the hunter didn't quite understand why.

"Well," she said, "I see you every time you go into the woods."

She wanted him to go home with her, for she lived only a few steps away. But the hunter realized what kind of woman she was, and walked away from her.

Every time afterward when he went out hunting, she came up to him and invited him home, but he always said no.

One day—and it was a cold, nasty, and windy day—the hunter thought it might be fun just to see what kind of house the woman lived in, and so this time he went with her. Before he knew where he was, he was standing in a hall so beautiful that he'd never seen its equal. Walls and benches shone as though they were made of gold, and it was warm and cozy in there as well.

After he'd been there once, he came back a second and then a third time, and before long he went as often as he could.

But the hunter was a married man, and his wife soon figured out that something was wrong. She tried, but couldn't get a word out of him. Then one day when she was home alone, an elegant lady came to see her—this woman looked very suspicious. After they'd been speaking a while, the wife said, "I just wish I knew what to do about my bull. He'll never stay at home. He always goes to the neighbor's cows and follows them around like a slave."

"Oh, that's no problem," answered the strange woman. "There's a cure for that." And she told the wife to get some mezereon and valerian† and give them to the bull; that way he'd be sure to stay home.

---

* *Skogsrå:* wood spirit; see Introduction, p. xxi.

† Mezereon is a small European shrub *(Daphne mezereum)* with purple flowers and an acrid bark used in medicine as a vesicatory (causes blistering) and irritant. Valerian is a plant *(Valeriana officinalis)* the root of which formerly was used as a carminative (relieves flatulence) and sedative, especially in nervous conditions.

The woman thanked her for the good advice and got herself some mezereon and valerian, but she gave it not to her bull but to her husband. After that he never went to the *skogsrå* again. Whenever he went into the forest, she stood right in his path just as before, but he always made a wide circle around her. She was very sad, and one day she went to the hunter's wife and said to her:

"Foolish me, unwary one,
To tell you of valerian and mezereon."

The Woman in the Hole

A very long time ago—it was around the time of King Olov Skötkonung*—a farmer pushed his mean old wife into a pit in a big swamp near their farm, and she never came back up again. The farmer started to miss her, and spent about three years braiding a rope, which he then lowered into the hole to help her up. Instead of the woman, the Evil One came crawling up the rope.

"Did you happen to see an old woman down there?" asked the farmer.

"I sure did!" answered the Evil One. "About three years ago an old woman came tumbling down, but she was so mean that I couldn't stand being with her. I had to get out of the house, so I grabbed the rope you dropped down and started climbing up. The old woman climbed after me, of course, but I cut the rope behind me, and she tumbled back down again. Whatever you do, don't make another rope; if she comes up, neither you nor I will have another happy day."

And so the farmer gave up the idea of rescuing the old woman.

---

* King Olov Skötkonung is thought to have died around the year 1020.

The Man Who Married the Mara

There is a creature that some call a *mara** who is said to ride people in their sleep. Once upon a time one of these *marar* chose a certain man to plague night after night. Finally, the man made up his mind to find out why. One night after he'd been troubled again, he got up, lit the lamp, and shut the windows, the doors, the damper, and all the other openings in the house. Then he noticed a small knothole, and he proceeded to plug that up too. He searched the house for days, seven in all, without finding what he was looking for.

On the evening of the seventh day, he heard whimpering that sounded as if it were coming from the stove. When he turned around, he saw a maiden who was very lovely and very naked. She sang:

> "Dear handsome young man,
> Please let me out again!
> I must be in my mother's sight
> Before the morning light."

"I won't let you go, you troll! But since you're so lovely, I'll marry you instead!"

And he gave her some clothes and sent for the parson, who first baptized her and then married them.

One day after they'd been married for seven years and had seven children, the wife noticed the small plugged hole. She asked her husband to take out the plug. When he did as she asked, she vanished before his eyes!

Then he realized that if he hadn't taken out the plug from the hole, she'd never have been able to get away—for this was the very hole through which she'd entered. He missed her terribly, for he held her very dear, and so he went out to search for his lost love.

He wandered about this way and that for seven years without finding any trace of her, and finally he returned home. On his arrival

---

* *Mara* (pl. *marar*): a nightmare hag.

he found the *mara* sitting in the same place that he'd caught her the first time.

She sang:

> "My mother's died and lies on a bier.
> I've lost my golden hair and am so sad!
> Please take me back and hold me near.
> She will be happy who now is sad!"

With these words she fell into his arms, and they lived together happily and well for many, many years.

And that's all I know!

The Hidden Key

Once there was a farm family who had an only daughter. One day there came calling a young man, who the mother believed had come to propose to her daughter. When she learned this for sure, she wanted to show how clever her daughter was, and she pointed to the spinning wheel, which stood ready with a full head of flax.

"My daughter spins three of those a day," she said.

The suitor thought that that was fine, but he still wanted to see for himself how skillful she was. When he was alone in the room for a moment, he took a key from a chest and hid it at the bottom of the head of flax.

After three weeks he visited again. This time he was told that after his last visit they'd lost the key to the chest and hadn't been able to find it anywhere. Now he knew just how clever the spinner—who the mother had said could spin three heads a day—really was, and he made sure not to propose to that girl!

"His Just Reward"

MORAL TALES

His Just Reward

A man went out into the forest one day looking for a runaway horse. At one point he had to climb across a cleft in the mountain, and that was when he found that a large snake had got its rear end caught in the crevice.

The snake said to the man, "If you help free me, I'll see that you get your just reward!"

The man took his staff and pried the rocks apart so that the snake could get out.

"Thanks," said the snake. "Now come over here and I'll give you your just reward."

The man asked what his just reward might be.

"Death," said the snake.

The man said that he wasn't sure that he wanted that, and he suggested that they ask the first creature who came along what one's just reward ought to be.

A bear came along, and the man asked the bear what one's just reward ought to be.

"Death," said the bear.

"You see?" said the snake. "Death *is* one's just reward! So now I'm going to take you."

But then the man replied, "Let's just walk a little farther and ask someone else."

After a while they met a wolf. And the man asked him what one's just reward ought to be.

"Death," answered the wolf. "That's everybody's just reward."

"There it is," said the snake. "Now you're mine!"

"Just a minute," said the man. "Let us say that the third creature we meet is the final judge, whoever it turns out to be."

In a little while they met a fox. The man asked the fox what one's just reward ought to be, and the fox answered just like the others.

"Death," he said.

"So now I'll bite you to death," said the snake.

When the fox heard that, he said, "Now wait just a moment. We must consider this case more carefully. First of all, what really happened?"

"Well," said the man, "the snake got its tail caught in a crevice."

Then the fox said, "Why don't we go back there to see exactly how it was."

Well, they went back, and the fox asked the man to pry open the rocks again with his staff, and then the snake should put his rear end right in between, just the way it'd been before. Then the man should let the rocks slip back a little.

"Was it tighter than this before?" asked the fox.

"Yes," said the snake.

"Let go a little more," said the fox to the man. "Was it tighter than this?"

"Yes."

"Then let go completely. Now, are you in good and tight?"

"It's worse than it was before!" said the snake.

"Well then, you might as well stay there. That way the two of you are even."

So the snake had to stay, and the man avoided getting his just reward.

Master Pär and Rag Jan's Boy

Once there was a man who was so terribly rich that no one could really say how rich he was. He owned big farms both here and there, and some were almost like palaces. People called him Master Pär—for master is what he wanted to be, and one of the finest too. There was also a poor tenant farmer who lived next to Pär. He had nothing but his wife and a bunch of kids. They called him Rag Jan.

Now this Master Pär was terribly stingy and conceited, and the poorer people were, the worse he treated them. But when he was with noblemen or other fine folk, he did it up in style and the drink flowed, lest it be said that anyone entertained better than Master Pär.

Even though he was so rich, he still was never satisfied. He envied Rag Jan all his many children—for he himself had no one who could take over all his farms and feed him when he wasn't able to manage any longer. His wife talked to all the wise men and women, and even the doctors, but no one could help her.

"Things always go wrong for me," Master Pär said. Every time Rag Jan had another child, he sang the same old song.

One evening a poor old crone came to Master Pär asking for a roof over her head for the night. "Impossible," he said. "I don't run an almshouse." And he shut the door in her face.

Then the old crone came to Rag Jan's with the same request.

Yes, she was very welcome, Rag Jan said, but his wife had just given birth to a boy, so he didn't know exactly where to put her.

"So that's what's going on," the old crone said. "Then I've come at just the right moment. I know how to take care of such things," she said as she came into the cottage.

"You know, that's just the nicest boy I've ever seen," she said. "Nice deserves nice, so what you've got to do is invite Master Pär to be his godfather."

Rag Jan and his wife looked at each other. The sun would sooner turn black than Master Pär agree to be the godfather of a poor farmer's boy.

"Well, he may be poor now," said the old crone, "but he'll be rich by and by. Master Pär, however grand a fellow he may think he is now, didn't exactly come into the world with clothes on his back either. So, Jan my friend, I think you should do as I say."

Rag Jan pulled his ear and scratched his head, but the old crone was stubborn, and since she was the sort of person who knows more than other people—she was one of the Finn people,* she was—Rag Jan went to Master Pär and told him what was on his mind.

"Have you gone stark raving mad?" he said. "Do you think that I want to be the godfather of a beggar's kid? Get packing, and be quick about it if you want to stay in one piece," he said, slamming the door with a crash.

"No matter," said the old crone when Jan got back, "it's still your boy who'll be his heir. All the wealth that Master Pär is scraping together will someday be his. But you'll have to keep your mouths shut about this. Otherwise it might not work."

Yes, they'd keep their mouths shut—that was certain.

---

* Finn people refers to Finns who immigrated to Sweden from the end of the sixteenth century to the middle of the seventeenth. Their language and culture differed from that of the Swedish majority, and, just like the Lapps, they were considered to have supernatural powers.

Out of her birch-bark knapsack the old crone pulled fancy little clothes for the baby. Then she carried him to the parson and had him christened Pär.

Master Pär continued to moan and groan about not having any children, and since his wife couldn't give him any, they agreed to buy themselves a foster child. It had to be a nice kid, of course—and not too expensive; so Master Pär went to Rag Jan.

"You've got so many children," he said.

"Yes, I have children the way you have farms: you can hardly count them," Rag Jan said.

"But I have none at all," said Master Pär. "Let me buy your smallest boy."

Jan was no businessman—at least not with that kind of merchandise—but then he remembered what the old Finn crone had said, and they agreed on a Christian exchange: Jan got a barrel of oats and Master Pär got the boy, and he promised to feed him until he died, and even swore to it.

After some time had passed, Master Pär began to sing the same old song again. The boy he'd bought wasn't his own flesh and blood, so his wife got busy again talking to doctors and wise folk. This time luck was with her, for whatever tricks they did, Master Pär got himself a little girl to rock to sleep. Of course, he was mighty pleased, but then he started thinking that he could do without that Rag Jan's boy. However, since he'd already taken him, he'd have to keep him until he got bigger and he could figure out what to do with him.

Naturally, Rag Jan and his old woman were pleased as punch that things had turned out the way they had. When they saw the boy playing with the sweet, beautiful girl, it seemed to them that they were already bride and groom; they were as sure of the Finn crone's word as if they already had all of Master Pär's money in their hands. But we all know what womenfolk are like: they can't keep a secret. And so one day the wife blabbed about what the Finn crone had predicted. After she'd said it, she could have kicked herself, but words don't come back—and these flew around the countryside until they reached Master Pär's ear. By then he'd forgotten that the boy was nothing but the son of a beggar. But now he remembered, and started thinking that when people get an inch they want a mile; the way that kid was playing with his girl, why one day he might get it into his head to marry her! This made Master Pär very nervous, and he began plotting to get rid of the boy.

Master Pär had a sister who lived north of the mountains, west of the lake, south of the great waterfall. One day he told the boy to take her a letter, and to guard it well. He didn't tell him what it said—that she should take the boy to the dock above the great waterfall and push him into the river!

The boy started off as fast as he could. By the time evening fell, he was in the middle of the forest without a place to sleep. But then he met an old Finn crone—yes, the very same one who, as his godmother, had brought him to the parson.

"Where are you going?" she asked.

"I'm taking a letter to Master Pär's sister who lives north of the mountains, west of the lake, and south of the great waterfall," he said. "Could I please stay at your house for the night?"

Yes, she lived nearby, the old woman said, and he was welcome to stay with her. As soon as he'd fallen asleep, she took the letter to a schoolteacher who lived in the Finn forest. She asked him to read it to her. "He knows how to do mischief, that Master Pär does," she said. "But he doesn't dare do it himself. Well, this time he won't get away with it."

She asked the schoolteacher to write a letter that said that Master Pär's sister should bring the boy up like her own until Master Pär himself came to get him. Then she hurried back, and when the boy woke up, he thanked her for her help and went on his way.

Master Pär's sister read the letter, and she cared for the boy as well as he could ever wish. The more time passed, the more she grew to like him, for he was kind and obedient, and had plenty of spunk.

But no matter how good things were, sometimes he got a bit homesick. If the truth be told, he thought about the girl, his old playmate.

One after another the years went by, and he grew into a big, strapping fellow. They didn't hear a word from Master Pär, who was at home thinking about marrying off his daughter. Though she was old enough to start looking for a husband, she wouldn't hear of it. But once in a while she did ask when the boy was coming back;

and the older she grew, the more often she asked, so that Master Pär finally started to worry that his sister hadn't done as the letter had said. What if he were alive! That would be a terrible state of affairs. So one day he drove off in a horse and buggy to his sister's to check.

When he arrived, there stood the boy in the yard. Master Pär exploded!

"Why didn't you do as I said in the letter?" he asked his sister.

"Didn't I bring him up exactly as though he were my own child, just as you asked?" she said, handing him the letter. Master Pär read and read until his eyes almost popped out of his head, for the letter looked exactly as though he'd written it himself.

"Why do things always go wrong for me?" he said. If he'd had the courage he'd have killed the boy right then and there, but he didn't, so he told his wife in a letter to take the boy to the blast furnace and push him in. If she didn't do this, she'd get the same treatment herself when he got home. He handed the boy the letter and told him to hurry home as fast as he knew how.

When evening began to fall, the boy found himself again in the middle of the Finn forest, where he met the old Finn crone.

"Where are you coming from now?"

"I'm coming from Master Pär, who's at his sister's, and I'm going home with a letter for his wife," he said. "Could I please stay at your house tonight?" Yes, he was welcome to, she said. But when the boy had fallen asleep, the old woman brought the letter to the school-teacher and asked him to read it to her.

"He's up to mischief again, and this time he's getting his wife to do the dirty work," said the schoolteacher.

"He won't get away with it this time either," the old woman said. She had the schoolteacher write another letter telling the wife to take the girl and the foster son immediately to the parson and have the banns posted for their marriage; if she didn't do it, she'd have to jump into the blast furnace. The old crone hurried back, and when the boy woke up in the morning, he thanked her and went on his way.

When the boy got home, Master Pär's wife was goggle-eyed with surprise, and even more so when she read the letter. Well, one hears a lot of crazy things in one's life, but this was the last thing she'd ever expected. However, she hardly wanted to be pushed into the blast furnace, so she called for her daughter, who now, oddly enough, suddenly wanted to get married. Off they went to the parson to post the banns.

On the day the first banns were posted, Master Pär's wife arranged a great party. There was such bright light burning in the windows when Master Pär drove up to the house that he thought a fire was raging. And when he found out what was going on, he got so mad that he almost burst.

He rushed up to his wife: "What kind of madness is this? Why didn't you do what I told you to do in the letter?"

"Didn't I go to the parson and post marriage banns for our girl and Rag Jan's boy, and make a real party?" she said, handing him the letter.

Master Pär read and read until he turned green and yellow; the letter looked exactly as though he'd written it himself.

"I think Old Erik* is up to his tricks, one after the other," said he, and then he called for the boy. "So you intend to become my son-in-law? It's not quite so simple. First you have to go to the giant at the end of the world who can answer all questions. Ask him why things always go wrong for me. If you bring back an answer, you can have my daughter, but not before then."

The boy was less than pleased at the thought of such a journey. The girl begged and pleaded with her father, and cried one flood of tears after another, but nothing helped—the boy had to go. Now Master Pär thought he'd won, for he knew that the giant was a man-eater.

It was a long trip to the end of the world. The boy had to pass through three kingdoms before he got there. When he arrived at the first castle, the king himself was standing at the entrance.

"Where are you off to?" asked the king.

"I'm going to the end of the world to ask why things always go wrong for Master Pär."

"If you're going to the end of the world, you might ask a question for me too. In my garden there's a strange apple tree; on one side the

* The Devil.

apples are red, and on the other they're white. Couldn't you find out why?"

"I'll try," said the boy. "If I get an answer to one question, I suppose I could get two just as well." The king fed him and gave him a sack of food to take along, and he thanked the king and went on his way.

When he'd walked a good while longer, he arrived at another castle and decided to stop there too. The king himself was standing at the entrance.

"Where are you off to?" asked the king.

"I'm going to the end of the world," said the boy, "to ask why things always go wrong for Master Pär."

"If you're going to the end of the world, you might ask a question for me too. On my land is a spring that used to have the most wonderful water; it was almost like wine. But now, in spite of all the digging I've done, it's nothing but a muddy puddle. Please, my friend, ask why that is."

"I suppose I can try. If I can get one answer, I can probably get more as well." The king took good care of him, and supplied him with another sackful of food. The boy thanked him and went on his way.

After he'd walked very far—even farther than far—he came to the third castle. The king himself was standing at the entrance, and asked him where he was going.

"I'm going to the end of the world," said the boy, "to ask why things always go wrong for Master Pär."

"If you're going to the giant at the end of the world, then won't you please ask him what happened to my daughter, who was lost seven years ago?"

"I'll try," said the boy. "If I get the answer to one question, I suppose I can get others as well." The king took very good care of him, and gave him a third well-filled sack of food to take along. He thanked the king and went on his way until he came to the tallest mountain in the world. This was where the giant lived who could answer all questions.

To get to the mountain one had to cross a great river. In the river was a ferryboat, and in the boat sat an ugly old woman. The boy asked her to ferry him across.

"So you're going to the giant, are you?" asked the old crone.

Yes, he was; he was on his way to ask why things always went wrong for Master Pär.

"Oh, my dear, would you please ask him how long I have to sit here? I've been here for three hundred years."

"I'll try," said the boy, and she ferried him across.

In the mountain was a door, and in the lock was a key. He gathered his courage and turned the key. Inside was a large room where the walls shone with the purest gold, and in that room sat a lovely maiden, spinning the finest gold thread on a distaff.*

"It's been a long time since I've seen a Christian," she said. "Dear friend, how do you happen to come here, and what do you want?"

"Well, I came with many greetings to the giant from Master Pär, and to ask him why things always go wrong for him. How can I meet the old man?"

"The giant? Oh, my dear child, you don't know what you're saying. He's gone for the moment, but when he gets back, he'll eat you right up in one gulp."

"That's too bad," said the boy. "But I still have to ask him all sorts of questions." He told her about all his adventures, and when he spoke of the king who lost his daughter seven years before, she exclaimed, "Oh, just imagine if that's my father! I'll help you all I can, and perhaps we'll be lucky enough to get away."

She pointed to a golden sword hanging on the wall.

"See if you can lift it," she said.

The boy tried, but it didn't budge.

"Take a drink from this bottle," she said. It helped: now he could take it down from the wall. "Take another drink," she said, and he did. Now he could lift it into the air. When he had drunk the whole bottle, he could pick it up and swing it as if it were a willow branch.

"Crawl under the bed and cover yourself with this bearskin, so the giant can't smell you," she said.

---

* A distaff is a staff for holding the flax, tow, or wool from which thread is drawn in spinning by hand or with the spinning wheel.

The boy crawled under the bed and pulled the skin over his body.

Just then the giant came stomping in. "Hmm, I smell the blood of a Christian," he panted.

"Yes, I'm sure you do," said the princess. "Your hawk came back a while ago with a big bone in its beak. I suppose it must have been a human bone since it makes your nose tingle."

"The smell wouldn't be so strong from just one bone," the giant said.

"No, but now I seem to recall that he had two."

"Well, I guess that would explain it," said the giant, and he sat down and told of all his exploits and how many humans he'd eaten that day. Then they went to bed, and as soon as they lay down, the giant fell asleep.

Suddenly, the princess awoke with a start. "Oh!" she screamed, tossing around in bed.

"What's the matter?" said the giant.

"I had such a strange dream!"

"What was it?"

"I dreamed that someone named Master Pär asked me why things always went wrong for him."

"That's because he doesn't want the son-in-law he's supposed to have," said the giant, and when he fell asleep again he started snoring so loud that the mountain shook.

Suddenly the princess started again.

"Oh! Oh!" she screamed, tossing around in bed.

"Now what's wrong?" said the giant, starting to get annoyed.

"I had such a strange dream!"

"Now what did you dream?"

"I dreamt that a king had an apple tree, whose apples were red on one side and white on the other. How can that be?"

"What a question!" said the giant. "That's because of all the gold and silver that was buried under the tree when all kings in the world were at war with each other." He turned toward the wall and started snoring again until the mountain wheezed and roared.

Suddenly the princess jumped again.

"Oh! Oh! Oh!" she screamed, tossing around in her bedclothes.

"What's wrong now?" the giant yelled angrily. He was beginning to get quite cross.

"Oh, I dreamt such a strange dream."

"What did you dream?"

"I dreamt that there was a king who had a spring with the clearest, nicest water in the world. But now it's nothing but a muddy puddle. Dear heart, how did that happen?"

"What a question!" said the giant. "That's because of the old crow they buried there. If they dig it up again, the spring will be as it was before. Now leave me in peace with all your dreams!" He turned back to the wall and started snoring till the rafters shook.

All at once the princess started again.

"Oh! Oh! Oh! Oh!" she screamed, and she tossed even more violently.

"Now what's the matter?" the giant screamed furiously.

"I had such a strange dream," said the princess.

"And what did you dream this time?" shouted the giant.

"Well, I dreamt that a king asked me what had become of his daughter who was lost seven years ago—and I just wonder what sort of king that is."

"What a question!" said the giant. "That was your father. But he can just keep wondering for all the good it will do him. Now you'd better leave me in peace with all your dreams." Then he turned toward the wall and fell asleep snoring so that the mountain rumbled and grumbled like thunder.

The princess gave one more start.

"Oh! Oh! Oh! Oh! Oh!" she screamed, leaping halfway out of bed.

The giant flew up.

"*Now* what's wrong?" he roared; he was completely beside himself with rage!

"Oh, dear, sweet, darling Papa," said the princess, "I started because I had such a strange dream."

"What's going on with all your dreaming tonight? You don't usually dream like this," he said. "What did you dream now?"

"Well, I dreamt that the ferry woman by the river asked me how long she has to sit there."

"What a question!" said the giant. "All she has to do is jump ashore first when she's ferried someone across, and say, 'Sit there as long as I've been sitting there,' and then she'll be free and the other one will sit in her place. But if you don't let me sleep in peace now,

I'll chop your head off." He took down the golden sword and put it next to him in bed. Then he started snoring with a crackling and a roaring like the loudest of thunder.

Now that the princess had gotten answers to all her questions, she slipped out of bed, and the boy crept out from underneath and picked up the golden sword. He chopped the giant's head off, and blood poured out all over the floor; if they hadn't gotten out of there quickly, they might have drowned.

When they came to the ferry woman, she asked the boy if he'd gotten her an answer. "First help us across, then I'll tell you." So the old crone took them across, and when they'd hopped ashore, the boy said, "Next time you ferry someone across, make sure to jump ashore first and say these words: 'Sit there as long as I've been sitting there.' Then you'll be free, and he'll have to sit instead."

"You should have told me that before," the old crone shouted after them.

When they arrived at the castle where the princess's father lived, you can imagine how they were welcomed. The king raved on and on, and insisted that the boy become his son-in-law and king after him. The princess also begged and pleaded as best she could, but neither could convince him; he told them that he had to go to Master Pär with his answer, for someone was waiting there for him.

Since there was no convincing him, the king gave him beautiful clothes, horses, and a carriage so that when he drove off, he looked like a prosperous gentleman.

He arrived at the second castle. When the giant's advice had been followed, the spring water turned as clear as wine. This king gave him great gifts too, and he went on to the third castle. He told them to dig on both sides of the apple tree, where they found so much gold and silver that words can't even describe it. The king gave him half, more than a horse could carry.

Now Rag Jan's boy was a real gentleman, and Master Pär had to doff his hat when the grand carriage arrived at his farm; he almost thought it was the king himself who'd come to call because he looked like such an important man. But when Master Pär saw who it was, imagine how his eyes bulged out of his face; and when he heard what the giant had said, he started making immediate preparations for a feast the likes of which no one had ever seen, for Master Pär did things in style. Master Pär's sister came, and the Finn crone, and Rag Jan and his wife and all their kids in spanking new clothes. There were seven parsons and seven sextons and seven cooks from Karlstad, and so many people that one couldn't even count their horses. And they played and danced and drank and ate as if they were at the king's own palace. What a tremendous party that was!

Now Master Pär ought to have been pleased; a better son-in-law he couldn't have gotten on this side of the end of the world. But he wasn't; the fact that his son-in-law was richer than he irked him, and when he thought of the boy leaving all of the giant's treasure behind, he felt a pain in his heart. So one day he got into his wagon and drove off, and not a soul knew that he'd gone to the end of the world to get the giant's fortune.

After he reached the river, he stepped into the ferry. The old crone told him to sit down, but as soon as he did, she quickly hopped ashore.

"Sit there just as long as I've been sitting there," she said—and so Master Pär had to sit in the ferry; and he's probably sitting there still, staring at the gold shining through the giant's open door.

But his daughter and Rag Jan's boy are doing just fine; and so is the one who told me all about it.

The Girl in the Robbers' Den

(§) nce there was a miller whose beautiful daughter was being courted by a handsome suitor. He came to see her often, but what he did or where he lived, no one knew. When she finally asked him about it, he told her to go into the forest the next day and follow a path of peas that he would drop to show her the way.

After a long walk she arrived at a large cave deep in the forest. In front of it stood an old man, who received her graciously and asked her what she was doing there. When she told him, he shook his head sadly, and explained with great tenderness the misfortune that had befallen her. The fact was that this was a robbers' den, and that their leader was her fiancé. These robbers butchered people and ate their

hearts, and when each of them had eaten nine hearts, he considered himself powerful enough to do anything he wanted and never be punished. Soon she too would be one of their victims.

The old man concealed her behind a large barrel, where she waited for the robbers in terror and fear. Before long they arrived, bringing along a poor child whom they immediately slaughtered. On her finger the child was wearing a ring, which flew right into the girl's bodice as she hid behind the barrel. The robbers looked for the ring, but couldn't find it.

Early the next morning the robbers went out hunting. The old man helped the frightened girl out of her hiding place, and she hurried off.

It wasn't long before the suitor put in an appearance at the miller's house. They prepared a great feast, and during it the miller's daughter said that she'd had a curious dream. She told of the adventures she'd had during her day in the robbers' den. Her fiancé changed color several times, and when she finally showed the ring, he couldn't deny it, and, as was proper, he was beaten to death by the guests.

Funteliten and His Mother

Once there was an old woman who had only one son. This son was pretty small and thin, so she called him Funteliten, Little One. But even though he wasn't very big or very strong, he was so full of the Devil that his mother couldn't manage him at all; he did the exact opposite of everything she said.

If she told him to go out to the woods, he'd hide the ax so that she couldn't find it for days, and then he'd say that uh, well, thieves and strangers had stolen it. He'd stay out with troublemakers and bad characters till all hours, and he'd only come home when he got hungry, and he wouldn't bring even a single piece of wood to keep him and the old woman warm. This happened time after time, and all the while the old woman never had any wood for her stove.

If she asked him to go fetch water, sometimes he'd drop the

bucket down the well, saying that uh, well, he just happened to let it go. Or he'd break it to bits and say that he'd tripped over it. Yes, there was just no end to the mischief that Funteliten would do.

The old lady beat him with a cane as much as she could, but it was hopeless. She tried sending him off to learn first one trade, then another, but that was hopeless too: after he'd been somewhere for a short while, they'd see what he was like and send him right back home. The old lady tried everything under the sun—but everything was hopeless!

Soon Funteliten reached an age when he should have been able to earn his keep and not depend on his mother and others to support him. The old woman got the bright idea to let him try his luck as a peddler. She gave him five riksdaler* and a bit of goods to start him off, and she also gave him six rules to live by. If he took them all to heart, he'd be sure to be rich and happy his whole life through.

These were the six rules:

1. Stay away from strong drink.
2. Stay away from big crowds.
3. Keep your purse closed as much as possible.
4. Respect older people and let them walk in front of you.
5. Don't pick up anything you haven't put down.
6. Don't tell people everything you hear, see, and know.

Funteliten swore that he'd follow all these rules, for he was happy to get the money.

The next morning, after eating breakfast and collecting his things, he kissed his mama goodbye and got ready to leave. She wished him well and reminded him to follow the six rules, and he promised never to forget them.

After a while on the road, Funteliten began to get hungry, and he went up to a cottage. When he got inside, he saw that it was an inn and asked if he could buy himself a little food to eat.

"I don't have any food to give you," answered the innkeeper, "but if you'd like a drink or two, that can be arranged."

---

* An old Swedish monetary unit; see note, page 87.

Then he asked her how far it was to the next town or farm, and she said it was a good three miles. He was tired, so he said, "Well, I don't mind if I do!"

After he'd had one drink, he wanted another, and when he'd had two, he wanted a third, which pleased the innkeeper, and she called him her "good fellow" and "nice son."

After he'd had his drinks, he was feeling very fine. At the other end of the table sat some gay blades and rough characters, playing cards. They asked him if he'd like to join them.

"Why not?" he answered, for by then he was feeling no pain.

He pulled up a chair, sat down with his new companions and started playing. After they'd played several games and Funteliten had lost all of them, the winners began asking for money, and the innkeeper joined right in with the others. So the boy had to open his purse for the first time, but what he had wasn't enough to pay even half of what he owed. That made them change their tune, and they beat him till he had to run away from his jolly companions.

But now Funteliten didn't know where to go and what to do. If he went back home to his mother, he knew he'd be scolded and perhaps get another beating, and he'd deserve it since he'd squandered her money and completely ignored her good advice. With his head still foggy with drink, he walked along wondering what to do.

"Well," he thought, "I suppose I'll just have to take what comes. I'm sure I'll be scolded, but I'm used to that. The beating I can usually run away from. Yes, I'll just have to go home."

When he arrived, his mother said, "Welcome home, my child! How was your journey?"

"Oh, Mama," her son answered, "it was pretty shitty."

"Then you didn't do what I told you to, you dummy, you nincompoop. You never think about anything but doing mischief from morning till night, you blockhead, you sow's ass—which you'll be for the rest of your life! Didn't you remember the six good rules I taught you?"

"Yes, Mama, I remembered them," said the boy.

"Then let me hear them. I don't believe you remembered even one."

"The first rule dear Mama taught me was to stay away from strong drink. I haven't had a drink of water since I left, and water is the strongest drink I know. It can destroy houses and farms, give power to mills and foundries, carry ships on oceans and lakes. I haven't touched the stuff, and it's the strongest drink I know."

"That's not what I meant, you rascal! What about the second rule? Did you remember that?"

"Yes, dear Mama," answered the boy. "To stay away from large crowds. I stayed away from churches and gallows hills, since they're the biggest crowds I know."

"That's not what I meant either," said the old woman. "Well, what was the third rule I told you? I suppose you've taken that to heart just like the other two, you pea brain. You won't amount to anything in this life, so help me God."

"Mama's third rule was not to open my purse too often. Well, I opened it only once, and it didn't have enough to pay even half of what I owed. Then I was beaten and had to run away. So dear Mama can't say that I wore out those purse strings by tying and untying them too often."

"You know that's not what I meant, you evil beast! You're making a laughingstock of me! You blockhead, you can't tell the difference between someone who looks after you and someone who takes advantage of you! I'm going to take you across the lake to a carpenter where you can learn to work with wood. See if you like that better than the easy life of a peddler."

"Yes, Mother," said Funteliten.

The old lady dressed herself in four or five old skirts, her thin old fur coat, and her flat old down-at-the-heels clogs. With her old snuff-box and handkerchief in one hand and her crutch in the other, she headed for the shore.

The lake had just frozen over, and it was as slippery as a mirror. The old woman said to her son, "Child, you're younger and lighter. Walk ahead and find where the ice is strongest."

"No, Mother, you told me yourself that the fourth rule was to respect old people and let them walk in front. Since my old papa died, there isn't anyone on earth I respect more than my old mother."

"How about that!" thought the old woman. "Maybe I can make a human being of him yet. I'd better walk in front."

So she walked out onto the slippery ice. At just that moment a powerful whirlwind grabbed her, spun her around a few times, and knocked her over. The ice broke, and the old lady fell in. She shouted for her son to help her, but he answered, "The fifth rule Mama taught me was never to pick up anything that I didn't put down. I never put as much as a wood shaving in that hole in the ice. But if you'll take my advice, you'll put yourself in God's hands and go to Hell! That's the best advice I can give you. And thanks for everything!"

The old woman started yelling at him and grabbing at the edges of the ice: "Oh, you good-for-nothing son-of-a-dog! You've never had anything in your head but jokes! If you yourself won't help me in my hour of need, at least run up to the farm and tell *them* to come and help me!"

"No, Mother," said the boy. "The last rule you taught me was not to tell everything I hear, see, or know. I promise that I'll never tell a single person that you're here. Only, as I said, take my advice and put yourself in God's hands on your way to Hell!"

And so Funteliten got rid of the nagging old lady, just the way many of us would like to who still have someone like that around.

The Girl Who Stepped on the Bread

The father of a servant girl on a farm died, and her mistress gave her three loaves of bread to take to the funeral, for the girl's home was very poor.

She was wearing a pair of new shoes, and so when she came to a stream, instead of saving the bread for her family, she put the loaves in the stream to serve as stepping-stones so as not to get her shoes all wet and dirty.

When she'd stepped on the first and the second loaves, and was about to step on the third, she found that she couldn't move: her feet were stuck. It was Sunday, and when the people on their way to church came by and saw her, they tried to pull her up but couldn't. The people sent for the parson, but he couldn't free her either. All he could do was pray for her as she sank deeper and deeper until she finally disappeared out of sight.

A Tale of Two Beggars

Once two beggars met on a road. They decided to keep each other company on their way to a nearby castle where a very rich prince lived. When they arrived at the castle courtyard, they sat down and waited until the prince came out and walked past them. At that moment one of the beggars said, "He whom the prince will aid, he has been helped!" The other one said, "He whom God will aid, *he* has been helped!"

The prince walked by, pretending not to have heard them, but a while later he sent out a servant with a huge loaf of bread for the beggar who'd said, "He whom the prince will aid, he has been helped!"

The other beggar got nothing, and after they'd rested, they went on their way again. The beggar who'd gotten the bread wasn't very strong. Soon he began to feel that the big bread was too heavy to carry, and offered to sell it to the other. The other beggar had thirty-three öre,* which he was willing to give for the loaf of bread, so the first beggar accepted this payment, and the loaf changed owners. Both beggars walked together a bit longer, but soon they parted ways.

When the one who'd bought the loaf started to get hungry, he sat down to eat, and after eating awhile he found a large lump of gold inside the loaf. Quickly he pulled it out, ran to the nearest town, and sold it. After that, he was a rich man.

The other beggar wandered back to the castle and again sat waiting until the prince walked by.

"He whom the prince will aid, he has been helped!" he repeated.

"Yes, but I've already helped you," said the prince. "I gave you a loaf of bread with a large lump of gold in it."

The beggar was astounded.

"I didn't know that! I sold it to my comrade for thirty-three öre!"

"Well, if you were that stupid, you won't get any more from me. That lump of gold was so large that you'd never have had to beg again," said the prince.

The beggar had to leave empty-handed. He was very sad, but now at least he understood that the other had been telling the truth when he'd said, "He whom God will aid, *he* has been helped!"

The Filthy-Rich Student

Once there was a student who gambled and partied from morning till night. Although his parents were rich and gave him all kinds of money, it was never enough. Finally, he had to write home and tell them that he was in quite a bit of debt. But his father refused to pay, and told him that he'd have to manage on his own. So there he was, with nothing left to do but hit the road.

He walked and walked, until finally he came to a forest where he met a fine gentleman. "What are you thinking about so deeply?" asked the gentleman.

---

* There are a hundred öre to one Swedish krona. At today's exchange rate, there are about seven Swedish kronor to a dollar.

"What business is it of yours?" replied the student.

"I might just be able to help you."

"Oh, that's not too likely."

"Well, it wouldn't hurt to try," said the gentleman. So all at once the student blurted out everything that had happened; he couldn't imagine how on earth he could get the money he needed.

"Is that all?" said the gentleman, who went on to say that such a problem could be easily solved.

"And just how is that supposed to happen?"

"Well, you can have as much money you want if you do as I say."

"And what would that be?"

"You must neither comb nor wash nor shave yourself," he answered. "Neither must you change your shirt or your socks or your hat, nor must you blow your nose for seven years. If you can do all that, then you'll be free to keep all your money; but if you fail, even once, before the seven years are up, then you're mine. What do you say?"

"And I'll really get the money?" asked the student.

"As much as you want."

"When will I get it?"

"As soon as you start."

These were hard terms, thought the student, and of course he realized what sort of gentleman he was dealing with. But when one is in debt, one gets into all sorts of difficult situations. So he agreed.

"Sign right here," said the gentleman, taking out a contract.

The very moment the student signed his name, he got his money. Then he left the wicked man and trotted along until he came to a town.

He went to a fur shop, where he asked if they had bearskins. Yes, the furrier had some. "Then make me a coat, and line it with linen," said the student. "And make me stockings that go far up my legs, and a bearskin hat too."

"It's not going to be cheap," said the furrier.

"That doesn't matter," answered the student. And he got his bearskin clothes and paid the price without haggling.

Thus it was that he started his new life. He neither washed nor combed nor shaved nor wiped his nose. His pockets were always full of gold; if he spent any, more came. He bought a large house and garden while he still looked fairly decent, and there he lived by himself, rarely venturing into town. Since he had so much money, he was allowed to do as he pleased. People thought that he was a bit cracked, but otherwise they said nothing against him; for he was never stingy to anyone, but gave everyone his due, and then some.

Once when he was in town, he went into a gambling house. The people there were frightened of him, but when he bought them all a drink, they calmed down. Just then, a millowner came out of the next room quite beside himself; he had just gambled away everything he owned. Pacing up and down the floor, he noticed the student, who asked what had put him in such a passion. The millowner told him how much he'd lost.

"A mere trifle!" said the student. "Here it is. Now go and try again." And he pushed him back inside.

A little later the millowner came out again in just as much—if not more—of a panic. Now he'd lost everything the student had given him! But the student repeated that it was a mere trifle, and that the millowner should go back in and try his luck one more time; he'd see to the money. So the millowner agreed, and later returned overjoyed because now he'd won everything he'd lost, and then some. He wanted to repay the student, who said that he should keep it for a rainy day.

"What a grand fellow he is, even if he's very ugly," thought the millowner. "It might be a good idea to learn more about him."

So he invited him home, and they left the gambling house together. The millowner asked him if he was married, and when the student said that he wasn't, he mentioned that he had three daughters; perhaps one of them would interest the student.

"Could be," he answered.

When the millowner told his daughters that he'd brought with him a suitor who was helpful, kind, and rich, everyone was delighted. "Go out and take a look at him for yourselves," he said.

The eldest went out to look, but when she saw the student, she said "Ugh!" and turned around again. The second one said "No!" and came right back. But the youngest greeted him kindly, for she knew how generous he'd been to her father.

"Come closer, my girl," said the student. She stepped closer.

"Would you consider having me?" he asked.

"Yes, since it was meant to be," she answered.

"Can you accept me as I am?"

She touched his face and said, "You are a human being."

The student took out a chain and locked it around her neck, saying, "When I come back and unlock this lock, then I'll be your husband." With those words he left. They heard nothing of him for three years, for that was as much time as he had left.

After the three years were over, the student was free. He'd been very careful, and the Devil had no claim on him. Finally, he could wash and cut his hair and shave and clean himself all over. When he looked quite elegant, he set out for the millowner's house; and when he arrived, he said that he'd been sent by one of his good friends, who had told him of the marriageable daughters in the house. He asked to see each one in turn. The eldest was sent in first. But as soon as he saw her he said "Ugh!" and sent her away. After her came the second one. "No!" said the student, and she had to leave too. Finally, he asked the youngest in a very kindly way if she would be his wife.

"No," she answered, "I'm already spoken for."

The student tried to tempt her, saying her betrothed was ugly and the reason she hadn't heard from him for so long was that he'd forgotten about her. But the girl stood her ground and simply repeated that she was spoken for; around her neck was a chain that she'd gotten from her fiancé. Even though the student standing before her was a very fine, handsome gentleman who might well have tempted her under other circumstances, she didn't give in.

Taking out a small key, the student walked straight up to her and unlocked the chain around her neck, saying, "I've finally come back. Let's celebrate our wedding!" And a wedding they had, and it was a fine one too, for the student had everything they needed, he did.

That night, as the student stood looking out into the garden with his bride at his side, the Devil poked his head out and said, "You see, I got two instead of one!"

And when they looked around, they saw that the two other girls had hanged themselves out of pure envy.

The Bad Stepmother

Once the father of a girl whose mother had died remarried, and so she got a stepmother. The stepmother also had a daughter, whose name was Malena. But the stepmother wanted to get rid of her stepdaughter, so one day she put a lot of good things into a heavy chest and told her, "This is all for you, if you get in with it." When the girl got in, the stepmother dropped the lid of the chest and squeezed the girl to death. Afterward, she cooked the girl and gave her to her father to eat. Malena collected all the bones and carried them outside.

A few days passed. One day, when the father was walking home from the forest, he saw a bird sitting on the roof, singing. The bird sang as people speak. It sang:

"My mother set a trap for me,
My father ate me up,
My sister Malena
Collected my bones
And put them in a silk scarf
And carried them under the juniper bush."

Then the bird threw a gold bell down to the father and flew away. When the stepsister went outside, the bird sang the same song, and it threw down a gold chain for her.

When the stepmother saw the fine presents, she too went outside, but this time the bird threw down a rock and killed her.

However it happened, the dead girl came back to life again, and afterward the family lived together in peace and harmony.

The Tale of the Copper Pot

A woman and her son worked in a large manor house. They were day laborers who had to do hard, backbreaking work, the way one always did in the old days on the large farms. These people were treated more like animals than people. They were very poor, of course, so poor that they almost didn't have their daily bread.

One day when the boy was walking to work, he felt sad and depressed, for he didn't know how they were going to manage. Suddenly, he met a man who asked him, "Why are you so sad?"

"Well," said the boy, "we're so poor that we have hardly anything to eat."

"Don't be sad anymore," said the man. "I'll give you a copper pot, and all you have to do is put her on the embers in the hearth and tell her to run off and get you anything you want, and she'll do it."

The boy was very grateful, and he ran home to his mother and said, "Look, Mother, now I'll get us some food."

"How can you do that?" the mother said. "That pot's totally empty!"

But the boy just put the pot on the embers, and she said, "I'm running. I'm running!"

"Please run to the manor house kitchen and get us some good food," said the boy.

The pot did as the boy asked, and returned with the most delicious food, and that night they ate until they were quite full. Every night after that, all they had to do was to put the pot on the embers, and she would run for food for them. At the manor house they began to wonder where all the food was disappearing to, for of course it was beginning to be noticeable.

When the woman and her son needed money, all they did was put the pot on the fire.

"I'm running, I'm running," she said.

"Please run up to the master's chest and get us some money," they told her, and off she went. But soon the master began to notice that the money in his chest was dwindling, so he decided to keep watch and find out who was stealing it. One day he heard rumbling in the chest, and when he went to open it, he saw a small copper pot digging around in his money. He grabbed her, but she was so strong that she dragged him with her, and there was nothing he could do. Before he knew it, he was sitting in the poor farmer's house, begging them to please let him go.

But the woman said, "As evil as you've been to us, that's how evil we'll be to you!"

The master told them that if they'd only let him go, he'd give them half of everything he owned. So they did, and later they were very well off, and that's the end of this tale.

The Two Chests

Once there was a king who had a real daughter and a stepdaughter. His second wife was a witch who wanted her daughter to be better and more beautiful than her stepsister, but the real daughter happened to be much more beautiful, and good and kind as well.

So the stepmother decided to get rid of the king's real daughter. She told both daughters to sit at the edge of the well spinning, and the one whose thread broke first would be pushed in. She gave her own daughter the finest linen, and her stepdaughter the worst scraps

from the bottom of the box. Of course hers was the first thread to break. Happily the stepmother pushed her into the well, and she sank all the way down to another world.

She walked along in this world until she came to a fence. "Step gently over me, for I am old and fragile," said the fence. She stepped lightly over the fence. "This will serve you well," the fence said. Then she came to a cow who was grazing with a milk pail on her horn. "Milk me and drink as much as you want, but hang the pail back on the horn," said the cow. She did as the cow had asked. "This will serve you well," said the cow. Then she arrived at an oven full of white-flour buns and delicious sugar cakes. "Eat as many as you wish, but don't take any with you," said the oven. That's what she did. "This will serve you well," the oven said.

When she'd walked a bit farther, she met an old man who offered to take her into service, and she accepted; later she found out that he was a giant. He ordered her to carry water in a sieve. At first she was despondent, but an old cat happened to be walking by, and he screeched, "Press clay into it! Press clay into it!" This she did, and whenever there was anything else she didn't understand, the cat had the answer to that too; in turn, she was kind and good to the cat.

When it was time for her to leave, the cat said, "The old man will bring a red, a blue, and a black chest for you to choose among. Take the black one, and when you go out, stand behind the door. He'll be coming after you with a red-hot poker to burn you, but he won't see you." The girl did as the cat instructed her; she chose the black chest and stood behind the door. The old man didn't catch her.

When she got back home from wherever she'd been, she wanted to open her chest. "You can do that in the pigsty," said the step-mother, for both she and her daughter were furious that the real daughter had returned. She went down to the pigsty, for the cat had told her to be alone when she opened the chest. When she lifted the lid, thick golden chains came pouring out and draped themselves around her neck, and beautiful rings slipped on her fingers; the whole pigsty was covered with so many beautiful things that it didn't look like a pigsty any more.

When the stepmother saw all this, she said, "My daughter's going down there too!" She pushed her own daughter down the well, and she too arrived in the other world.

When she came to the fence, it said, "Please step gently over me, for I am old and fragile." But she kicked it, and the old fence fell down. "This will serve you well," said the fence. Then she came to the cow with the pail on its horn. "Milk me and drink as much as you like, but hang the pail back on the horn again." She milked and drank, but afterward she threw the pail and the milk on the ground. "This will serve you well," said the cow. Then she came to the oven. "Eat as much as you want, but don't take anything with you," the oven said. But she ate all she could, stuffed her pockets, and threw the rest away, leaving the oven empty. "This will serve you well," said the oven.

On her way she met the same old man, who hired her as a maid. She was ordered to carry water in a sieve, and the cat tried to teach her how to do it, but she yelled, "Get out of my way, stupid cat!" and struck and kicked him. She couldn't do anything right! The old man beat her, and the cat tried to help her again, but she always did the opposite of what he said. When the time of her service was up, the cat told her to take the black chest and hide behind the door. But she chose the red one, and the old man chased her with the poker and burned her so that her clothes started smoking and her body was covered with welts.

When she finally got home, the best room in the castle had been prepared for her. But when she opened the lid of the chest, out poured toads and snakes, which crawled all around the room. Long snakes wrapped themselves around her neck and arms. She hadn't listened to the advice of the wise old cat, and he who listens to good advice is all the wiser for it.

Godfather Death

A poor man's wife gave birth to a son. But since the couple already had seven children, they weren't very happy about number eight. The man went out collecting money for christening clothes and food, but no one wanted to be godfather to the beggar's son, for no one wanted to give him a christening gift.

Weeping from sadness and loneliness, the man walked into a big forest. There he met a man whose eyes were as brilliant and blue as the spring sky, whose hair was like gold, and whose voice was lovely music. The handsome man asked, "Why are you crying so much?"

"No one will be godfather to my little son," the poor man said.

"I will," said the shining creature.

"Who are you?" asked the man.

"I am the Good Lord," he answered, and the flowers burst into bloom and the birds sang even more beautifully.

"Well," said the beggar, "if you are God, I don't want you for his godfather. You aren't just. To some you give wealth and happiness, to others poverty and misery." And, crying, he continued on his way.

Then he met a man with eyes that glowed like burning coals. Where he walked the flowers wilted, and snakes coiled in the grass around him.

"Why are you crying?" he said, and a horrid smell of sulphur came out of his mouth.

"No one will be godfather to my son," the beggar said.

"I can be," said the horrible creature.

"Who are you?"

"I am the Devil," he answered, grinning wickedly.

"I don't want you as the godfather of my son; in the end, you reward the people who serve you by tormenting them for eternity."

Later the poor man met a tall, thin figure with a scythe on his shoulder. A chilly fog seemed to come from his mouth, and the grass and flowers froze where he walked.

"Why are you crying so hard?" he said in a cold voice.

"I have a son who is about to be baptized," said the beggar, "but no one will be his godfather."

"I will be the godfather to your son," the gloomy man said.

"Who are you?"

"I am Death," said the man, and a cold gust of wind blew from his mouth. Now the beggar was happy. "Yes, I'll be glad to have you as the godfather," he said. "You treat everyone equally, and play no favorites between highborn and lowborn."

So Death carried the beggar's son at the baptism, and afterward he said, "When my godson turns eighteen, bring him to the place where we met, and I will give him a christening gift."

When the boy was eighteen, his father brought him to the spot where he'd first met his godfather. "My godson will become a doctor," said Death, "and as a christening gift I will give him the power to know if a sick person will die or get well. If he sees me standing at the head of the sickbed, the sick person will die, but if I stand at the foot, he will live."

Soon the boy's fame spread far and wide. As soon as he entered a sickroom, he could say if the patient was going to recover or die—and he was never wrong.

Now it happened that the king's most important advisor took sick. Without this advisor the king couldn't govern his country, so he promised two barrels of gold to anyone who could cure him. When the doctor entered the sickroom, he saw his godfather standing at the head of the bed. The doctor begged him to move to the foot, but he wouldn't, so the godson decided to trick him. He told the servants to turn the bed so that Death was standing at the foot instead of the head; immediately the king's advisor revived, and the doctor got the promised reward.

Death was furious at his godson for tricking him out of what was rightfully his. "If you do that again, you yourself will die."

After a while the king's only daughter took sick. The king said that he couldn't live without her, and he promised half his kingdom and the princess's hand to whoever could make her well. When

Death's godson stepped into the princess's room, he saw his godfather standing at the head of her bed. He fell to his knees, and begged and pleaded with Death to move to the foot of the bed, but he refused. So the doctor decided one more time to turn the bed so that Death was standing at the foot. The princess revived, and a wedding was prepared for her and the doctor who'd saved her.

On the wedding night, while the doctor was sleeping with his beautiful bride, there was a knock on the door. Godfather Death motioned to his godson, who got up and followed him into a cave under the earth. There he saw acres and acres of burning candles. Some had just been lit, while others had burned down almost to their holders.

"What does this mean?" asked Death's godson.

"These are the life candles of human beings," his godfather said.

"Whose is this one?" The godson pointed to one whose flame was barely flickering.

"Yours," said Death, and then pointed to a big candle which had been lit so recently that the flame hadn't quite caught properly. "This one belongs to your son."

The godson fell down before his godfather and begged him to place a new candle in his holder, but Death didn't answer. The flame flickered one last time and went out, and at that moment the godson fell dead.

From this we learn that there is no way to influence or outsmart Death.

The Bear and the Woman

A long time ago a woman was out in the fields tending her cows. As they were grazing peacefully, along came a big, bad bear. The woman, who was pregnant, was so frightened that she couldn't move; she collapsed on a grassy hill, expecting the worst from the wild beast.

Closer and closer came the bear until finally he was right in front of her. She already felt his panting breath, and in her despair, she called to God to protect her. The bear lifted his huge paw, but what happened? Carefully and gently, he placed it on her knee and licked her clenched hands. Astonished, she looked into his imploring eyes. He began to lick his paw, and now she noticed that it was bloody. She gathered up her courage and took a closer look. She could see that a large splinter was stuck in the bear's paw, so she quickly took hold of it and pulled it out.

The bear licked her hands again, took his paw from her lap, and walked away. Surprised and happy, the woman thanked God that the danger had passed. Later, when she was returning home with her cows, the bear came along carrying a large horse thigh in his mouth. He walked up to her and laid it at her feet. Obviously he meant it to be his token of gratitude to her for pulling the splinter out of his paw.

The Boy, the Old Woman, and the Neighbor

Once there was an old woman who was keeping company with the old gent next door. Her husband she neglected something awful; she gave him so little food that he was turning pale blue with hunger.

One day she and her husband hired a servant boy who wasn't too pleased about this state of affairs. He soon figured out what the wife was up to, and decided to set a trap for her. One day when the husband and the servant boy were ploughing a field, the boy said that he was thirsty and asked to go home for a drink.

When he got home, he told the woman that her husband had sent him home for food, so she gave him some bread and butter and a piece of cheese. On his way back to the field, he ate the bread and butter, but he broke the cheese into little pieces, which he threw in the road.

After they'd finished their work and headed for home, the boy walked in front, leading their horse, while the husband lagged behind. When he saw the cheese in the road, the husband thought it a pity that it was lying there getting ruined, and he started picking up the bits. The woman noticed that her husband was walking along picking something up, and she asked the boy what it was.

"Well," he said, "your husband found out that you've been keeping company with the old boy next door, so he's collecting rocks to throw at you. If you confess your crime and beg him for mercy, maybe he'll spare you this time."

Scarcely had the old woman heard what the boy was saying before she ran off, screaming with fear. The husband heard her yowling as if knives had been stuck in her, and he hurried toward home to find out what was going on.

"The farm's on fire!" answered the boy.

At this, the husband took off after his wife to find out where the fire was. But when she saw him running after her, she ran even faster. They ran around and around the buildings, but he was a faster runner than she, and started catching up. When she saw that there was no escape, she threw herself onto her knees and begged him in God's name to spare her this time: she'd never do it again. The husband simply thought that his wife had gone crazy!

Then the boy came along and told his master what was going on, and he asked him to spare her if she promised never to see their neighbor—and to give them both plenty of food from now on. Happy that the punishment wasn't worse, the old woman promised. From that day on, the man and the boy got all the food they wanted, and the woman stopped seeing the old geezer next door.

The Salt Mill

Once there were two brothers, one rich and the other miserably poor. On Christmas Eve the rich brother lit his candles and put all sorts of good food on the table. But the poor brother had neither candles nor firewood nor anything to eat. He went to his brother and asked him for a little food, but his brother said that he couldn't spare a thing. The poor brother didn't give up; he kept nagging and asking for help until finally the rich brother threw a ham at him, saying, "Why don't you go to Hell with it!"

The poor brother did exactly that: he went to Hell. When he arrived at a certain woodpile in Hell, he met an old man with gray hair and a beard that reached down to his feet. The poor brother greeted him and asked if this was Hell. Yes, so it was, he replied. But when the old man saw the ham, he told the poor brother to be on his guard, for at that particular time there was a great shortage of ham in Hell, and he could be certain that the little devils would do anything to get it. They mustn't have it unless they gave him the old grinding mill standing in a corner in Hell.

Inside Hell, he was immediately surrounded by a gang of little demons who started ripping pieces from the ham, shouting, "How much for the ham? How much for the ham?"

The brother swung at them with the knobby stick he carried, and shouted that he wouldn't give them the ham unless they gave him the old grinding mill. That was far too much to ask, they said, but since he wouldn't give in, they finally had to let him have it. Throwing the ham right into the middle of the crowd, he grabbed the mill and bolted for the door. When he got outside Hell to where the old man was standing, he asked him what the mill was good for. "It can grind anything you tell it to grind," said the old man, and he showed him how to start and stop it. The brother thanked him for the information and hurried home.

Back home everything was cold and dark in the poor brother's house. He'd been gone so long that his wife and children sat crying, fearful that something terrible had happened to him. He told them not to cry or be sad; soon they'd have heat and light. Placing the mill on the table, the poor brother ordered it to grind firewood. Immediately, the mill ground out the best dry wood that you could wish for! After that he told it to grind candles and all sorts of good food, and the mill ground everything he asked for. Now they had so much of everything that the king himself couldn't have wanted more.

On Christmas day the poor brother invited his rich brother to visit. When the rich brother saw all their wealth, he was dying of curiosity. So they showed him the mill, and the poor brother commanded it to grind out a few silver trinkets. His eyes round with envy, the rich brother tried to persuade the poor one to sell him the mill. At first he was told that it couldn't be bought for love nor money, but he nagged and nagged, offering more and more money, until finally the poor brother said that even though his brother had been cruel and mean to him, he was still his flesh and blood, and so he'd sell it to him for the highest amount he'd offered. This delighted the rich brother, but even though he hurried home with his new possession, it wasn't until summer that he could bring himself to try it out.

One day during haymaking he told his wife to join the other harvesters gathering in the hay; he'd stay home and do the chores, as well as prepare the dinner. His wife was happy to do this, for he was always complaining that she didn't do enough work at home.

The husband cleaned and fussed and did small chores, and before he knew it it was time to make dinner. His plan was to let the mill prepare the dinner, so he put it on the table and told it to grind out herring and porridge. And so it did; herring and porridge poured out of the mill until all the pots and dishes were full. He tried to stop it, but his brother hadn't told him how, so it continued to grind and grind and grind. Though he put out every dish he could find, they too were filled in a matter of minutes, and soon the herring and porridge started to overflow onto the floor. In a few minutes he was in herring and porridge up to his knees.

He opened the doors to the other rooms, and the herring and porridge followed behind until it reached up to his chin. Luckily, he made it to the front door, and rushed out and away down the road. But the wave of herring and porridge pursued him, and after he'd run for a while, he saw his wife and the harvesters on their way home for dinner.

"Get out of the way, or you'll drown in herring and porridge!" he shouted, and rushed off down the road.

They thought he'd gone mad, and continued toward home. Soon, however, they were met by the torrent of porridge, and now they were the ones who had to take to their heels.

Meanwhile, the rich brother ran off to the poor brother's house, and asked him to come quickly and turn off the mill. But his brother answered that he had no intention of doing that, for once he'd sold the mill, he didn't want to have any more to do with it. After begging and pleading, the brother who now owned the mill said that he'd give it back for nothing if only the flood of herring and porridge would stop. When his brother heard this, it didn't take him long to stop it. This time he kept the mill for a good long time, and it ground out everything he asked, and he became a rich, powerful man.

Around that time, a sea captain from England came to their town after having heard of the miraculous mill. He went to its owner and offered to buy it, but was told that it couldn't be bought for love nor money. But the captain offered so much that finally its owner was persuaded to part with it.

The captain took it on board his ship and sailed away. However, the poor brother had neglected to tell him how to turn it off. When the captain was out in the middle of the ocean, he ordered the mill to grind out salt. He had no idea that it would grind so fast, and figured that he'd have a full load only when he got to the harbor.

But he had a surprise in store: within only a few days the ship was so full of salt that it looked like it might sink. The captain couldn't stop the mill, and the crew couldn't even manage to dump all the salt into the ocean. The result was that the ship sank with captain, crew, and mill.

Now that mill stands at the bottom of the ocean still grinding out salt, and that's why the ocean is salty.

Old Nick and the Widow

Once a rich farmer and a poor widow were neighbors. He was a mean old man, for after he mowed his hay early in the year, he let his cattle loose; as there was nothing but a broken-down fence between their farms, the animals would cross over and eat the widow's uncut hay. When she complained of this to the farmer, he just answered, "Well, if you don't take better care of things, you have no one but yourself to blame!"

During haymaking time the next year, the farmer had just finished mowing when a strange man came to the widow and offered to cut all her hay.

"Of course it's a fine thing to get some help," she said, "but I have to be honest and tell you that I've nothing to pay you."

"Oh, that's not so important," the fellow said, and took off for the field with his scythe. But before he left, he told the widow to bring him his food, and she promised that she would.

When she brought his breakfast, however, she found him just resting there by the field. It was the same thing when she brought the other meals, but she said nothing. At the evening meal he finally stood up and said, "Go to your neighbor and tell him that if he hasn't gotten his animals off your field before sunset, their legs will be chopped off."

The widow told her neighbor, but he just laughed and left the animals where they were. It went just as the mower had said, and after sunset he and his crew set to work, and a proper job they did— for before the sun came up, the entire field had been cut.

And Old Nick wanted no payment.

The Lazy Boy and the Industrious Girl

I was sitting on a bench in a park in Vänersborg* in the beginning of the 1880s. Soon after I arrived, a couple of the town's artisans came and sat down on the bench. They discussed social questions for a while, and finally one of them told this story.

In the Beginning it was decided that one person must labor for another. When Jesus walked on earth with His disciples, they came to a field where the grain was being cut. The servant boy cut the grain, but always rested when he got to one end of the field. The

---

* Vänersborg is a town in Dalsland in western Sweden.

servant girl, on the other hand, worked so hard that the sweat poured off her without a minute's pause.

Then the disciples said to the Master, "You ought to give that girl a reward for all her hard work."

"Yes," said the Master, "she'll get the lazy boy for a husband."

"But isn't that being unjust toward the girl?" the disciples said.

"No," said the Master. "You see, it's the lot of one human to carry another through life."

The Parson's Wife Who Had No Shadow

A parson married a woman who'd asked a witch to help her avoid having children. The witch had told her to take some stones and throw them over her left shoulder into a well, and then listen for what she would hear. She heard screams from three of the stones, and returned to the witch to tell her all about it. The witch told her that these were the screams of the three children she would have had—but now she'd killed them.

One day when the parson and his wife were walking in the garden, he discovered that she had no shadow: he had one, but she didn't. He walked all the way around her looking for the shadow, but there wasn't any. He realized that she must have done something unusual, and insisted that she tell him what it was. Oh, he was so angry with her—for he had so much wanted to have children—that he divorced her. He also told her that it would be as impossible for her to go to Heaven as it was for flowers to grow on the stone ceiling of his bedroom.

She had to go away and beg for her living, and she suffered greatly. Ten years passed, and then one day a woman came to the parsonage asking to spend the night there. She was so ragged and miserable-looking that the servants said she couldn't stay, for they didn't dare let anyone who looked like that into the house. Finally, however, they took pity on her and told her that if she wanted to lie behind the stove and be absolutely quiet, she could stay. So she went and lay down behind the stove.

The next morning she didn't get up. The parson came in and asked if strangers were there. The servants denied it, but he insisted that someone must be there. So they had to tell him about the woman behind the stove. When they went to look, they found that she was dead.

That morning, when the parson had awakened, he'd seen the most beautiful flowers growing on his ceiling, and he'd understood that what she'd done had been done in ignorance, and therefore she had been forgiven.

The Despised Rake

Once a servant girl who had gone away to service came home to visit. Looking very handsome and acting in a high and mighty manner, she stepped into the small, low-ceilinged cottage just as her mother was in the midst of baking and raking coals out of the oven. Of course the mother was happy to see her, and they chatted on and on, and that's when the mother noticed that the maid had started talking fancy. After her mother had finished raking out the oven and placed the rake, head down, beside the oven, the girl went up to the rake and acted as if she didn't even know what an odd thing like that was called. As she stood there speculating and wondering and pretending to have forgotten all about it, she accidently stepped on the head of the rake so that the shaft flew up and struck her, and then she yelled, "Ouch, the devil of a rake shaft attacked me!" When she got mad, she had no trouble remembering its name!

The Tale of the Sculptor's Beautiful Wife

Once there was a sculptor who made statues just like the ones that you can still see today here and there. He had a wife so beautiful that the parson, the sexton, and the organist all wanted her.

She complained that they were always running after her and coming to see her, so she and her husband decided to play a trick on them. She made a date to meet them one Saturday night, when they'd all get their chance to be with her. The sculptor went out to have a few drinks, and she stayed home to receive them. She'd scheduled it so that they'd arrive with a half-hour between each visit.

The parson was the first to come. She told him that she wouldn't let him touch her unless he took off all his clothes. When he was ready, the sexton knocked on the door and asked to come in. So she said to the parson, "Oh, gracious me! Here comes my husband! What will we do now? You'll just have to go out there." And she opened the door to the sculptor's studio, and threw the parson's clothes in behind him; he'd have to stay there until later.

As soon as the sexton came in, he wanted her right away. But he got the same story: he had to get undressed too, for otherwise she wouldn't let him. So of course he did, and no wonder, since she'd gotten the parson to do it already.

Then the organist knocked. Again she said, "Gracious, my husband is coming!" Out into the studio went the sexton too. Again the same thing happened, and this time the husband knocked, and she said, "Gracious, my husband is coming!" So the organist had to go the way of the other two. When her husband came in, his wife had the coffee waiting, and he and the people he'd brought along sat down at a table to drink coffee grogs.

After they'd been drinking for a while, they went out to the studio to look at his sculptures. The sculptor brought along a candle and lit it so they could see what they were doing. There seemed to be a lot of sculptures. When they got to the organist, they stopped to look at him, and the guests asked what kind of sculpture that was. "Ah," said the sculptor, "that's my candlestick," and he stuck the candle in the organist's ass. The organist stood quite still while the candle continued to burn.

Then they went to look at the other two "sculptures." The guests asked what they were, and the sculptor answered, "Adam and Eve." Then they said, "But that's wrong, for they both have sticks." So he said, "That's no problem. I can fix that in a jiffy." He went to fetch his hammer and chisel and was about to chop off the parson's stick. But before he could start, off ran the organist with the candle in his ass, and the other two followed right behind, with the organist lighting the way.

At the Sunday service the parson was shabbily dressed, for he'd lost all his clothes. The other two were shabbily dressed as well; they'd all been wearing their Sunday best. When the parson went to sing at the altar, he sang, "I had a terrible adventure last night." And the sexton answered, "And so did I, did I, did I." All the organist could say was, "Diddledee, diddledee, diddledee dee—diddledee, diddledee, diddledee dee."

And that was the end of that story. I heard it when I was very young.

The Big Turnip

Once upon a time, in the days when Saint Peter and Our Lord walked on earth, there was a rich farmer and a poor farmer who farmed the same piece of land. Together they'd cleared and burned off the field, and now they were planning to sow turnips. On Midsummer Night's Eve, they both went out to sow—first the rich man and then the poor.

On his way the rich farmer met Saint Peter and Our Lord.

"How do you do, my friend! Where are you headed?" Our Lord asked.

"I'm off to sow a turnip," answered the farmer.

"Then one turnip is all you'll get," said Our Lord.

A while later they met the poor farmer.

"How do you do, and where are you going?" asked Our Lord.

"I'm going out to sow turnips," answered the poor man.

"Then turnips it shall be!" said Our Lord.

Later, when the farmers went to harvest their turnips, the rich man found on his field only one solitary turnip—the biggest turnip that anyone had ever seen; on the poor man's field there was a good crop of ordinary-sized turnips. But the rich farmer was greedy, and he forced the poor one to exchange with him so that he got the ordinary turnips and the poor man got the big turnip. Because the rich farmer was more powerful, the poor man had no choice but to go along with him.

That night he lay in bed, sighing deeply.

"What are you groaning about?" asked his wife.

"I have the best of reasons," he answered. "Our Lord made many turnips grow on my field, but our rich neighbor has taken them, and all we got is his single solitary turnip. How will we feed all our children?"

"Calm down, the Good Lord will watch over us. Anyway, I have an idea. Why don't you take the turnip to the king? He's probably never seen anything like it, and he may pay you well for it."

"I'll try that," said the old man, and fell asleep.

In the morning he harnessed his old mare to the wagon and went to town. The king received him with great kindness and gave him a whole bag full of silver coins for the turnip.

The farmer went home, overjoyed, and when he arrived, he went to his rich neighbor to borrow a bushel measure.

The neighbor became very curious. Why would a poor farmer want a bushel measure? When he learned that the poor farmer needed it to measure money, he was filled with resentment and envy.

"If the king can give away that much money for a turnip," he thought, "what wouldn't he give me for my beautiful horses? I think I'll go and give them to him."

The next day he ordered his boy to hitch up the wagon and accompany him and his beautiful horses to town.

When they got to court, the rich farmer presented the horses to the king.

"And what shall I give you in return?" asked the king, adding quietly to himself, "I think I see the lay of *this* land!"

Then he whispered something to one of his courtiers. A little while later, two courtiers came in carrying a big bundle wrapped in a cloth.

"Here you are, my friend. I'll give you something that cost me several thousand riksdaler,*" said the king to the farmer. "But you mustn't open it till you get home; otherwise someone might steal it."

The rich farmer bowed and scraped humbly before the king, and then went on his way. When he got home, he called his wife to stand at his side while he unwrapped his precious gift. Just imagine what happened when he looked inside and saw—of course—his own gigantic turnip!

---

* An old Swedish monetary unit; see note on page 87.

"Yet a Little While, and the World Seeth Me No More"

PARSONS,
THE GOOD LORD,
AND
THE EVIL ONE

"Yet a Little While, and the World Seeth Me No More"

Once there was a minister who was so short that he had to place an empty herring keg upside down on the pulpit to stand on while he said his sermon. One Sunday as he was standing there, he read, "Yet a little while, and the world seeth me no more." * At that very moment the bottom of the herring keg collapsed, and the minister disappeared!

The Devil and the Tailor

A long, long time ago, so long ago that the Devil wore a *koperklortel*,† he went one day to visit a tailor. He wanted to make a deal with this tailor. You see, at that time the Evil One used to snoop around looking for sinners because he didn't have enough of them back home in the Smoky Place.

Like I say, one day he came to this tailor and asked him, "Will you sell your soul to me? I'll give you a big bundle of money. I'm very rich."

He pulled out a fistful of thousand-riksdaler‡ coins from his pants pocket and showed them to the tailor. But even though the tailor had no desire to sell his soul to Horn John, he had nothing against the money, so he mulled it over a long while before he answered. Finally, he said, "If you can beat me in a sewing contest, you can have me when you want. But if you lose, I'll take the money you just showed me."

"That's a deal," the Evil One answered. As you probably can

---

* John 14: 19.

† *Koperklortel*: dialect term for an unspecified piece of clothing, perhaps some sort of copper girdle, that the Devil presumably wore.

‡ An old Swedish monetary unit; see note on page 87.

tell, he was just as proud and conceited as he had been at the beginning of the world when he sinned against Our Lord.

"Now, when we have our sewing contest," the tailor said, "we must sit on the church roof. There we'll have enough room not to get in each other's way as we swing our arms around."

"That's fine with me," said the Evil One.

"And we've got to use long threads in our needles, so that we don't have to thread them so often when we get going," the tailor said.

"That's terribly good advice," replied the Evil One, and proceeded to unwind nearly a whole spool of thread and to thread it through his needle. The tailor just pretended that he'd taken a long piece of thread.

When they started to sew, the Evil One had to crawl down from the church roof and walk far out into the graveyard for every stitch he pulled through the fabric; he'd let the tailor fool him into taking such a long piece of thread! He hustled and bustled and ran up and down as fast as he could, but he lost anyway, and he had to give the tailor the fistful of money. But that was no blessing, because it turned out to be nothing but coal bits and wood chips.

Kitta Gray

Kitta Gray was an ugly but very shrewd old crone. She outsmarted even the Devil himself.

One time she made a bet with him that she could beat him in a footrace. They chose to run through a swamp—it was the swamp down by Klöse in Västergötland, by the way—and Kitta Gray promised that if the Devil won she'd give herself to him.

When the race started, they both ran off into the swamp. Before long Kitta Gray started falling behind, but the Devil didn't notice; he was too busy racing ahead. When he reached the finish line, he was surprised to find the old woman already there, peeking out from behind a bush. Then they ran back again, and the old woman fell behind once more, and the Devil pulled ahead. But when they ar-

rived at the finish line, there she was again, thumbing her nose at him. And they continued on in this way, back and forth, back and forth, until the Devil, who was completely exhausted, finally had to give up.

The fact is that Kitta Gray had a sister who looked so much like her that you couldn't tell them apart, and she and her sister had positioned themselves at either end of the swamp. That was the way Kitta Gray fooled the Devil.

In that same region lived a merchant whose business was doing very poorly. One day the Devil showed up and offered to help him. When the merchant complained that he had no customers no matter how good his merchandise was, the Devil told him that he'd get him so many customers that he wouldn't be able to meet the demand. The merchant didn't believe it; he said that if the day ever came when he ran out of goods to sell, that day the Devil could come for him.

From then on, business began to pick up. One day the merchant saw that he'd sold almost everything. Now he started to get worried, for he realized that he'd sold his soul to the Devil. Then he thought of Kitta Gray. He sent for her and told her how things were. She said, "Make a glass cabinet and put me inside. Then tell people that I'm for sale."

When the Devil arrived, thinking that he was about to claim his victim, he asked the merchant how business was going.

"Very well, except for one item that seems to be terribly hard to sell."

When the Devil asked what it was, the merchant showed him the cabinet in which Kitta Gray sat laughing. When the Devil saw her, he said, "Anyone who knows Kitta Gray would never, ever buy her."

And he rushed out the door, never to return.

The Pregnant Parson

A parson had a beautiful daughter whom he watched over with loving care. But he was also as stingy as a miser, and the only farmhand he would hire was one who was afraid of womenfolk; for the parson was so stingy that he wouldn't pay for more than one bed for the girl and the farmhand.

One day a Västgöta* came along looking for work.

"Are you scared of womenfolk?" asked the parson.

"No, is there any reason I should be?" the man replied, throwing out his chest and acting real manly.

"Well then, I don't want you," said the parson.

But when the farmhand saw the lay of the land, he left, and came back again later to ask for work.

"Are you scared of womenfolk?" the parson asked.

"Oh, bless me, yes! If you have any of those, I don't want to be here," he said.

So he got the job. He was to sleep in the same bed as the girl, but since he was so scared of womenfolk, there was no danger, as I'm sure you can see.

But the girl must have observed what the parson and his wife did every now and then, and when some time had passed, she asked the farmhand what they were doing.

"Well, they're brushing each other," he said.

"Won't you give me a brushing?" the girl said. "They seem to be having a good time."

"Oh, heavens no! That brush is too expensive," he said.

"Well, how much would a brush like that cost?"

"Not less than a hundred riksdaler," he said.

So the girl went and took a hundred riksdaler from the parson, and slipped them to the farmhand. And then you should have seen them brushing!

After a while the parson got suspicious and kicked the farmhand off the farm. But the girl thought that the brush belonged to her, so she ran after him. When they got to a stream, the farmhand shouted that he was throwing the brush into the water, and the girl jumped in and started searching for it. However, it happened that the parson came along, and when he heard what an expensive brush the farmhand had thrown into the water, he undressed and joined in the

---

* A Västgöta is a person from Västergötland in southwest Sweden.

search. But when the girl saw what he had underneath his shirt, she went right up and grabbed it and gave herself a real thorough brushing.

Now the parson was worried. Since he'd been underneath, he was sure that he'd be the one to get pregnant. And when he started swelling up and getting fat, he peed into a bottle and sent it to a wise man to find out what the matter was.

On the way, however, the messenger boy dropped the bottle and spilled its contents. Since he didn't want to go all the way back, he put the bottle under the rump of a cow who was just then taking care of a little business, and he took this to the wise man.

The wise man mumbled and recited from a book, and finally said that whoever owned what was in the bottle would give birth to a red and white calf. The boy brought back this message to the parson.

As you can imagine, the parson was horrified, so he left home because he didn't want his parishioners to find out what was about to happen.

During his wanderings he came upon a man who had hanged himself. Stingy as he was, he noticed that the man was wearing a pair of brand-new boots, but since it was cold, the legs had frozen and he couldn't remove the boots without cutting the legs off at the knees. So that's what he did, and then he trudged off—boots, leg stumps, and all.

That evening he was given lodging on a farm where they were waiting for the cow to calve.

That's right!

The parson placed the boots by the stove to thaw the legs, and lay down to sleep.

But that night the cow calved, and the calf got up and hopped and staggered around the floor the way calves do. It was cold outside, so the servant girl carried it inside to keep warm. Suddenly, the calf licked the parson right in the snout, and he woke up.

"The damn thing has come!" he thought. "Now I'm done for!"

And he ran out the door, forgetting boots and everything.

But in the morning when the servant girl came in, the calf was standing there licking the boots. She raced over, looked at the leg stumps, and got completely terrified.

She ran to the farmer shouting, "Oh, my God! Please forgive me!

I brought the calf into the kitchen with the vagabond, and do you know what it did? It ate the man, and now there are only boots and leg stumps left!"

Forging with Sand

Once there was a blacksmith who was making scythes, but he couldn't temper them. Finally he had to ask the Devil, but the Devil wouldn't teach him the trick. Someone volunteered to help the smith, and made him a scythe out of wood and painted it to look like it had been tempered.

"Hang it up above the door of the smithy," he said.

So the blacksmith nailed it up.

Before long the Devil himself came along, and believing it was a real scythe, he said, "So you've used sand!"

That was the way he was fooled, for now the blacksmith knew how to do it.

The Parson, the Sexton, and the Devil

I almost forgot to tell you what happened when our parson decided to drive the Devil out of the church. I'd better tell it, for it's as good a ghost story as any.

Well, it so happened that we'd gotten ourselves a new sexton,* and a real joker he was, who liked to think up one bit of mischief worse than the next. He'd heard that the parson had been bragging about being able to drive out ghosts and such. "It'd be fun to actually

---

* In earlier times in Swedish Lutheran churches, the sexton, or parish clerk *(klockaren)*, took care of various church-related affairs, including preparing for the service, bookkeeping, and sometimes even playing the organ.

see Our Father do that," thought the sexton, and started figuring out how to arrange it.

So one Saturday night right after sunset the sexton was walking in the graveyard when he saw the parson's big black sow, which was also roaming around in there.

"I've got it!" he said, and opened the church door.

"Walk right in," he said to the sow, and pushed it into the church. "Now the parson will have his hands full."

He locked the door, put the key in his pocket, and walked up to the parsonage. The parson was sitting there relaxing when the sexton walked in.

"Something strange is going on in church," the sexton said. "When I walked past the door, there was such a terrible racket. I was going to hang up the numbers for tomorrow's psalms, but I had to beg God to protect me."

"You don't say!" said the parson.

"Oh yes I do!" said the sexton, and looked so distressed that the parson didn't know what to think.

"Very well then," he said. "God willing, I'd better go and fight it out." He put on his coat and collar, and stuck a book under his arm. "If you come along, you'll see what kind of powers have been bestowed upon me."

The sexton pretended that he didn't want to come, but at last he let himself be persuaded.

When they arrived, there was an awful ruckus. The sow was thrashing about, knocking down everything she could reach; you can imagine that she didn't care much for being alone in the church.

"Have you got the key?" said the parson.

"Yes," the sexton said, unlocking the door.

The parson stood in the doorway and was about to start reading, but he hadn't said a word before the Black One came rushing out like mad right between the parson's legs, and the sow shrieked and the parson was frightened, and that's how he sat on the back of the sow and was carried away.

"Tell them at home that the Devil took me!" the parson yelled.

"I'll make sure of that," answered the sexton. And he did.

The Sermon About Nothing

Once there was a minister who was asked to give a trial sermon in the cathedral. The bishop didn't give him the text until he was on his way up to the pulpit, and when he unfolded the paper, one side was blank. When he turned it over, he found that the other side was blank too.

The minister said to himself, "Well, if it says nothing, it was from nothing that God created Heaven and Earth."

And on this theme he delivered a sermon that won him the ministry.

Sven Fearless

A long time ago one of the citizens of this country was a very rich gentleman who owned a grand manor house. But he got little pleasure from it, because the Devil himself liked to spend the night in one of the rooms, and of course no human could stay there.

Now you shouldn't think that this gentleman was a good friend of the Devil. On the contrary, he promised his only daughter as well as a generous dowry to anyone who would dare to spend a night in the room and show that he was a match for the Devil. Many tried, but the Devil wrung their necks, every one of them; in the morning they all lay stone dead on the floor.

A poor widow lived near the manor house with her three sons. The youngest was named Sven, but over the years they'd taken to calling him Sven Fearless; it was he who decided to try his hand at scaring the Devil out of the rich man's house. When Sven's two older brothers heard about this, they asked to come along, not because they were brave but because they hoped to trick Sven into doing the work while they grabbed the prize.

Sven wasn't especially keen on having them along, but since they insisted, he finally agreed on the condition that they act as his helpers.

When he arrived at the manor house, he asked for lodging for himself and his two servants. The gentleman answered that it wasn't a good idea, for as things stood, anyone who stayed there and tried to outsmart the Devil lost his life.

"Is that all?" answered Sven Fearless. "Then I think I'll give it a try. But if I succeed—as humble as I am—I would like that reward."

The gentleman promised that he'd have it, for you can imagine how he felt with the Devil in his house.

Now Sven Fearless asked the gentleman to put a carpenter's vise and three newly slaughtered, unplucked geese in the room. He also asked for permission to light a fire so that he could cook the geese.

When night fell, Sven Fearless brought his two less-than-fearless brothers into the room. After plucking one of the geese, he told his eldest brother, "It's time to bring in wood for the fire. Would you like to stay here with our brother, or go to the attic for wood?"

"I'm not staying in the Devil's room without you," answered the eldest, and went up into the attic. He figured that it would be a while before he'd have to come back down again.

But when he reached the attic, he got so scared of the dark that he just grabbed a few logs and tried to hurry back down again. But when he put his foot on the ladder, one of the Devil's men yanked it, and he fell down and split open his skull. He died on the spot, and the Devil's henchmen dragged his body away.

"He's taking awfully long with that wood," said Sven Fearless to his other brother. "If you stay here with the geese, I'll go see what's going on."

"No, I can do that," answered the brother, for he thought, "If I get out of here, I won't come back before it gets light in the east!" But when he started up the attic steps, one of the Devil's men caught him, wrung his neck, and made off with his body.

"Seems like I'd better fetch the wood myself," said Sven after waiting for his brothers. He climbed the ladder, followed by the Devil's man.

"Come on down! It's me, Sven Fearless, calling you!" said Sven, thinking that his brothers were in the attic. When the Devil's henchman heard who he was, he got scared and tried to turn back, but Sven Fearless kicked backward with his iron-capped boot heel and sent him flying all the way out into the courtyard as though he were nothing but a wisp of straw. Then Sven Fearless got the firewood himself, carried it back down into the room, lit a fire, and sat down to pluck the second goose.

The door flew open, and the Devil himself came in.

"What's going on here?" he asked Sven Fearless.

"I'm just plucking a goose. I mean to cook three, but there's one more that still needs plucking. If you do it, I'll give you a taste of the roast."

One of the geese was already turning on the spit over the fire. When the Devil smelled the meat cooking, he wanted some, so he sat down to pluck the third goose. "I'll still have time to wring the fool's neck," he thought.

"What are you doing?" shouted Sven Fearless. "The way you pluck that goose, you're tearing out the delicious lard! Let me have a look. Yes, your claws are much too long. Come here, I can cut them with this pair of scissors."

The Devil had to admit that his claws really were far too long for the job, so he let Sven fool him into placing all ten claws into the vise. And Sven, he tightened it for all he was worth, you can depend on that!

The Devil, he hopped and he screamed and he hissed, but Sven Fearless kept him there while he turned the spit, and the goose smelled more and more delicious.

Finally, the Devil had to beg for mercy. He promised to agree to anything if only Sven would let him go. So Sven demanded that he leave the manor house and its grounds forever.

"All right, but couldn't you just leave me the hill farthest from the farm?" said the Devil. "And if I ever trespass on your territory, I'll be your prisoner, but if you ever walk on that hill, you'll be mine."

"It's a deal," answered Sven Fearless, for he liked to be fair to everyone, and even the Devil deserved his due.

So Sven let him out of the vise. You can imagine that it didn't take the Devil long to slink away to nurse his sore fingers.

At daybreak Sven Fearless went to the gentleman and claimed his daughter's hand as well as the large dowry.

Soon afterward, the gentleman died and Sven inherited the manor house and all its grounds. One day he and his wife went driving in a carriage to survey the estate. He'd brought along a gun, thinking that he might shoot a hare for dinner. When they got to the Devil's hill, he saw a hare sitting there, and he grabbed his gun, jumped out of the carriage, and ran up the hill.

"Now you're mine!" shouted the Devil, for it was he who'd had the cunning idea of changing himself into a hare.

"Yes, you've got me now," answered Sven Fearless. "All I ask is to be allowed to say goodbye to my wife. Then I'll go with you."

"Since you gave me this hill, I'll grant your wish," said the Devil.

So Sven Fearless went to his wife and told her the trouble he was in. But he also told her that he thought he could fool the Devil one more time—with her help.

Well, she was more than willing to do anything for her husband, for she'd come to love Sven Fearless dearly.

Sven picked her up and put her over his shoulder so that her feet pointed toward the Devil.

"What have you got there?" asked the Devil when he saw Sven returning.

"Oh, well, these are just my scissors," answered Sven. "I travel with them everywhere."

"No! No!" screamed the Devil. "Away with you and your scissors! I've had enough!"

And he ran down the hill, never to trouble Sven Fearless again.

The Tale of the Parson and the Sexton

Once upon a time like all other times, there was a parson who said in his Sunday sermon that he who gives with a pure heart whatever he can will be rewarded tenfold.

When the sexton got home and thought about the parson's words, he took his only cow and led her over to the parson's house. The parson thanked him warmly and the sexton went home. But since the sexton's cow was bigger than the parson's cows, she got to wear the bell, and toward nightfall she returned to the place she knew best.

Now the fact is that wherever the bell cow goes, there go all the other cows, and so when the sexton saw his cow returning with the parson's ten cows, he led them all inside. The parson sent his servant over to the sexton's house to get his cows back, but the sexton wouldn't return them. Then the parson himself came calling, all high and mighty, demanding his cows back. "Are you crazy?" answered the sexton. "As you yourself said in church today, he who gives whatever he can with a pure heart will be rewarded tenfold. That's what I've done, and so the animals are mine."

"Very well," said the parson after thinking it over. "But why don't we say that whichever of us gets up first tomorrow morning gets the animals?"

The sexton agreed. Hardly had the parson gone home before the sexton went to the parsonage and climbed up into a pear tree right in front of the parson's bedroom window.

When night fell, the parson asked a maid to stay with him and help wake him up. After a while he asked the girl if she'd ever heard or read about the time Pilate rode into Jerusalem. Yes, she'd heard about that. Then he asked her if she'd like him to show her the way Pilate rode into Jerusalem, and the girl agreed. After Pilate had made his journey, the parson needed to go out to pass water and see if the sky was getting lighter. When he'd finished and was about to go inside, the sexton coughed and blew his nose very hard to make the parson notice.

"What, are you here?" he said.

"Yes," said the sexton, "I've been here ever since Pilate rode into Jerusalem."

"Oh well, since perhaps you've seen and heard a thing or two, by all means keep the animals."

The sexton honestly felt that he deserved the cows, so he didn't hesitate.

> And they sat in the barn,
> They mended their shoes,
> And if they haven't died
> Then they're still alive.

The Farmer Who Sold His Soul to the Devil

Once there was a farmer who made a pact with the Devil. The Devil would help him become rich and powerful if he'd sell his soul to him after a certain number of years. The farmer was lucky and successful at everything he did, and became wealthy and powerful. But when his time was growing near, the Devil came to remind him of his end of the bargain.

"But I still have so much to accomplish," said the farmer. "Won't you please give me a few more years?"

"On one condition," replied the Devil. "If, on the day I come to claim you, you can meet me in a carriage harnessed to animals stranger than the ones I have, I'll give you what you want. If not, you'll have to come away with me down to Hell."

And with that the Devil disappeared.

After a few days passed, the farmer began to grow uneasy. He didn't know what animals to harness to his carriage. When the day finally came, he pulled out his carriage onto the road, jumped in, and ordered his wife and maid to come out and help him. He told them to grab hold of the crossbar and pull the carriage witn their backsides facing front and their upper bodies bent down over their hands. Finally, he pulled their skirts all the way up to cover their heads, and told them to start moving.

He'd barely gotten settled in the carriage when a coach harnessed to two magpies pulled up. As soon as the two wagons met, the coach stopped and the Devil stepped out. When he saw the farmer's draw horses, he said, "Never saw anything like those horses before! Because you're so clever, I'll give you the extension you want."

Then the Devil disappeared, coach and magpies and all.

The Night-Blind Parson

In olden days, when ministers used to get around on foot, there once was a parson whose eyesight was so bad that people said he was night-blind. Whenever he went to visit his parishioners, his sexton had to go along with him. But this parson was so stingy that he wouldn't carry a sack of food for himself or pay the sexton anything for giving him food out of his sack.

"Just you wait," thought the sexton. "One of these days I'll pay you back in kind."

One day the sexton came to the parson, looking so forlorn and pathetic that poor farmers would cry and rich ones weep—that's how miserable he looked. When the parson asked what the matter was, the sexton said he'd heard prophecies that the world would be destroyed by a new Flood at harvest time.

When the parson heard this, he got very upset; since he didn't know much about the Prophets, he believed that everything they said always came true. Now he was completely convinced that the end of the world was at hand, and he asked the sexton in a pitiful voice what the two of them should do to avoid getting drowned.

The sexton suggested that they find a tall mountain, put a boat on top, and wait there for the Flood. So the next day they started out on their journey.

But even now the parson was so stingy that he didn't bring along a food sack; his plan was to live off the sexton and all the people they met along the way. But that rascal of a sexton hadn't brought along any food either; he'd decided that he'd rather starve than give the parson one single bite.

So they walked along, up hill and down dale. They didn't find any mountains, and the parson decided that none of the hills they saw was high enough. Soon it was past noon, and the parson's belly was spinning like a cat. The sexton had carefully avoided towns and farms, so finally the parson had to admit that he was famished. The sexton bent down, picked up a handful of sheep pellets, and pretended to eat them. Thinking they were boiled horse beans,* the parson quickly gobbled up a handful before he stopped to examine them more closely. And then he chastised the sexton severely for his gluttony and unclean tastes!

---

* Horse beans are large, smooth, flat beans (*Vicia faba*) used as a food staple in parts of Europe; they are also called broad beans or fava beans.

Toward evening, the sexton brought them to a farm where he knew there were warm beds and good food. But before they went in, he warned the parson not to be too greedy, in part because it wasn't fitting for a man of the cloth, in part because he'd be too heavy to run in case the Flood began in the middle of the night.

Now it happened that this parson could never really tell when he'd had enough to eat. So he asked the sexton to step on his foot when it was time to stop eating, and this he promised to do.

Inside the farmhouse, their hosts invited them to sit down at the table, and they made them comfortable in every way. By this time the sexton himself was ravenous, and he didn't have the heart to starve the parson any longer. But then the cat started stepping on the parson's feet. Of course the parson thought that it was the sexton, and since he himself didn't know when to stop, he figured that now was the time, even though his stomach was sending him a clear message that said, "I want more!"

Later that evening the bench by the stove was made up for the two travelers, and the farmer and his wife slept in their alcove in the living room. But, as we know, the parson was almost night-blind, so he always brought along a string, which he tied to the bedpost and the door, or wherever he thought he'd need to get to in the middle of the night. After the farmer and his wife had fallen asleep, he asked the sexton to tie the string to the door handle so that he could find his way outside if he had to go, and this the sexton did.

In the middle of the night the parson woke up, complaining that he was starving. To get some peace the sexton whispered that there was food on the counter next to the door. All the parson had to do was follow the string, and he'd find what he wanted.

So the parson got up and tiptoed over to the counter. The first thing he found was a jug that was wide at the opening but narrow around the neck. He pushed his hand down inside and discovered some porridge, so he grabbed a handful but then couldn't get his hand out again. However, he wasn't about to open his hand—that's how much he wanted that porridge.

Rousing the sexton out of his warm bed, he begged him to help him out. But when the sexton woke up, his old mischievousness came back, and instead of getting the parson's hand out of the jar, he moved the end of the string to the farm couple's bed. The woman was lying on the outer edge of the bed with her nice side turned toward her husband, just as proper women do.

The porridge jug was overflowing, but the parson still had no intention of opening his hand.

"It's getting all over me!" he whispered.

"Then go over to the end of the table. There's a towel. I'll move the string," that rascal of a sexton said, but instead of doing that, he just went back to bed.

The parson followed the string to where the farmer and his wife lay sleeping. In his sleep the farmer had pulled most of the cover off his wife, and the poor parson, who couldn't tell a nightgown from a dish towel, fumbled with the woman's nightgown and the sticky porridge jar until the poor woman began to feel something cold on her, and she turned around in bed to warm her other side. This woke her husband, who accidentally touched the woman's smeared nightgown. He scolded her something awful, accusing her of making on herself, and told her to go straight to the well and clean up.

The woman couldn't help thinking that she'd done something bad in her sleep, so she climbed out of bed. The sexton, who'd been watching all along, guided the parson into a corner, and while she stood fiddling with her slippers, he moved the string again and tied it to the well in the yard. Thinking that the woman had gone into the kitchen, the parson once again listened to the sexton, who told him to follow the string out to the yard where he could get the jug off and eat the lovely porridge.

When he got out there, the woman stood crying by the well while she washed the porridge off the bottom of her nightgown in the water trough. Suddenly, thinking that she was the well beam, the parson smashed the jug right into her "good afternoon," and she let out a shriek. This time the farmer and the dog both woke up, and they started barking for all they were worth. When the farmer came out and found the parson with his woman, things went from bad to worse, and finally both parson and sexton were kicked right off the farm.

The next night the sexton and the parson came to a household where no one was at home; the people were laborers who worked at the nearby estate. In the kitchen stood a large kneading trough, and when the parson saw it, he was as happy as a lark, for he thought that it might save his life in case the Flood came that night. He told the sexton to make a bed for him in the trough and hang it up under the ceiling with some cow tethers that were lying in the kitchen. This the sexton did, and before long the parson was lying in the hanging cradle, safely awaiting the end of the world. The sexton made himself a bed in a room off the kitchen.

Later that night the young town blacksmith came up to the window of the sexton's room, quietly calling for the farmer's daughter; she was his sweetheart, and he thought that she was at home alone because she'd been sick the day before. The sexton opened the window a crack to hear what the fellow wanted.

"Are you still so sick, you poor thing?" whispered the blacksmith.

"My whole body is hurting," moaned the sexton.

"Would you like a snack? I've brought you a taste of beer and a bit of bread and butter," said the blacksmith.

"I'll give it a try," the sexton promised, sticking his hand out the window and pulling in a mug and a long sandwich as thick as an oak plank. The sexton quickly finished off both wet and dry; then he said thank you and gave back the mug.

"You might at least get up on your knees and give me a kiss," said the blacksmith.

"I've got such bad breath," answered the sexton, for he had bristles like a pig around his mouth, and didn't want to give himself away.

"I don't mind," said the blacksmith, who was quite mad about the farmer's daughter.

And now the Devil got into the sexton again, and he put his backside out the window. But first he told the blacksmith that he—meaning the girl—was swollen around the cheeks. The blacksmith greedily kissed what was offered, but then he noticed that this didn't really feel like the girl's face. But he didn't let on, and went home, promising very sweetly to come back very soon.

Too full of food and mischief to fall asleep, the sexton lay there wondering how he could fool the blacksmith again. Before he knew it, the smith returned, begging for another kiss. The sexton stuck the same face as before out the window. But now the blacksmith took a red-hot iron that he'd hidden behind his back, and gave him such a hot kiss that he started screaming for all he was worth, "Water, water!"

This woke the parson, who thought that the Flood had come. He pulled out his trusty pocket knife and cut the tethers so that the trough could float. But he fell to the floor so hard that his heart flew right into his throat, and all thoughts of the Flood went straight to Hell!

The Burning Lake

Two students decided to go to a parson and tell him a story so outrageous that he'd pay them just to keep it quiet.

The first student went to the parson and related two strange events that he'd just heard about. The first was that God in Heaven had died, and the second was that the Sea of Galilee had caught fire and burned. The parson refused to believe him. Later, the second student went to see the parson, who asked him if he'd heard these strange rumors: Could God in Heaven be really dead, and the Sea of Galilee burned to a crisp?

"Well," said the second student, "I didn't see it with my own eyes, but I'm sure it's true. When I was in Nazareth a few days ago, the entire marketplace was filled with fried fish, and the angels were buying up all the black cloth in town for mourning clothes."

The parson gave them both a large sum of money so that they wouldn't pass this news on; otherwise, he'd never be able to preach again.

The Bishop's Visit

Once there was a parish in which the farmers complained that their parson wasn't good enough, and they wanted another. So they sent for the bishop.

It so happened that the parson had a very beautiful wife, and the bishop went up to her and grabbed her breasts. "What do you call these?" he asked.

"The Bells of Bethlehem," answered the wife.

Then he grabbed her a little farther down. "And what do you call this?" he said.

"Joshua's grave."

He wanted to put his staff into Joshua's grave, and so he did. All the while the parson lay in the next room listening to everything.

Later, when the bishop was about to go to sleep, he checked to see if the parson was asleep, and accidentally singed his beard and hair with his candle. But the parson kept his eyes closed.

The next day, Sunday, the parson took his revenge. He started his sermon this way: "And a strange man came to me last night. He singed my hair, he fried my beard, he rang the Bells of Bethlehem, he put his staff into Joshua's grave. And this will be the subject for today's sermon."

The bishop stood up and said to the congregation, "This man is so learned that you'll never be able to understand what he's saying. But I understand him very well!"

And after that the parson was allowed to stay and continue his ministry.

One More Schnapps

Once there was a boatswain—and he was only one among many—who was awfully fond of tobacco and schnapps. The problem was that these were the very things that he had most trouble getting. So one day he got the idea that maybe the Devil could help him. The next time he met him, he said, "Listen up, you old Devil, will you make a contract with me?"

Well, the Devil is always ready to do that, so he asked the boatswain what he had in mind.

"I want three wishes," said the boatswain. "And if I can wish for something that you can't give me, then I'll go free. Otherwise you can have all of me."

"Sounds good to me. Just wish away!" the Evil One said, ready to go along with the deal.

"First of all, I want all the tobacco in the world," said the boatswain.

This he was granted.

"Then I want all the schnapps in the world," the boatswain said.

Very well, he was granted that too. Now the boatswain stood pondering for a while.

"Hurry up! I'm waiting," said the Evil One.

"Well then, give me just one more drink," said the boatswain.

That made the Devil so furious that he ran off howling, for he knew the boatswain had made a fool of him.

The Hare in the Treetop

Once there was a farmhand who made a deal that the Devil could have him if he couldn't come up with something that the Evil One wasn't able to do.

When the Devil came to fetch him, the farmhand told him to chase a hare up into the tallest tree he could find. The Evil One started gathering together lots and lots of hares; in fact, he gathered together all the hares in the entire county. Hares were running everywhere, but it never got so crowded that any one of them had to climb up into a tree. Finally, the Evil One got so exhausted that he gave up.

Exchange Heads with the Devil

Once upon a time Our Lord and Saint Peter went walking in Småland where all the tall pine trees grow. They heard some people having a terrible row in the forest, and Our Lord told Saint Peter to go and find out who was fighting, and try to see if he couldn't possibly make peace.

Saint Peter found the Devil and a Smålänning* at each other's throats. When he asked them to behave themselves, they both started bawling him out, saying that he wasn't worth more than a rotten herring. This made Saint Peter angry, and since he couldn't get them to shut up no matter how he tried, he chopped off both their heads.

After he'd returned to Our Lord and told him who'd been fighting, and that, in order to get some peace, he'd chopped their heads off, Our Lord said, "You shouldn't have done that. It's never a good idea to get involved with the likes of them. It's pretty late now"—it was around seven-thirty at night—"but early tomorrow morning, as soon as you get dressed, go back there and put their heads back on. If you touch your sword to their necks, they'll come alive again."

Saint Peter did as he was told, but when he got there, he couldn't tell which head belonged to the Devil and which one to the Smålänning. As luck would have it, he switched them.

That's how it happens that Smålänningers always have something of the Devil in them, and that those who know a thing or two about the Evil One insist that he is a lot like a Smålänning.

---

* A Smålänning is an inhabitant of Småland in southeast Sweden.

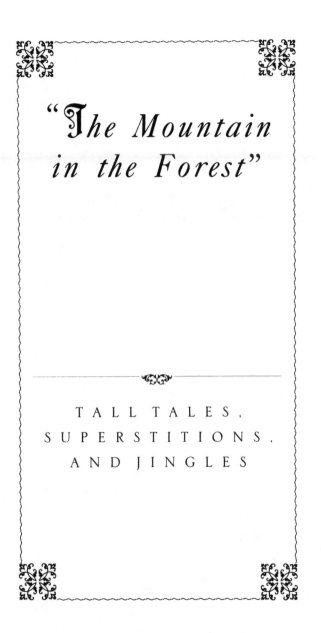

"The Mountain in the Forest"

TALL TALES,
SUPERSTITIONS,
AND JINGLES

The Mountain in the Forest

In the forest stands a mountain—never did I see such a lovely mountain. The mountain stands deep in the forest.

On the mountain there is a tree—never did I see such a lovely tree. The tree on the mountain, the mountain standing deep in the forest.

On the tree there is a branch—never did I see such a lovely branch. The branch on the tree, the tree on the mountain, the mountain standing deep in the forest.

On the branch there is a twig—never did I see such a lovely twig. The twig on the branch, the branch on the tree, the tree on the mountain, the mountain standing deep in the forest.

On the twig there is a nest—never did I see such a lovely nest. The nest on the twig, the twig on the branch, the branch on the tree, the tree on the mountain, the mountain standing deep in the forest.

In this nest there is an egg—never did I see such a lovely egg. The egg in the nest, the nest on the twig, the twig on the branch, the branch on the tree, the tree on the mountain, the mountain standing deep in the forest.

In this egg there is a bird—never did I see such a lovely bird. The bird in the egg, the egg in the nest, the nest on the twig, the twig on the branch, the branch on the tree, the tree on the mountain, the mountain standing deep in the forest.

On this bird there is a feather—never did I see such a lovely feather. The feather on the bird, the bird in the egg, the egg in the nest, the nest on the twig, the twig on the branch, the branch on the tree, the tree on the mountain, the mountain standing deep in the forest.

On this feather there is a louse—never did I see such a lovely louse. The louse on the feather, the feather on the bird, the bird in the egg, the egg in the nest, the nest on the twig, the twig on the branch, the branch on the tree, the tree on the mountain, the mountain standing deep in the forest.

On this louse there is a spot—never did I see such a nice spot. The spot on the louse, the louse on the feather, the feather on the bird, the bird in the egg, the egg in the nest, the nest on the twig, the twig on the branch, the branch on the tree, the tree on the mountain, the mountain standing deep in the forest.

The Old Lady's Cat

Once there was an old crone who had a cat. "If you'd like a little porridge for dinner, I'll make it for you," the old crone said.

"Jam, jam," said the cat.

"I have to go out and milk my cow," the old crone said.

"Jam, jam," said Kitty.

While the old woman was out milking, the cat ate up both porridge and pot. Then he went out to where the old woman sat milking. The old woman said, "What have you been up to, Kitty, that you're so fat?"

"I've eaten up the porridge and the pot, and if you're not quiet, I'll eat you too," said the cat. "Gulp," he said, and ate up the old lady, the bucket, the cow, and the calf—everything.

He walked around for a while until he met a rabbit. The rabbit said, "What have you been up to, Kitty, that you're so nice and fat?"

"I've eaten the porridge and the pot, the old crone and the bucket, the cow and the calf. If you're not quiet, I'll eat you too. Gulp," he said, and ate up the rabbit.

The Snake Cookers

In my childhood, people believed that if you found a white snake,* you should take it home and cook it, then dip a piece

---

* A white snake is an albino or very light-colored snake. According to the folklorist Gustav Henningsen, it was a commonly held folk belief that one could gain "second sight" and exceptional wisdom from eating such a snake, considered the "king of snakes."

of bread in the broth and eat it. This would give you great wisdom; you'd know things that no one else would understand.

Once a girl found such a snake, which she proceeded to cook. But she left the pot alone for a short while, and when she returned, someone else had dipped into the pot and got the wisdom, which only the first person to dip could get.

The Goat Who Wouldn't Go Home

Once there was an old pensioner who had a goat named Tinkla, and Tinkla wouldn't walk home when she was in the forest, because Tinkla's little feet were cold. The pensioner went to the fox and said, "Fox, bite Tinkla. Tinkla won't walk home at night, because Tinkla's little feet are cold."

"No, I won't," said the fox.

Then the old man went to the hunter and asked the hunter to shoot the fox, for the fox wouldn't bite Tinkla, and Tinkla wouldn't walk home from the forest, because Tinkla's little feet were cold.

"No, I won't," said the hunter.

Then the old man went to the stick and asked the stick to beat the hunter, for the hunter wouldn't shoot the fox, and the fox wouldn't bite Tinkla, and Tinkla wouldn't walk home from the forest, because Tinkla's little feet were cold.

"No, I won't," said the stick.

Then the old man went to the fire and asked the fire to burn the stick, for the stick wouldn't beat the hunter, and the hunter wouldn't shoot the fox, and the fox wouldn't bite Tinkla, and Tinkla wouldn't walk home from the forest, because Tinkla's little feet were cold.

"No, I won't," said the fire.

Then the old man went to the water and asked the water to put out the fire, and so on.

"No, I won't," said the water.

Then the old man went to the ox and asked the ox to drink the water, for the water wouldn't put out the fire, and so on.

"No, I won't," said the ox. Then the old man went to the rope and asked the rope to tie the ox, for the ox wouldn't drink the water, and so on.

"No, I won't," said the rope.

Then the old man went to the rat and asked the rat to gnaw the rope, for the rope wouldn't tie the ox, and so on.

"No, I won't," said the rat.

Then the old man went to the cat and asked the cat to catch the rat, for the rat wouldn't gnaw the rope, and the rope wouldn't tie the ox, and the ox wouldn't drink the water, and the water wouldn't put out the fire, and the fire wouldn't burn the stick, and the stick wouldn't beat the hunter, and the hunter wouldn't shoot the fox, and the fox wouldn't bite Tinkla, and Tinkla wouldn't walk home from the forest, because Tinkla's little feet were cold.

"Yes, I'll do it," said the cat, "for a little sweet milk."

So the cat went after the rat, and the rat after the rope, the rope after the ox, the ox after the water, the water after the fire, the fire after the stick, the stick after the hunter, the hunter after the fox, and the fox after Tinkla, *and then Tinkla walked home.*

"Eat the Bread Too!"

Some people were out in the fields bringing in the hay. They'd brought along a little boy and left him by himself at the edge of the field with a jar of milk with some pieces of bread in it. He sat there eating with a spoon when along came a snake, who poked his snout into the jar and started drinking the milk. For a while the boy sat watching while the snake drank. But then he hit him on the head with the spoon, saying, "You've got to eat the bread too, you pushy piece of string!"

The Little Old Woman

Once there was a tiny little old woman who had a tiny little cottage and a tiny little barn, a tiny little cow, a tiny little milking stool, a tiny little milking bucket, a tiny little milk dish, a tiny little milk strainer, a tiny little cat bowl, and a great big cat.

The little woman went to milk the little cow, and when she came back she put the milk bucket on the table and went to fetch dish and strainer to strain the milk. But the big cat lapped up all the old woman's milk. So she stamped her foot and screamed, "Scat, cat!"

And the cat was so scared that he ran into the forest and never dared come home again.

The Three Lying Old Women

Once three old women were sitting together in a cottage. All three of them were great liars.

The first woman said, "Oh, if you only knew how good my eyesight is even though I'm getting quite old! When I stand on the ground below the church tower, I can see perfectly clearly the mosquitoes sitting there yawning on the spire."

The second woman said, "I can't pride myself on my eyesight, but I do have such incredibly good ears that when I lie in bed I can even hear the fleas pissing in the straw bedding."

And the third one said, "I can't pride myself on my eyesight or my hearing, but I have unusually good teeth. As old as I am, I can still bite through the thickest part of an iron rod any time I want to, and it doesn't hurt my teeth the least little bit."

The Biggest Stable and the Biggest Pot

Up in Great Juktan in Sorsele* lived some people who were so wealthy and their stable so large that if a cow got impregnated by the stable door, she'd give birth before they had time to lead her into her stall at the opposite end. The kettle in that stable was so large that when it boiled on one side, there was ice for skating on the other!

The Black Cow, the Pot, and the Cheese

Next to Black Mountain was a small lake called Black Lake, and next to Black Lake was a small cottage where there lived an old man and his old wife. Giants lived in Black Mountain, and it

* Stor-Juktan (Great Juktan) in Sorsele is a part of Lappland.

often happened that they came to borrow things from the old man and woman; when the giants were brewing, for instance, they borrowed the couple's big copper kettle. They always came at night and were very quiet. The old man and woman never denied them anything, for they wanted to stay on good terms with them.

One day the giants gave the old man and woman a black cow to thank them for being so helpful. And what a cow it was! They got so much milk from it that they didn't know what to do with it. They had to get a large pot—so large that it took three blacksmiths three years to make it. Then they decided to make cheese. The pot was filled with milk, and when the cheese rennet was to be put into the milk, they had to spread it with a horse and wagon. The horse was pregnant, and she gave birth in the pot. After they'd been eating the cheese for three years, they finally found the mare's dead foal.

And there was so much butter! They made a hill of butter, and people came from far and wide to buy it. But they had no scales, so to measure out a pound the old woman rode a sleigh from the top of the mound, and the butter that she scooped together at the bottom she called a pound. If someone wanted only half a pound, the old woman just rode the sleigh from halfway up the mound. It was as simple as that.

Black Mountain and Black Lake are still there, but the giants and the old man and woman are gone, and so is the black cow. Thank goodness this tale is still alive.

Boots for the Son in America

Once a boy wrote home from America to his father that he had bad boots. The father wanted to send him a pair of new ones, but since he'd heard that the telegraph was much faster than the mails, he threw the boots up onto the telegraph wires so that they would get to America quickly. Before long, a tramp came by, and when he noticed the splendid new boots, he pulled them down and threw his old, worn-out ones up there instead. When the old man saw the worn-out boots a little while later, he believed that the son had gotten the new ones and sent the old ones home.

That Was the End of the Tale

A boy walking along a road found a locked chest. After he'd walked awhile longer, he found a key.

"What if it fits?" said the boy.

He placed the chest on a rock and put the key in the keyhole. "Crack," it said, and the chest opened.

Guess what was in the chest? A tail! And if the tail'd been longer, then so would this tale.

Notes

The following notes are brief and factual, limited to information about informants and collectors as well as the particular sources where the variants were found. These sources may be either a published collection of tales, a journal, or an archive. Finally, we list the catalogue number from *The Types of the Folktale* (Helsinki: Folklore Fellows Communications 184), a classification and bibliographical system compiled by Antti Aarne in 1910, and translated and enlarged by Stith Thompson in 1928. In 1960, Thompson published the latest version, including many new indices. Another index referred to here is Reidar Th. Christiansen's *The Migratory Legends* (Helsinki: Folklore Fellows Communications 175, 1958), in which an extension of the number system of the Aarne-Thompson catalogue is used.

Animal Tales

Small Birds Can Kill Too! Told and recorded by Axel Romdahl, Gotland. From the Säve Collection, Uppsala University Library. Collected by Per Arvid Säve, ca. 1850. Aarne-Thompson type catalogue no. 248.

The Rooster Wins the Race Told by informant from Anundsjö County, Ångermanland. Recorded by Ella Odstedt, 1928. Uppsala Institute of Dialect and Folklore Research, ULMA #2002:2 (archive). Published in *Svenska landsmål och svenskt folkliv*, vol. 5, *Sagor från Ångermanland*, Stockholm, 1931 (journal). Aarne-Thompson type catalogue no. 230*.

The Fox, the Bear, and the Honeycomb Told by Johan Nord, Källunga County, Västergötland. Recorded by C. M. Bergstrand, 1934. Institute of Folklore in Gothenburg, DAG #3304 (archive). Aarne-Thompson type catalogue no. 15.

How the Bear Got His Stubby Tail Told and recorded by Richard Bergström and Johan Nordlander, 1885, from Ångermanland. Published in *Svenska landsmål och svenskt folkliv*, vol. 5, *Sagor från Ångermanland*, Stockholm, 1931 (journal). Aarne-Thompson type catalogue nos. 1 and 2.

The Fox and the Rowanberries Told by Johan Zakarias Bång, Lycksele County, Västerbotten. Recorded by J. Nensén, 1823. Uppsala University Library. Published in *Svenska Sagor och Sägner* 9, *Sagor från Åsele Lappmark*, Kungliga Gustav Adolfs Akademin för Folklivsforskning, Stockholm, 1945 (publication series). Aarne-Thompson type catalogue no. 9.

"They're Sour," Said the Fox Told by informant from Småland. Recorded by Gunnar Olof Hyltén-Cavallius, ca. 1840, and published in *Wärend och wirdarne: ett försög i svenskt etnologi*, vol. 2, Stockholm, 1844–49. Aarne-Thompson type catalogue no. 59.

The Fox and the Crane Invite Each Other to Dinner Told by Märta Bergvall, Edsele, Ångermanland. Recorded by Frans Bergvall, 1957. Uppsala Institute of Dialect and Folklore Research, ULMA #23399 (archive). Aarne-Thompson type catalogue no. 60.

Why the Hare Has a Cleft Lip Told and recorded by Fabian Karlsson, Konga County, Småland, 1940. Institute of European Ethnology and Folklore in Lund, LUF #M6422:7 (archive). Aarne-Thompson type catalogue no. 70.

If It Were Summer . . . Told by Gamle gubben (Old Man) Eklund, Dalhems County, Småland. Recorded by Sofia Petersson, Dalhems County, Småland, 1925. Collected by Waldemar Liungman and published in *Sveriges Samtliga Folksagor*, vol. 1, Stockholm, 1949. Aarne-Thompson type catalogue no. 81.

The Wolf and the Fox Told by an informant from Halland. Recorded and collected by August Bondeson and published in *Svenska folksagor från skilda landskap*, Stockholm, 1882. Aarne-Thompson type catalogue no. 120.

The Wolf Who Wanted to Become Stronger Told and recorded by P. Dahlström, Västergötland, 1936. Institute of Folklore in Gothenburg, DAG #3725 (archive). Aarne-Thompson type catalogue no. 153.

The Billy Goat and the Wolf Collected by Gunnar Olof Hyltén-Cavallius and published in *Wärend och wirdarne: ett försög i svensk etnologi*, vol. 2, Stockholm, 1863–64. Aarne-Thompson type catalogue no. 132.

Hold the Wolf by the Tail Told by an informant from Småland. Recorded by Hilda Lundell and Elise Zetterquist, Kläckeberga County, Småland, ca. 1880. Published in *Svenska landsmål och svenskt folkliv*, vol. 9, no. 1, Stockholm (journal). Aarne-Thompson type catalogue no. 1229.

Trolls, Giants, Ghosts, and Other Beings

To Squeeze Water from a Stone Told by Jan Petter Andersson, Ödeborg County, Dalsland. Recorded by Arnold Olsson, Svarteborg County, Bohuslän, 1932. Institute of Folklore in Gothenburg, DAG #2917 (archive). Aarne-Thompson type catalogue no. 1060.

The Girl Who Wouldn't Spin Told by an informant in Skåne. Collected by Eva Wigström. Published in *Svenska landsmål och svenskt folkliv*, vol. 1, *Sagor och äfventyr upptecknade i Skåne*, Stockholm, 1884 (journal). Aarne-Thompson type catalogue no. 500.

The Boy Who Worked for the Giant Told by August Jacobsson, Tanums County, Bohuslän. Recorded by David Arill, 1920. Institute of Folklore in Gothenburg, DAG #138 (archive). Aarne-Thompson type catalogue no. 1000.

Little Hans Told by Elisabeth Bolin, Gotland. Recorded by Per Arvid Säve. Published in *Svenska Sagor och Sägner* 10, *Gotlandska Sagor*, Kungliga Gustav Adolfs Akademin för Folklivsforskning, Uppsala, 1952 (publication series). Aarne-Thompson type catalogue no. 507A.

Onen in the Mountain Told by an informant from Småland. Collected by Carl Wilhelm von Sydow, 1947. Institute of European Ethnology and Folklore in Lund, LUF #10630 (archive). Aarne-Thompson type catalogue no. 328.

The Gullible Troll Recorded by Ernst Jotson, Wrigstadt County, Småland, 1916. Institute of European Ethnology and Folklore in Lund, LUF #870 (archive). Aarne-Thompson type catalogue no. 1030.

The Clever Boy Told and recorded by Ivar Mattsson, Askums County, Bohuslän, 1918. Institute of Folklore in Gothenburg, DAG #37 (archive). Aarne-Thompson type catalgue no. 1035.

The Bäckahäst (legend) Told by Mlle. Norberg, Norrbyås County, Närke. Collected by Gabriel Djurklou, Närke. Published in *Svenska Sagor och Sägner* 5, Kungliga Gustav Adolfs Akademin för Folklivsforskning, Stockholm, 1943 (publication series). Migratory legend no. 4090.

The Skogsrå at Lapptjärns Mountain (legend) Told by Rickard Jansson, Gustav Adolfs County, Värmland. Recorded by Helmer Eriksson, Råda County, Värmland, 1925. Collected by Waldemar Liungman and published in *Sveriges Samtliga Folksagor* vol. 1, Stolkholm, 1949. Aarne-Thompson type catalogue no. 1131.

To Catch Smoke (legend) Told by Anders i Björkhagen, Västergötland. Recorded by Algot Andersson, Västergötland, 1935. Uppsala Institute of Dialect and Folklore Research, ULMA #23575:173 (archive). Aarne-Thompson type catalogue no. 1176.

The Tale of the Troll Woman (legend) Told by Helena Johnsson, Tåby County, Östergötland. Recorded by Agda Andersson, Tåby County, Östergötland, 1925. Collected by Waldemar Liungman and published in *Sveriges Samtliga Folksagor*, vol. 1, Stockholm, 1949. Aarne-Thompson type catalogue no. 1148A.

The Tale of Speke (legend) Told by Samuel Johansson, Västerlanda County, Bohuslän. Recorded by Hulda Hammarbäck, Västerlanda County, Bohuslän, 1926. Collected by Waldemar Liungman and published in *Sveriges Samtliga Folksagor*, vol. 1, Stockholm, 1949. Aarne-Thompson type catalogue no. 760.

The Gypsy Girl and Her Dead Fiancé (legend) Told by Johan Dimitri-Taikon. Recorded by Carl-Herman Tillhagen and published in *Taikon berätter: Zigenarsagor* (Gypsy Tales), Stockholm, 1946. Aarne-Thompson type catalogue no. 365.

Hobergsgubben (legend) Told by Johannes Andersson, Örsköld County, Dalsland. Recorded by Tage Heimer, 1927. Institute of Folklore in Gothenburg, DAG #1960 (archive). Aarne-Thompson type catalogue no. 1165.

The Trolls and the Bear (legend)   Told by Anders Andersson, Rödinge County, Skåne. Recorded by Nils Bengtsson, Skåne, 1932. Institute of European Ethnology and Folklore in Lund, LUF #3450 (archive). Aarne-Thompson type catalogue no. 1161.

The Giant's Toy (legend)   Recorded by Margit Neuman, Lycksele County, Lappland. Uppsala Institute of Dialect and Folklore Research, ULMA #2151:3 (archive). Aarne-Thompson type catalogue no. 701.

True Dummies and Clever Folk

The Tale of the Crooked Creature   Told by an informant from Skåne. Collected by Oscar Swahn and published in *Svenskt Skämtlynne*, Stockholm, 1884. Aarne-Thompson type catalogue no. 1203.

Wise Klara   Told by Lovisa Säve, Gotland. Collected by Per Arvid Säve. Published in *Svenska Sagor och Sägner* 10, *Gotlandska Sagor*, Kungliga Gustav Adolfs Akademin för Folklivsforskning, Uppsala, 1952 (publication series). Aarne-Thompson type catalogue no. 883B.

The Stupid Boy Who Didn't Know About Women   Recorded by Samuel Jakobsson, Tegneby County, Bohuslän. Institute of Folklore in Gothenburg, DAG #1543 (archive). Aarne-Thompson type catalogue no. 1545B.

Counting the Stars in Heaven   Told by Andreas Karlsson, Blekinge. Recorded by Brynhild Wilén, Blekinge, 1920. Institute of European Ethnology and Folklore in Lund, LUF #2601 (archive). Aarne-Thompson type catalogue no. 922.

Fools   Recorded by S. Lampa, Läske-Längjum County, Västergötland, 1897. Uppsala Institute of Dialect and Folklore Research, ULMA #111:237c (archive). Aarne-Thompson type catalogue no. 1290.

The Princess of Catburg   Told and recorded by Bengt Söderberg, Skärstad County, Småland, 1927. Institute of European Ethnology and Folklore in Lund, LUF #745 (archive). Aarne-Thompson type catalogue no. 545A.

Pretend to Eat, Pretend to Work   Told and recorded by Carl Johan Salomonson, Västergötland, end of nineteenth century. The Segerstedt Collection, Kungliga Vitterhets Historie och Antikvitets Akademien, Stockholm (library). Aarne-Thompson type catalogue no. 1560.

Lazy Masse   Told and recorded by Carl von Zeipel, Uppland. Published in *Svenska Sagor och Sägner* 4, *Sagor ur G. O. Hyltén-Cavallius och George Stephens Samlingar*, Kungliga Gustav Adolfs Akademin för Folklivsforskning, Stockholm, 1942 (publication series). Aarne-Thompson type catalogue no. 675.

Big Tomma and Heikin Pieti   Told by Heikin Pieti, Lappland. Recorded by Anshelm Eriksson, Vittangi Kapells County, Lappland, 1925. Collected by Waldemar

Liungman and published in *Sveriges Samtliga Folksagor*, vol. 1, Stockholm, 1949, Aarne-Thompson type catalogue no. 1535.

For Long Springday   Recorded by Bengt Söderberg, Skärstad County, Småland, 1928. Institute of European Ethnology and Folklore in Lund, LUF #806 (archive). Aarne-Thompson type catalogue no. 1541.

The Students and the Eclipse of the Moon   Told by Elna Bengtsson, Skåne. Recorded by Nils Svensson, Skåne, 1929. Institute of European Ethnology and Folklore in Lund, LUF #41 (archive). Recorded in Swedish only. Aarne-Thompson type catalogue no. 1627*.

The Numbskull Who Thought He Married a Man   Told by Oskar Andersson, Källsjö County, Halland. Recorded by Gunnar Johansson, Halland, 1925. Collected by Waldemar Liungman and published in *Sveriges Samtliga Folksagor*, vol. 1, Stockholm, 1949. Aarne-Thompson type catalogue no. 1686**.

Tälje Fools   Told by an informant from Uppland. Recorded by Gunnar Olof Hyltén-Cavallius and George Stephens. Published in *Svenska Sagor och Sägner* 4, *Sagor ur G.O. Hyltén-Cavallius och George Stephens Samlingar*, Kungliga Gustav Adolfs Akademin för Folkslivsforskning, Stockholm, 1942 (publication series). Aarne-Thompson type catalogue no. 1281 (and 1200-1-43-88, 1310).

The Thief's Three Masterpieces   Told and recorded by Mickel i Långhult, Småland. Collected by Gunnar Olof Hyltén-Cavallius and George Stephens. Published in *Svenska Sagor och Sägner* 1, *Mickel i Långhult Sagor*, Kungliga Gustav Adolfs Akademin för Folkslivsforskning, Stockholm, 1939 (publication series). Aarne-Thompson type catalogue no. 1525A–D.

The Girl and the Calf's Eyes (legend)   Told by Oscar Andersson Berg, Hällestad County, Östergötland. Recorded by Ebba Nilsson, Östergötland, 1927. Institute of European Ethnology and Folklore in Lund, LUF #2199 (archive). Aarne-Thompson type catalogue no. 1685.

The King, the Headsman, and the Twelve Robbers (legend)   Recorded by Gabriel Djurklou, Närke. Published in *Svenska Sagor och Sägner* 5, Kungliga Gustav Adolfs Akademin för Folklivsforskning, Stockholm, 1943 (publication series). Aarne-Thompson type catalogue no. 952.

Twelve Men in the Forest (legend)   Recorded by Olof Petter Pettersson, Åsele Lappmark. Published in *Svenska Sagor och Sägner* 9, *Sagor från Åsele Lappmark*, Kungliga Gustav Adolfs Akademin för Folklivsforskning, Stockholm, 1945 (publication series). Aarne-Thompson type catalogue no. 958.

The Wise Daughter (legend)   Told by Anna Olsson, Bro County, Värmland. Recorded by R. Nilsson, 1931. Institute of Folklore in Gothenburg, DAG #2475 (archive). Aarne-Thompson type catalogue no. 875.

Bellman Stories (legend)   Recorded by Carl-Herman Tillhagen and published in *Skæmtsomme eventyr fra Danmark, Norge og Sverige*, Copenhagen, 1957. Aarne-Thompson type catalogue no. 1698A*.

How to Win the Princess

Twigmouthius, Cowbellowantus, Perchnosimus   Recorded by Gabriel Djurklou, Närke, and published in *Sagor och Äventyr*, Stockholm, 1912. Aarne-Thompson type catalogue no. 1641C.

The Princess Who Always Had an Answer   Collected by Sven-Öjvind Swahn, Blekinge. Published in *Svenska folksagor* by Jan-Öjvind Swahn, Stockholm, 1986. Aarne-Thompson type catalogue no. 853.

The Boat That Sailed on Both Land and Sea   Told by a schoolboy from Rönneslöv County, Halland. Institute of European Ethnology and Folklore in Lund, LUF #7364 (archive). Aarne-Thompson type catalogue no. 513B.

The Liar   Told by an informant in Skåne. Recorded by Eva Wigström. Published in *Svenska landsmål och svenskt folkliv*, vol. 1, *Sagor och äfventyr upptecknade i Skåne*, Stockholm, 1884 (journal). Aarne-Thompson type catalogue no. 852.

Ash Dummy Chops Down the Oak and Becomes the King's Son-in-Law   Told by an informant from Barva County, Södermanland. Recorded by Gustaf Ericsson, metalworker and folklore collector in the districts of Åkers and Rekarne, Södermanland, between 1860 and 1880. Uppsala Institute of Dialect and Folklore Research, ULMA #Ericsson 12, p. 433 (archive). Aarne-Thompson type catalogue no. 577.

The Princess with the Louse Skin   Told by Per Lindberg, Almundsryd County, Småland. Recorded by Birger Andersson, Småland. Institute of European Ethnology and Folklore in Lund, LUF #1770 (archive). Aarne-Thompson type catalogue no. 621.

Sheepskin Boy   Told and recorded by Torsten Svidberg, Gryteryds County, Småland. Institute of Folklore in Gothenburg, DAG #448 (archive). Aarne-Thompson type catalogue no. 301.

The Princess Who Danced with a Troll Every Night   Told by Anna Charlotta Nilsson, Kimstads County, Östergötland. Recorded by Emelie Jonson, Norrköping, Östergötland, 1925. Collected by Waldemar Liungman and published in *Sveriges Samtliga Folksagor*, vol. 1, Stockholm, 1949. Aarne-Thompson type catalogue no. 306.

Stuck on a Goose   Told by Holmeig Takaryd, Asarums County, Blekinge. Recorded by David Nyström, Hallabro County, Blekinge. Institute of European Ethnology and Folklore in Lund, LUF #637 (archive). Aarne-Thompson type catalogue no. 571.

The King's Hares Told by an informant from Skåne. Recorded by Eva Wigström. Published in *Skämtsägner från Skåne*, Stockholm, 1882. (*Bidrag till vår odlings häfder*, edited by Artur Hazelius, vol. 2, 1, *Ur de nordiska folkens lif*, 1.) Aarne-Thompson type catalogue no. 570.

Prince Greenbeard Told and recorded by Sven Sederström, Småland. Collected by Gunnar Olof Hyltén-Cavallius and George Stephens. Published in *Svenska Sagor och Sägner* 2, *Sven Sederströms Sagor*, Kungliga Gustav Adolfs Akademin för Folklivsforskning, Stockholm, 1938 (publication series). Aarne-Thompson type catalogue no. 900.

Tales of Heroes and Heroines

The Three Swords Told and recorded by Mickel i Långhult, Småland. Collected by Gunnar Olof Hyltén-Cavallius and George Stephens. Published in *Svenska Sagor och Sägner* 1, *Mickel i Långhult Sagor*, Kungliga Gustav Adolfs Akademin för Folklivsforskning, Stockholm, 1937 (publication series). Aarne-Thompson type catalogue no. 300.

The Peasant Girl in the Floating Rock Recorded by Carl Fredrik Cavallius, Småland. Collected by Gunnar Olof Hyltén-Cavallius and George Stephens. Published in *Svenska Sagor och Sägner* 3, *Sagor från Småland*, Kungliga Gustav Adolfs Akademin för Folklivsforskning, Stockholm, 1939 (publication series). Recorded in Swedish only. Aarne-Thompson type catalogue no. 746*.

Manasse and Cecilia Told and recorded by Jacob Wallin, Stenkyrka County, Gotland, ca. 1840. Collected by Per Arvid Säve. Published in *Svenska Sagor och Sägner* 10, *Gotlandska Sagor*, Kungliga Gustav Adolfs Akademin för Folklivsforskning, Uppsala, 1952 (publication series). Aarne-Thompson type catalogue no. 611.

The Princess in the Earthen Cave Told by an informant in Småland. Collected by Gunnar Olof Hyltén-Cavallius and George Stephens and published in *Svenska Folk-Sagor och Äfventyr*, Stockholm, 1844–49. Aarne-Thompson type catalogue no. 870.

The Silver Dress, the Gold Dress, and the Diamond Dress Recorded by Carl Fredrik Cavallius, Småland. Collected by Gunnar Olof Hyltén-Cavallius and George Stephens. Published in *Svenska Sagor och Sägner* 3, *Sagor från Småland*, Kungliga Gustav Adolfs Akademin för Folklivsforskning, Stockholm, 1939 (publication series). Aarne-Thompson type catalogue no. 510B.

The Boy in the Birch-Bark Basket Told and recorded by Hulda Berg, Stenbrohult County, Småland, 1926. Collected by Waldemar Liungman and published in *Sveriges Samtliga Folksagor*, vol. 1, Stockholm, 1949. Recorded in Swedish only. Aarne-Thompson type catalogue no. 554B*.

The Castle East of the Sun and West of the Wind in the Promised Land   Told by Johannes Glader, Dalsland. Recorded by August Bondeson and published in *Historiegubbar på Dal*, Stockholm, 1886. Aarne-Thompson type catalogue no. 400.

Prince Vilius   Told by August Jacobsson, Tanum, Bohuslän. Recorded by David Arill. Institute of Folklore in Gothenburg, DAG #138 (archive). Published in "Ur den västsvenska folksagodiktningen," *Folksägen och Folkdiktning i Västra Sverige, Göteborgs Jubileumspublikationer*, Gothenburg, 1923. Aarne-Thompson type catalogue no. 425.

The Three Sons Who Each Had a Foal, a Puppy, and a Sword   Told by Maja Stina Svensdotter, Kristianopel County, Blekinge. Recorded by Herman Geijer, 1922. Uppsala Institute of Dialect and Folklore Research, ULMA #708 (archive). Aarne-Thompson type catalogue no. 303.

The Twelve Kidnapped Princesses   Recorded by Albrekt Segerstedt and published in *Svenska Folksagor och Äfventyr*, Stockholm, 1884. Aarne-Thompson type catalogue no. 302.

The Tale of White Bear   Told by Jakob Gustav Cläesson, Göteborg. Recorded by Sigrid Eriksson, Åmål, Dalsland, 1925. Collected by Waldemar Liungman and published in *Sveriges Samtliga Folksagor*, vol. 1, Stockholm, 1949. Aarne-Thompson type catalogue no. 934B.

Little Rose and Big Briar   Told and recorded by Sven Sederström. Collected by Gunnar Olof Hyltén-Cavallius and George Stephens and published in *Svenska Folk-Sagor och Äfventyr*, Stockholm, 1844–49. Aarne-Thompson type catalogue no. 403A.

Metamorphoses

The Serpent Prince   Told by an informant from Landskrona, Skåne. Recorded and collected by Eva Wigström and published in *Folkdiktning, Samlad och upptecknad i Skåne*, vol. 1, Copenhagen, 1880. Aarne-Thompson type catalogue no. 433B.

The Widow's Son   Told and recorded by John Svensson, Hoby County, Blekinge. Institute of European Ethnology and Folklore in Lund, LUF #658 (archive). Aarne-Thompson type catalogue no. 314.

Gray Cape   Told by Anders Backman, Dalsland. Recorded by August Bondeson and published in *Historiegubbar på Dal*, Stockholm, 1886. Aarne-Thompson type catalogue no. 710.

The Animal Husbands   Told and recorded by Amalia Nyquist, Svanskogs County, Värmland, 1926. Collected by Waldemar Liungman and published in *Sveriges Samtliga Folksagor*, vol. 1, Stockholm, 1949. Aarne-Thompson type catalogue no. 552B.

Prince Faithful   Recorded by Carl von Zeipel, Uppland. Collected by Gunnar Olof Hyltén-Cavallius and George Stephens. Published in *Svenska Sagor och Sägner* 4, *Sagor ur G. O. Hyltén-Cavallius och George Stephens Samlingar*, Kungliga Gustav Adolfs

Akademin för Folklivsforskning, Stockholm, 1942 (publication series). Aarne-Thompson type catalogue no. 531.

The Rats in the Juniper Bush   Collected by Carl Wilhelm von Sydow, 1950. Institute of European Ethnology and Folklore in Lund, LUF #11406:20 (archive). Aarne-Thompson type catalogue no. 402.

Tales of Men and Women

Like a Cold Wind in Warm Weather   Told by an informant from Häggenås County, Jämtland. Recorded by Herman Geijer, 1916. Uppsala Institute of Dialect and Folklore Research, ULMA #869:6 (archive). Aarne-Thompson type catalogue no. 923.

The Quick-Learning Girl   Told by an informant in Skåne. Recorded and collected by Eva Wigström. Published in *Svenska landsmål och svenskt folkliv*, vol. 1, *Sagor och äfventyr upptecknade i Skåne*, Stockholm, 1884 (journal). Recorded in Swedish only. Aarne-Thompson type catalogue no. 1463B*.

The Girl Who Gave a Knight a Kiss Out of Necessity   Recorded and collected by August Bondeson and published in *Halländska Sagor*, Stockholm, 1880. Recorded in Swedish only. Aarne-Thompson type catalogue no. 879A**.

The Fussy Fiancé   Told and recorded by A. G. Andersson, Hjulsjö County, Västmanland, 1859. Published in *Fornminnen och Folktankar* 9, Lund, 1922 (journal). Aarne-Thompson type catalogue no. 1459**.

Pär and Bengta   Told by an informant in Skåne. Recorded and collected by Eva Wigström. Published in *Svenska landsmål och svenskt folkliv*, vol. 1, *Sagor och äfventyr upptecknade i Skåne*, Stockholm, 1884 (journal). Aarne-Thompson type catalogue no. 1408.

Who's Got the Dumbest Husband   Told by Oscar Nilsson, Jörlanda County, Bohuslän. Recorded by Anna Gustavsson, Solberga County, Bohuslän, 1926. Collected by Waldemar Liungman and published in *Sveriges Samtliga Folksagor*, vol. 1, Stockholm, 1949. Aarne-Thompson type catalogue no. 1406.

Geska   Told by informant from Blekinge. Recorded and collected by August Bondeson and published in *Svenska folksagor från skilda landskap*, Stockholm, 1882. Aarne-Thompson type catalogue no. 1383.

The Stingy Farmer   Told by Helena Jonsson, Tåby County, Östergötland. Recorded by Agda Andersson, Kuddby County, Östergötland, 1926. Collected by Waldemar Liungman and published in *Sveriges Samtliga Folksagor*, vol. 1, Stockholm, 1949. Aarne-Thompson type catalogue no. 1407A.

The Man and Woman Who Changed Jobs   Recorded and collected by Gabriel Djurklou. Published in *Svenska Sagor och Sägner* 5, Kungliga Gustav Adolfs Akademin för Folklivsforskning, Stockholm, 1943 (publication series). Aarne-Thompson type catalogue no. 1408.

The Contrary Old Woman (legend)   Told by Lars Sedlund, Fjällsjö County, Ångermanland. Recorded by Ella Odstedt, 1929. Uppsala Institute of Dialect and Folklore Research, ULMA #2668:14 (archive). Aarne-Thompson type catalogue no. 1365A.

The Tale of a Suitor (legend)   Told by Hilda Ohlin, Billinge County, Skåne. Recorded by Helga Persson, Skåne, 1932. Institute of European Ethnology and Folklore in Lund, LUF #3669 (archive). Aarne-Thompson type catalogue no. 1453***.

The Hunter and the Skogsrå (legend)   Told by an informant from Öland. Recorded by Eva Wigström, Skåne, before 1884. Published in *Svenska landsmål och svenskt folkliv*, vol. 2, *Sagor, Sägner och Visor*, Stockholm, 1884 (journal). Recorded in Swedish only. Aarne-Thompson type catalogue no. 1349E*.

The Woman in the Hole (legend)   Told by an informant from Gillberga County, Värmland. Recorded by Johan Egardh and published in *Prosten Göransson: En sägenomspunnen värmlandspräst*, Stockholm, 1935. Aarne-Thompson type catalogue no. 1164.

The Man Who Married the Mara (legend)   Recorded by Gunnar Olof Hyltén-Cavallius and George Stephens, and published in *Svenska sagor*, Stockholm, 1965. Migratory legend no. 4010.

The Hidden Key (legend)   Told by Hilda Ohlin, Billinge County, Skåne. Recorded by Helga Persson, Skåne, 1932. Institute of European Ethnology and Folklore in Lund, LUF #3669 (archive). Aarne-Thompson type catalogue no. 1453.

Moral Tales

His Just Reward   Told by Jacob Glader, Dalsland. Recorded by August Bondeson and published in *Historiegubbar på Dal*, Stockholm, 1886. Aarne-Thompson type catalogue no. 155.

Master Pär and Rag Jan's Boy   Told and collected by Gabriel Djurklou, Närke, and published in *Sagor och Äventyr*, Stockholm, 1883. Aarne-Thompson type catalogue no. 461.

The Girl in the Robbers' Den   Recorded by Gunnar Olof Hyltén-Cavallius and George Stephens. Published in *Svenska Sagor och Sägner* 4, *Sagar ur G. O. Hyltén-Cavallius och George Stephens Samlingar*, Kungliga Gustav Adolfs Akademin för Folklivsforskning, Stockholm, 1942 (publication series). Aarne-Thompson type catalogue no. 955.

Funteliten and His Mother   Told and recorded by Mickel i Långhult. Collected by Gunnar Olof Hyltén-Cavallius and George Stephens. Published in *Svenska Sagor och Sägner* 1, *Mickel i Långhult Sagor*, Kungliga Gustav Adolfs Akademin för Folklivsforskning, Stockholm, 1937 (publication series). Aarne-Thompson type catalogue no. 910A.

The Girl Who Stepped on the Bread   Told by Frederika Pålsson, Knäreds County, Halland. Recorded by Harald Nilsson, Laholm, Halland, 1927. Institute of Folklore in Gothenburg, DAG #1368 (archive). Aarne-Thompson type catalogue no. 962**.

A Tale of Two Beggars   Told by Olof Andersson, Sanne County, Bohuslän. Recorded by Arnold Olsson, Svarteborg County, Bohuslän, 1927. Institute of Folklore in Gothenburg, DAG #1612 (archive). Aarne-Thompson type catalogue no. 841.

The Filthy-Rich Student   Collected by Richard Bergström and Johan Nordlander in Värmland. Published in *Svenska landsmål och svenskt folkliv*, vol. 2, *Sagor, Sägner och Visor*, Stockholm, 1885 (journal). Aarne-Thompson type catalogue no. 361.

The Bad Stepmother   Told by Erika Sedlund, Fjällsjö, Västerbotten. Recorded by Bertil Nygren, Västerbotten, 1929. Uppsala Institute of Dialect and Folklore Research, ULMA (archive). Aarne-Thompson type catalogue no. 720.

The Tale of the Copper Pot   Told by Johan Danielsson, Slätthög County, Småland. Recorded by Olle Levander and Martin Larsson, 1931. Institute of European Ethnology and Folklore in Lund, LUF #3060 (archive). Aarne-Thompson type catalogue no. 591.

The Two Chests   Told and recorded by Maria Aronsson, Råggård, Dalsland, 1944. Uppsala Institute of Dialect and Folklore Research, ULMA #16716 (archive). Aarne-Thompson type catalogue no. 480.

Godfather Death   Told and recorded by Amalie Nyqvist, Svanskog, Värmland. Institute of Folklore in Gothenburg, DAG Liungman #505 (archive). Aarne-Thompson type catalogue no. 332.

The Bear and the Woman   Told by Ida Heimer, Håbol, Dalsland. Recorded by Tage Heimer, 1922. Uppsala Institute of Dialect and Folklore Research, ULMA #377 (archive). Aarne-Thompson type catalogue no. 156.

The Boy, the Old Woman, and the Neighbor (legend)   Recorded by Olof Petter Pettersson. Published in *Svenska Sagor och Sägner* 9, *Sagor från Åsele Lappmark*, Kungliga Gustav Adolfs Akademin för Folklivsforskning, Stockholm, 1945 (publication series). Aarne-Thompson type catalogue no. 1725.

The Salt Mill (legend)   Recorded by Olof Petter Pettersson. Published in *Svenska Sagor och Sägner* 9, *Sagor från Åsele Lappmark*, Kungliga Gustav Adolfs Akademin för

Folklivsforskning, Stockholm, 1945 (publication series). Aarne-Thompson type catalogue no. 565.

Old Nick and the Widow (legend) Told by J. A. Holmgren, Gällareds County, Halland. Recorded by Gunnar Johansson, Kjällsjö County, Halland, 1925. Collected by Waldemar Liungman and published in *Sveriges Samtliga Folksagor*, vol. 1, Stockholm, 1949. Recorded in Swedish only. Aarne-Thompson type catalogue no. 820B.

The Lazy Boy and the Industrious Girl (legend) Told and recorded by O. G. Svensson, Vänersborg, Dalsland, 1930. Institute of Folklore in Gothenburg, DAG #2246 (archive). Aarne-Thompson type catalogue no. 822.

The Parson's Wife Who Had No Shadow (legend) Told by an informant from Junsele County. Recorded by Ella Odstedt, 1928. Published in *Svenska landsmål och svenskt folkliv*, vol. 5, *Sagor från Ångermanland*, Stockholm, 1931 (journal). Aarne-Thompson type catalogue no. 755.

The Despised Rake (legend) Told by J. A. Holmgren, Gällered County, Halland. Recorded by Gunnar Johansson, Kjällsjö County, Halland, 1925. Collected by Waldemar Liungman and published in *Sveriges Samtliga Folksagor*, vol. 1, Stockholm, 1949. Aarne-Thompson type catalogue no. 1628.

The Tale of the Sculptor's Beautiful Wife (legend) Told by Edvard Svensson, Knäred County, Halland. Recorded by Harald Nilsson, Lund, 1930–35. Institute of European Ethnology and Folklore in Lund, LUF #5025 (archive). Aarne-Thompson type catalogue no. 1730.

The Big Turnip (legend) Recorded by Carl Fredrik Cavallius. Published in *Svenska Sagor och Sägner 3*, *Sagor från Småland*, Kungliga Gustav Adolfs Akademin för Folklivsforskning, Stockholm, 1939 (publication series). Aarne-Thompson type catalogue no. 1689A.

Parsons, the Good Lord, and the Evil One

"Yet a Little While, and the World Seeth Me No More" Recorded by Frans Bergvall, Edsele, Ångermanland, 1965. Uppsala Institute of Dialect and Folklore Research, ULMA #26017 (archive). Aarne-Thompson type catalogue no. 1827.

The Devil and the Tailor Told by an informant from Västergötland. Recorded by Oscar Swahn and published in *Svenskt Skämtlynne*, vol. 11, Stockholm, 1884. Aarne-Thompson type catalogue no. 1096.

Kitta Gray Told by Maria Andersson, Hjärtums County, Bohuslän. Recorded by Gustava Matilda Karlsson, Hjärtums County, Bohuslän, 1926. Collected by Waldemar Liungman and published in *Sveriges Samtliga Folksagor*, vol. 1, Stockholm, 1949. Aarne-Thompson type catalogue no. 1074.

The Pregnant Parson   Recorded by Carl-Herman Tillhagen and published in *Skæmtsomme eventyr fra Danmark, Norge og Sverige*, Copenhagen, 1957. Aarne-Thompson type catalogue no. 1739.

Forging with Sand   Told by Magnus Norlund, Nora County, Ångermanland. Recorded by Ella Odstedt, 1932. Uppsala Institute of Dialect and Folklore Research, ULMA #4978 (archive). Aarne-Thompson type catalogue no. 1163.

The Parson, the Sexton, and the Devil   Recorded by Oscar Swahn and published in *Svenskt Skämtlynne*, vol. 12, Stockholm, 1884. Aarne-Thompson type catalogue no. 1838.

The Sermon About Nothing   Recorded by Frans Bergvall, Edsele, Ångermanland, 1965. Uppsala Institute of Dialect and Folklore Research, ULMA #26017 (archive). Aarne-Thompson type catalogue no. 1825B.

Sven Fearless   Told by an informant from Hjärnarps County, Skåne. Recorded by Eva Wigström. Published in *Svenska landsmål och svenskt folkliv*, vol. 1, *Sagor och äfventyr upptecknade i Skåne*, Stockholm, 1884 (journal). Aarne-Thompson type catalogue no. 326.

The Tale of the Parson and the Sexton   Told by Samuel Jakobsson, Tegneby County, Bohuslän. Recorded by Carl Johansson, 1925. Institute of Folklore in Gothenburg, DAG #1133 (archive). Aarne-Thompson type catalogue no. 1735.

The Farmer Who Sold His Soul to the Devil (legend)   Recorded by O. M. Ohlin, Hällerstads County, Skåne, 1925. Collected by Waldemar Liungman and published in *Sveriges Samtliga Folksagor*, vol. 1, Stockholm, 1949. Aarne-Thompson type catalogue no. 1091.

The Night-Blind Parson (legend)   Told by an informant from Skåne. Recorded by Eva Wigström. Published in *Svenska landsmål och svenskt folkliv*, vol. 1, *Sagor och äfventyr upptecknade i Skåne*, Stockholm, 1884 (journal). Aarne-Thompson type catalogue no. 1775.

The Burning Lake (legend)   Recorded by Johannes Börjesson, Hyssna County, Västergötland, 1926. Collected by Waldemar Liungman and published in *Sveriges Samtliga Folksagor*, vol. 1, Stockholm, 1949. Aarne-Thompson type catalogue no. 1920A.

The Bishop's Visit (legend)   Told by Gubben (Old Man) Ivar, Svinhult County, Östergötland. Recorded by Carl Segerstål, Östergötland. Institute of European Ethnology and Folklore in Lund, LUF #1559 (archive). Aarne-Thompson type catalogue no. 1825A.

One More Schnapps (legend)   Told by an informant from Halland. Recorded by August Bondeson, Halland, before 1882 and published in *Svenska folksagor från skilda landskap*, Stockholm, 1882. Aarne-Thompson type catalogue no. 1173A.

The Hare in the Treetop (legend)   Told by an informant from Lappland. Recorded by Bertil Nygren, Lappland. Uppsala Institute of Dialect and Folklore Research, ULMA #4296 (archive). Aarne-Thompson type catalogue no. 1171.

Exchange Heads with the Devil (legend)   Told by an informant from Osby County, Skåne. Recorded by Eva Wigström, 1882. Published in *Skämtsägner från Skåne*, Stockholm, 1882. (*Bidrag till vår odlings häfder*, edited by Artur Hazelius, vol. 2, 1, *Ur de nordiska folkens lif*, 1.) Aarne-Thompson type catalogue no. 1169.

Tall Tales, Superstitions, and Jingles

The Mountain in the Forest   Told by Sofia Holmkvist, Sibbarps County, Halland. Recorded by Olga Holmkvist, Falkenberg, Halland, 1926. Collected by Waldemar Liungman and published in *Sveriges Samtliga Folksagor*, vol. 1, Stockholm, 1949. Recorded in Swedish only. Aarne-Thompson type catalogue no. 2041*.

The Old Lady's Cat   Told by Maja Stina Svensdotter, Blekinge. Recorded by Herman Geijer. Uppsala Institute of Dialect and Folklore Resarch, ULMA #708 (archive). Aarne-Thompson type catalogue no. 2027.

The Snake Cookers   Told by an informant from Brunns County, Västergötland. Recorded by E. Larsson, Varberg, Halland, 1926. Collected by Waldemar Liungman and published in *Sveriges Samtliga Folksagor*, vol. 1, Stockholm, 1949. Aarne-Thompson type catalogue no. 673.

The Goat Who Wouldn't Go Home   Told by Cissa Svensson, Tving County, Blekinge. Recorded by Ruth Nelsson, Blekinge. Institute of European Ethnology and Folklore in Lund, LUF #714 (archive). Aarne-Thompson type catalogue no. 2015.

"Eat the Bread Too!"   Told by Sven Andersson, Skärstad, Småland. Recorded by Sven Liljeblad, 1925. Institute of European Ethnology and Folklore in Lund, LUF #875 (archive). Aarne-Thompson type catalogue no. 285.

The Little Old Woman   Recorded by Hulda Berg, Stenbrohults County, Småland, 1926. Collected by Waldemar Liungman and published in *Sveriges Samtliga Folksagor*, vol. 1, Stockholm, 1949. Aarne-Thompson type catalogue no. 2016.

The Three Lying Old Women   Recorded by Olof Petter Pettersson from Åsele Lappmark. Published in *Svenska Sagor och Sägner 9, Sagor från Åsele Lappmark*, Kungliga Gustav Adolfs Akademin för Folklivsforskning, Stockholm, 1945 (publication series). Aarne-Thompson type catalogue no. 1920E*.

The Biggest Stable and the Biggest Pot   Told by an informant from Norsjö, Västerbotten. Recorded by Bertil Nygren. Uppsala Institute of Dialect and Folklore Research, ULMA #4299 (archive). Aarne-Thompson type catalogue no. 1960EF.

The Black Cow, the Pot, and the Cheese   Told by "Per vid Skärsjön," Brunskogs County, Värmland. Recorded by Olof Hagberg, Brunsberg, Värmland, 1926. Collected by Waldemar Liungman and published in *Sveriges Samtliga Folksagor*, vol. 1, Stockholm, 1949. Aarne-Thompson type catalogue no. 1960AFK.

Boots for the Son in America   Told by C. O. Olsson, Hälstads County, Östergötland. Recorded by Gustaf Olsson, 1924. Institute of European Ethnology and Folklore in Lund, LUF #1586 (archive). Aarne-Thompson type catalogue no. 1710.

That Was the End of the Tale   Told by Henrik Andersson, Onsala County, Halland. Recorded by Agnes Andersson, Onsala County, Halland. Collected by Waldemar Liungman and published in *Sveriges Samtliga Folksagor*, vol. 1, Stockholm, 1949. Aarne-Thompson type catalogue no. 2250.

Bibliography

The bibliography contains editions of Swedish tale collections, secondary reference works, and library collections used in the preparation of this volume. Many of the tales used derive from the following three archives:

Dialekt- och Folkminnesarkivet i Uppsala (ULMA) (Uppsala Institute of Dialect and Folklore Research).

Lunds Universitet, Etnologiska Institutionen med Folklivsarkivet (LUF) (Institute of European Ethnology and Folklore in Lund).

Institutet för Folklore (DAG) (Institute of Folklore in Gothenburg).

Publications and Library Collections

Aarne, Antti, and Stith Thompson. *The Types of the Folktale.* Helsinki: Folklore Fellows Communications 184, 1966.

Arill, David. "Ur den västsvenska folksagodiktningen." In *Folksägen och Folkdiktning i Västra Sverige.* Gothenburg: Göteborgs Jubileumspublikationer, 1923.

Austin, Paul Britten. *The Life and Songs of Carl Michael Bellman.* Malmö: Allhem Publishers; New York: American-Scandinavian Foundation, 1967.

Bondeson, August. *Halländska Sagor.* Stockholm: Albert Bonniers Förlag, 1880.

———. *Historiegubbar på Dal.* Stockholm: Albert Bonniers Förlag, 1886.

———. *Svenska folksagor från skilda landskap.* Stockholm: Albert Bonniers Förlag, 1882.

Booss, Claire, ed. *Scandinavian Folk and Fairy Tales.* New York: Avenel Books, 1984.

Bringéus, Nils-Arvid. *Gunnar Olof Hyltén-Cavallius: En studie kring Wärend och wirdarne.* Stockholm: Nordiska Museets Handlingar 63, 1966.

Christiansen, Reidar Th. *The Migratory Legends: A Proposed List of the Types with a Systematic Catalogue of the Norwegian Variants.* Helsinki: Folklore Fellows Communications 175, 1958.

———. *Studies in Irish and Scandinavian Folktales.* Published for Irish Folklore Commission by Rosenkilde & Bagger, Copenhagen, 1959.

Djurklou, Gabriel. *Sagor och Äventyr.* Stockholm: P. A. Norstedt & Söners Förlag, 1912.

Dorson, Richard M., ed. *Folklore and Folklife: An Introduction.* Chicago and London: University of Chicago Press, 1972.

Dundes, Alan, ed. *Cinderella: A Casebook.* Madison: University of Wisconsin Press, 1988.

Egardh, Johan. *Prosten Göransson: En sägenomspunnen värmlandspräst.* Stockholm, 1935.

Fornminnen och Folktankar (journal). Lund, 1914–44.

Fredén, Gustav. *Östen om solen, norden om jorden: Randanteckningar till folksagens historia.* Stockholm: P. A. Nordstedt & Söners Förlag, 1982.

Hazelius, Artur, ed. *Ur de nordiska folkens lif.* Stockholm: F. & G. Beijers Förlag, 1882.

Herranen, Gun, ed. *Folkloristikens aktuella paradigm*. Turku: Nordic Institute of Folklore, 1981 (NIF Publications 10).

Herranen, Gun, and Lassi Saressalo, eds. *A Guide to Nordic Tradition Archives*. Turku: Nordic Institute of Folklore, 1978 (NIF Publications 7).

Holbek, Bengt, and Birgitte Rørbye, eds. *Nordisk Folkediktning og Folkemusik*. Copenhagen: Nordic Institute of Folklore, 1972 (NIF Publications 1).

Honko, Lauri, ed. *Folklore och Nationsbyggande i Norden*. Turku: Nordic Institute of Folklore, 1980 (NIF Publications 9).

———. *Metodiska och terminologiska betraktelser i folkloristik*. Stockholm: Institutet för folklivsforskning, 1980.

Hyltén-Cavallius, Gunnar Olof, and George Stephens. *Svenska sagor*. Vols. 1–4. Edited by Jöran Sahlgren. Stockholm: Bokförlaget Prisma, 1963.

———. *Svenska Folk-Sagor och Äfventyr*. Vol. 1. Stockholm: A. Bohlins Förlag, 1944.

———. *Wärend och wirdarne: ett försög i svenskt etnologi*. Stockholm: P. A. Nordstedt & Söners Förlag, 1844–49.

Høgset, Oddbjørg. *Erotiske folkeeventyr*. Oslo: Universitetsforlaget, 1977.

Klintberg, Bengt af. *Svenska folkesägner*, 2nd ed. Stockholm: P. A. Nordstedt & Söners Förlag, 1972, 1977.

———. *Folkloristiska grundfakta*. Stockholm: Institutet för Folklivsforskning, 1983.

Kvideland, Reimund, and Henning K. Sehmsdorf, eds. *Nordic Folklore: Recent Studies*. Bloomington: Indiana University Press, 1989.

———. *Scandinavian Folk Belief and Legend*. Minneapolis: University of Minnesota Press, 1988.

Liljeblad, Sven, ed. *Svenska Folksagor*. Vols. 1–4. Stockholm: Gidlunds Förlag, 1981.

Lindow, John. *Swedish Legends and Folktales*. Berkeley: University of California Press, 1978.

Liungman, Waldemar. *Sveriges Samtliga Folksagor i ord och bild*. Vols. 1 and 2. Stockholm: Lindfors Bokförlag, 1949–50.

———. *Sveriges Samtliga Folksagor i ord och bild*. Vol. 3, *Varifrån kommer våra sagor?* Uppsala: Almquist & Wiksells, 1952.

Müller, Folke, ed. *John Bauer: En konstnär och hans sagovärld*. Stockholm: Bokförlaget Bra Böcker and the National Museum, 1982.

Nellemann, George, and Johannes Nicolaisen. *Etnologins forskningshistoria: En översikt*. Stockholm: Institutet för Folklivsforskning, 1976.

Nyman, Åsa. *De etnologiska undersökningarna i Uppsala: Organisation och utveckling 1878–1978*. Uppsala: special printing from *Svenska landsmål och svenskt folkliv*, 1978–79.

Petersen, Per. *Sagans teorier*. Uppsala: Etnologiska Institutionen, 1980.

Propp, Vladimir. *Morphology of the Folktale*. Austin and London: University of Texas Press, 1968.

Schön, Ebbe. *Älvor, vättar och andra väsen*. Stockholm: Rabén & Sjögren Bokförlag, 1986.

Segerstedt, Albrekt. Collection. Kungliga Vitterhets Historie och Antikvitets Akademien, Stockholm.

———. *Svenska Folksagor och Äfventyr*. Stockholm: Albert Bonniers Förlag, 1884.

Svenska landsmål och svenskt folkliv (journal). Stockholm, 1878 et seq.

Swahn, Jan-Öjvind, ed. *Folksagor ur oknyttens värld*. Höganäs: Bra Böcker Folksagor, pt. 7, 1989.

———. *Svenska folksagor*. Stockholm: Albert Bonniers Förlag, 1986.

Svenska Sagor och Sägner (publication series). Edited by Jöran Sahlgren and Sven Liljeblad. Kungliga Gustav Adolfs Akademin för Folklivsforskning. 1–9, Stockholm, 1937–45; 10–12, Uppsala, 1952–59.

———. *Trollen, deres liv. land och legender.* Stockholm: Bonnier-Fakta, n.d.

Swahn, Oscar. *Svenskt Skämtlynne.* Vols. 1–12. Stockholm: Albert Bonniers Förlag, 1884.

Säve, Per Arvid. Collection. Uppsala University Library.

Thompson, Stith. *Motif Index of Folk Literature.* Bloomington: Indiana University Press, 1955.

———. *The Folktale.* New York: Holt, Rinehart & Winston, 1946.

———. *One Hundred Favorite Folktales.* Bloomington: Indiana University Press, 1968.

Tillhagen, Carl-Herman, L. Bødker, and Svale Solheim, eds. *Skæmtsomme eventyr fra Danmark, Norge og Sverige.* Copenhagen: Hans Reitzels Forlag, 1957.

———. *Taikon berättar: Zigenarsagor.* Stockholm: P. & A. Nordstedt & Söners Förlag, 1946.

Virtanen, Leea. "The Function of the Children's Tradition." In *Children's Lore.* Helsinki: Studia Fennica 22, 1978.

Wigström, Eva. *Folkdiktning, samlad och upptecknad i Skåne.* Copenhagen: Karl Schönbergs Bokhandel, 1880.

Wolf-Knuts, Ulrika. *All världens epos.* Åbo: Åbo Akademis Bibliotek, 1985 (NIF Publications 15).

The Illustrators

V. Andrén: 72.

John Bauer: pp. 14, 46.

Elsa Beskow: pp. 187, 188, 192, 193, 209, 210, 212, 217, 357.

Bertil Bull Hedlund: pp. 2, 6, 37, 64, 69, 77, 90, 100, 165, 177.

Albert Engström: p. xxiv.

Edvard Forsström: pp. 119, 121.

Pehr Hilleström: p. 96.

P. D. Holm: p. xix.

Carl Larsson: p. 26.

J. F. Martin: p. 94, copperplate engraving/etching after relief medallion by Johan Tobias Sergel.

Severin Nilsson: p. xvii.

Einar Norelius: pp. 18, 29, 44, 56, 63, 79, 84, 107, 131, 137, 149, 153, 161, 174, 180, 199, 213, 223, 241, 272, 275, 278, 292, 297, 306, 310, 316, 323, 329, 334.

Jenny Nyström: pp. 41, 249, 251, 256, 308.

Bengt Arne Runnerström: pp. 50, 300.

Permissions Acknowledgments

Grateful acknowledgment is made to the following for permission to translate into English previously published material:

Dialekt- och Folkminnesarkivet i Uppsala (ULMA) (Uppsala Institute of Dialect and Folklore Research): Selections from *Svenska Landsmål och Svenskt Folkliv* (Swedish Dialects and Folk Traditions), vols. 1 and 2 (Eva Wigström); vols. 2 and 5 (Richard Bergström and Johan Nordlander, Ella Odstedt); vol. 9, no. 1 (Hilda Lundell and Elise Zetterquist); and from ULMA.

Kungliga Gustav Adolfs Akademien: Selections from *Svenska Sagor och Sägner,* 1–12, Kungliga Gustav Adolfs Akademiens collections.

Lunds Universitet, Etnologiska Institutionen med Folklivsarkivet (University of Lund, Department of European Ethnology): Selections from LUF and from *Fornminnen och Folktanker* (Lund, 1914–1944).

Norstedts Förlag AB: "Herrkarls-Pär och Tras-Jan's-pojken" and "Kvistmuntus, Koböljantus, Abborrnäsius" from *Sagor och Äventyr* by Gabriel Djurklou. Copyright © 1912 by Gabriel Djurklou. "Flicken och hennes döde fästman" from *Taikon berättar: Zigenarsagor* by Carl-Herman Tillhagen. Copyright © 1946 by Carl Herman Tillhagen. Published by Norstedts, Stockholm. Translated into English by permission.

Hans Reitzels Forlag A/S: "Prasten der skulle føde" and "Bellmanhistorier" from *Skæmtsomme Eventyr fra Danmark, Norge og Sverige,* edited by L. Bødker, Svale Solheim, and Carl-Herman Tillhagen. Translated by permission of the publisher.

Professor Jan Öjvind Swahn: "Prinsessan som aldrig blev svarslös" and "Kvistmuntus, Koböljantus, Abborrnäsius" from *Svenska Folksagor* by Jan Öjvind Swahn (1986), 4th edition published by Carlsson's Förlag. Translated into English by permission of the author.

Lone Thygesen Blecher and **George Blecher** are prize-winning translators from Swedish and Danish. Their translations include the novels *After the Flood* by P. C. Jersild and *The Thirty Years' War* by Henrik Tikkanen, as well as a number of plays and film scripts. Their children's-book translations *If You Didn't Have Me* by Ulf Nilsson and *The Battle Horse* by Harry Kullman both received the Batchelder Prize from the American Library Association, and they were cited as distinguished translators by the International Board of Books for Young People. George Blecher is also a widely published fiction writer and journalist, and Lone Thygesen Blecher is a teacher. They both live in New York City.